Beacon of Hope: Episode II

Labyrinths of Radiance and Shadow

Jeffrey A Hallett

ISBN: 979-8-9921902-0-5   (paperback)
       979-8-9921902-1-2   (eBook)

Library of Congress Control Number: 2025900346

Illustrations by Jessica Nagel (@colorful.and.wild)
Cover Art by Holly Dunn (@hollydunndesign)
Developmental editing by Amelia Beamer
"Rene's Note" by Sarah Richardson (@sarascript)

Dragon's Trove Press, Livermore, CA, USA

Chapter List

Illustration List

Acknowledgements

As with "Paths into Darkness and Light", it took a village to help me get this across the finish line. Without them, it wouldn't have become a sequel of which I could truly be proud, so my unending appreciation and thanks go out to:

Bernie, my writing buddy and mentor, for his staunch encouragement and for being a sounding board for my crazy ideas,

Elyse, for her continued patience and support in reading snippets and segments along the way, giving feedback and critique whenever needed,

My editor, Amelia, for her wisdom and unique insights that let me raise the stakes for my characters and myself,

My illustrator, Jess, for continuing to give old friends and new characters life with her creativity,

My beta readers, Sabrina and Trista, for their investment of time and candor,

And to my cover designer, Holly, for giving this series the beautiful look it deserves.

Thank you all, and to my other friends and family who were cheering me on. I could not have done it without you.

Forward

They say lightning doesn't strike twice, but for me, it did. As I said in the preface of *Paths into Darkness and Light*, writing a book was a dream on my bucket list for years. All it needed was an idea, and eventually it came. It was fun to invent Beacon and explore what it meant for an average person to come to terms with suddenly becoming exceptional, choosing to use those abilities openly to make a difference, growing as a person, and learning where her strengths, weaknesses, and moral boundaries lay.

Writing these stories also gave me a chance to experiment with some of the familiar superhero tropes and put my take on the ones I'd always found unsatisfying. *Paths* was a rewarding learning experience, but when the book was done, I figured that was it. Bucket list checked.

Lightning did strike again, though. I'd become too invested in these people not to take them to the next level. Clearly, they also felt they still had stories to tell, so this book began unexpectedly with a single chapter out of the blue just before *Paths* was released. Tricia had earned her stripes, and it was time to raise the stakes for her, for the people around her, and for myself as a writer, to develop a story now that depends on a greater ensemble of characters, and puts Tricia into a situation that deeply challenges her to survive and grow by leaning into more of what makes her a true heroine: her heart and her spirit.

I hope you enjoy this story and the characters in it, familiar and new, as much as I did writing it.

Who knows, maybe lightning can strike a third time... we will see.

The end never justifies the means because there is no end; there are only means.

– Penn Jillette

Those who find their light go into the darkness to find it.

– Unknown

It is not our abilities that show who we truly are; it is our choices

– Albus Dumbledore,
Harry Potter and the Chamber of Secrets,
J.K. Rowling

Prologue

New Chatham Colony
The New World
1702

The woman stood in the makeshift dock of the hastily converted parish courtroom. She was disheveled and dirty. Her auburn hair, a mass of snarls and tangles, fell down around her face and shoulders. Her face and arms bore smudges of dirt mixed with dried blood. The arm of her dress was torn, exposing her shoulder, and a welt had blossomed in the side of her jaw where they had struck her. She was tired and weak from the cold dampness of her cell and the lack of food or water. Her arms hung limply at her sides, no longer able to hold up the weight of the iron manacles at her wrists and the chains binding them to her waist.

Across from her sat the colony magistrate. He took turns studying the writ of accusation on the judge's bench before him and assessing her. His once-white wig was now stained with streaks of dirty white and brown. Despite her exhaustion, her deep green eyes met his gaze defiantly, and she did her best to keep her chin up and her back straight. *Thou mayest take my life*, she thought to herself, *but thou shalt not break me.*

"Alicia Whitby," the magistrate finally said, letting the writ settle on the surface of the bench and fixing his gaze on her over the rim of his thin-rimmed glasses. "Thou art accused of practicing witchcraft and being in communion with Satan and the hosts of darkness. What is thy plea?"

It had been inevitable that she would find herself here. Alicia knew that. They had come for her just after sundown, carrying torches. They had demanded she come out of her home, and when she had stepped out to face them, they ambushed her and fastened the manacles about her wrists, locking the chain itself around her waist. They then dragged her, shouting and cursing her, to the gaol, where they threw her into a cell, alone and cold.

As Alicia sat in the cell, blood ran down her hands and fingers from where the rough metal of the cuffs dug into her skin and tore it raw. She could not even heal herself. Iron confounded her gift. If Alicia was in direct contact with the metal, she could barely even call upon it. When it did respond to her, it was wild and chaotic, and the pain it caused was excruciating, far worse than the cuts and gouges she felt on her wrists. All she could do was tear some strips of cloth from her petticoat and wrap her wrists as best she could to soften the bite of the cold, sharp metal and contemplate her fate.

"Madam Whitby!" The magistrate said more forcefully, breaking her reverie. "I ask again. How dost thou plead?"

Alicia cleared her dry, raspy throat. "I deny the accusations, my Lord," she said as confidently as she could in her exhausted state. "I use my skills and gifts solely in the service of the Lord and in the service of this colony and its people."

The townspeople gathered behind her grumbled and murmured in response, but the magistrate waved them down into silence. "Very well," he said. "Let those who would give testimony for or against come forward."

Alicia let her mind wander as various members of the colony came forward to bear witness. None of them surprised her. Most she knew bore her some grudge: a man whose attentions she had spurned, or women bitter with jealousy for one thing or another, and others simply seeking attention.

Her relationship with the other colonists had always been tenuous at best. Her late husband, Roger, was the third son of Lord and Lady Whitby. They had a modest estate in Southern Wales. Roger, being the third son, though, did not stand prominently in line for inheritance or title, but he was ambitious and determined to make a situation for himself separate from his father's holdings. When he learned of the opportunities offered by the New World, potentially in timber, mining, or even gold, he was eager to make his way there, and his father had ample connections to ensure he was awarded passage, a grant of land, and a small fund to seed his ventures.

When Alicia and Roger arrived in New Chatham, most of the colony assumed she was privileged and, of course, resented them as such. Nothing could have been further from the truth. Alicia's father was a sheep farmer, and her mother was a midwife, a very skilled midwife who also had a knack for herbal treatments and remedies for a variety of minor illnesses and maladies. Alicia's mother trained her thoroughly as a young girl, and she would never have even met Roger Whitby had Lord Whitby not learned of her mother's reputation and asked her to help alleviate Lady Whitby's chronic inflammation of the gut, and had her mother not brought Alicia with her to assist and to learn.

Roger was immediately smitten with Alicia and, after a brief courtship, asked her to marry him and come with him to the colonies. When Roger made his intentions to marry known to his father, Lord Whitby gave a simple sniff of disapproval but consented. Alicia's mother had been of tremendous service to his wife, and since Roger was third in line, marrying a common girl wouldn't be much of a scandal. Besides, the two of them would be leaving for the Americas soon anyway, and any gossip would die off quickly after they were gone.

Sadly, it took a tragedy for the colonists to start to see Alicia differently. Shortly after their arrival and the completion of the construction of their home, a plague struck the colony. Roger was one of the first afflicted and passed within a few days. Alicia was heartbroken, but while some of the treatments she learned from her mother were not enough to save Roger, she worked tirelessly to bring aid to others in the colony. Many lives were saved with her help, and after the plague had passed, Alicia used a small portion of Roger's endowment to buy some livestock, establish a garden, and begin to build a reputation for herself as a midwife and herbalist just as her mother had.

Alicia's reputation with the colony changed even more dramatically after the storm. She was gathering mushrooms and other ingredients in a thickly secluded area of the nearby forest when a massive thunderstorm broke, taking her by surprise. Before she could seek shelter, a bolt of lightning struck the glade where she was standing. The edge of the blast caught her, sending a surge of energy through her body and throwing her violently into a thicket at the edge of a stream.

As she lay on the edge of death, drifting in and out of consciousness, she was sure she heard a voice, a voice that she later believed could only be of God Himself, call out to her. "Alicia," it said, "accept this gift, and the power that comes with it, to help thy neighbors. Accept it and use it wisely, with compassion and mercy."

Weakly, Alicia nodded and, in her delirium, answered, "Yes, Lord. I shall. Thy will be done."

Instantly, she felt power flow from the ground beneath her and course through her body. She was healed, and Alicia came to realize she could not only heal herself, but she could sense any illness or injury in plants, animals, or people. Her gift grew quickly within her, and she learned she could not only detect these maladies but heal them even unto the brink of death.

Of course, Alicia dared not display her gift openly in the colony. They were a superstitious lot, and she knew they would not understand, so she learned to use it deftly and inconspicuously. Even though she could only use it sparingly, the colony saw fewer stillborns and less illness, even averting an outbreak of what the village doctor was sure was consumption. People came to trust Alicia, seeking her remedies and wisdom for matters both small and grave, all of which she was glad to provide at little or no return for herself.

That was when things took a turn for the worse for her.

For as many as accepted and appreciated Alicia's skills in the colony, there were others, some very prominent, who resented her. Reverend Pickering saw fewer of the colonists seeking his counsel in favor of the more open and less judgmental Alicia Whitby. Doctor Slattery, who relied on trade for his services, needed to start finding other means to make ends meet as more people sought out Alicia's less expensive, and often more effective, care. Of course, there were those who bore petty grudges and jealousies and were more than willing to spread rumors and gossip just out of spite to see the young widow make her way successfully and influentially. On top of this, some of the colony councilmen had their eye on her holdings, which would transfer to the colony itself in the event of her demise.

It was only a matter of time before the conspiracy grew, and they came for her.

The last of the witnesses finished giving testimony. Altogether, eight brought testimony against her, while two spoke in her favor. Because of her skills, one grateful family was raising two healthy twin boys instead of having to bury them. The other nearly lost a leg to a glancing axe swing. Doctor Slattery wanted to amputate, but they had begged Alicia to intervene. If he lost his leg, it would condemn them to poverty and begging, so she agreed, knowing the risk to herself. After several of her poultices, in concert with small doses of her gift, administered subtly to avoid discovery, the wound reached the point where it would heal on its own, and he could once again walk. Alicia smiled and nodded in gratitude to each of them as they spoke on her behalf.

But there are too few, she realized sadly.

The magistrate cleared his throat. "The witnesses have been heard," he said. "Madam Whitby, what say ye in your defense?"

Alicia considered for a moment and took a deep breath. "It is difficult, my Lord," she finally said. "All I have heard is fancy and speculation, much laced with malice and bitterness. No witness corroborates another. There is no evidence. There are only stories that are, at best, figments of fancy and speculation and, at worst, deliberate falsehoods laced with malice and borne of spite and greed. All I can say is that my skills and gifts are from the Lord God, and I use them freely for the benefit of the colony and for His glory and honor, nothing more." She looked into the magistrate's eyes. "Could one who communes with Satan so freely honor God?"

"What of the goat you were seen raising from the dead?" shouted Reverend Pickering. "The spirit seen leaving its body?"

"It was not dead," Alicia said truthfully. "The kid had consumed a noxious weed. Yes, it was failing, but by forcing it to vomit, I was able to relieve it of the poison before it passed beyond hope. That is all the good witness saw." Less truthful; yes, she had used her gift to extract the poisons from that baby goat, and she cursed herself for being so careless as to be seen.

"Wouldst thou have us believe thou canst make a goat cast up its cud?" Reverend Pickering demanded with a ridiculing sneer.

Alicia shrugged. "'Tis but a simple technique. Perhaps thou shouldst step forward so that I may demonstrate." Pickering huffed as the crowd tittered with amusement.

"And the curing of consumption?" The magistrate asked. "The doctor assures that such a feat would be unnatural indeed."

"If it were consumption, then it certainly wouldst be," Alicia agreed calmly, choosing her words carefully. "If, however, Doctor Slattery were in error regarding his diagnosis, then it wouldst not be miraculous or unnatural at all. If this trial be about medical competence, then perhaps Doctor Slattery shouldst be standing here before you, my Lord, instead of me."

"Of all the impudence," Slattery exclaimed again while the colonists in the gallery murmured and chuckled softly.

"Perhaps then thou canst explain why thy garden is so much more lush and bountiful when others wither in the hot sun. Why are thy livestock fatter and more robust than any other in the colony?" challenged the Reverend once again. "Explainest thou this!"

"I careth for them as I do the people of the colony," Alicia replied. "With naught but my skill and compassion."

"And your exceptional youthfulness and comely appearance. How dost thou account for that?"

"The same," she said. "I careth for myself in the same manner." She forced herself to remain calm and to hold her voice even, but she already knew she was lost. "Any blessings I receiveth are by the grace of God alone."

"Any blessings thou receivest," accused the Reverend, "are from the Prince of Darkness in payment for thy deceptions that lure and sway the people from the Church and from God!" The crowd murmured angrily in agreement.

The magistrate held up his hand, and the room quieted. "Alicia Whitby," he said solemnly. "The testimony hath been heard and the evidence recorded. As thou hast no defense to tip the scales, I find ye guilty of practicing witchcraft and sentence thou to be burned at the stake post haste."

Alicia's chin dropped to her chest as the crowd roared and jeered, shouting, "Burn her" and "Destroy the witch". Rough hands grabbed her arms and hauled her down from the dock, through the crowd, and pushed her out the door into the square in front of the parish house.

Before her, in the center of the square, a thick pole had already been erected. *They knew my fate all along,* she thought as they dragged her toward it. They forced her to stand on a short stool and removed the shackles and chains. With the iron gone, her gift burst into life within her as they forced her hands up over her head and bound them tightly to the pole. She cried out as the ropes bit into her already tattered skin. They then kicked the stool out from under her feet, leaving her to dangle against the pole while they piled thick bundles of wood around her.

Her gift raged and churned within her. *Use me,* she felt it beg, urging her to let it save her, but she forced it back. *No, Father,* she prayed silently. *I pray Thou doest not use the gift Thou gavest me to harm these people, even though it cost me my life. Forgive them.*

When the piles of branches and logs were assembled at her feet, Pickering himself stepped forward from the jeering crowd with a torch in his hand. "Burn, meddlesome witch," he said with a malicious smile on his face, and tossed the torch into the wood. At first, the wood smoldered, releasing thick tufts of smoke, but quickly it began to crackle and finally caught fire.

As the flames grew, smoke billowed up into Alicia's face, causing her to cough. The higher the flames rose, the more her gift swelled and struggled, desperate to save her, and she quickly realized it would soon be beyond her ability to hold it back. The fire blazed higher, the crowd shouted its approval, and Alicia wept. She wept not just from the stinging smoke and embers in her eyes or the scorching heat on her face and arms. She wept because the gift that had been given to her to be in service of His mercy and grace would now become an instrument of His righteous wrath and judgment.

When the flames licked her bare legs, she could hold it back no longer. With a final breath, Alicia cried out, "Thy will be done!" and the raging power within her erupted outward in a billowing torrent of fire, smoke, and death.

Izzy

If Crystal Bay had a side on the right side of the tracks and one on the wrong side of the tracks, Izzy figured she was probably walking down the middle of the tracks themselves. *Figuratively, of course*, she thought, walking down the late evening sidewalk, kicking the random stray rock or abandoned beverage cup. Unlike the part of the city a few blocks over, the windows didn't have bars on them. At least most windows didn't. The building faces were old and in need of some paint and sprucing up, but this area was far enough removed from the more affluent parts of the city that the owners either couldn't afford it or didn't think it was worth it, or both.

Some of the shops stayed open a little later as well. This section catered to the working class of Crystal Bay. Most of them had day jobs with long hours, so any time they had for shopping was in the evenings or on the weekends. However, they didn't stay open too late. Once the evening gave way to night, more of the undesirable elements started to come out. *I'm probably considered one of them*, Izzy thought to herself, kicking another stone against the brick facade of the building next to her.

She wouldn't have picked being here out of choice, but the shelters on the other side of town were dismal, dirty, and downright scary. Of course, the wealthier parts of town didn't need shelters for wayward girls, so there was really no help for her there. It could be worse. She could've stayed at home.

Izzy glanced at herself in a big storefront window and stopped for a moment. Her reflection's big, hazel eyes watched her run her fingers through her hair. It was getting longer now, but she was uncertain about whether she still wanted short hair anymore or whether it was time to let it grow out, maybe dyeing it as well, to avoid being recognized by anyone who might be looking for her.

If anyone even is...

Long hair would be nice to have again, she mused, twisting some of the longer dark brown strands around her index finger. For years, she'd cut it short, and for good reason, but maybe she was past that now. Letting it grow out might help her leave all that behind her. *I'll think about it*, she decided, and kept walking.

She had kept it short on account of her brothers, mostly her older brother, in hindsight. Izzy-only her mother had ever called her Isobel-had three brothers, one older and two slightly younger. Her mother had left when she was very young. Her father was a construction worker who also liked to drink a lot and gamble a lot, and when he did them together, he got sloppy at both. Then budgets got tight, and tempers flared around the house. Izzy remembered her mother leaving one night with a split lip after a particularly vicious argument. She never heard from her again. Izzy loved her mom and frequently missed her to the point of crying, but as she got older, Izzy realized her mom was the smart one and had given her an example for how to deal with what was going on at home.

Her father clearly would have preferred to have had only boys. They got away with whatever they wanted, and any extra money they might've had went to sports and clubs (they were far too stupid for any academic extracurriculars). Izzy got hand-me-downs and consignment shop bargains.

Her brothers were rowdy and aggressive and often liked to pretend to be knights or barbarians or goblins on some medieval quest. As the only girl, though, Izzy was the designated "damsel in distress" when her brothers wanted to play their role-playing games. As the damsel in distress, Izzy often found herself tied to a chair or stuck in the small storage closet "dungeon" in the basement, or—and this was the worst—forced to endure the "torture chamber" where they tickled her almost to the point of peeing herself. As stressful as all this was, at least she had school and friends there, so she tolerated it, knowing it wouldn't last forever. Nothing lasts forever; her mother had shown her that much.

And it didn't. She found it actually started to get worse, especially as they all got older, and Izzy started filling out as girls usually do once they reach puberty. She began to find the lingering looks, snickers behind her back, and the jokes and innuendoes about her body more uncomfortable than funny. Playing the damsel in distress with her brothers became increasingly unnerving as well. That's when she cut her hair short; the less she looked like a girl, perhaps the less they would notice she was one. Wearing some of her older brother's baggy old clothes helped a lot, too.

While she felt physically safer, the abuse continued, just in a different form. Now that she looked a little more like a tomboy, her brothers started mocking her as a lesbian, calling her "Lezzy" instead. Of course, her father said nothing, only telling them to stop it when they got so loud he couldn't hear the television anymore. The name-calling didn't bother her, though. She knew who and what she was, and again, if it kept them from taking any unwanted interest in her, it was worth it. Besides, they were all getting older, entering high school, so it wouldn't last forever.

And, again, it didn't. The camel's back finally broke one hot summer day. Izzy was again the damsel in distress, tied to a table in their mock torture chamber, being incessantly tickled by her brothers. Her stomach hurt, and her voice was so raw from forced laughing that she could hardly speak anymore. All she could do was wheeze out "No...no more...please" when they took a short break, but her protests only seemed to egg them on even further. Finally, they stopped. She lay there panting. Her flimsy tank top was soaked with sweat from the heat of the day and her struggles against the tickling. Then, her brother leaned over her and leered at her. It was a look she'll never forget. As he stared at her lying there, he grinned and called back over his shoulder to the others, "Hey guys, maybe what Lezzy here needs is a reminder about what being girls and boys is all about." They all laughed. Izzy's eyes grew wide as she slowly shook her head, silently mouthing "No."

Still leering menacingly, he reached down and slipped one finger inside the top of her tank top, peeling the sweat-soaked fabric away from her skin. She shook her head harder and tried to pull away as tears started to run down her cheeks, but she was still roped down to the table. She begged him to stop, sliding as far from him as her restraints allowed. Grinning, he then plunged his hand inside her top. Izzy shrieked. Fortunately, her brothers weren't skilled at all, and when she twisted to get away from his touch, the flimsy knots finally gave way. Clenching her sagging top tightly in her fist, she shoved him back and ran to find their father. She could hear them laughing behind her as she scrambled up the stairs from the basement.

Izzy found her father in the living room, working his way through a six-pack of Rheingold, watching professional wrestling. Fighting through the sobs, she told him what happened. He sat there and looked at her while she told the story, and when she had finished, he shook his head and chugged down the last of the bottle in his hand. Setting the dead soldier, as he called them, on the table, he looked her up and down and, with a shrug, asked her, "Well, what did you expect would happen?"

Her jaw dropped. "What?" She stammered in disbelief and disgust. "What do you mean?"

"Look at yourself," he said. "Walking around wearing skimpy clothes, letting them play those games with you. You're begging for it. If you don't want that kind of attention from boys, and you kinda act like you don't, then don't act like you're giving it away for them to take."

It was time to go. Over the next few days, Izzy did some research online. Crystal Bay, she found, looked like an ideal place to get a fresh start. Since Beacon had come on the scene, it was rated as one of the top cities in the country, and it didn't hurt that Izzy was a huge Beacon fan, having seen her on the news streams multiple times.

Meeting her would be so cool!

With someone like Beacon watching over it, Crystal Bay was a place Izzy was sure she could feel safe, and a city like that was bound to be loaded with opportunities for someone like her. Plus, it was close enough that she could get there fairly easily with her limited funds, yet far enough away that it felt like she had truly escaped.

Perfect!

She quietly packed her backpack with some essentials and hid it under her bed, ready for when the moment came.

And that moment did come soon enough. Just a few nights later, her father came home drunk, thrilled that he'd landed a big score in his weekly poker game. He then celebrated with a few whiskey shots and passed out in his armchair. After her brothers had gone to bed, Izzy retrieved her backpack, snuck downstairs, cleaned her father's winnings out of his jacket pocket, and huffed it down the bus station. Next stop, Crystal Bay. She boarded the bus and vowed to herself that she would never come back.

All things considered, Izzy considered herself luckier than most girls in her situation. Most ended up in the seedy shelters, but her research had paid off, and she found a spot in one of the nicer ones here in the "middle of the tracks." The bed was clean and comfortable, and she could get two square meals a day.

She had also managed to find ways to pull in some cash. Technically, since she wasn't yet eighteen, she couldn't work without a parent's consent, but a friendly smile and a little playful banter had gotten her some off-the-books work cleaning up and taking out the trash after hours for a few of the diners and coffee shops near the shelter. The cash they paid her helped her buy some better clothes, and by adding a donation to the shelter on top of the chores all the girls had to do to stay there, she felt she had created a pretty stable and secure situation. *See?* she told herself, *it didn't last forever after all.*

Of course, Izzy had heard all the horror stories of trafficking, drugs, prostitution, and the like. Since most of her work hours were well after the dark blues of evening faded to full night and the meager yellowish streetlights finally flickered into life, creating even more shadowy nooks and crevices, she was especially careful to avoid the alleys and other questionable places. She wanted to have a life, and staying clear of trouble was a big part of building one.

Unfortunately, despite her caution and heightened awareness, Izzy was utterly oblivious to the man sitting in the car across the street, studying her when she pushed the diner front door open for work.

Izzy couldn't be entirely to blame for overlooking him tonight, as she had every night for the past week. He was very discreet, using different cars and wearing different jackets or hats each night. He was good at this—very good actually—and knew how to make sure she didn't see him, or even if she did, that she wouldn't take any notice of him. Here, from the car, he could see Izzy clearly through the diner's front window as she slipped on an apron and rolled up her sleeves. The owner turned off the neon OPEN sign in the window, and she went to work, smiling, completely unaware that he was watching.

He quickly checked in on his commpod, leaned back in the seat, and closed his eyes. She'd be at least a couple of hours, so he knew he had some time to get a little rest before he had to follow her back to the shelter. Tailing her back probably wasn't really necessary; by now, he had a pretty complete picture of Izzy's routine, but still, he was a professional, and every bit of information they could gather about her and her patterns would be useful when the time came for her to join the program.

While Izzy slept in after her late night shifts, and Tricia Carling was supposedly at a doctor's appointment, Beacon sat in the small trailer set aside for her to prepare for the ribbon-cutting ceremony for the new children's medicine research wing of the University hospital. The facility was the latest gift to the city from her charitable foundation, Beacons of Light. Inside the trailer, Xia was putting the final touches on her hair while Casey was out somewhere meeting with the event organizers and coordinating final details.

Technically, neither Xia nor Casey worked for the foundation itself. Since Beacon first met them at her debut interview on CrystalClear, Xia had struck out on her own and was doing freelance work. Casey was still an employee of the media company, though, and not associated with the charities in any way. However, it was one of the perks of being the city's foremost (and only) superheroine; Beacon got to pick her own team for these public appearances, and she made sure Xia and Casey were with her for every one of them.

Beacon absentmindedly watched Xia work her hair, carefully adjusting and layering the streaks of blonde and ebony. Finding plausible excuses to cover for these appearances during the work week was tricky at times. Fortunately, she could play the doctor's visit card this time, and, just to make sure no one got too inquisitive about it, she dropped the one word that would stop any further questions about her appointment dead in their tracks: gynecologist.

Of course, Tricia never actually needed to see the doctor. In the nearly a year since the accident that started her transformation into Beacon, she had not had so much as a sniffle. Something about her abilities gave her a heightened resilience and durability, and even in the rare cases where she might be injured during her exploits, her healing ability allowed her to recover at a highly accelerated rate.

Not needing to see a doctor routinely was perfectly fine with her, of course. It wasn't just the embarrassing visits to the gynecologist she sought to avoid. It was all doctors in general. The memory of her time after her accident was still very fresh in her mind; she had endured several weeks of poking and prodding and testing to make sure she was fully recuperated and that there were no lingering aftereffects. *Little did they know*, she mused.

Once she was finally cleared, she'd had enough of the medical profession to last her a lifetime. On top of all that, she always carried the worry that some random examination or test might inadvertently reveal something about her unique nature and expose her. No, anything she might need from a medical perspective, Marni could provide more comfortably and with less risk.

Xia's perky voice brought Beacon back to the present. "I could just cut this off, you know," she said, tugging on the playful lock that routinely misbehaved and gave Xia fits styling her hair.

Beacon looked up at her in the mirror. "You always say that."

Xia shrugged. "Just hoping you will give in someday and let me really give you a good styling. You have awesome hair. I could do wonders with it," she boasted with a mischievous smile.

"I think it's fine the way it is," Beacon said curtly, and seeing Xia's face fall, immediately regretted it. She closed her eyes beneath her mask, took a deep breath, held it for a few seconds, and then exhaled through her nose. Beacon turned and put her hand on Xia's forearm. "I'm sorry, Xia. Look, you're fantastic. If there was anyone I'd want to style my hair, it would be you. Honestly. I didn't mean to sound snippy." She turned back toward the mirror and studied the woman looking back at her. "I guess I'm just not feeling like myself today."

Xia gave her shoulder a short empathetic squeeze. "It's ok. We all have those days." She smeared a small dab of gel on her hands. "Let's just tame this little beast, and we can talk styling another time."

"Deal," Beacon replied, forcing a half-hearted smile.

The door to the trailer popped open. "About ten minutes until show time, ladies," Casey said, climbing up the steps. As she pulled the door closed behind her, Casey must've sensed some tension in the room. She looked at Xia, then at Beacon, then back at Xia again. "Did I miss something?"

Beacon continued to look at herself in the mirror. "No, we're good," she replied. Xia looked at Casey and shrugged.

Casey pulled a chair up beside Beacon and sat down. "Uh-huh," she said, leaning in. "We have a few minutes, Queen Bee. C'mon, spill the tea. What's up?"

Casey's pet name for her always made Beacon smile, even if this time it was a weak attempt. "It's just that I'm not sure what I'm doing here," she finally said with a sigh, turning to face Casey. Xia had just finished tacking down the last few strands of Beacon's hair and shuffled around beside Casey. She leaned against a short cabinet to listen. "I mean, I'm thrilled about the new children's wing. It's really wonderful, and a lot of fantastic people worked incredibly hard to make it happen. Why aren't they cutting the ribbon to commemorate it? I really had nothing to do with it...nothing at all, actually, and yet here I am getting rolled out like a trick pony for show."

Casey looked at Beacon calmly and nodded. "Yes, a lot of people did work hard, and trust me, they are here, but *you* are the inspiration. Without you, none of this happens."

Beacon scoffed. "Seems like they could put just about anyone in this costume, and it would have the same effect."

Xia shook her head. "No," she said emphatically. "No, it wouldn't. They'd know. You matter much more than you think you do in all this. If it was anyone but you, they'd feel cheated, and they wouldn't pitch in anywhere nearly as much. You bring the special sauce that makes this foundation work."

Casey nodded and piled on, "Look, I know it isn't like jumping from rooftop to rooftop at night and bringing down bad guys. I'm sure that feels more like you're personally doing something, but because you do that, it's _you_ that people see when they look up. You make them feel safer and like they can make a difference, too. That's you, all you, and no dressed-up model or cardboard standee can replace that." Xia nodded vigorously and gave Beacon a thumbs-up.

Beacon pressed her lips together in a half smile. _These guys are the best. I still feel like a prop, but they are right—it's important to keep the spirit alive._

Casey's hand suddenly jerked to the commpod in her ear. "Time to go," she said and stood up.

Beacon stood up with her and clapped her hands together. "All right then," she said, dredging up some enthusiasm, "we've got a hospital wing to open."

Casey led Beacon out of the trailer door. Beacon could hear the crowd murmuring somewhere off to the side, but from where she was standing, she couldn't see them. Her trailer was sequestered down behind the platform where the commemoration ceremony would take place, keeping Beacon out of sight until it was time for her big entrance. Above her and to her left, she could just see the end of the large red ribbon that she would be cutting shortly.

Thunk thunk thunk echoed from the speakers as someone tapped the microphone. "Gosh, I wish they wouldn't do that," Casey whispered to Beacon, forcing her to stifle a snicker.

Then, she heard a man's voice over the loudspeaker. She recognized it as the hospital's chief administrator. He was MC-ing the events for the day. "Ladies and gentlemen, welcome today for the commemoration ceremony for the new children's medicine research wing here at our esteemed Crystal Bay University Hospital. With these new facilities, we hope to grow the knowledge to fight and cure many childhood diseases and conditions that still plague our children. We hope that the research we do here will make many of these ailments a distant memory in our lifetime." The crowd answered with applause. The administrator went on for several more minutes, thanking the Beacons of Light foundation and individually recognizing several members of the team who had coordinated the project and worked tirelessly to make it a success.

"And now," he said, taking a deep breath, "without further ado, to perform the ceremonial ribbon cutting, I'd like to bring out our guest of honor. Our very own Angel of Light, the Crystal Bay Crusader herself...Beacon!"

As he said her name, Beacon could just see his hand gesture in her direction over the edge of the platform. Casey tapped her elbow and gave her a big smile and thumbs up. Drawing on both her energies, Beacon leaped high into the air over the platform. Checking her landing spot, she trickled a small flow of levitation to descend slowly. The crowd exploded when they saw her suspended above them and cheered her all the way to the platform. As she touched down softly next to the hospital administrator, she smiled broadly and waved, inciting more shouts, whistles, and clapping.

After several seconds, she approached the microphone. She briefly considered tapping it just for Casey's benefit, but refrained. "Thank you! Thank you, everyone," she said, stilling the crowd. "It's a huge honor to be here. I can't say enough how proud I am of the foundation and the hard work these people have put in for such an amazing project. Please, let's give them another round of appreciation. They are the real heroes here today!" She clapped, looking toward the team sitting to her right, and the crowd enthusiastically joined her.

"I'm also incredibly proud of the city of Crystal Bay and deeply grateful for all of you, too. Without all of you contributing money and volunteering your precious time, projects like this aren't possible. This—" she gestured behind her "—is all because of you." She clapped again, and again, the crowd echoed her applause.

The administrator approached the microphone next to her. "Thank you for those words, Beacon. And now, it's time to dedicate the new wing by cutting the ceremonial ribbon." He waved to the side of the stage, and two stagehands carried out a very large set of metal scissors onto the platform.

Well, as long as I'm here, let's make it a real show, shall we? she thought. She smiled at the administrator, held out her hand, palm out, toward the large scissors, and shook her head playfully. The two scissors-bearers stopped and looked at each other, not knowing what to do next. Likewise, the administrator smiled hesitantly, clearly surprised and confused, but he played along.

With a flourish, Beacon pointed her index finger toward the ribbon, carefully aiming over the crowd, and drew on the flows of energy within her. A thin, white-hot beam shot from her finger and neatly sliced the ribbon in two. The crowd gasped in amazement and then erupted, roaring and squealing its approval.

Laughing and clapping softly, the administrator retook the microphone. "Excellent. Well done. Thank you for that, Beacon." Beacon smiled and stepped back as the administrator turned to the crowd once more. "That concludes the ceremony itself. In the pavilion behind me, we have set up a small reception area where, for a small donation to Beacons of Light, Beacon will be signing autographs and will be available for photographs. Thank you again for coming!"

He turned and shook Beacon's hand. As the crowd started to mingle and disperse, he motioned toward the back of the platform toward a small private entrance to the reception area.

Giddyap, little pony. Show's not over yet.

District Attorney Harris sat at his desk. Across the room, the large monitor on the wall showed the live stream of the hospital commemoration ceremony where Beacon had just sliced the ribbon using her powers. Harris grinned. *She may hate these public appearances*, he thought, chuckling to himself, *but she is a natural.*

The desk before him was covered with case sheets from the empty folio on the corner. Some had photos, some didn't. He scanned them over again. Homeless people, addicts, orphans, prostitutes. All very different people, but with one thing in common: they were all missing.

The other thing that connected them was the fact that, as far as he could tell, there was nothing connecting them...except a hunch.

What he saw in the files also confirmed something else that the police commissioner had told him: these disappearances had been going on for months. Most of them had gone completely unnoticed until a few random witnesses had finally come forward, and the investigators started finding more of them. Sadly, cases like this quite often don't even get a second look; it wasn't uncommon for people in these parts of town living these kinds of lives to just go off the grid unexpectedly. Harris shook his head as he thumbed through them. *Sad, but true.*

Typically, this kind of thing is handled by the police, and the District Attorney's office wouldn't be involved until charges needed to be filed, but the folio delivered by the courier had a short note attached to the front from the commissioner himself explaining why it had landed here:

> We've hit a dead end on this one, but we believe there might be more going on here. It might be time to pull in someone who can get more of a rooftop view on this situation for us.
>
> Perhaps you can get in touch with our friend in the black and yellow suit and see if she can help.

The more Harris looked over the contents of the folio, the more the hunch grew, and the more he thought the commissioner was right. He looked up at the monitor again just in time to see Beacon wave once more to the crowd and leave the stage "Yup," he muttered to the screen, "going to go over this a bit more myself, but pretty sure you're going to be hearing from me in a few days, my friend."

Shifts

Tricia hesitantly pushed the door to the outer office open and peered inside. It had been nearly a year since she had last been here, and that visit had been under very different circumstances. Doctor Alexei Demerov had presided over the last complex then, and he had been the one to place her and her lab on probation following her accident. Since then, however, Doctor Demerov had stepped down after Rene Thornton's association with the Liberators of Gaia had been exposed, and Doctor Clarissa Patel had recently been appointed to replace him.

As Tricia surveyed the outer office, she immediately found Brenda, the chair's executive assistant, sitting in her familiar place on the far side of the room just outside the door to the inner office. With all the changes that had happened, seeing her there was somehow comforting. *Thank goodness some things don't change,* she thought as she stood in the doorway.

Brenda looked up, and when she saw Tricia standing there, she broke out with a big smile. "Come on in, Doctor Carling," she said, waving Tricia into the room. "Doctor Patel is just finishing up a call. Please take a seat. She'll be done any moment." Her welcoming tone helped settle some of the butterflies fluttering in Tricia's stomach in anticipation of her first formal meeting with the new chairperson.

"Thanks, Brenda," Tricia replied, settling into a chair near the coffee table. Despite the change in leadership, this part of the office remained familiar, albeit brighter and more spacious. The drawn curtains let the bright afternoon sun fill the room, casting a warm glow on the familiar surroundings. Tiny particles of dust glowed midair as they danced in the light.

"Nice jacket," Brenda said, breaking the silence as Tricia settled into the chair. "Very smart."

"Thanks," Tricia replied, reflexively reaching up and smoothing out the nonexistent wrinkles in the sleek material with her palms. The jacket was brand new. She had bought it over the weekend just for the meeting. Marni had helped her pick it out. It was one of the new lapel-less jackets that had become the latest fashion sensation.

Tricia had thought it might be a bit too radical for her, but Marni was adamant. "The style just screams 'forward thinker,' and it fits you like a glove," she insisted. She also said the shimmering navy blue fabric and the royal blue silk top she wore beneath it just made Tricia's eyes pop. *Who was I to argue?*

"Have you met Doctor Patel before?" Brenda asked.

"No, not since the welcoming reception a couple of months ago, and that really wasn't much more than a hello-and-handshake thing."

"Doctor Patel, you'll find, is somewhat less formal than Doctor Demerov, but I'm very sure that blazer will make a good impression," Brenda said.

Tricia smiled. Although Doctor Patel had been here just slightly over two months now, Tricia still didn't know very much about her. Doctor Patel had immediately started sending out regular videocasts and holding regular virtual town halls for the lab complex, so Tricia had seen a bit of her in action. Her initial impressions of Patel were favorable, but video and in-person were two very different things.

Of course, she'd read the brief biography that had been circulated when Doctor Patel joined. It talked mostly about how she had taken a career in industrial research rather than academia, and while it highlighted some of her accomplishments as head of research for some major corporations and had some political appointments as a technology advisor, it told Tricia nothing about what kind of a person she was or what she might expect from this first meeting. Tricia had even made a point to casually ask the other lab directors who had met with her already about their impressions, but their perceptions varied from "congenial" and "friendly" to "imposing" and "intimidating", none of which was very useful to help her prepare.

Whatever preparation Trica had been able to do would have to suffice, though, as the door to the inner office opened, and Doctor Patel swept into the room. She paused briefly to welcome Tricia with a warm smile but held up one finger, silently asking Tricia to give her just a minute. Tricia nodded in response, and Doctor Patel bent down to talk to Brenda. To give them some semblance of privacy, Tricia deliberately tried to focus her attention elsewhere, but even so, Tricia couldn't help but take the opportunity to study Doctor Patel as she and Brenda talked.

Doctor Clarissa Patel was a striking figure, as stark a contrast to the previous lab chair as one could possibly get. Her lavish black hair spilled over her shoulders, framing her piercing black eyes and the smooth dark complexion of her face. Only a few gray hairs hinted at her age; she appeared far younger than she likely truly was. She wore a simple black skirt and a sleeveless orchid button-down blouse adorned with only a single gold pendant around her neck. Simple, practical, stylish. Tricia guessed Doctor Patel to be about her height (without the black heels she was wearing), but a bit less slight of build and curvier. Judging from the definition of her exposed arms and calves, she took her personal fitness quite seriously. Given the animated manner in which she spoke with Brenda and how she punctuated her words with her hands, Tricia was certain Doctor Patel's intensity was not restricted to just the gym.

After a few exchanges, Doctor Patel stood up and turned to face Tricia. She smiled broadly as she walked over to meet Tricia. Tricia rose to greet her, quickly twisting the stray strands of hair that were patting her cheek to secure them behind her ear.

"So good to finally meet you, Doctor Carling," Patel said, extending her hand.

Tricia took her hand and smiled back. "Likewise, Doctor Patel," Tricia replied, giving her a firm handshake.

"Please, call me Clarissa." Doctor Patel glanced downward momentarily before quickly restoring eye contact. "Nice jacket, by the way."

"Thank you," Tricia replied. She glanced briefly over Doctor Patel's shoulder to where Brenda was sitting. Brenda grinned and winked at her.

"Shall we?" Doctor Patel gestured toward her office door. Tricia nodded and followed her in.

Just as Clarissa herself was a stark contrast to her predecessor, Tricia was amazed at how the inner office had changed since the last time she had visited. The heavy drapes had been replaced with blinds and light curtains, creating an atmosphere bursting with light. The office now smelled of sandalwood and lavender instead of leather and musk. One side of the room now held a small alcove clearly designed for video conferencing, where Tricia assumed Clarissa prepared her newly regular videocasts and conducted the virtual town halls. In both style and demeanor, Clarissa Patel was the opposite of Alexei Demerov, but in no way less professional or deserving of respect.

The walls and shelves that once had held Doctor Demerov's awards and certificates now held plaques for patents, engraved crystal awards, and numerous photos of Doctor Patel with several very prominent corporate executives, multiple leading scientists, and even two presidents, presumably the same ones on whose science and technology councils she had served. Many people disparaged Patel's time in industry and politics, claiming they didn't prepare her to run the university laboratory complex, but it was clear to Tricia that Clarissa was highly accomplished in her own right. Whether she was qualified to run the labs or not, Tricia knew it would be a tremendous mistake to underestimate her.

Clarissa gestured to the chair in front of her desk for Tricia to take a seat. She then grabbed a large spring comb clip off her desk, gave her thick hair a practiced twist, and secured the black rope securely behind her head. "Would you like some tea?" she asked Tricia casually.

Tricia hesitated—she wasn't much of a tea drinker but felt it would likely be rude to refuse—and Doctor Patel immediately picked up on the pause. "If you're worried about having caffeine so late in the day," she said, "it's completely herbal. I found this lovely little shop just off campus that makes and sells these exquisite blends. I'm absolutely in love with the place."

Tricia smiled. She not only appreciated Clarissa's passion for a good hot beverage but was also amused at her concern about caffeine. Truth be told, Tricia wouldn't mind a bit of a boost, even this late in the day. Since Alex had been on vacation, Jamal had picked up the morning coffee-making duties, and sadly, what he brewed was more akin to liquid suffering than what could be considered coffee. Tricia had even tried coming in early to beat him to it, but more often than not, she hadn't been successful, so involuntarily, Tricia found herself cutting back lately, mostly out of pity for the lining of her stomach.

"Sure," Tricia replied with a smile, "I'd love to try it."

Clarissa nodded with a smile and went to the small sideboard against the window that had been transformed into her tea station. She then began what Tricia could only describe as a ritual bordering on ceremony. Watching her, Tricia was struck again by the stark contrast between Demerov and what she'd seen of Patel. Whereas Demerov embodied the very essence of staunch academia, the purity of science, and research for research's sake, Patel was clearly the face of embracing a progressive mindset, open collaboration, and making a positive impact on the world.

Despite all that, though, she was also deliberate and calculating. Tricia watched her make the tea; every scoop precisely the same, the water poured just a certain way. Clarissa picked up a stiff bamboo brush and stirred each cup gently and evenly. It dawned on her then that Patel wasn't just making tea; she was preparing tea, preparing an experience, preparing herself. *And preparing me*, Tricia realized.

Satisfied the cups met her expectations, Patel turned and handed Tricia a plain, handleless cup. The bouquet of the tea hit her immediately, and she bent down to inhale the vapors more deeply. *Bergamot...star anise...cardamom,* she thought, noting each of the blended scents as she recognized them. Several she could not. *From the color, I'm guessing saffron as well?*

Tricia took a careful sip. It was still scalding hot, but even in that tiny taste, the flavors danced on her tongue. *And ginger,* she marveled. *It's a feast for the senses. If it made sound, it would be nothing short of Vivaldi's Four Seasons,* she mused and hummed softly to herself.

Clarissa had already taken the other seat in front of her desk, facing her. She smiled in anticipation of Tricia's reaction. "Do you like it?" She asked expectantly.

"It's delightful," Tricia responded, giving her a big smile. "Thank you for preparing it."

Clarissa beamed and took a sip of her own tea. She closed her eyes, indulging herself a moment of complete satisfaction and contentment before starting the meeting. Setting the cup down, she reached over to her desk and fetched her commpad and a small set of reading glasses. She flipped the chain over her head and let the glasses rest on her chest.

"You know," she began, "I've been especially looking forward to getting to know you better, Tricia."

"Why is that?" Tricia asked, taking another sip of her tea. *It really is amazing. We may need to add a tea option to the break area,* she thought as Doctor Patel scanned her commpad.

"Well, you see, Doctor Demerov didn't leave much behind in the way of notes before he left, but in the few he did leave, he had some very good things to say about you."

Tricia couldn't help but look surprised. "Really?" She asked.

"Mmm-hmmm," Clarissa replied, nodding her head. She perched her reading glasses on the end of her nose and scrolled on the screen in front of her. After a few swipes, she stopped and read:

> "...despite having to put Doctor Carling on probation to reinforce the importance of following protocols, Tricia Carling and her team are among the finest examples of the upcoming talent we have in the laboratory complex. She and they embody the potential we have to advance the frontiers of science and to further the university's reputation in the scientific community as a whole in the future."

"Wow," Tricia said. "I had no idea he thought that highly of me...us. I'm really honored. I didn't know him well, but he was a great scientist."

Patel nodded. "I didn't know him well personally either, but I knew him by reputation." She tapped the commpad. "He had very high standards and didn't dole out praise often. You should take it as the highest compliment. Anyone who could get Alexei Demerov to write this is someone I think is worth getting to know."

The two women proceeded to chat informally for the better part of an hour. Clarissa shared her background, which, in Tricia's mind, easily justified most of the plaques, awards, and photographs she had around her office. Clarissa was also keenly interested in Tricia's academic journey and asked a lot of probing questions about her aspirations, both personal and professional, her vision for the lab, and where she might see herself in the near future. Throughout the conversation, Tricia gained a deep appreciation for another one of Clarissa Patel's distinguishing characteristics: the value she placed on networks and relationships. She had gotten a hint of this from the various town halls and video blogs Clarissa had done, but seeing it in person, it was clear she not only valued relationships but was also extremely polished and adept at forging them. *This is someone I could learn a lot from*, she decided well before the end of the conversation.

"Thank you so much for the opportunity to get to know you a bit better, Tricia," Clarissa said. She quickly checked the time on her commpad. "There is one more topic I want to make sure we get to in the time we have left today, which, I'm afraid, is running a bit short. I am making sure that when I meet with each of the lab directors, we take time to discuss some of the strategic changes I will be leading in terms of how we fund the labs going forward."

Uh oh, Tricia thought, *the "f" word*. Most of Tricia's colleagues were quite comfortable with the typical one, but when 'funding' came up, that's usually when people started scrambling, and, in her experience, the bickering started.

"You see," Clarissa started, lifting the chain of her reading glasses up off her neck and setting them, along with her commpad, down on the edge of the desk next to her, "even before Doctor Demerov's departure, the trustees were growing increasingly concerned about the tremendous investment the university makes in the research lab complex versus how little return the university actually gets back from it."

"But the research done here has contributed significantly to the scientific community, hasn't it? My understanding is that the work done here is highly respected and admired," Tricia chimed in. "I mean, after all, we do have four Nobel laureates. The Advanced Genetics Lab won the Lasker Award twice, if I recall, and the Nuclear Physics lab received the Wolf Prize just last year."

Clarissa nodded, "True, true, and that does help in terms of securing donations and grants, but the trustees have felt for a while that we could be doing a better job of leveraging the intellectual property we create to increase funding more directly. Right now, the university as a whole is very dependent on its trusts and donations, as well as tuition and sports, to fund both the labs and the student programs. If we could make the labs more self-sustainable financially, we could not only increase the funding for the research but allow the university to channel more of the general funds into the student programs, offer more scholarships, expand extracurriculars, that kind of thing."

She sat back in her chair a bit more, assuming a slightly more relaxed posture. "That's why I've been brought in. They would like me to apply my experience and connections to find partners in the corporate world who would be interested in licensing or acquiring our research results. This means, as a whole, we will put more energy into promoting research programs that we believe will be of interest to corporations for commercial purposes."

Some obvious questions immediately came to Tricia's mind. *Not sure how well she'll take these, but her reaction will tell me what she's really like,* she thought and went for it.

Tricia sat forward a bit and looked Doctor Patel in the eye. "So, the funding part makes a lot of sense, and I'm definitely behind approaches that would get more money for the labs and better fund student programs. However, I'm concerned that if we focus too much on profit rather than scientific advancement, won't that take away what makes us special? I mean, we can research the radical concepts that a company with financial obligations to stakeholders couldn't justify. Also, what will that do to the labs that are more theoretical in nature? Would they get pushed to the back in favor of the ones that have more obvious applications for their research?" She then held her breath, waiting for Clarissa's reaction, and mentally crossed her fingers.

Clarissa smiled. Leaning forward, she replied, "You know, of all your colleagues with whom I've met and have run this past so far, you are the first one who thought of that question, or at least, the first one who has had the courage to actually ask it."

Carling for the score! Tricia thought, happy she didn't just sink her career in their first meeting.

Clarissa spread her hands. "There has to be a balance, of course. Our first mission is to advance science and learning, but we do have limited resources. While we may need to avoid funding investigations that don't go anywhere after a reasonable period of time, this is really about capitalizing on results that demonstrate some financial potential.

"Let's face it, Tricia, when the time comes for budgets to be tightened, and we'd be foolish to think they won't be—" Clarissa raised an eyebrow and tipped her head to the side in a small shrug "—the labs that generate income will fare far better in that process than the ones that don't. Yours is one of the highly promising ones, and we want to make sure it gets all the support it needs, don't we?"

"Of course, Clarissa," Tricia agreed emphatically.

"Further," she continued, "even if funding weren't the primary driver, making an impact on society with our work requires both research *and* development. To make the world a better place, our research needs to be applied to real-world problems and made usable. The university simply doesn't have the core competencies to commercialize and distribute, so we still need partners that can."

Spoken like a true executive...she's not wrong, though.

"That makes sense," Tricia agreed, "but what about the researchers themselves? If a company decides to pick up their work, what happens to them?"

What happens to me? she added mentally.

"It depends on the nature of the agreed partnership," Clarissa explained. "In most cases, companies will simply license the IP, and the university is free to continue doing whatever research they want. If a business partner wants more exclusivity, well, then the team would be free to pursue other grants or projects, or they could potentially negotiate with the company to join them and continue as part of their R&D staff."

Tricia stiffened a bit and observed that Clarissa picked up on it immediately. Clarissa reached over and put her hand on Tricia's forearm. "It wouldn't be so bad, I promise," she reassured Tricia with a smile. "I may be a bit biased in my belief, but I think talented people like you could learn a lot from a tour in the private sector. It would provide a chance to build some skills that are not typically developed strongly at the university, skills such as management disciplines, leadership, and how to take a more economic perspective in decision-making and setting priorities."

Anticipating Tricia's follow-up question, Clarissa quickly added, "Of course, if someone made that career choice, it goes without saying that the door would always be open for them to return and bring those skills back to help make our programs here even more successful."

Tricia relaxed a bit and nodded. Clarissa searched her face for a moment and asked, "Does that sound reasonable? Do you have any other thoughts or questions around that?"

"Hmmm, no. Not right now," Tricia replied, gently shaking her head. "It's just a lot to take in. I'll need some time to process it all and what it might mean for me...for all of us." Then, tacking on a smile, "I'm sure I will later, though."

"That's perfectly fine," Clarissa said, returning the smile. "We will definitely have the chance to talk about it more. In fact, probably sooner than you might have originally thought."

"What do you mean?" Tricia asked, cocking her head and furrowing her eyebrows slightly.

"Your work has already drawn the attention of a few interested parties. I'm going to ask Jack, your lab admin, to coordinate with Brenda to start scheduling some walkthroughs. I will also have them set up some time for us to prepare and make sure the lab and the team are ready."

"How soon?" Tricia asked.

"One is exceptionally eager to see what you've done and is pushing to come in sometime in the next couple of weeks," Clarissa answered. "Don't fret. We will do it when we are ready, but we will do our best not to make them wait any longer than we have to, right?"

Tricia nodded, somewhat stunned by the aggressive timeline. "Yes, of course."

"Very good." Clarissa quickly checked her watch, looked at Tricia, and stood up, gesturing toward the door. "My apologies, but as much as I've enjoyed our meeting today, I do have an appointment in a few minutes and would appreciate a bit of time to get ready."

Rising to meet her, Tricia replied, "Oh, certainly. Of course." Her mind was reeling, but the meeting had gone well, and she was determined to end it on a solid note, despite the tornado in her brain. She pushed it aside and extended her hand. "I really enjoyed getting to know you better as well, and we will do whatever it takes to impress anyone interested in our work," she said, forcing a smile.

"I know you will," Clarissa said, giving Tricia's hand a solid pump in return.

Brenda greeted Tricia as she let herself out, closing the door behind her. "So, how did it go?"

"Well," Tricia answered, lowering her voice, "it went a lot better than the last time I was in this office."

Brenda chuckled. "I'm sure it did. She's quite a presence, isn't she?"

"She definitely is," Tricia agreed, "but yes, I feel it went pretty well and that we really got off on the right foot. She clearly has some big changes in mind that I'll need some time to wrap my head around, but I think I'm going to learn a lot from her."

"No doubt," Brenda agreed.

On the way out, Tricia decided to make a brief stop in the restroom. Before facing the world again, she needed a brief moment to decompress in private. When she walked in, she took a moment to inspect the stall door that had borne the brunt of her frustration and angst the last time she was here. *They did a nice job fixing it,* she noted, running her hand over it lightly. The last time she saw that door, or rather its predecessor, most likely, it was lying on the floor up against the side of the toilet with a section of her handprint impressed into the metal. She was sure that, to this day, the maintenance person who'd found it still had no explanation for how it got that way and that it remained both a mystery and a good story he or she told on occasion.

Tricia went to the sink and let the cool water run over her hands briefly before splashing some gently on her face. She then pulled down a paper towel and patted her face and hands dry, letting the details of the conversation play over and over in her head. Finally, she put her hands down on the counter and stared at her reflection, much like she had done a year ago.

It's all happening so fast, so suddenly.

It's my life's work! They can't take it away from me.

Yeah, they could, and I could do nothing to stop it.

Would I be prepared to leave the university? Leave the team?

What if the team leaves me?

She hung her head for a moment and took a deep breath. She then faced herself in the mirror. *Easy does it, Trish. Don't get ahead of yourself. There are still a lot of bridges to cross before any of this matters. One step at a time.*

She nodded once to herself and tossed the damp wad of paper towel into the trash. *Yes,* she affirmed as she pulled open the door. *Just take it one step at a time,* and let the door swing closed behind her.

Tricia tugged the black elastic armband up over her left bicep and smoothed the sleeve of her *gi* underneath it. Sensei Tim handed out the armbands to the black belt candidates that he selected to assist him with teaching the class. Since Tricia had officially become a candidate a couple of months ago, he had selected her nearly every week, either to help with the regular open class she and Marni took together, or with the advanced select class he had invited her to join last year.

She pulled down on the hem of her jacket and tugged the ends of her brown belt to cinch in the knot at her waist. Tricia ran her thumb over the stripe. It had taken her two attempts to earn the black stripe on the belt, the stripe that marked her as a black belt candidate, and the way Tricia had failed still ate at her every now and then. It was the sparring portion of the test. She was ahead by two points and got cocky, opting for a high-risk maneuver to end the match quickly rather than be smart and patient. She slipped and lost her footing. Worse, she barely caught herself before she instinctively drew on her powers to recover.

In the end, she went down, and her opponent caught her with a wrist lock on the mat, forcing her to tap out. Sensei had given her a thorough dressing down for being so reckless, but since she'd done exceptionally well on the other parts of the test, he only made her repeat the sparring portion. She won that second match easily and earned the stripe, but the fact that she had once again almost slipped with her abilities sharply reminded her of the importance of the discipline she was still developing.

Despite the fact that Tricia had previously assisted Sensei with multiple classes, she still couldn't shake the butterflies she got each time he called her forward to receive the armband. Sensei had made it clear to her and the other candidates that how they led the class and helped teach the other students was as much a part of earning the belt as the techniques and sparring. "Mastery is more than our personal proficiency," he frequently reminded them. "It is about how we enable and develop the proficiency of others." As the leader of a team herself, Tricia could not have agreed more.

Looking toward the back of the room, she spotted Marni still getting ready. Their usual pre-class catch-up had been interrupted when Sensei called her to the front of the room. Marni looked up and made eye contact. Tricia smiled at her, but Marni could only muster a slight curl at the end of her mouth, leaving her eyes melancholy. *Something's clearly on her mind*, Tricia thought, but before she could consider it further, Sensei called the class to order.

"Form up, people!" His deep voice boomed out from the front center of the room. All the chit-chat suddenly stopped, and the class settled into neat lines and rows facing him. They knew better than to lollygag once he'd called them to attention. Tricia, along with the other students Sensei had selected to assist tonight, lined up to his right in front of the class. She noticed that Marni didn't take their usual spot, choosing instead to stay near the back of the room. *Definitely, something is going on with her.*

"Carling," Sensei said, drawing her mind back to the class. "Lead the warm-up if you please."

"*Hai,* Sensei!" Tricia shouted, clapping her hands to her sides and bowing slightly. Sensei bowed back, and Tricia jogged to the front center spot. She exhaled sharply and turned to face the room.

"Ok, everyone, let's start with some stretches. Horse stance, please." Tricia and the rest of the class settled into the stance. She pulled her left arm across her chest. "Arm stretch, left first, and hold...."

As soon as class was over, Tricia quickly returned the armband to Sensei Tim, thanked him for the chance to help him lead the class, and made a beeline to the back of the room where Marni was packing her gear away. Tricia squatted down next to her. "Hi there," she said, stripping off her belt and *gi* jacket.

"Hey," Marni said sullenly, not looking up.

Tricia swapped the clothes in her hand for the hoodie in her bag and pulled it on over her head. "So," she said with slightly exaggerated enthusiasm, "do you want to get a quick drink on the way home?"

"I dunno," Marni replied, still looking down at her bag. She zipped it forcefully for emphasis. "Do you *have* the time?"

Tricia's brows knitted a bit, and her face fell, clouded with a touch of sadness. "C'mon, Marns," she said, putting her hand on Marni's shoulder. "Don't be like that."

Marni turned to look at her. At first, her face was stony, but her gaze softened when she saw the hurt on Tricia's face. Marni sighed, and her shoulders slumped slightly. "Yeah, sure, let's."

Tricia had walked to class, so Marni drove them to a small place just off campus. The ride was a quiet one. It reminded Tricia of the ride they'd taken just about a year ago after the class, where Tricia had accidentally used her powers for the first time at Marni's expense. That was a very quiet ride as well, but Tricia suspected the hurt Marni was feeling now was deeper and more serious than a simple bruise on her chest from a careless punch.

When they arrived at the bar, Tricia went up to get them some drinks while Marni scouted out a table toward the back. She apparently needed no coaching to find a somewhat secluded spot where they could talk with some measure of privacy. Two glasses of Malbec in hand, Tricia made her way over to where Marni was sitting.

"Malbec," Tricia announced, setting a glass in front of Marni and taking the chair across from her. "Just what the doctors ordered." It was one of their standing jokes, but Marni didn't even crack a smile.

"Ok, Marns," Tricia said. "What gives? Did I say something? Did something happen at the hospital?"

Marni swirled her glass and stared down into the deep red liquid. Finally, she sighed. "Are you aware you won't be in our class after a few weeks? That once you pass your black belt test—and you will pass it with flying colors, I'm sure—you'll have to transition out of the open class?"

There it is, Tricia thought. "Yes, Marni, I am very aware of it," she replied, a hint of genuine sadness in her voice. "It's been on my mind ever since I was accepted as a candidate. I just didn't want to make a big deal out of it."

She patted Marni's hand and forced a smile. "Besides, who knows? Sensei has been asking me to help teach a lot. Maybe after I pass, I'll still get to come as an assistant teacher. John is moving away after he gets married, so Sensei may be looking for a replacement."

Marni looked up at her. Her eyes were turned down, missing their usual sparkle, and her lips were pressed together in a line. "Attending class with you as a teacher will *not* be the same as taking the class *with* you, Tricia. You know that." She huffed as she fidgeted with the stem of the wine glass in her hand. "I shouldn't even have to bring it up."

Tricia nodded as Marni pressed on. Her eyebrows furrowed, and her expression shifted from sadness to irritation. She finally took a sip of wine and pushed the glass to the side.

"You know what the thing is about all this, Tricia?" she said angrily. "Remember that when we started, this was *my* thing. I wanted you to do it *with* me. I practically had to twist your arm to get you to do it. Do you remember that?"

"Yes, I do remember," Tricia admitted.

"And then, the next thing you know, you ran with it. Sensei invited you to his special—" Marni made air quotes with her fingers "—advanced class, and then you're jumping from one belt to the next like a bug on a hot rock. Pile all the extra practice you get with your, um, extracurricular activities on top of it, and you just took off."

Tricia pursed her lips. The accusatory tone rubbed her the wrong way, but she bit her lip. *Easy does it, Trish. Marni needs to get this off her chest.*

"It wasn't intentional, Marni. You know I needed this. I needed this training to get the other things that were happening to me under control."

"I get that," Marni shot back. "I really do, but it just felt like you left me behind. Recall I didn't know anything about what was happening to you until much later... when you finally got around to telling me." She took another swig of her wine, a much bigger one this time. "Honestly, even knowing now doesn't make it all feel any better either."

"What did you want me to do?" Tricia asked, her irritation now starting to show. "Hold myself back? Not test when I was ready? Not advance?"

Marni sighed again and shook her head. "No, of course not, and frankly, that's the real kicker in this whole thing. You're amazing, Tricia." Tricia sat back, surprised. "No, I really mean it," Marni continued. "The way you move, the control you show, how you string techniques together so effortlessly. It's awesome. I can see why Sensei pulled you into the advanced class. He saw it, saw your potential."

A tear welled up in Tricia's eyes. *Didn't see that coming,* she thought, smiling. "Thanks, Marni. I...I didn't know you thought that."

Marni nodded, smiling now herself. "I'm so proud of you, everything you've accomplished, but it still doesn't make dealing with the fact that you'll be moving on from this without me any easier."

Tricia pressed her lips together to keep from crying. She reached across the table and took Marni's hand. "I know. I've felt the same, but I also know that no matter what else changes, it's you and me. You mean the world to me, and that isn't going anywhere. We *will* find something else that can be ours, something else that we can do together."

Marni nodded, "I hope so, but it's not going to be easy. Your schedule is pretty full, day *and* night, and not the way a nighttime schedule should be full either, I might add." She winked and chuckled. "It's pretty hard competing with jumping around the rooftops of Crystal Bay."

Tricia snickered. "I can see how you'll feel that way, but we will figure it out...all of it. We *will* make it work, I promise," Tricia assured her, patting her hand again for emphasis.

Marni let out a short exhale, obviously feeling some weight leave her shoulders. "I'm sure we will. And I'm sorry for just unloading all this without any warning. I guess it's all the change that's been going on for a while now, and it finally just caught up with me. The thing with our class just pushed it over the edge. I shouldn't have let it get this far. I'm sorry."

"All good," Tricia said and held up her glass. Marni clinked it in return. "It's been a week, but I can fill you in on that later."

Marni nodded. She quickly checked her watch and gulped down the last of her wine. "Sorry to emote and run, but I've got an early shift at the hospital tomorrow, so I need to bounce." She gathered her things, and Tricia stood up, and after a quick hug, Marni turned toward the door to leave.

After taking a couple of steps, Marni stopped and turned back toward Tricia. "I know this probably seems very selfish," Marni said with a sigh, "but things *have* changed. It's not your fault, but like it or not, things are different, and even though you'll never stop being my sister, I just need some time to wrap my head around it. I hope you understand that."

"No, I get it," Tricia replied. "It's not being selfish at all. I understand. Really, I do." Marni smiled weakly and nodded in both agreement and relief. "We are still getting together for our usual appointment later this week, aren't we?" Tricia asked hesitantly.

"Of course," Marni answered, broadening her smile. "Regardless of any of this, you're still a tough nut we have to crack, Tricia, and we have a lot of work to do to sort out what's really going on with you and your, um, condition."

"Great," Tricia replied. "And don't worry about this," she added, waving her hand over the table. "Go ahead and take off. I'll handle the check."

"Thanks," Marni said gratefully. "Do you want a lift home?"

Tricia pondered for a second and then shook her head. "Nah. We're close, and it's a nice night. I can walk from here."

Marni nodded, and Tricia watched her walk out the door. *She is my sister*, she thought. *And my rock. I'd be lost without her. Maybe things have changed, but I'm not going to let that push her away, not if I have anything to say about it.*

Not by a long shot.

Return

Her eyes snapped open as she gasped in a large breath. She pushed herself up, propping herself up on one elbow, and pulled open the front of her shirt. She looked down and felt her chest. There was a small circular scar just to the left of her breastbone. It was barely noticeable, but she knew exactly where to look.

What? Where?

She felt a hand on her shoulder. A woman's voice softly said, "Shhhhh." She turned her head slowly, straining the tense muscles in her neck, to look up at the woman. She blinked a few times to focus her eyes on her. This woman was in her mid-thirties. Her medium brown hair was pulled back into a short ponytail. Her piercing gray eyes met hers, silently commanding her to relax. *A nurse?*

The woman methodically helped her sit more upright and adjusted the angle of the bed so she could sit properly. She then took a plastic cup of water with a straw from the small table next to the bed and handed it to her. She sipped eagerly.

After quenching her thirst, she asked, "Where am I?"

The woman held up one finger to ask her to be patient and then walked to the far side of the room. She tapped a commpod in her ear and said something too softly for her to hear. She then turned back toward her and clasped her hands behind her back, waiting.

Sipping the water again, the woman looked around. The room was austere but clean. Leads and wires running from small patches on various parts of her body and neck were connected to a small bank of monitors on a rack next to the bed. She studied them briefly; all the indicators read normal. There was a small window with sheer white curtains, but the room was much brighter than could be accounted for by the light streaming in through it. She could see no other obvious source of illumination, though.

A hospital? Some kind of clinic? she wondered, but deep down, she decided it wasn't, at least not in the conventional sense.

Her black hair, usually pulled up, was splayed out on the pillow behind her. *Longer than I usually wear it,* she observed, and ran her fingers through it. *It has been recently trimmed, though.* She noticed also that the nail polish she'd been wearing had been removed, and she'd been given a manicure, both quite recently.

Just then, she heard a buzz followed by a loud click. A man entered the room. He was probably her age, or slightly older, with some gray at the temples of his short, cropped dark hair. He wore a simple jacket over a mock turtleneck shirt, slacks, and polished shoes.

"Hello, Doctor Thornton," he said as he walked to her bedside. He gestured with two fingers to the woman waiting across the room. She nodded and rolled a short stool over to the bed for him. He undid the button on his jacket, sat on the stool, and extended his hand toward her.

Rene gave it a tentative shake. "Thanks, I think," she responded. "Where am I? *How* am I here?"

"We will get to 'where' in due time, Doctor Thornton," he replied. "As to 'how', you were brought here after your, um, policy disagreement with the Liberators of Gaia at Meyer's Tower."

"Policy disagreement?" Rene said with a sneer. "I was shot."

"Yes, you were," he agreed.

"How then?"

"You were nearly out of reach when the responders arrived on the scene. The Liberators were long gone by the time they arrived. Some of our people were in the responder unit—we've been watching for a while, you see—and were able to administer some Neurostatin to induce biological stasis until you could be treated for your wounds. They also saw to it that you were officially declared dead on the scene and then brought you here for additional care."

Rene stifled a short laugh.

"Something about that amuses you, Doctor Thornton?" Sorensen asked stiffly.

"No, no," Rene said, "Just appreciating the irony in that." She chuckled again, recalling her encounter with Beacon in her lab, where Rene had essentially tried to do the same thing to her to keep Beacon prisoner while Rene carried out her plot with the Liberators of Gaia. "Never mind," she added with a dismissive wave of her hand. "Did they make it? The Liberators, I mean."

"They did escape from Meyer's Tower, but, in the end, they were in no real danger."

"How do you mean?" Rene asked, a bit more urgently.

"Beacon was able to use her abilities to stop your device," he replied.

"I see," she acknowledged. *Clever girl, Tricia.*

As if he could read her mind, he followed on, "Yes, Doctor Carling proved to be quite resourceful. She continues to be as well."

"Oh, so you know about Tricia?" Rene asked. "I suppose, then, you may as well call me Rene."

"In time, perhaps. You may address me as Director Sorensen. Yes, we know all about Doctor Carling, the accident, and the abilities she developed as a result of it. We've been following her and her alter-ego intently."

He shifted on his stool. "The DA has been running interference on her behalf, but we have ways of knowing things beyond his level of influence," Sorensen said with a coy smile.

Interesting...and potentially useful, Rene pondered for a moment and took another few sips of water. She thought back on the scar, her hair, and her nails. "Sorensen, how long have I been here?"

"*Director* Sorensen," Sorensen corrected, leaning towards her and clasping his hands between his knees. "It's been nearly a year since Meyer's Tower, Doctor. You've been here, with us, receiving care since that time, but we've now come to the point where we think we have use for you, so it was time to bring you back."

She scowled a bit. "Use for me?"

Sorensen nodded. "You see, we know all about you, too. We know about your past, your substantial academic credentials, and your numerous—and quite impressive, I might add—achievements. We also know about your activities with the Liberators and what you were really trying to accomplish. It's all those skills and more we are hoping to tap into for our work here."

"So, you need me to help you study Tricia? Her abilities?" she asked hesitantly. *Finally, we are cutting to the chase*, she thought.

"In a manner of speaking," he admitted. "We are still determining the best way to go about that." He shifted on his stool again, sitting more upright. "We are fairly sure Doctor Carling – Beacon – will not be entirely receptive to working with us, so we have not yet made contact."

Rene smirked a bit, "Well, surely you have ways of...convincing her, don't you?"

"How well did 'convincing her' work out for you, Doctor Thornton?"

Rene huffed a bit. "Fair point."

"No," Sorensen went on, "Before we attempt any kind of coercion, we need to be absolutely sure what we are dealing with. While we know quite a bit about her abilities already, there are aspects of her that remain a mystery, and the risk of moving too soon is unacceptably high right now."

"What are we doing then? Are you asking me to help study her? Figure out how to get her to cooperate with whatever you're planning? What?" Rene asked impatiently.

"In part, but while we wait to make contact with Beacon, we aren't exactly standing still either," Sorensen replied vaguely.

"For example, Doctor Carling was not the only product of the accident at her imaging lab that day."

Rene's eyes widened, and she straightened her back, leaning toward him. "You mean there's someone else? Someone else like Tricia?"

Sorensen nodded. "While she has, unfortunately, been drawing a little too much attention to herself lately, the other one, contrary to Doctor Carling, has chosen to be more clandestine about her abilities and has stayed out of public view.

"Despite having experienced the same accident, her abilities are significantly different than Doctor Carling's... Beacon's. We made contact with her several months ago, and after some persuasion, she has been working with us covertly, performing the odd errand for us here and there. While she doesn't know the bigger picture—and likely won't ever know the bigger picture—we are convinced that when the time is right, she will be cooperative and useful in our studies...in *your* studies should you choose to work with us."

Rene crossed her arms. "Okay, Sorensen, can we cut to it? What are you trying to do? Figure out what makes them tick? Replicate or nullify their powers? What?"

Sorensen smirked. "Not quite, Doctor Thornton. We don't need to figure out how to replicate their powers. That part we already understand, at least, for the most part."

"What then?"

"We want to know why their powers haven't killed them."

Rene squinted. "To what end?" she asked slowly and intently.

Sorensen smiled, sat back on the stool, and looked at his watch. "That's probably enough for today, Doctor. It's your first day out of the Neurostatin, and we don't want to tax you until you fully regain your strength."

He stood up and pushed the stool back towards the woman who had been waiting patiently off to the side during their conversation. She returned it to the corner and joined them at Rene's bedside. "Don't worry, though. We will have some additional conversations soon enough."

Rene sat back on the inclined bed. "Very well. What happens next?"

Sorensen buttoned his jacket. "You'll stay with us here until we are convinced you are fully recuperated. In the meanwhile, Sofia here—" he gestured toward the gray-eyed woman "—will look after you and assist you with anything you need." Sofia gave Rene a nod and a half-smile and then refilled Rene's water cup.

"Once you have recovered and we have reached an accord, you'll be transferred to other accommodation."

Rene looked him squarely in the eye. "And if we don't reach an accord?"

Sorensen returned her gaze. "Well, Doctor Thornton, it might be more accurate to say that you'll be moved to some other accommodation regardless. Reaching an accord, or not, simply determines what manner of accommodation you'll receive and how long you'll be staying there."

Rene's stomach tightened a bit, but she was determined not to show any measure of fear or intimidation. "I look forward to our next conversation, then," she said to him, forcing a sly smile.

Sorensen nodded. "As do I, Doctor. Rest well," and he turned away from her. He knocked on the door and was quickly rewarded with a buzz-click, allowing him to open the door and leave.

Curiouser and curiouser, Rene mused, taking a few more deliberate sips of her water.

Beacon planted her foot on the edge of the rooftop, thrust with a burst of dark energy, and soared. She spread her arms wide and savored the feel of the wind whipping through her hair and the sound of her cape flapping behind her. This was freedom.

Sure, she was technically on the clock during her evening patrols, but it was her clock.

Her time.

Her place.

The rooftops of Crystal Bay were hers and hers alone.

Overhead, the constellations glimmered in the indigo evening sky. Beacon knew them from her childhood. The Hunter, with his diamond belt, the Eye of the Wolf shining brightly just to the side and below him. The Bull and the Twins just over and above The Hunter. The head of The Lion was just peeking over the horizon.

On the opposite side of the sky, she saw the Blacksmith's Hammers between the Anvil and the Forge. The Hammers were especially important to her as the star at the tip of one of the handles always showed North, helping guide her on her patrols.

The street zipped beneath her, empty at this time of night except for a few late-night drivers and a handful of city workers doing maintenance or other work that kept the city humming. They went about their business, oblivious to her passing overhead, and Beacon did the same.

As the next rooftop loomed in front of her, she tucked into a forward roll. At precisely the perfect moment, Beacon extended her body and, with a soft touch of levitation, landed deftly on her feet. *And she sticks the landing. The crowd goes wild,* she thought gleefully to herself with a playful grin. Yes, it was flashy and unnecessary, but she was entitled to a little silliness once in a while, too, especially on these slower nights.

Beacon sighed. Slow was probably an understatement. She's seen barely a mugging all week. *Maybe I've been doing my job too well,* she lamented. Shame quickly followed lament; a lack of crime wasn't anything to be sad over, but still, if she wasn't needed to patrol anymore, were the charities and public appearances all she had left?

I hope not...a fate worse than death.

There are other places...other cities for someone like me to make a difference.

But Crystal Bay is my home.

I really don't have to worry about that, just yet, do I? Beacon asked herself with a sigh and shook her head. *It'll pick back up. It always picks back up eventually.*

This had happened before. Shortly after she started her patrols, the crime rate plummeted, and she remembered the thrill of seeing her work and dedication really pay off. It was short-lived, however. After a brief lull, it was clear the criminals had just gotten a bit smarter; they had learned her patrol routes and were only changing up where and when they decided to prey on people again. It was like trying to get rid of rats—you plug up one hole, and they simply find another.

"You can't just stop crime," Marni had said to her on several occasions when Tricia ranted about the situation. "You can stop some of it, but until you fix the root causes and give the criminals a more profitable alternative, they'll keep coming back. No matter how many you put away, others will come to take their place."

She was right, of course, and through the Foundation, they'd been successful in funding social programs targeted at poverty, joblessness, homelessness, drug addiction, and mental health.

Those efforts certainly had not gone to waste. Many people, particularly those in Crystal Bay's more underprivileged and underserved sectors, had benefited significantly from them, but if they had any meaningful impact on violence and hate, well, Beacon sometimes had a hard time seeing it.

If that weren't discouraging enough, a new type of miscreant had been spawned, this one apparently by Beacon herself: the sport criminal. These were people who didn't commit crimes for money or gain. They were in it for the thrill, to see if they could get something past the resident superheroine, to claim a trophy.

On the positive side, these people were not committing violent crimes, focusing more on petty theft, but still, how do you fight that? Normally, to shut down attention-seekers, you stop giving them attention, but violent or not, there are still victims, and ignoring it was not really an option. *No matter what I do, there always seems to be something else.*

Beacon breathed in deeply, puckered her lips, and let it slowly trickle out. *Regardless,* she thought to herself, *there's still work to be done and people to protect, and crying about it won't help.* Beacon turned, but before she could leap to the next rooftop, she heard a commotion from the street to her side and paused to listen.

"Stop it! Leave me alone!" she heard a young female voice call out.

"You know what we want," a boy's voice replied, followed by more scuffling.

Beacon scowled and quietly walked to the edge of the building to get a better look. As she approached the edge, though, her scowl faded to exasperation when she heard a giggle.

"Shhh," another boy's voice said in a rough whisper. "You'll blow it!"

I thought we were past this crap, Beacon thought, and after invoking her suit's camouflage with a small trickle of energy, crept to the edge and looked down. Sure enough, below her on the street was a group of two boys and a girl, likely in their early teens. The boys were pretending to push the girl around and making mock threats while the girl feigned calls of protest. Their facial expressions told Beacon all she needed to know.

"Spoofers," she muttered to herself, put her palm to her face, and slowly shook her head.

'Spoofing' was a term coined for simulating a crime to get attention, or, more specifically, Beacon's attention. Shortly after she first started to gain popularity, some of Beacon's more enthusiastic fans started pulling these kinds of stunts, impersonating crimes, hoping she would 'catch' them so they could get a picture or maybe even an autograph.

It was infuriating, if not dangerous, as it diverted her attention away from actual crimes that needed her intervention. A flurry of these cases quickly led to the city council passing Beacon's Law, which was just an extension of the laws that already forbade fake calls to emergency lines or pulling fire alarms as a prank, to make these kinds of incidents targeted at 'duly recognized agents of the city' subject to criminal charges. After a few arrests, some very prominent coverage of the offenders in the city's new streams, and some stiff sentences to set an example, spoofing died out, or, at least, most of it had.

Today seemed to be one of the rare exceptions. *I could simply ignore it,* she thought, watching the kids roughhousing on the street below, *but it is a slow night after all...*

Beacon released the mimesis of her suit and hopped over the edge of the roof, using her levitation to land softly next to the trio. As expected, as soon as one of the boys saw her, his hand shot up, holding a small commpad with a camera. He was fast, but Beacon was faster, and just as he started to click the button to snap her photo, a bright white flare burst from her hand, blinding the camera and forcing the teens to shield their eyes and look away.

"Ok, enough," she said, still bathing them in the intense light from her hand. "Put those in your pockets now and keep your hands where I can see them."

The kids tucked their devices into their pockets and stood before her, hanging their heads sheepishly. Beacon looked at them with her hands on her hips. "What do you think you're doing out here?" she asked sternly. "You know this kind of thing is illegal, don't you?"

"Awww, we didn't mean anything by it," the taller of the two boys said. "My sister here is a big fan, and she just wanted to meet you and maybe get a photo, that's all."

Beacon looked over at the girl. The girl looked up at her with big puppy-dog eyes, gleaming with hope. *Nope,* Beacon steeled herself against her melting heart. *I have to be tough about this.*

"What you all are doing isn't very smart," she told them. "It's late, and I'm out here for a reason, you know. Your parents are probably worried sick. I have half a mind to call them and tell them what you've been up to tonight."

"No, please," the girl started, but the other boy interrupted her.

"Don't freak out, guys. She's not going to call our parents," he said smugly, crossing his arms. "How can she? She doesn't even know who we are."

Beacon looked at him, and a small smile curled her lips. "Oh really?" she asked him, returning his smug attitude. "I do have superpowers, you know."

"Not mind reading ones," he replied with a sneer.

She leaned over slightly and looked him in the eye. "Is that a chance you want to take...Trevor?"

Trevor's eyes bugged out of his head, and his jaw dropped. Satisfied with his reaction, Beacon stood back up and crossed her arms. *That's right, Trevor,* she thought, watching him gape at her in disbelief. *Next time you pull a stunt like this, don't bring your backpack with your name embroidered on it.*

"Shut up, Trev!" the girl yelled, wheeling on him. "You're just making it worse!" She turned back to Beacon, and her tone softened. "Please don't tell them, Beacon. We snuck out, and they'd kill us if they found out." The girl shuffled her feet nervously. "I'm Ginny, by the way, and that's Wally." She pointed to the taller boy, and he gave Beacon a small wave.

Beacon pursed her lips and nodded, and the girl relaxed slightly. "Why would you do this anyway?" she asked them. "If you want a picture so badly, why not just come to one of the charity events? We do them all the time."

"We can't afford those," Wally answered. "Those are for rich people. We figured something like this was the only way we could help Ginny meet you."

Beacon frowned slightly beneath her mask. *Note to self: I need to talk with the team about how we can make some of these events more accessible.*

"Ok," she said. "I have an idea. First, though, there won't be any photos tonight." Ginny's face fell all the way to the ground. Beacon reached down and lifted her chin to look into her eyes. "If I were to reward something that was wrong, no matter how innocently you meant it, that wouldn't be right now, would it?" Ginny nodded her head sadly.

"But, I'll tell you what," Beacon said, looking around at each of them in turn. "Talk to your parents about getting involved with one of the charities. Volunteer some time. If you do that, and bring proof that you did to one of the upcoming events, I'll personally see to it that you get the VIP treatment. How does that sound?"

Ginny beamed and nodded vigorously. "Yeah, sounds good," Wally agreed.

"Great," Beacon said and looked around for a street sign, noting the number on the building next to where they were standing. "We are at 203 Montgomery St. You come to an event and tell the people at the ticket booth we met at this address. I'll make sure they are on the lookout for you."

"Honest?" Ginny asked. "You'd really do that for me? For us?"

"Honest," Beacon answered with a smile. "Now, are you kids going to be all right getting home without getting into any more trouble?"

They nodded. "And you promise me you won't do anything like this again, right, Trevor?" she asked with a grin.

"Uh-huh," Trevor answered, still a little embarrassed. "We won't."

"All right then, go on home," Beacon said, giving them a wave of her hand. "I hope to see you all again very soon." With that, the teens mumbled some 'thank you's and scampered away, leaving her behind on the sidewalk.

Beacon leapt back up to the rooftop and watched after them while they crossed the next street and walked away from her, talking excitedly and laughing as they receded into the distance. When they were finally out of sight, she chuckled, shaking her head slowly,

Back to work, she thought, but before she could make the jump to the next rooftop, the commpod in her ear chimed. "Who is it?" Beacon asked, already knowing the answer.

"District Attorney Harris," the mechanical female voice responded.

"Answer it, please," she instructed and stepped away from the edge of the building while the call connected. When she finally heard the line open, Beacon greeted her caller, "DA Harris, to what do I owe the pleasure?"

"Busy night?" she heard him ask.

"Not so much," Beacon replied nonchalantly. "Just a bunch of kids spoofing for a photo."

He laughed on the other end of the line. "Do I need to clear any space down at Juvenile Detention?"

"No," she said, chuckling in return. "I gave them something else to do instead, a way to earn one instead of screwing around on the streets late at night."

"Smart idea. Hope it works out for them," Harris said. "So, as usual, not a social call. We need your help with something."

"I figured," Beacon said. "We never talk anymore," she added with a chuckle. "What's going on?"

"There have been a series of disappearances. Mostly runaways, homeless, those kinds," he said grimly.

"How many?" Beacon asked.

"We aren't sure."

"How long has it been going on?" she tried again.

"We aren't sure."

Beacon huffed. "What *are* you sure of, then?"

"We know it's probably been going on longer than we think and that there are likely more people missing than we think," he replied. "We've only just become aware that this has been going on, and while there isn't any pattern we can figure out yet, the cases have been clustering around a few specific demographics. Unfortunately, it isn't that uncommon for people like that to go off the grid. They are barely on the grid as it is, and they often just move on or something else on their own. Makes them very hard to track or trace on even the best of days."

"I see," Beacon replied, "out of sight, out of mind, huh?"

"Yeah, I get it," Harris answered with some measure of frustration. "I'm not happy about it either, but let's not get into a debate right now about social programs, okay? We're piecing things together, but we are still very short on real information."

"Ok, fair enough," Beacon agreed. "Any idea what's happening with them?"

"No. We have our usual suspects when things like this happen, but the trails on activities like trafficking, prostitution, and drugs are all cold. We are pretty sure it's not any of the typical channels we ordinarily connect with random abductions."

Beacon paused for a moment to think and digest the conversation so far. After a few seconds, she asked, "So what do you want me to do?"

"We need you to keep your eyes and ears open," Harris said. "You get around in parts of the city more freely than the police typically can. See if you can find out about anyone else who might've gone missing, anyone who might've seen or heard something, anything that might put more paint on the canvas for us."

"And if I have to grease a few palms to get information?"

"I'll take care of it per our usual arrangement," Harris reassured her and then, before she could say it, mockingly added, "Yeah, yeah, after all, only the superheroes in the comic books are secretly billionaires."

Beacon chuckled. "You know it."

"I have always wondered how you get your stuff, though," Harris probed with teasing curiosity.

"Santa brings it for me," Beacon replied. "I am on the nice list, after all."

"I'm sure you are," Harris said with a laugh. "But still..."

"Look, Harris," Beacon said firmly, "you, of all people, know it takes a village for a city to have a superheroine. You've contributed to it yourself, so I'm sure you especially can appreciate how important it is that everyone's involvement in this not become public knowledge, right?"

"Indeed, I do," Harris agreed. "You're right. As a prosecutor, you'd think I'd know the meaning of not asking questions to which you really don't want the answers, but curiosity is part of the package for a District Attorney. You'll let me know if you hear anything, then?"

"You know I will," Beacon said. "Talk soon," she added and closed the call with a tap to the commpod tucked beneath her mask.

Beacon shook her head. *Disappearances now? Trafficking? Something worse?*

When it rains, it pours.

She looked up, her eyes tracking down the street next to her.

Perhaps, she thought, *let's make sure those kids are getting home safely first. I don't need to see them show up in Harris' case files.*

Motivations

A sneakered foot slammed into the belly of the boy lying
on the ground. He groaned and rolled over, clutching
his midsection.

*The owner of the foot, a tall, slender older kid with an
impressive case of blooming acne, chuckled heartily. "Give it to
us, you little puke," he sneered, looking down. "We ain't got all
day, and I'm getting tired."*

Sorensen watched his younger self in the haze. The scene
wasn't complete; it was as if a fist had ripped a portion of a
memory from his mind and shaped it for the dream. Only a
few of the hall lockers were visible, and large portions of the
hallway were just undefined blackness, but he didn't need all
that background to recognize he was back in middle school,
watching a scene that had played out repeatedly while he was
a child.

*A larger boy, who at the time seemed like nothing short of a
stunted gorilla, bent down and slapped the boy lying on the
ground. Then, grabbing him by the front of his shirt, hauled*

him up to his feet. "Yeah," *he hissed through his stained teeth,* "give it to us. All of it." *His breath stank of sourness and rot.*

Sorensen watched his boyhood self finally nod, holding back a torrent of tears, and reach into his pocket for his wallet. He knew that wallet contained the allowance his parents gave him each week to cover his lunches and a little extra for other small things a boy that age might want or need, but today, like so many days before, it was going to stop a beating instead.

The smaller boy took the money out of the wallet with shaking hands and reluctantly gave it over to the taller kid. The two bullies laughed, and the bigger of the two threw the younger boy into the lockers behind him. He hit hard, his head clanking against the locker door, and sank to the floor while the other two congratulated each other and walked away with his allowance and a week's worth of lunches in their hands.

Sorensen watched and fumed. These dreams were becoming more routine now. At first, they were daunting, uncomfortable, even frightening at times, but now they simply served as reminders and affirmations of his course. Like Ebenezer Scrooge, they frequently started with scenes like this from his childhood, but there were no spirits guiding him. It was just him and his past, alone.

The scenes he frequently relived, like this one, weren't unique in his childhood either. The middle school and junior high students shared a wing at the small public school he and his sister attended after moving to this town so many years ago. He was small for his age, and being the new kid on the block instantly drew the attention of the bigger junior high students who often bullied and hazed the middle schoolers. In this case, he had the misfortune of getting on the radar of Todd Samuels and his hulking sidekick 'Booger' Warburton. They took no small pleasure in making his life miserable and routinely took things from him—books, food, money, whatever—not because they needed it, but because they could. He wasn't their only target, but he was by far their favorite.

Sorensen watched the images of himself sniveling on the floor with his back to the row of lockers that lined the school hallway and the backs of his tormentors walking away. As kids are, within a few years, all this went away on its own. Even a couple of Neanderthals like Todd and Booger grow up, and as they moved on to other things, the habitual bullying eventually tapered off on its own. The memory of it, and the seed for revenge it left behind, did not.

Sorensen smiled to himself. A few years later, the principal had gotten an anonymous tip, and when he checked Todd's and Barney's (he'd left the 'Booger' moniker behind when he left junior high) commpads, he had found just what the tip said he'd find; numerous indecent and illicit pictures taken candidly of young girls in the girl's bathroom and locker rooms. Of course, they denied everything, but a quick forensics check of the data proved they were genuine, and Todd and Barney ended up spending some time in juvenile hall and doing community service...after being expelled, of course.

They should have taken better care of their devices, shouldn't they? Or better yet, not have picked on the wrong person in the first place. Frick around and find out, he thought, and abruptly the scene shifted.

The same boy sat on the floor of his room at home. A younger girl sat next to him with an arm around his shoulders and her head resting on his shoulder. He was crying, and she, as she often did, was comforting him. Similar to the scene at the school, the room was incomplete; the irregular edges of a black void abruptly cut off portions of the walls and bedroom furniture. Off to the side, around a small table floating in the dark void, sat two middle-aged, smartly dressed adults, a man and a woman. They were talking amongst themselves, clearly oblivious to the two children nearby.

Sorensen again watched himself in tears after yet another school incident, sitting with his sister. She was younger than he was, but she was as full of compassion as she was intelligent, and she was always there for him. She celebrated his achievements with him, supported him in his low times, and when he had some scheme or project he wanted to work on, she was by his side.

He glanced over at the image of his parents sitting off in the distance, just as they so frequently had done in real life, and frowned with scorn and derision. Unlike his sister, his parents were never there for him. They sat there as he always remembered them, dressed as if they were about to receive the key to the city. They were always preoccupied with events at their country club, activities at the church they attended, or their careers. His father's response to the only time Sorensen had told them about getting bullied at school was that he needed to stand up for himself, that the best way to overcome a bully was to confront them. "One good punch in the nose is all it takes," he'd said.

He wasn't entirely wrong, Sorensen thought, *but why stop with just a punch to the nose?*

His sister, though, had always listened, always comforted, was as much everything for him as his distant, self-absorbed parents never were.

Until...and the scene shifted once more.

His sister, many years older now, stood in the family living room with their parents, smiling. She was accompanied by a young man roughly her age, perhaps a year or two older. She was holding up her hand, her left hand, for her parents to see. The sunlight refracted off the ring on her finger, erupting in small flares around the ceiling and walls. They all laughed and giggled and hugged each other in celebration.

All except for Sorensen himself. As he watched the jubilant scene unfold, he frowned again. His younger self had played along, pretending to share in his sister's joy, but inside, Sorensen knew he was seething.

This was the day his world nearly came apart, the day the interloper, the intruder into his family, had made the mistake of proposing to his sister. It was bad enough that she had been spending more and more time with him, which meant being there for Sorensen less and less, but now he intended to take her away for good. Of course, she had said 'yes'—she didn't know any better—but it was completely unacceptable and could not be tolerated.

And the scene again shifted.

It was a dismal gray day. The vision was broken between segments of empty black and pieces of trees, hills of green, and gravestones. The young woman was crying, pressed against his younger self. He had his arm around her. He rested his cheek against the top of her head as she sobbed into his jacket. She was dressed all in black, and it was his turn to comfort her while they stood beside the coffin, waiting for it to be lowered into the ground.

Ashes to ashes...

Dust to dust...

Sorensen felt a sense of pride and accomplishment whenever he relived this moment. Her fiancée, the interloper, had fallen victim to a hit-and-run after dropping his sister off at home after a date late one evening. She was devastated, but she would eventually move on, and, more importantly, that man who had dared to insert himself between them would not be taking her away from him now.

The driver had never been identified, and Sorensen knew he never would be. The people he had started working with, and continued to work for even now, were remarkably efficient with matters like this.

After the accident, many strings had been pulled to get his sister into the right position with the right company. That company was then acquired, making sure she could take a key role in Sorensen's program.

Of course, he'd taken other measures as well to guarantee his sister would remain at his side.

Right where she should be.

Right where she belongs.

Forever...

...the loud chime from the table next to his bed shattered the images in the dream, snapping him awake. He shook his head once, rolled over, and picked up the commpad. Noting the urgent incoming call, he tapped the screen to accept it. Sofia's face filled the screen.

"Sorry to disturb you, Director, but there's been an incident," she said calmly.

"What kind of incident?" he asked impatiently, rubbing the remains of his broken sleep out of his eyes.

"In the testing rooms," she replied.

"Ugh, the boy?" Sorensen asked with a scowl.

Sofia's image nodded in affirmation. "Yes," she said. "The team is requesting that you come down right away."

"On my way," he said with a huff of disgust. "And while I have you," he added after a brief pause, "what is the latest update on Doctor Thornton? Has she fully recovered?"

"Mostly, Director," Sofia answered. "Her strength and endurance still need work, and she'll require some physical therapy for a while, but otherwise she's fit. The doctors cleared her to resume a normal routine a few days ago. We have already relocated her to more standard accommodations."

"Excellent," Sorensen replied. "I believe we are overdue in orienting Doctor Thornton to her new role with us. Set that up for tomorrow, Sofia. The sooner, the better."

"Of course. Consider it done," she replied and ended the call.

He sat up and stretched. Setbacks with their test subjects, like this boy that he was going to hear about shortly, were still too much of a regular occurrence for his taste. *No matter,* he thought to himself as he started to dress. *We will clear this up and keep moving. Regardless, it's nearly time for the next phase to begin. Once Thornton and a few other key people are fully on board, these incidents will cease to be a problem, and my vision will all but be assured.*

A world without taking, without people preying on the weaknesses of others.

A world that will no longer take from me.

Not her.

Not anything.

And not just from me—not from anyone else either.

A world of fairness and justice.

But there is a lot of work to do, he shrugged, *a lot of problems to solve, obstacles to overcome, hard decisions to make.*

And it's on me to make them, so if, at least for a while, I have to be the one to do the taking, to seize the advantage, to make the difficult and questionable choices, to see that vision realized, so be it.

Not bad, not bad, Rene thought as she examined herself in the mirror. *You clean up pretty well, for a dead woman, that is.* She ran her fingers through her hair, tucking a wayward strand back into place, and then tugged on the tips of her blouse collar to straighten it properly.

After the doctors had cleared her, they'd moved her to a new room, likely the same kind they used for any staff that lived on-site at The Workshop. a nickname for this facility that she'd casually picked up from them. Rene had learned from an early age that the best way to learn was to listen, but in a way that people didn't know you were listening, and that skill had served her well over the past few days.

The room was simple and austere, but that suited her just fine. If she had her way, she wouldn't be in it long enough to develop any sense of attachment that would push her to any need to decorate. She would have to bide her time, though. It was unlikely someone was just going to open the door for her and let her walk out, at least not right away.

Her hair, on the other hand, was very new for her. When she'd been brought out of biostasis, it had been down to her waist, the longest it had ever been in her life, even when she was a young girl. Rene sighed. *I always liked wearing it long.* She sighed again. Back then, everyone complimented her on how thick and luxurious it was, including her foster parents...unfortunately.

Those compliments from her foster parents, especially those from her foster father, had become increasingly uncomfortable as she'd grown up. The encouragement they gave her to wear it long progressively changed from casual to insistent to outright demanding that she wear it down and loose. It came to the point where every time he noticed it, she would cringe and look for any way she could to hide it. The humiliation and self-consciousness became oppressive, so much so that even after her foster father's attentions crossed the line that ultimately led to charges being filed, and she was finally able to escape that place for good, she never wore it down again.

So many years later, those feelings still lingered. During her recovery, she'd put it into a thick braid. Besides making her hair less noticeable, this style of choice had a practical aspect as well. The braid kept her hair out of the way during the physical therapy sessions she had endured to overcome the atrophy in her muscles and stiffness in her joints that came with such a long period of inactivity. The braid had fulfilled its purpose, but now that she had been cleared, that heavy mass hanging down her back was just a constant source of agitation in a variety of ways.

Sofia, in her typical efficient manner, had connected her with a member of the staff who had experience working as a stylist before joining The Workshop. Under normal circumstances, Rene would have opted to go back to her standard shoulder-length style that she often tucked up into a bun, but here, she felt something slightly less conventional might serve her better. The woman had happily obliged, and what Rene saw in the mirror now was her black hair shaped into something between a textured lob and a shaggy pixie. Not only would it be very easy to care for, but it was decidedly more casual and, more importantly, less intimidating. If she looked less like someone to be taken seriously, someone would eventually make that mistake and let their guard down.

The rest of the outfit was also courtesy of Sofia. The clothes weren't anything to rave over, but they were neat and functional. The lilac cotton blouse and trim black slacks fit her perfectly, and in the same manner as her hair, the flat black shoes worked to soften her image and blend in.

Yes, perfect, she thought as a sharp knock came at the door. "Come in," Rene said as she made a few final adjustments in the mirror.

After a click of the lock—Rene had noted that her new apartment was no less of a cell than the medical room had been—Sofia entered. "Are you ready, Doctor Thornton?" she asked, folding her hands in front of her.

"Indeed, Sofia," Rene said as she put down her hairbrush and turned away from the mirror to face her. "As ready as I'll ever be. Thanks again for the clothes and other accommodations. It's nice to feel human again."

"You're very welcome," Sofia said with a slight smile. "Shall we go? Director Sorensen is waiting in his office."

"Yes, of course," Rene replied, following Sofia's gesture to lead the way. Sofia pulled the door closed behind them, and Rene fell in next to her as she led the way down the hall. Sofia was still a bit of a mystery to Rene, compassionate and thoughtful on the one hand but stoic and stiff on the other, efficient and practical but rarely smiling or jovial, and undoubtedly a valuable source of information if she could only get through that shell.

"Anything I should be aware of when I meet Sorensen?" Rene asked casually as they walked down the empty hallway. "Any advice that might make things go more smoothly?"

Sofia stared straight ahead as she considered the question. "Just one thing, Doctor Thornton," she finally answered cooly and evenly. "Director Sorensen is impressed with your background and scientific prowess and is quite eager to have you contribute your skills to our work here. We are doing very cutting-edge work in areas that are an excellent fit with your expertise, and when he talks about our work here and how you can contribute to its success, take him at his word. In that regard, he will be completely sincere and honest with you."

Sofia then turned and looked Rene dead in the face, and for a moment, Rene's blood ran cold from the look in her eyes. "However, if you should ever get any impression that he is offering you a choice about your future with us here, you should assume you've misunderstood him somewhere along the line."

Rene returned her gaze silently. After a brief pause for effect, Sofia turned away to look forward again, but Rene's eyes lingered on Sofia's expressionless face a moment longer.

That goes both ways, my dear. Trust me.

After a few hours, Rene found herself back in Sorensen's office. The tour had been thorough, if anything; Sorensen was definitely very proud of the Institute for the Advancement of Human Potential and what he had built here. The handful of people she had met seemed quite capable. The labs themselves were beyond state-of-the-art. All the equipment was top of the line, much of it advanced beyond anything Rene had ever seen before. She could only guess at the potential applications for some of it.

However, as much as Rene felt Sorensen had done his very best to show off how exceptional the facility was, it was also apparent to her that Sorensen had been equally careful to deftly deflect her attention away from certain areas. It was obvious to her that there were things he did not intend to divulge until he knew where she stood.

Of course, that did nothing except pique her curiosity. *There's clearly more going on here than meets the eye,* she thought as she sat down across from Sorensen. *I'm going to have to be very careful to avoid the same fate as the overly-curious cat, though, that's for sure.*

Sorensen sat down across from Rene. He wore a very proud, almost smug, smile as he looked across his desk at Rene. "So, Doctor Thornton, what do you think of our facility?" he asked, interlacing his fingers expectantly.

Rene forced a smile. "It's very impressive," she replied with no small measure of sincerity. "High-energy physics, molecular biology, state-of-the-art genetics, a laboratory that would put any university or corporate research center to shame. It's all very impressive indeed. I just have one question," she continued, resting her chin on her fingertips. "What exactly are you doing here in the name of 'advancing human potential'?"

"I see you live up to your reputation for directness," Sorensen said with a chuckle. "Excellent. That's something I can work with. It's all because of your friend, Beacon, actually."

"I'm not sure you could classify our relationship as 'friends,'" Rene scoffed. "But that aside, what does this have to do with her?"

Sorensen sat back and folded his hands into his lap. "Well, if you ask the people who fund our operation here, they would say her abilities are far too valuable to be left with one person. Some would say they are too dangerous as well, but most of them are very interested in what they believe comes with her powers: healing, physical robustness, probably advanced immunity to disease, maybe even prolonged life expectancy. These are all things that people with money and power crave, not only for themselves but as something they can exploit to give themselves more money and more power."

"Very likely," Rene said coyly with a half-smile. "Which is exactly why people like that shouldn't have them, but if I'm reading you correctly, I'm certain the real answer lies elsewhere. What you've told me sounds more like a story to keep the money flowing."

Sorensen tipped his head slightly to the side and regarded her momentarily. "Quite right, Doctor Thornton," he finally said. "Very perceptive, and before you ask, no, it isn't the military either. Many of our benefactors do see the potential of harnessing her abilities and selling them for military applications as a highly lucrative enterprise. They wouldn't be wrong either, I might add. However, my vision and true motivation are far more ambitious than that...and something that I think is very near to your heart too, Doctor."

"Oh? I'm all ears," Rene said with a touch of playful sarcasm.

Sorensen huffed in amusement. "Like you, I see the damage people's baser nature causes to society at large. As soon as there is the slightest advantage or power imbalance, the stronger exploit the weaker. The result is crime, oppression, violence, corruption, and a multitude of other hateful acts that undermine what would otherwise be a peaceful society."

"Agreed," replied Rene.

"Police are overworked, and resources are stretched too thin," Sorensen continued. "However, as we've recently seen, someone like Beacon, with her unique powers and strong moral compass, tips the scales back to the center. Crystal Bay is a living example."

"Yes, of course," Rene agreed, "but it seems our Angel of Light is stretched a bit thin already, don't you think?"

"Indeed," Sorensen said, leaning forward on the desk. "She is, but if we could harness her powers and replicate them in others, we would have an entire legion of parahumans we could deploy across the country, the world, to do the same. Tip the scales back everywhere."

"Parahumans?" Rene asked skeptically, furrowing her eyebrows. "So your answer to curing society's ills caused by an imbalance of power between people is to give superpowers to a select group of people? *That's* your plan?" Rene shook her head in disgust. "You know what happens when you give power to people. They *use* it...for *only* themselves. Beacon isn't the rule. She's the *exception* to the rule."

Sorensen held up his hands, conceding the point. "Yes, yes, that's generally true, but we wouldn't be so arbitrary," he countered. "We would vet our parahuman candidates to make sure they were trustworthy and take measures to ensure we could control them so they wouldn't go rogue."

"I'm not sure any such people actually exist," Rene argued. "Everything I did leading up to Meyer's Tower was predicated on the fact that people are irrational, selfish animals who will act purely in their own short-term self-interest at the expense of each other and even their own long-term survival as a species. Even if you found a few you could trust to be your super police force, I don't think you could make a difference on a global scale. People would resist it."

"Much of what you say is true, but we have seen, fairly recently in fact, that with the right messaging and information management, people can be persuaded to accept just about anything. The truth is nothing more than what you convince people is true. Once they can see what our group of parahumans can actually do, and with the right political and thought leaders on board, I'm very certain that not only will people accept it, they will actively embrace it."

"So, you need to control politicians and influencers, as well?" Rene sneered. "Good luck with that. They are the worst of the worst when it comes to setting aside personal agendas for the greater good."

"Perhaps," Sorensen said confidently, "but leave that to me."

He's delusional, Rene thought as she pondered him for a moment. "Very well then, Director Sorensen," Rene said. "Assuming you can do all that, what will my role be in all of this? You went through a lot of trouble to bring me here when you already have an incredible facility with some top-tier researchers and staff. Why me?"

Sorensen nodded once and sat back in his chair. "It is just as I told you when we first brought you out of stasis. While we've made some excellent progress so far, we have hit some obstacles. The staff can fill you in on the specifics, but put simply, subjects that begin to acquire abilities lose control of them before they can stabilize. The result is almost always fatal, in most cases quite spectacularly, and usually not just for the subject either. We have lost some very good staff members in the process." Sorensen gestured toward Rene. "I believe that you are uniquely qualified to help us solve these few remaining problems."

"In what way?" Rene asked.

"Not only is your practical knowledge of biogenetics unparalleled, but your direct personal experience with Beacon herself—the world's only functioning parahuman—I believe, sets you apart in terms of the experience and skills needed to move us forward," Sorensen replied.

Rene laughed. "Seriously, Director Sorensen, my 'direct experience' with Beacon did not turn out very well, now did it?"

"Be that as it may," Sorensen said evenly, "I do believe you are the right person for the job. The circumstances here will be quite different and wholly in your favor. Plus, if it helps to know, there is one other person I'm actively working to bring on board as well, someone I believe will be an invaluable asset to your research and who will give you an edge you didn't have in your prior encounter."

"Who?" Rene asked, genuinely curious.

"All in good time," Sorensen said smugly. "So, Doctor Thornton, what do you think?"

I think you're absolutely certifiable, she thought as she studied his face. Sorensen just calmly looked at her over the top of his steepled fingers. Clearly, the next move was hers.

"Despite some skepticism, I admit I am genuinely intrigued," Rene said, carefully measuring her words and ensuring her face didn't give away any of her real feelings. "May I have some time to consider it?"

Sorensen's face darkened. "No, Doctor Thornton," he said coldly. "I'm afraid not. You see, we don't have time to debate decisions that should be obvious. You were brought here for a specific purpose, and if you aren't willing to serve that purpose, then I will find another purpose for you here, one that is far less enjoyable."

Rene suppressed an involuntary shiver as Sorensen continued, "For example, we are always in need of test subjects. It would be fascinating to see what kind of powers you would develop, Doctor Thornton. That is if you survived the procedure and didn't destroy yourself in the process." He leaned forward and stared directly into her eyes. "Of course, if for some reason you weren't suitable for that, or for any other purpose, then unfortunately, we don't have the luxury of carrying around any dead weight here at The Workshop. Do you understand my meaning, Doctor Thornton?"

"Perfectly, Director Sorensen," Rene said. Sofia's warning echoed through her mind while she kept an iron grip on her composure.

No fear.

Do not give him the satisfaction.

Be a rock.

"So," Sorensen said with a malevolent smirk. "I'll ask again. What do you think, Doctor Thornton?"

Rene paused for a second before replying. "I think I'm the right woman for the job, Director," she said with a forced smile and extended her hand toward him.

Sorensen stood, took her hand, and gave it a solid shake. "I'm glad to hear it, Doctor. Welcome to the team."

"Glad to be a part of it," she said, still forcing the smile.

At least, until I can figure something else out.

Intersections

"As advertised," Beacon muttered to herself as she landed gracefully in the dimly-lit parking lot. The alert had come through her commpod that a robbery was in progress just a few blocks from where she had been patrolling, and she had responded immediately. The strobe light flashing in the windows of the building in front of her and the high-pitched screech of an alarm coming from inside told her she was in the right place.

It appeared, though, that she may already be a bit late to the party. The car parked across the lot from her was already running, and a few darkly-clad men were scrambling to get into it. She could hear the driver yelling at them to hurry up.

"What? Leaving so soon?" she shouted at them. "I only just got here."

At the sound of her voice, their heads jerked around, turning in unison to look at her like a pack of meerkats. She heard one of them swear, and as the last man scrambled into the car and the driver hit the gas, one of them took a potshot at her. The engine roared, and a cloud of blue smoke poured out of the tailpipe as the tires squealed on the pavement.

The bullet was an easy dodge. "Lame," she scoffed with a snort of derision. It wasn't even a good attempt, but as the vehicle started to pick up speed, Beacon realized that split-second of distraction may have been all they needed. If she didn't catch them in time, and they managed to escape into the street, overtaking their vehicle in a high-speed pursuit and bringing it to a stop safely would be far more difficult. Best to finish it now before they got that far.

"Time to slice, dice, and julienne fry," Beacon muttered to herself and prepared to do what she'd done dozens of times before: drive a beam of heat and light into the rear tire, disabling the vehicle before it could leave the lot.

Urgently, she shifted the currents of energy within her from her speed toward her finger and pushed, but in her haste, she pushed too hard, and the flows tangled and snarled. Watching the car continue to accelerate, she tried to force them, knotting them even further.

Frak! Beacon thought, growling in frustration. *They are getting away!*

Then, she felt it—a sensation quietly deep within her.

Twist

She didn't understand it, but she was out of time. Beacon relaxed, and in her mind, she let the gnarled flows twist. Instantly, they untangled and smoothed out, twirling and knitting themselves into an interwoven helix. Through the filters in her mask's visor, she could see the pattern overlaying her hand, beautiful and throbbing with power.

Then, just as she said, "Whoa," in amazement under her breath, the pattern tightened, and a beam of searing white energy erupted from her finger toward the back of the car.

Unfortunately, her wonder at her new discovery was quickly supplanted by shock and awe. Doing what it was designed to do, the micro-collimator she had developed from the lab's imaging systems and had installed in her glove to help her do just this—give her the ability to focus her energy projection more intensely and precisely—sensed the energy discharge. It activated and attempted to concentrate the energy even further.

The resulting power was staggering. Beacon screamed as the collimator overloaded, sending intense waves of pain up her arm. In a glorious burst of radiant energy, the hyper-focused discharge decimated the entire rear tire, melting the steel rim and part of the axle and tearing off the rear quarter panel along with a sizeable chunk of the underlying frame. The back end of the shattered vehicle dropped sharply and hit the pavement with a loud crash, spewing sparks on the asphalt until it ground to a halt, colliding with the side of a building just at the exit to the street.

Almost afraid to look, Beacon glanced down at her wounded hand. The glove's fingertip was charred and splayed open. Her own finger looked intact, but it, too, was badly burned, and she could see pieces of the collimator array embedded in her skin.

Stunned and uncertain of what to do next, Beacon looked up toward the crippled getaway car. The men inside were obviously dazed from both the shock of seeing their car reduced to a smoldering ruin and the impact with the building. They were going nowhere for the moment, but they'd recover soon, and she was in no shape to take them on.

Fortunately, the timely arrival of the police lifted the decision of whether to fight or not from her shoulders. Two squad cars, lights flashing and sirens wailing, careened into the lot. They screeched to a halt next to her, and two officers, guns drawn, jumped out of the car and looked at her.

"There," she said and pointed toward the wrecked vehicle. When the officers saw it, their jaws dropped. The back was still smoldering, and the dazed would-be thieves were groaning, rubbing their necks and shoulders.

The officers looked back at her slowly, their faces silently asking what had happened here. Suppressing the anguish of her throbbing hand, Beacon simply gave them a weak smile and a half-shrug and, cradling her hand, leapt to the top of a nearby roof and disappeared.

The slab of metal started to glow dimly at first, but within seconds it was a bright orange, then yellow, then white. Rivulets started to form on its smooth surface, and tiny wisps of smoke began to steadily spiral upward toward the ceiling. Finally, molten globs oozed down onto the table surface, and the beam of white light emanating from Tricia's newly-gloved finger punched through the other side, carving a neat half-inch diameter hole in the silvery metal.

Tricia released the helical weave of energy before it could score the wall behind and turned toward Harold. "Brilliant!" she exclaimed giddily.

"That's incredible," Harold said, staring at the cooling metal resting on the table before them. It was now a dull red, fading rapidly by the second. Sooty black marks marred the smooth surface, radiating outward from the hole she had made. The melted drops were now small, solid beads. Harold nudged them across the tabletop with the tip of his finger.

He turned to face Tricia, who was beaming with excitement. "That's anodized tungsten, Tricia. It has a melting point of over thirty-seven hundred degrees Kelvin, and you punched a hole through it in a matter of seconds like it was butter."

Tricia nodded vigorously.

"The amount of power that takes," he said, shaking his head. "It's phenomenal."

Tricia ran her hands up and down the new black and yellow-edged gloves covering her forearms, then interlocked her fingers and squeezed.

"How do they feel?" Harold asked.

"Great," Tricia replied, flexing her fingers a few times.

Harold grinned. "Fits almost like..."

"...a glove," they finished together and laughed.

"It had to be said," Harold chuckled.

"I suppose it did," Tricia replied.

Harold had been a little stiff when they first started working on her Beacon costume, but as they'd spent time together, he had loosened up, and more of his sense of humor had started to come through. It was quirky and a little dry, but it always made her laugh.

Her old gloves, destroyed in her encounter with those thieves a few days before, lay on the table next to them. The index finger on the right glove was gone, and the material itself, otherwise nearly indestructible, was frayed well past the knuckle, almost down to the palm.

Fortunately for her, the glove had absorbed most of the energy. If it hadn't, its replacement would have only needed four fingers.

As it was, even with her healing abilities, it had been days before her finger and hand felt normal again.

When she showed Harold the ruined handwear, he transformed immediately into a delightful mixture of child-like amazement and intense curiosity, and, watching his reaction, she couldn't help but snicker.

He asked Tricia if he could keep that glove and run tests on the damaged fabric—of course, she agreed—and also offered to help her craft a new set. His craftsmanship had thoroughly impressed her. With a very practiced and precise hand, he slightly modified her old pattern, and, in a matter of a few hours, Beacon had a new set of gloves that she honestly believed looked and fit better than her original set ever did.

"Did you notice the palm?" Harold asked tentatively.

"I did," Tricia answered. She opened her hand and looked into her open palm. "I was going to mention it. This padding feels like some kind of silicone, but it's more flexible. Lighter."

"Stronger, too," Harold said, smiling. He held her hand in his palm and traced the palm and finger pads with the index finger of his other hand. "Except it isn't silicone. It's actually multiple layers of the material itself, but treated so it fuses into a thicker and more wear-resistant form. It has the same energy transference properties as the original material but is significantly stronger and more durable."

Harold picked up a piece of scrap metal. It was wickedly ragged and sharp on one side. "Here, try it out," he said as he placed the serrated edge in her palm. "Give it a twist. Really dig in," he emphasized, simulating a twisting motion with his hands.

Tricia looked at him sideways, but trusting him, she gripped the threatening edges with both hands, drew on the flows around her, and twisted the metal scrap just as if she were wringing out a wet towel. She winced slightly, expecting the jagged edge to poke and jab into her hands, but caution quickly gave way to surprise and delight as the metal wound like a ribbon in her hands with no discomfort whatsoever.

"That's amazing, Harold," she exclaimed, handing the deformed scrap metal back to him. He tossed it casually back into the scrap bin. "I barely felt those sharp edges through the gloves."

"Yes, they should protect you much better than the couple of simple layers you'd used on the older pair. I dare say you could have torn that metal in half and not run any risk of cutting yourself or damaging the gloves."

"Very cool," Tricia said, admiring the glove on her hand. "These will definitely come in handy," she added, giving him a playful smirk.

Harold laughed. "Good one!" he said. "You know, I have some ideas about how we could do the same thing with your boots. We can replace that bulky foot piece with a new sole made from an even thicker version of that palm padding. We can mold it to the shape of your foot for even more support and comfort. Besides being lighter, it would also give you better traction and grip. Further, it would hold up to the abrasion caused by your hyperspeed much better than what you have now."

"You don't say," Tricia replied. "Sounds interesting."

"Well, we could discuss them more if you want," Harold said with some hesitancy. He looked away nervously. "Maybe over dinner sometime?"

Dinner, yeah sure, Tricia thought absently, making a fist with her new glove, testing the fit one more time, and then froze.

Wait, what?

Is he suggesting...

Is he thinking what I think he's thinking?

She opened her hand and looked up at him. "Do you mean, like on a date, Harold?" she asked.

Harold leaned back slightly, and a flustered look crossed his face. "I mean, yeah, I guess so," he stammered as he nervously pushed his fingers through his hair, and a subtle redness crept up into his cheeks. "I mean, if it isn't weird or anything. If it is, we can forget it, of course."

Tricia smiled. "No, no, it isn't weird," she replied, likewise brushing back the strands of her own hair that had fallen into her face. "It's just a bit of a surprise, that's all."

What do I say?

He's kind but rather shy.

Generous. Thoughtful.

Work relationships are always asking for trouble. Dating within the superheroine support team is probably downright stupid.

He's funny. I do like being around him.

I don't want to mess this up.

I really, REALLY don't want to mess this up.

Then don't mess it up.

"Sure," Tricia answered. Harold visibly relaxed, taking his first breath in what had likely been several seconds. "But, let's make it lunch, ok? As you know, my evening dance card is rather full these days, and lunch will just be, well, easier right now."

"Sure," Harold said, his eyes downturned. "I understand."

"No," Tricia said, reaching out to touch his arm. "I mean it. Please don't read anything into what I'm saying, Harold. I do want to go, but things are crazy right now."

Harold looked up to meet her gaze as she continued, "Patel is setting up these visits to the lab to try to get some investor funding flowing into the lab coffers. In fact, there's one coming up in a few days. We are spending every spare minute getting ready for it, and—" she tipped her head closer and lowered her voice "—I'm sure you understand I can't let my other...extracurricular activities slide either, right?"

"No, no, of course not," he replied.

"Ok, great. If it's all right with you, please just give me a few days to get ready for this upcoming dog and pony show, and I promise I'll get back to you to set up lunch, ok?"

"Yeah, that'll be just fine, Tricia," Harold said with a bit more confidence creeping back into his voice. "Just let me know a good time that will work for you."

"I will, I promise," Tricia assured him.

Harold smiled. "I completely understand the pressure you're under, too. Patel talked to me about the very same thing in my meeting with her last week, and ..."

Harold was still talking, but Tricia wasn't listening anymore. *A date*, she thought to herself as she started to unroll the glove down her arm.

What am I thinking?

Dating—romance of any kind—had been strictly off the board since she'd started her activities as Beacon. It was taking too much of a chance, and she didn't really have time for it anyway, but here she was, agreeing to a date.

What am I thinking?

Nothing against Harold, she thought as she slipped the glove off her hand, *but I think I'd rather be facing the Liberators of Gaia again...nuke and all.*

Tricia shivered as she looked inside the imaging field chamber that dominated the center of her lab. Before her floated a large glowing polyhedron. Suspended in the middle of the Hot Spot, as they affectionately called it, the shape slowly rotated, its surface pulsing and shifting through the various colors of the spectrum. It was beautiful, but it was also the same shape they used in their experiment a little over a year ago, the experiment when they first tried to fuse dark energy with their holographic emitters, the experiment that had gone terribly wrong, changing her forever. Every time she saw this shape, the memory of that day and the agony she endured haunted her even now.

"How are things looking, Jamal?" Tricia called out, still watching the angular bob and roll slowly in front of her. She was certain they'd corrected the problems that led up to her accident, and they had made amazing progress since then, but some latent fear lingered in the back of her mind anyway. No matter how confident she was, part of her still did not want to take her eyes off of it, afraid of what it might do if she did.

"Five by five, Doctor C," Jamal replied from the primary imaging console. "It's as solid as a rock...literally."

"Power level is spot on, too," Alex added.

"Are we ready for this?" Tricia asked the team. "Doctor Patel and the Draconyx team will be here any time now."

"Looking good on this end," Nikki chimed in. Nikki had just been an intern at the time of the accident last year. Tricia knew she still partially blamed herself for what had happened, for the error that swapped some critical experimental parameters and created the feedback loop that caused the overload.

It really wasn't her fault; Tricia knew better than to have proceeded with a new configuration without running the simulations to verify them, but at the time, it was "no guts, no glory", and they all had gotten caught up in the heat of the moment. Fortunately, she'd gotten over her guilt and become an exemplary addition to the team, eventually deciding to stay on for her doctoral thesis.

"Ok, Jamal, load the demo configuration," Tricia said. Jamal nodded and pressed a few buttons on his console. The large glowing shape promptly dissolved into a simple hemisphere roughly the size and shape of a kitchen mixing bowl.

Jamal chuckled. "They are gonna love this," he said, grinning in anticipation. "Show me da money, Daddy Warbucks!"

"Let's hope so," Tricia replied. "Alex, polarize the glass. We'll draw the curtains for our little show after the tour."

"Will do, Doctor C," Alex said, and at her command, the glass walls of the Hot Spot started to dim until they went completely black. "Where are they now?"

Tricia checked her watch. "Doctor Patel was giving them the standard introductory presentation in her office, and then they were going to walk over here. Based on the original agenda, I'd think they'd be here any time now.

"Remember, team," Tricia reminded them all. "We want them to leave here without their socks and with open wallets." They all chuckled. "Let's give them a show they won't forget."

"They're here," Alex said with a hint of excitement in her voice and gave a nod toward the door.

Tricia and the rest of the team turned to see Clarissa Patel pull open the main laboratory doors. *Very corporate*, Tricia mused as the three visitors, the ones she knew would be assessing her lab and their work for further investment, filed into the lab ahead of Doctor Patel.

The first of their visitors wore thin wireframe glasses. They rested more on his very plump cheeks than on the bridge of his nose. His jowls hung slightly over a shirt collar that was a smidge too tight. He wore a green and white striped tie that was too wide and tied so short it barely reached the top of his round belly. His jacket was a bit too small to cover it either.

Behind him entered a woman. She was clearly older, with graying shoulder-length hair. She had an austere look about her. Her pantsuit was perfectly tailored, and she wore a striking red blouse underneath the jacket.

Just ahead of Doctor Patel entered an imposing, taller man, lean but with broad shoulders. He had short, dark hair that was graying slightly at the temples. His eyes immediately surveyed the room, finally resting on Tricia herself, the edges of his mouth curling slightly when he saw her. He had a presence about him; not only did Tricia feel he was the type of person who took command of a room when he entered it, but that he felt he was entitled, if not required, to take it.

Tricia stepped forward to meet the entourage just in front of the small break area at the front of the lab. Clarissa Patel stepped up to stand beside her. "Doctor Carling, I'd like to present our distinguished guests from Draconyx Enterprises." She gestured first toward the rotund man in the glasses. "This is Doctor Samuel Robinson, Chief Scientist at Draconyx."

"Pleased to meet you," Robinson said, giving Tricia's offered hand a single shake in greeting.

Clarissa presented the woman next. "This is Marlene Albright, Chief Financial Officer and head of Business Development for Draconyx."

"My pleasure," Tricia said, shaking her hand.

The woman nodded toward her with a slight smile. "Likewise. A pleasure to meet you, Doctor Carling."

"And last, but certainly not least," Clarissa began, gesturing toward the taller man, the third member of the Draconyx contingent.

"Sorensen," the man interrupted, stepping forward and grasping Tricia's outstretched hand. His hand swallowed hers in a warm, firm grip. "Director Sorensen. I oversee our Institute for the Advancement of Human Potential laboratory and special research programs."

"Pleased to meet you, Director," Tricia said politely, but when she tried to disengage the handshake, he maintained a secure grip on her hand.

"I can't say enough what a distinct pleasure it is to finally meet you, Doctor Carling," he said, smiling and staring directly into her eyes. "It's very rare that we get to meet someone of your unique talents."

"I'm very flattered, Director Sorensen, of course," Tricia said, flustered. Once again, she tried to draw her hand back, but the prolonged handshake persisted. "You say 'human potential', Director, but I thought Draconyx was primarily involved in security and defense," she said, trying to deflect how uncomfortable the handshake was becoming for her.

"Yes, that is our primary business," Sorensen replied, finally releasing her hand but not relinquishing the lock his eyes held on hers, "but we also believe that the world will be safer and more secure if we can also improve the human condition. That's a mission I'm sure you can relate to, is it not, Doctor?"

"I certainly can," Tricia answered, returning his penetrating stare, determined not to wilt under his piercing gaze.

"I'm very glad to hear that, Doctor Carling," Sorensen replied smoothly. "It's one of the reasons I'm sure you and your work would be a great addition to our research programs and why I want to make sure I become very familiar with everything, and I do mean *everything*, that has come out of this lab."

What does he think he knows?

"Well, that is what we are here for, isn't it, Director Sorensen?" Tricia asked, refusing to give an inch. She stood at least half a foot shorter, but somehow it felt as if she was practically nose to nose with him as the intensity of their conversation escalated.

"Doctor Carling," Clarissa broke in, trying to release some of the tension that was obviously building between the two.

"Perhaps you could introduce the rest of your team to our guests?"

"Of course," Tricia replied, relieved. "Here we have Jamal Okunye, our software and general systems engineer." Jamal gave a small wave.

"Next," Tricia said, indicating Alex, "is Alexandra Garcia. Alex is our electronics guru."

"Hi," Alex said, also giving a wave.

"And Nikki Robbins is a PhD candidate working with us. Her thesis is in combinatorial energy wave mechanics."

"Pleased to meet you," Nikki said with a polite smile.

Tricia turned back toward the visitors. "Our other colleague, Steve DiCicero, is currently defending his doctoral thesis, so he can't be with us today, but he's been a tremendous contributor. We expect to be calling him 'Doctor Steve' very soon."

"You must be very proud," Marlene said.

"Very much so, Ms. Albright," Tricia replied. "Not just of Steve, but of the entire team. Everything you'll see today is a result of their hard work and scientific prowess."

"Well, very good," Clarissa said brightly. "Shall we get started then?"

"Certainly," Tricia said. She turned toward her team and waved them forward. "Alex and Jamal, would you like to show our guests around?"

"Absolutely, Doctor C," Jamal said excitedly and looked to the three visitors. "If you'll follow Alex and me, please." The Draconyx contingent followed Jamal, Alex, and Nikki as they started pointing out and explaining various features of the lab.

When the group had walked far enough away to create some privacy, Tricia leaned over to Clarissa, and, still watching her guests' backs and lowering her voice, asked, "That was...different. Anything specific I should know?"

Clarissa raised an eyebrow. "Nothing I can think of, Tricia," she answered also in hushed tones. "I think the demo will go over very well, and as for anything else, I promise to step in more quickly if it looks like things may be, um, getting out of hand, shall we say?"

"Appreciate it," Tricia said, and the two of them followed to catch up with the tour.

The tour had taken a little longer than expected, but the group had ended up at the Hot Spot not too far off schedule. *Show time,* Tricia thought. She took a deep breath; now that they were finally here, it was her turn. The visitors had been very engaging and curious, and Alex, Jamal, and Nikki had done a wonderful job at showing the Draconyx people the lab, pointing out the exceptional aspects of how they worked, and answering their questions, but the Hot Spot was Tricia's baby. The team knew it. Without anyone needing to say a word, they stepped back in unison to let Tricia take point on the demonstration they all felt would be the highlight of the visit.

Tricia stepped forward to face the small cluster of visitors and motioned toward the darkened glass panels of the Hot Spot just behind her. "And this is the star of our show," she said with a proud smile. "This is the imaging field chamber. Here, we conduct our experiments in virtual instrumentation, what we call Immersive CoSimulation, by infusing ordinary holograms with dark energy." She saw Doctor Robinson perk up. Sorensen's eyes were acutely riveted to her as she spoke. "However, rather than bore you all with some long-winded presentation, we thought it would be much more fun and interesting to just show you what we do here."

Tricia nodded to Jamal, who had taken a seat behind the primary control console while she was talking. He nodded back, pressed a few controls, and the chamber's walls started to clear. Simultaneously, the door to the chamber slid open, dramatically revealing the floating hemispherical bowl inside.

"Please," Tricia said, gesturing with her hands toward the open door. "Won't you please come in?"

Marlene Albright hesitated. "Are you sure it's safe?"

Tricia chuckled. "Yes, of course," she replied. To demonstrate her point, she entered the chamber and stood next to the projected solid, facing back toward them. "Please, join me," she encouraged them.

Sorensen wasted no time entering the chamber and rapidly scanned the interior. Marlene Albright entered next, some hesitation and concern still lingering on her face. Doctor Robinson shuffled in right behind her. The three of them formed a line just to the side of the door against the inner perimeter of the chamber, facing Tricia. Doctor Patel and the rest of the team huddled around the console behind Jamal, where they could clearly see and yet still hear what was being said during the demo. Jamal also wore a headpiece tied into the auditory system of the Hot Spot itself, ready to support Tricia during the demonstration.

"As you know," she started, "we can create any visual structure we wish using light holograms, but a singular limitation in their usefulness has always been that they lacked substance." Tricia brushed her hand through the floating shape next to her. It waivered slightly but was otherwise unaffected.

"However, if we fuse the hologram with a carefully synchronized field of dark energy at the correct resonance frequency—" Tricia said, nodding toward Jamal.

Jamal returned the nod and responded by manipulating the controls on the console. Tricia felt the dark energy swell inside the shape next to her. She knew it wasn't something that the others could see or sense in any way, but her unique relationship to the flows of energy around her gave her a more unique perception. Part of her wanted to reach out and steal the energy for herself, but she deftly shrugged her desire to the side and continued.

"—the construct takes on the characteristics of an object that is more solid, more real." Tricia again brushed her hand toward the floating shape, but this time, instead of her hand passing through, the object slid through the air when she touched it.

Marlene Albright gasped, and even stuffy Doctor Robinson perked up as Tricia casually pushed and prodded the object through the space in front of her. Tricia smiled slightly. *Got them,* she thought proudly.

"Ms. Albright, would you care to come give it a try?" Tricia invited the wide-eyed woman. Albright glanced toward each of her colleagues, and, getting no sense that either of them wanted to go instead, she stepped forward. She slowly reached out with her forefinger extended and gently touched the side of the floating shape. It shifted slightly, and with a playful smile, she pushed harder with her finger on its edge, chuckling in delight as the object moved under her touch.

Albright looked up at Tricia with a childlike grin. "It's absolutely amazing, Doctor Carling, but why doesn't it fall?"

Doctor Robinson broke in before Tricia could answer. "Because the simulation isn't programmed for it to fall," he offered haughtily.

"Actually, it is, Doctor Robinson," Tricia countered. "The simulation is programmed to respond properly to our known laws of physics. The issue here is much more foundational. The object you see in front of you is entirely constructed of woven energies. It has no mass."

Robinson nodded his head slowly as the implications of her statement sank in. "Of course. No mass, so the laws of Newtonian physics don't apply to it."

"Correct," Tricia replied.

"But, your hand pushes it," Sorensen said, eager to join the debate. "That means there is some force at work, does it not?"

"Normally, yes," Robinson replied. "However, since the object has no mass, when she touches it, it essentially becomes an extension of her hand." Tricia nodded in agreement as he continued, "It moves only as her hand moves while they are in contact, but on its own, it has no momentum, no inertia, and gravity cannot affect it." He walked over and poked the virtual bowl. "See? After I push it, it stops moving as soon as I'm no longer touching or pushing on it. If it had mass, it would continue to glide since I've imparted a force that translates into velocity, which, in turn, would give it momentum. None of that applies here."

Sorensen nodded in comprehension as Tricia took a marble-sized steel ball bearing out of her pocket and picked up where Robinson had left off, "To further the point, watch what happens when we give the construct some mass to work with." She carefully set the ball bearing inside the floating hemisphere. As soon as she released it, the virtual bowl and its contents plummeted to the floor. The bearing bounced slightly on impact and hit the side of the bowl, tipping it over and spilling the steel ball out onto the floor. The ball rolled toward Tricia, coming to a stop when it hit the side of her foot.

The group jumped slightly when the construct and its contents hit the floor. Despite the fact that the bowl was made entirely of energy, the illusion was solid enough to make a rather loud and unexpected clatter when it hit, and the sharp clack produced by the steel ball itself further punctuated the startling clamor.

Tricia squatted down to pick up the ball and returned it to her pocket, taking some small satisfaction in how the crash had startled them. "Jamal, reset the construct for us, please," she said, standing back up. The bowl on the floor dissolved, and a second later, it reformed right side up, floating in the center of the chamber again, just as it was when they'd entered the room.

Albright cocked her head to one side, puzzled. "Couldn't you have just picked it back up again?" she asked.

"I'm glad you asked," she replied with a coy smile. "That's another interesting issue we are working on. Yes, I could have, but presently, it's much trickier than it looks."

"How so?" Albright asked.

"Please come and see for yourself, Ms. Albright," Tricia invited. "Try to grasp the bowl by the lip or sides."

Albright stepped forward and did as Tricia suggested, but each time she tried to squeeze down on the edge of the construct, it squirted out from between her fingers. After a few tries, she stopped and gave Tricia a mild look of frustration and confusion. Robinson and Sorensen likewise turned to Tricia for an explanation.

Tricia paused a few seconds for effect, briefly stealing a glance at Patel and her team outside the chamber. They were positively beaming, and Patel gave her a nod of approval.

"Friction," Tricia said, looking at each of her guests in turn. "Not only do these constructs have no mass, they also have a perfectly zero coefficient of friction."

Tricia reached around the floating bowl and scooped it closer to herself. "You see, our entire concept of gripping a physical object depends significantly on the friction between our fingers and the surface of the object we are trying to grasp," she explained. "Recall trying to pick up a bar of soap in the shower. The slick nature of the wet soap lowers the static coefficient of friction, making it very challenging to pick up with wet hands." The analogy hit home, and the Draconyx team nodded in agreement.

Tricia cupped the bottom of the floating bowl in one hand and, even though she knew it would be cheating a bit, she channeled a tiny flow of dark energy into her hand, bonding the bowl to her palm. She took the steel bearing back out of her pocket and gently set it inside the bowl. "In this position, my hand is directly under the mass of the steel ball, so the construct and the downward force of the ball are perfectly balanced against my fingers."

She then placed her other hand gently on the side of the bowl and continued her explanation, "But, if I now slide my hand more to the side, that balance is disrupted and without friction, this will likely slip out of my hands and fall to the floor again." She released the anchoring flow of dark energy and slowly slid her hand up the bowl's side. As her hand moved, the bowl started to slip. Tricia instinctively tried to hold onto it, but the more she tried, the more the bowl slipped, and the more frantic her attempts became. Within seconds, the bowl had crashed again, and the steel ball was rolling across the smooth floor.

"So, to make our vision of virtual instrumentation come true," Tricia said in conclusion, "we still have a few key problems to solve, and hopefully, a partner like Draconyx would be ideal to help us make this dream a practical reality."

The three visitors paused briefly and then broke out into a short round of applause. "That was truly remarkable, Doctor Carling," Albright said. "Truly remarkable."

"Yes, I have to admit that was quite impressive," echoed Doctor Robinson.

"Thank you," Tricia said, motioning for them all to leave the imaging chamber. "Thank you very much. The team has worked hard, and we are quite pleased with our progress here. We're very excited about realizing some of the possible practical applications for this technology."

When they had exited the Hot Spot, Sorensen turned toward Tricia and extended his hand. Tricia looked at it hesitantly, then finally relented and took it to return the handshake. He squeezed it firmly, again intently looking into her eyes as if he were searching for something behind them. "I must say, Doctor Carling," he said smoothly. "I had fully expected to be impressed when I came here, and I'm very pleased to see that expectation was fully justified...in every way."

"Thank you, Director," she replied politely, but in his eyes, she saw something that made her skin crawl. She saw the look of a predator, something on the prowl, and for a moment, knew exactly how the mouse feels when greeted warmly by the cat.

He nodded back and increased the pressure on the handshake. "Of course," he said, looking deeper into her eyes, clearly anticipating some reaction. "I cannot say how much I'm looking forward to our next meeting and exploring how much of a boon you...and your work, of course...will be to *our* efforts as well."

He's testing me, she realized as the pressure of his grip continued to increase.

He's deliberately trying to bait me.

Tricia Carling was certainly no mouse, but as much as she wanted to respond, to hear the bones in his hand crackle and grind, to wipe that smug smile off his face, she knew that to take the bait would not be in hers, or the team's, best interests. Instead, she just smiled politely, refusing to give him the satisfaction of responding to his intimidation.

True to her word, Clarissa Patel stepped in between them and put her hand on Sorensen's arm. "Thank you, Doctor Carling and team, for that incredible demonstration of your virtual instrumentation research." She then turned to the rest of the Draconyx group. "I think this would be an excellent time to return to my office and discuss next steps. Shall we?"

"Yes, let's," Albright said and, after thanking Tricia once again, started to walk toward the door. Robinson mumbled a final thank you and turned to join Albright. Sorensen released Tricia's hand, and after giving her one last nod, turned to follow his colleagues. Patel shot Tricia a quick look of apology and ushered them toward the door.

Tricia put her hand into her lab coat pocket, resisting the desperate urge to run to the break area to wash it. The rest of the team stepped up behind her, and together, they watched the visitors leave. When the door had swung closed behind them, Alex broke the silence. "Well, that wasn't weird at all," she said sarcastically.

Jamal huffed out a breath in agreement. "Do you think all of these visits will be like that?"

"No, I don't think they will," Tricia replied quietly, still watching the laboratory door.

No, they won't, she thought to herself, *because this wasn't a business visit. They weren't here for the lab or the science.*

He was here for me. This was personal.

And I'm sure this isn't the last I will hear from Director Sorensen and Draconyx either.

Taken

U mbra's boots clicked on the cement as she walked briskly down the sidewalk. The tails of her long coat flapped lightly in the night breeze, and her long black hair flowed out behind her. Usually, when she was being Umbra, she preferred her hair pulled up into a knot behind her head. That look, she felt, created more of an impression of authority and power, but for tonight's mission, it was loose down her back and shoulders. Tonight required a softer, more approachable look.

It was only a three-block walk from the drop-off point to the Sirens coffee shop, but she didn't want to be late. When her contact picked her up, he told her that her target had already arrived at the shop. The girl was waiting for her shift to start, and he had told Umbra that other members of the team were already in position to make sure that when Umbra arrived, they would have the place to themselves. He was confident everything would go as smooth as silk.

Still, Umbra felt a little anxious. She didn't want the girl to wait too long. Despite the team's best efforts, anything could happen, and she wanted the mission to go by the numbers. The Director was showing a lot of faith and trust in her, but Umbra knew that his faith and trust were only as good as the last mission, so as she rounded the corner, and the Sirens came into view just a short distance ahead, she picked up her pace, determined to arrive before something could throw a wrench in the plans.

Of course, it would have been faster to just travel directly to the Sirens for her rendezvous, but Umbra had never been there before. To travel safely using her powers, she needed some familiarity with her destination, some feel for it, or, at a minimum, a clear line of sight to where she wanted to go. In the spaces between, things tended to drift and become disoriented, so without a clear mental image for her to focus on, it was frighteningly easy to end up somewhere else or, worse, inside something else.

Truth be told, she felt no small measure of pride in these recruiting assignments. Getting new recruits into the program was critical to the work they were doing and what they were trying to achieve for everyone. Sure, the recruits often, well, resisted, but Umbra was sure that once they understood the mission and how important their contribution would be, they'd appreciate the chance to participate and be part of something bigger like she was.

Deep down, she also believed what Director Sorensen had told her about the recruits themselves; many of the recruits were people down on their luck—homeless, poor, or runaways like this girl—and joining The Workshop, as they called it, really gave them an opportunity they needed for a fresh start. She was honored to be entrusted with these assignments that were so vital to both The Workshop's vision and the futures of the recruits themselves.

As she walked up to the front of the Sirens shop, she was relieved to see that the team had done its part. Umbra glanced inside and saw her recruit, Isobel, sitting alone at a table towards the back, enjoying a beverage before her shift started. Other than her and the night manager behind the counter, the shop was empty.

Umbra took a breath and brushed her hair back with her fingers. *Welcome to the program, Isobel*, she thought as she pushed open the door and walked in.

Izzy inhaled the steamy vapors coming off the top of the coffee she held in her hands and smiled. She was happy and grateful for it. Not only was it a treat, a free treat, but it was wonderfully warm. She wrapped her fingers around the cup to prevent even the tiniest bit of warmth from escaping unused. It wasn't particularly cold this time of year in the city, but she knew she'd lost weight since leaving home. She was doing better now, but besides being a bit too thin, her shirt was light, hanging loosely off her shoulders, and the air conditioning was running uncomfortably high.

She checked the clock on the wall; her shift would be starting soon. Mike, the night manager, was wiping down the counter in front of her. *He's a good guy*, she thought, finishing her pastry and washing it down with another sip. He was sympathetic to young people in her situation and found ways to help when he could. In Izzy's case, that meant a cash job off the books cleaning up between shifts and a free coffee and pastry while she waited. She nursed it, relishing both the taste and the chance to just sit peacefully with nothing but her own thoughts. The days were crowded and noisy, and soon this shop would be bustling with people coming off evening shifts, but for now, she had it to herself.

Izzy heard the bells on the door jingle and looked up to see a woman enter the shop. She couldn't help but stare. The newcomer was striking: perhaps a few years older than she was, tall, dark, dressed in black. Her dark blue top matched the streaks in her thick black hair. Izzy watched her as she approached the counter and placed an order. She was definitely not the kind of person who usually came in here, especially at this time of night. The evening customers were primarily blue-collar, some nurses from the nearby urgent care clinic, some security guards from the local shops, that kind of thing. *This woman is something else entirely,* Izzy thought, furrowing her eyebrows with suspicion. *What brings her here, I wonder?*

Mike brought the woman her order. She thanked him and turned sharply, her long coat flourishing around her. To Izzy's surprise, the woman walked up to her table. "Do you mind if I join you?" The woman asked.

"Sure," Izzy said hesitantly, somewhat lost for words. "I guess." *But why?*

"My name's Darci," the woman said, smiling as she pulled out the chair across from Izzy and sat down. "It's Isobel, right? I've been looking forward to meeting you."

"Izzy, actually," Izzy replied. Her eyes narrowed a bit. "Why is that?" Flags were starting to go up in the back of her mind. Big bright red ones.

"Well, you see, Izzy," Darci answered, "I represent an institution that's dedicated to improving the world for everyone. We have a variety of programs that are all about people finding their full potential and then showing them how to apply that potential toward helping others. I think you'd be a perfect addition to what we have going on there."

Great! She's some kind of religious nut job. Izzy rolled her eyes. "Sounds like some kind of cult," she sneered, sipping her coffee.

Darci laughed. "No, no. It's nothing like that. I assure you. It's nothing hokey or cultish. The Foundation for the Advancement of Human Potential is all about scientific research. It's not religion of any kind."

The alarm bells got louder in her mind. "What kind of research?" *And why me?*

Darci swirled her coffee and drank. "You know, genetics, physiology, some psychology, that kind of thing," she answered, gesturing with her hands vaguely.

No, I don't know, actually, Izzy thought. "So, what's in it for me?"

"That's the best part. We have a wonderful facility. A room of your own, not like that shelter. A quiet place to sleep. Hot meals. A gym. Everything you could want, and all you have to do is help us with our research. Sounds pretty good, doesn't it?"

Darci gestured toward herself. "I mean, I look like I'm doing all right, don't I? Seriously, this is going to give you a chance to explore capabilities you don't even know you had, let you achieve things you didn't even know were possible."

Izzy cocked her head slightly. *She's got some good points there. Maybe that would be better than the shelter, but something still smells fishy.* Before she could answer, she looked past Darci and saw Mike behind the counter raise his hand and wave to her. *Saved by the bell,* she thought thankfully. Izzy gave Mike a short nod and watched him walk into the back room, leaving the two of them alone in the store.

Izzy stood up and swigged down the rest of her coffee. Darci stood up with her. She was a good four or five inches taller, forcing Izzy to look up slightly to talk to her. The red flags were still flying, but she had a solid excuse to end this conversation before it got any weirder.

"Look," Izzy said, putting an urgent tone to her voice. "My shift is about to start, so I gotta get going. Maybe you can leave me a card or something, and I can think about it? I can call if I'm interested?" she smiled weakly.

"That won't be necessary, Izzy," Darci told her, looking down into her eyes. Darci's face had shifted; her smile was suddenly more menacing, more knowing. Izzy's mouth went dry. "You see, when we invite people to join our program, we don't really take 'no' for an answer."

Frightened now, Izzy tried to move away, but as she stepped, she saw Darci flex her wrist. Out of nowhere, coils of pure blackness entwined around Izzy's body, pinning her arms to her sides and binding her knees. She squirmed and tried to escape, but whatever this woman, or whatever she was, was doing to her, she was firmly in its grasp. Panic welled up in her. She was the damsel in distress all over again, but much, much worse. Izzy knew it wasn't a game this time. It was real.

Izzy opened her mouth to scream, but before she could make a sound, her bonds shifted, spinning her and pulling her tightly up against Darci. Darci clamped a hand over her mouth, stifling any call for help.

"Now, now," Darci whispered into her ear, "don't make this any harder than it has to be. I really do believe this is going to be an amazing experience for you. You'll thank me later. I'm positive of it."

Frantically, Izzy's terrified eyes frantically searched the shop, but there was no one to help her. She could only whimper softly as Darci raised her free hand in a wide, sweeping gesture. Seemingly at the woman's call, Izzy watched the very shadows in the room swirl toward her and encircle them both. In desperation, she struggled one more time to no avail, and with a blast of bitter cold and darkness, the Sirens shop disappeared around her.

The old man whistled as he walked down the nighttime sidewalk. Despite his tattered clothes, he was feeling pretty happy with himself at the moment. It had been a good day. Tom, as the nicer people called him, or Stinky Tom, as the not-so-nice people called him, had picked up enough money from panhandling to get a square meal and score the cheap bottle of liquor that he had wrapped up in a brown paper bag tucked under his arm. He smiled. Tom wasn't even his real name. That's just what people called him. Since people treated things that had a name, like a stray dog or feral cat, better than things that didn't, he didn't mind being Tom. As long as they gave him things, they could call him whatever they wanted.

Tom didn't even really consider himself homeless. He had a good place staked out in an alley nearby. It was dry and sheltered from the weather. He hated the city shelters. Too many nosy people trying to tell him how to run his life. He liked his freedom too much, but he had to admit, when he needed to clean up—to be less stinky, even for him—the shelters were good for that. The other thing that made his alley such a good place was also his final stop for the day, the Sirens coffee shop that sat on the corner.

Tom would never consider buying anything in there on what he scrounged day to day. It was far too expensive, but sometimes at night, he could score a handout from the day-old baked goods or produce they might be throwing out anyway. Sometimes, they might even give him a cup of warm coffee to go with it. Not the frou-frou stuff. Plain black, just as Tom liked it.

The handouts had gotten more plentiful lately, too. A new girl had started working there some nights, doing cleanup after hours. Young, pretty, with short, dark brown hair. She always greeted him warmly with a "Hello, how are you, Tom?" and made sure he got something good when she was there. He smiled again. *Nothing warms an old man's heart like a pretty girl with a smile, especially when she was a soft touch,* he thought with a cackle, knowing too that this was one of the nights she typically would be working. It was going to be a really good day, he could tell.

As Tom approached the front of the Sirens shop, his mood brightened. *Yup, there she is*, he thought excitedly, already anticipating whatever goodie she would slip his way. He cupped his hands around his eyes against the glass to block out the glare of the streetlights overhead. Through the front plate window, he could see the brown-haired girl sitting at one of the tables toward the back. *Lizzy? Ellie? What's her name again?* He couldn't remember, but it didn't matter. It looked like she had brought a friend, too. Sitting with her was another young woman with dark skin and long black hair, wearing a black coat and high black boots. *Lucky me*, he thought, and whistled softly. *The only thing better than getting a pastry and a coffee from a pretty girl*, he mused, grinning broadly, *was getting them from* two *pretty girls.*

He paused at the window and watched them talk for a couple of minutes. Finally, the man behind the counter gave the girl the usual signal that he would be closing shortly and that it was time for her to start working. That was usually his cue. Tom watched the two women stand as the man went into the back office. *Shame,* he thought, pouting slightly. *Guess her friend won't be sticking around after all.* Tom shrugged it off.

It didn't matter. Once he saw his friend go into the back, Tom would make his way around to the side door in his alley and wait for her to open the door. His mouth was already watering, looking forward to his late-night snack.

Suddenly, his anticipation was shattered by terror. Without warning, the black-haired woman grabbed the girl, spinning her around. Dumbstruck, he watched the woman raise her arm, and the room swirled with inky blackness. Tom could see the panic in the girl's eyes as she struggled to break free, but her struggle was brief. The shadowy maelstrom swallowed the two of them, and when it cleared, the shop was empty.

Tom's eyes bugged out of his head, and his jaw flopped open in shock. He stumbled back from the window, dropping the bottle under his arm. It hit the concrete and smashed inside the bag with a loud crash. As the contents leaked out on the sidewalk and the smell of cheap whiskey filled the air, Tom gave a small shriek and ran into the alley. He threw himself into his makeshift bed in the back corner and pulled his ratty blanket up over his head. Tom was never a religious man, but in that moment of sheer panic, he clasped his hands tightly together and begged God in Heaven with every fiber of his being that the dark woman, that spawn of Hell itself, had not seen him and that she would not come back to take him as well.

Beacon landed deftly on the top of the Sirens coffee shop. It was one of her routine places to start an evening patrol. Not only was the location favorable, but it was very convenient if she needed to grab a bite to eat afterward. This was one of those nights.

The rumble in her stomach made her glad she had chosen it as the starting point for tonight's patrol, and she wasted no time retrieving her bag from the corner where it had been safely waiting for her to return. She took a quick look around to check if there was anyone about at this late hour who might see her. Satisfied no one was, she crouched down out of sight and pulled back her mask.

Tricia gave her hair a vigorous fluffing with her fingers and took a deep breath. *It was a good night*, she reflected as she opened her bag. She'd broken up a couple of attempted muggings early. Given how quiet her nights had been lately, that would have been a win all by itself. However, tonight she'd gotten a bit lucky and dropped in on a major drug deal. Beacon had been tracking some of the drug traffic lately and already had a hunch something major would be going down soon, but tonight she'd been in the right place at the right time and caught them red-handed in the middle of a major deal.

When the police showed up, Beacon had been able to hand them some high-profile dealers, a lot of money and drugs, and a relatively pristine crime scene. Everyone was happy, well, almost everyone. The dealers were pretty miserable, and she took no small satisfaction in that.

Harris will have a field day with this, she mused as she took her tracksuit out of the bag and shook it out. Tricia carefully tugged the track pants on over her costume. "Feels good to finally have another big win," she muttered to herself, zipping the legs closed. A collar like this definitely helped tamp down some of the doubt she'd been feeling lately about the impact she was having, so much so that she had decided to declare victory and call it an early evening as well as a rewarding one.

As Tricia pulled out the jacket, a sound caught her ear. She paused, listening carefully. To her, it sounded vaguely like crying or whimpering. She followed the faint sound to the edge of the rooftop overlooking the alley next to the coffee shop. *Definitely, down there,* she decided, and slipping on her jacket and making sure her costume was completely out of sight, she drew a small amount of dark energy and lowered herself gently into the dark alley below.

Tricia tracked the sound to the back corner of the alley. The carefully arranged boxes and personal effects made it obvious to her that someone likely lived there. Huddled in the corner itself on a tattered, bare mattress was a figure covered in an old, threadbare blanket. Whoever was shaking under that blanket was, no doubt, the source of the terrified sounds she was hearing.

She knelt down next to the figure and gently touched what she thought was a shoulder beneath the blanket. The figure jumped a bit, startled, and clenched the blanket even tighter. "Are you all right?" she asked softly.

"Are you one of *them*?" a shaky, raspy voice replied.

"One of who?"

"Demons, o' course!" the voice exclaimed.

"No," Tricia replied, gently pulling down on the blanket. "No, I'm not."

The figure let her lower the blanket slowly, revealing an old man, scruffy and unshaven, with eyes as large as saucers. Wet streaks glistened in the dim light on his cheeks. The look of terror on his face softened slightly when he saw Tricia over the top of the blanket. "An angel, maybe?" he asked.

Tricia smiled. "Not quite," she said reassuringly. "Let's stick with Tricia for now, ok? What's your name?"

The old man lowered the blanket a bit more. "T-t-tom," he said, stammering slightly. "No, no, it's Randall, actually...Randy. Folks just call me Tom." He suddenly clutched the blanket tightly again. "Are you sure? The other one didn't look like a demon either, but she was. I swear, she *had* to be."

"Yes, I'm sure," Tricia replied. "Now, Randy, what other one? What happened to frighten you so much?"

Randy told Tricia his story, hesitantly at first, but as he told it, he got more energetic and animated. Eventually, he released his grip on the blanket altogether so he could gesture with his hands as he talked. Tricia listened patiently as he told her about his brown-haired friend, the woman he'd seen with her, and how he had seen her spirit them both away.

"Izzy...Izzy is her name," Randy said, concluding his story. "I couldn't remember before, but it's Izzy for sure. As for the other one, I dunno what she was, but only a witch could have done what I seen, coulda made 'em both disappear like that."

Vanished into thin air, Tricia realized, recalling her conversation with Harris, *like the others.*

"That's quite a story," Tricia told him, patting his shoulder. "If I'd seen that, I would be pretty scared too." She paused for a second, thinking, while Randy stared into her eyes. The old man was clearly feeling better, but he was still pretty agitated, and despite his detailed story, Tricia had a few questions. This man, though, wasn't the one to answer them.

"Look, you've had a rough time," she finally told Randy. "Why don't you let me go inside and get you something? Would you like that?" Randy nodded. Clearly, the promise of a snack displaced any residual apprehension he was feeling. Tricia smiled and squeezed his shoulder. "Ok then. You wait here, and I'll be right back, ok?" Randy nodded again, apparently choosing to trust her over his fear, and Tricia stood up. She checked quickly that her costume was still fully covered by her tracksuit and turned to walk up the alley toward the Sirens' front door.

Tricia pushed the front door open and was greeted by the jingle of a small bell dangling from the door retractor. She chose this Sirens routinely as a starting point for her patrols in this part of the city not just for its location but because it was also one of the few late-night shops. It was in a prime location to service people coming off their evening shifts, part of the reason she'd chosen it as one of her routine patrol points.

Seems kinda dead, though, she thought to herself as she walked into the empty shop, but then realized she was typically here a bit later. The usual patrons were probably still on their shifts working. *That must be it.*

In response to the bell, a man, presumably the night manager, came out of the back office and took up position behind the register. Tricia didn't recognize him, but again, she wasn't here at her usual time either. "Can I help you?" he said, sounding a touch impatient. *Yeah, probably getting close to the end of his shift, too,* she assumed. *Best to catch this fly with a little honey.*

"Sure can," she said, giving him a big smile. "I'll take two of those breakfast sandwiches, a large black coffee, and a bottle of water."

"Do you want those sandwiches heated up?" he asked, stifling a yawn.

"Yes, please," she answered. He rang up the order, and she paid with a tap of the commpod in her ear. "Hey, wondering too if you can answer a question for me. Does a girl named Izzy work here? Young? Short dark brown hair?"

"Who wants to know?" he asked, furrowing his eyebrows.

"My name's Tricia Carling. *Doctor* Tricia Carling," she answered and reached out her hand, hoping the title drop would be enough to get him to open up.

He ignored the extended hand, but apparently, the title did its job. "Yeah, she works here some nights. Cleans up, does dishes, sweeps and mops, that kind of thing between shifts."

"Is she here tonight?" Tricia asked.

He thought for a second, studying her a bit. "She was, but she bailed before her shift. Kinda surprising, actually. She's a pretty hard worker. Smart. Good-natured. Reliable, you know the type. I went into the back for a second, and when I came out, she was gone." He snapped his fingers. "Just like that."

Tricia nodded. "Was she alone?"

"Come to think of it, no, she wasn't," the manager replied. He was clearly starting to run out of patience with the line of questioning. "Usually, she is. Keeps to herself, but tonight she was with another girl. Maybe a few years older. Dark-skinned. Long black hair with blue streaks in it. Black coat. Tight black pants and boots. Pretty." He frowned at Tricia again. "What's this all about? Is Izzy in trouble?"

"I hope not," Tricia replied. "I'm going to go outside and make a call while those sandwiches are heating up. Back in a minute, okay?"

Tricia didn't wait for his response. She turned and went out front. When the door closed behind her, she swapped the commpod in her ear for the special Beacon commpod in her bag. Slipping it into her ear, she tapped on it. *What are the odds he might actually be up?* she wondered as she heard the first ring tone, and chuckled softly. *Not good.*

After a few rings, the call connected, and her assumption was confirmed. "I really hope this is something good," a groggy voice answered. "Do you know what time it is?"

"Did I catch you napping, Harris? Some of us work at night, you know," she said, having fun at his expense. "Didn't interrupt anything, did I?"

"Unfortunately, no, just some badly needed beauty sleep. Guessing that suit of yours doesn't come with a watch, does it?" He grunted. "What's up?"

"Well," Tricia said, "for starters, you're going to be handed a solid case against some major drug dealers in the morning. That's something to look forward to."

"Finally busted them, did you?" Harris replied, sounding slightly more awake. "That is good news, but you know I would have found out about that in the morning anyway." She heard him stifle a yawn. "Why did you really call?"

"I might have a lead for you on those disappearances," she said with a more serious tone. "It's not a lot, but it's something to work with."

"Okay, now that is some good news. What do you have?"

"First, in any of the reports, was there any mention of anyone else seen with any of the people who disappeared?"

Harris paused. "Come to think of it, just one. One witness thought they saw a woman dressed in black with one of the people right before they disappeared."

Tricia huffed. "Yeah, that fits. The bad news is that there's another disappearance to add to your list, a young girl named Izzy. You're going to want to get someone down here to the Sirens in Midtown, just off Lexington. A homeless guy in the alley claims he saw her tonight talking with a woman who fits that description. Says they disappeared right in front of him. The manager confirms both women were there, but they had suddenly gone when he came back out front."

"Whoa, wait," Harris jumped in. "What do you mean 'disappeared in front of him'?"

"Yeah, that's the interesting part," Tricia answered. "Based on his description, I suspect we may have another person with abilities here in Crystal Bay."

Harris was silent for a few seconds. "That's pretty fantastic, Beacon. How could there be someone else like you? What happened with you was such a fluke...a freak accident. How would that even be possible?"

"I don't know, but a year ago, you would have said a woman running around in black and yellow tights that could quench a nuke was pretty improbable, too." Tricia ran her fingers through her hair, pushing it back over her head, and exhaled slowly. "I know how it sounds. Maybe the guy is drunk or off his rocker. You have people who can talk to him and figure that out. He didn't smell like he'd been drinking, though, and he was genuinely terrified when I found him. He saw something, something that scared him half to death. I'm inclined to put some credibility to his story, and it does fit with what you just told me about the other victims."

"All right," Harris replied. "We'll look into it. At the very least, we can see how far we get with this other woman's description. See if we can tie her to anything else."

"Sounds good," Tricia said. "I'll keep nosing around, too. Maybe I can get a lead on her or any other people who have vanished mysteriously that haven't been reported yet."

"Ok, but be careful," Harris said with an uncharacteristic concern in his voice. "If there is another person like you out there, and she's not friendly, well, make sure you avoid any unpleasant surprises, all right?"

"Copy that," Tricia answered and disconnected the call. She took a deep breath, tipped her head back, and let it out slowly. *Just when I thought things couldn't get any weirder,* she thought. The implications of the night's events rattled her, but she'd have to deal with them later. Quickly composing herself, she went back inside, picked up her order, and took it back around into the alley to an awaiting Randy.

"Here you go, Randy," she said and handed him the steaming cup and one of the sandwiches from the greasy paper bag. "Some friends of mine will come by tomorrow to talk to you about what you saw tonight. You be sure to tell them exactly what you told me, okay? Don't leave anything out."

"Uh-huh", Randy agreed, tearing open the paper bag and scarfing some of his sandwich. He washed it down with a large swig of coffee, cringing a bit when the hot liquid hit his tongue. "Do you think she's coming back?" he asked tentatively.

"I don't think so," Tricia replied reassuringly, trying to sound confident for his sake and peace of mind. "Just in case, though, I have another special friend who'll check on you here and there and make sure you're ok if that's all right."

Randy took another bite. "Is she an angel?" he asked, mumbling through a glob of half-chewed sandwich. "Some people call her that," Tricia smiled and gave his shoulder another squeeze. "You take it easy, okay?" Randy nodded. Tricia turned, slung her bag over her shoulder, and walked up the alley toward the street.

When she reached the main street, she stopped and looked up. The city lights obscured all but the brightest stars, but she found them beautiful anyway. *Could there really be someone else like me?* she thought, asking the stars.

The idea of someone else like her filled Tricia with both excitement and trepidation. *I might not be alone with this anymore, but if she exists, what can I expect from her? Where did she come from? What are her intentions? Friend, or foe?*

She huffed, took a bite of her sandwich, and slowly shook her head as she started toward home. *Whatever she is, and whatever she's up to, first impressions aren't promising, though...*

Overtures

*I*t could be worse, Izzy thought to herself as she forked a healthy portion of scrambled eggs into her mouth. The food was decent, and she could have anything she wanted and as much as she wanted. The best part was she didn't have to prepare it herself or worse, prepare it for her ungrateful father and brothers who were more apt to criticize her cooking skills (which honestly weren't bad) than say 'thank you' for getting a decent meal put in front of them.

It was the same for her clothes. They weren't fashionable by any stretch of her imagination. In fact, they reminded her of those baggy outfits patients and surgeons wore on those doctor shows her mom used to watch during the day. However, they were soft and clean, and again, she didn't have to do the laundry either. They even smelled nice.

Once she'd gotten over the initial shock of being kidnapped from the coffee shop, it honestly hadn't been that bad. Sure, she was a prisoner, and the thought of that woman, the one who took her, and the things she could do terrified Izzy still, but since she'd arrived, she'd been treated very courteously by the staff, and she'd actually come to feel oddly safe here. Her room was a bit boring, but it was clean, quiet, and, most importantly, hers. They respected her privacy, and she wasn't afraid that someone would barge in unexpectedly to terrorize or humiliate her like her brothers did at home.

Yes, it could be a lot worse.

Izzy greedily finished off the rest of her breakfast, and no sooner than she pushed back her plate, a knock came at the door. "Isobel?" a woman's voice said through the door.

"Uh-huh," Izzy called back.

The door swung open, and a plump Asian woman entered the room. She was wearing a lab coat and dark blue pants, pretty much what Izzy assumed was the standard dress code around this place. "Shall we?" the woman said, motioning toward the door with a big, friendly smile. "You've got a big day ahead of you."

Great, more testing, Izzy thought to herself disgustedly. She mustered a small smile in return. "Yup, sure," she replied and pushed herself up from the table to meet the woman at the door.

Ugh, testing, she thought as they walked down the now familiar beige hallway past the rows of white doors. Each door had an electronic lock on the outside. Some had a red tag on the outside, while others were green. Izzy had figured out already that the tags indicated which rooms were occupied and which weren't. Part of her hoped she might meet one of the others, maybe someone like herself, but so far she had only seen the staff.

This place came with something else she had never experienced in her whole life, something that she now looked forward to every day. While she was out, someone would come and service her room, just like she was some celebrity or VIP in a fancy hotel. When she returned, her bed would be made with fresh, crisp sheets, her dishes would be gone, and her dirty clothes would be replaced with clean ones, neatly folded in the small closet. *It isn't horrible,* she pondered. *Well, except for the being kidnapped part, that is.*

The barrage of medical tests she'd endured since arriving was the only other downside so far. For days, it had been one thing after another: scans that produced all kinds of funky images, machines that recorded her heart or brain or anything else she could think of, and endless fluid and tissue samples. Her arms were feeling quite sore in spots from the needle punctures.

Still, the medical people had treated her very kindly through it all. One older doctor was quite surprised to hear that she'd not had any regular physicals, especially the ones for women's health, at her age. Izzy had just shrugged. Her brothers played sports, and her father liked going to the games, so they got regular physicals. She didn't. She only saw the doctor when something was wrong, and even then, her father told her to just tough it out more often than not.

Here, though, it seemed her well-being was very important to them, and in spite of any neglect for her health up to this point, the doctors were pleased with her results. They told her that her "baselines", whatever those are, were outstanding and, other than being slightly underweight, that she was in excellent physical health. That was something positive anyway.

"So, why is it going to be a big day?" Izzy asked the woman walking next to her.

The woman looked over at her, still smiling. "Pardon? Big day?"

"Yeah," Izzy said. "You said today was going to be a big day. What's going to happen?"

"Oh, oh, yes, of course," the woman replied with a shake of her head. "The Director will be meeting with you when we get where we are going, so it is probably best to let him fill you in on that. He is looking forward to meeting you very much."

Izzy grunted, but as she turned to go down the corridor she'd taken every other day, the woman gently caught her elbow. "Nope, this way today," she said, tipping her head toward the hallway straight ahead. Izzy's eyebrows ticked upward, and she followed, curious and slightly unsettled, about the unexpected change in routine.

At the end of the hallway, they came to an elevator door. The woman held her commpad up to the panel next to it, and after a few seconds, the doors slid open, and they went inside. At the bottom of a short ride down, they exited into yet another beige corridor, albeit a much shorter one. There were only two doors, and in contrast to the doors on the other level, these were much heavier-looking and slid into the wall to open. One of them was already standing open, and the woman gestured for Izzy to go that way.

Izzy started to enter the room, but when she surveyed the inside of the room, she stopped suddenly, bracing her hand on the door frame. Butterflies swarmed in her stomach, making her queasy. The room was moderately lit, but she couldn't see any obvious lighting fixtures. One side of the room was clear glass, or what looked like glass. Behind it was a man, also in a lab coat, busying himself with various instruments set into an array of panels. In the center of the room was a chair that reminded Izzy of some nightmarish dentist chair. It had thick black padded cushions on an articulated frame of dull gunmetal gray. The chair reclined slightly and had arced appendages of metal and glass rising up from beneath it like some demon's hand reaching up to grasp the chair and whoever was sitting in it and drag them to the underworld.

"Wh...wh...what is that? What's going on here?" Izzy stammered.

"Don't worry, Isobel," the woman said gently. She reached up behind Izzy and gently pulled her hand down from the door frame, and with her arm wrapped around Izzy's lower back, gently nudged her into the room. "This is where your procedures will be performed."

Izzy resisted the nudging and pressed back against the woman's arm. "What procedures?"

"The Director will be here any minute, and I promise he will explain everything," the woman replied, continuing to guide the squirming Izzy toward the chair. "Isobel, *please*," she insisted with a sterner but still gentle voice, and squeezing Izzy's arms, "There's really nowhere to go, so let's get you comfortable. Honestly, it will be ok. Trust me."

Izzy looked into her eyes, then at the chair again, then back at her. Seeing that the woman was right, that there was in fact no recourse, Izzy took a deep breath and finally relented, letting the woman guide her into the chair. Izzy climbed up into the chair and settled her head back into the cushioned headrest. It cradled her head comfortably, she had to admit, and as the woman clicked one control after another on the back of the chair, it adjusted to fit her body, settling her head, back, arms, and legs even further into a relaxing position.

"Better?" the woman asked.

Izzy nodded and shifted herself to nestle further into the thick cushions. They were soft and conformed to every curve of her body. If it weren't for the swarm of butterflies earnestly churning in her stomach, it would have been tempting to just take a nap.

She didn't have much time to relax, though. Just as she finished settling into the cushy chair, a middle-aged man walked into the room. He instantly reminded Izzy of her uncle back home, the one who sold cars, except this man was much more fit and had a more expensive suit. His electric blue tie practically glowed against the dark blue of his immaculate suit, and his short salt-and-pepper hair was perfectly trimmed. He also wore the same big welcoming smile as her uncle, except behind this man's smile lurked something darker.

"Hello, Isobel," he said warmly as he walked up next to her. He motioned to the woman before extending his hand toward Izzy. "I'm Director Sorensen. I run the facility here. So sorry we haven't had a chance to get acquainted before now, but it's been very hectic around here lately. You've come at just the perfect time."

Izzy smiled weakly and returned the handshake as the woman returned with a rolling stool. "Thank you, Angelica," the man said and sat down next to her. He unbuttoned his jacket and rolled himself up next to Izzy.

"So, Isobel, how has your stay with us been so far? Are you being treated well? Is your room comfortable?" he asked amiably.

"I suppose," Izzy said. *Other than it being a prison cell.* "What am I doing here? What's going to happen to me? Am I going to be sold to some sheik in the Middle East or something?"

Sorensen chuckled. "No, no, nothing like that, Isobel. I assure you. Here at the Institute for the Advancement of Human Potential, we are all about taking people, people like you and me, to a new level of human performance."

"You mean like athletes? Steroids? That kind of thing?" Izzy asked.

"No, not like athletics. Something superior entirely," Sorensen answered.

A wave of realization swept over Izzy. Her eyes widened. "You mean like that woman who took me? Like that?!?"

Sorensen smiled and nodded. "Umbra, Ms. Jackson, was already gifted when she joined us, but yes, Isobel, just like that."

"You've got to be *kidding*?" Izzy blurted out, gripping the arms of her chair. "She's horrible. Terrifying. Why would you want to have more people like *her*!? I still have nightmares about her."

"Now, now, there's no need to be concerned about Ms. Jackson, Isobel," Sorensen assured her. "I'm sure she seemed that way in your encounter at the coffee shop, but trust me, she's one of the good guys." Izzy scrunched her face in a frown and crossed her arms over her chest, not buying his attempt to reassure her.

"Besides," he continued, "even if she is a bit menacing, just look at her. Beautiful. Powerful. Strong. Being intimidating like that isn't a bad thing, is it? You can bet that no one takes advantage of her, do they?"

"I suppose not," Izzy admitted reluctantly.

"No, they do not," Sorensen said. "Umbra is here because she *wants* to be here. She believes in what we are doing. No one forces her.

"As for why, well, to be honest, Isobel, the world's not a nice place. People robbing and hurting other people, taking advantage of each other. People mistreating and abusing each other. Even family members hurting and abusing the ones they are supposed to love and protect." Izzy jerked slightly at the reference. "You've been on the street. You've seen all this firsthand, haven't you?"

"Yeah," Izzy agreed mournfully, "yeah, I have."

"The police are overwhelmed. The government doesn't have enough money. Sadly, some people do care, but there are too few of them," Sorensen continued. "Simply put, they need help, and that's where we come in. Imagine a team of gifted people out there stopping the bad people. Muggings, drugs, rape, all of it. Imagine what that would be like."

"Oh," Izzy said, brightening slightly. "You mean like Beacon? That amazing woman in Crystal Bay, the super one?"

"Yes, yes, exactly like her," Sorensen said, slapping his knee lightly. "Powerful and intimidating, exactly like Beacon and Ms. Jackson, but teams of them, everywhere, doing what she does. Helping people. Seeing to it that justice is served. Doesn't that sound amazing?"

"It kinda does," Izzy admitted. "Beacon is incredible. She really brings the heat to those scumbags. But what does that have to do with me? I'm nothing like her."

Sorensen leaned in a bit and put his hand on hers. "Imagine, Isobel, if *you* were like one of them."

"Me?"

"Yes, you, Isobel. That's what we do here. That's what these procedures we are performing will do. We take healthy, smart, good-hearted people like you and make them exceptional, make them *para*human, by giving them gifts and abilities they can use to help others. Doesn't that sound awesome?"

Izzy nodded. "Kinda," she said. "Kinda, yeah, but why me?"

"Because you're just the kind of person we want in our program, Isobel," Sorensen replied smoothly. "You're bright. You have initiative. You're not afraid to do what you feel is right. You're young and healthy and, frankly, have many of the genetic markers that are favorable to what we do here.

We...I...believe you have exactly what it takes to be someone incredible and use these gifts wisely."

Exactly what it takes...to be like Beacon? Or even the scary, darker woman, Umbra? Really?

To dish it out instead of taking it...

She closed her eyes and took a deep breath as she came to a decision. "It's going to hurt, though, isn't it?"

Sorensen shrugged a bit. "There will likely be some...discomfort...but won't it be worth it? To be like Beacon or Ms. Jackson, where no one will ever lay a hand on you again? To not rely on an uncaring father to protect you from your own brothers? To help other young women like yourself never have to feel afraid? To stand up for what's right? For yourself? Maybe even deal some back to those who deserve it? Wouldn't that be worth a small amount of pain?"

Yes, yes, it would, Izzy thought as she stared at him. *Wait, how does he know about my brothers? My father? Who is this guy?*

"Are there others?" She asked instead, pushing the rising doubts aside.

"We only know of two," Sorensen replied. "There could be more, of course."

"No, I mean here," Izzy clarified. "Are there others *here*? Others who have been changed? Can I meet them?"

Sorensen shook his head. "None that you can meet now, but don't worry, very soon you will be part of a very elite and special group of people. A new family that watches out for each other."

Izzy heard a soft chime go off inside Sorensen's jacket. In response, he paused to regard her for a second and then squeezed her hand and stood up. "Unfortunately, I have to leave now. I have a crucial meeting with someone very special that I'm working hard to convince to also join our program here, and I don't want to be late."

Sorensen patted Izzy's shoulder gently. "I'm going to leave you in Angelica's and Josh's capable hands now. I must say, I'm really looking forward to seeing how your transformation will turn out and what an amazing and powerful woman you'll become."

Izzy watched Sorensen leave the room and pondered the future he had placed before her. When Angelica returned from putting the stool back into the control room, she placed a hand on Izzy's shoulder. "So, quite the program we have going on here, wouldn't you say? Are you ready?"

Izzy nodded slightly and swallowed. "I suppose," she said hesitantly and managed a weak smile. *Not that I have much choice,* a small voice inside reminded her.

But that strength...power...freedom...would I say 'No' if I did?

"Great. I told you it was going to be a big day. Let's finish getting you ready, shall we?" Angelica suggested and gently pressed Izzy down into the chair. Once nestled into the cushions, Angelica tipped the chair back gently, moving Izzy into a more reclined position.

It'll be ok, Izzy told herself, staring up at the blank ceiling as she heard a loud click. The arced appendages that had looked like monster fingers before gently rotated to close into a series of circles over her, one just above her forehead, two more over her chest and stomach, and the last one at her hips. The clear sections of the rings glowed slightly in alternating blues, whites, and greens.

Angelica then pulled a strap out of the bottom of the armrest and wrapped it around Izzy's wrist, fastening it again to the bottom. "Wait. What's this for?" Izzy asked nervously.

"Just a safety precaution, Isobel. Nothing to worry about," Angelica said as she fastened a similar strap over the other wrist, and then over each of her two ankles on the foot rests. "If you were to move during the procedure, you could injure yourself or damage the equipment." Angelica leaned slightly over Izzy and smiled down at her. "We wouldn't want that to happen, now would we?"

Izzy shook her head and swallowed hard. Angelica clicked another control on the back of the chair, and the straps retracted sharply, locking Izzy into the chair. She jumped, and the butterflies in her stomach suddenly transformed into a swarm of bats. Any emerging sense of safety she might have been feeling was instantly shattered. In that moment, Izzy was transported back to her dungeon basement with her brother leering over her, once again completely at someone else's mercy. This time, though, she was sure that whatever was coming next wouldn't tickle.

Izzy gritted her teeth, struggling to control the panic welling up in her as Angelica joined Josh in the control room. She saw his hand flip a switch on the console, and his voice filled the room. "Ok, Isobel. We're ready to start. On the count of three. One..."

She pressed her eyes closed, squeezing out a tear that trickled down her cheek.

I will be strong...powerful...

"Two..."

Izzy gripped the arms of the chair tightly, digging her fingers into the cushion.

No one will ever hurt me again...

She never heard 'three.'

A searing wave tore through her body. Her muscles spasmed, arching her back and wrenching her wrists and ankles against the straps. Izzy's vision exploded in a scorching white light, and the last thing she remembered before consciousness mercifully slipped away was the sound of her own screams.

"So, honestly, Tricia," Marni said, perched on the edge of her lab stool. "I don't know where we want to go from here."

Tricia sat in a chair across from her in one of the university hospital's genetic labs, digesting what they had been discussing about Marni's research into the sources and potential side effects of her abilities. She pursed her lips, staring up at the ceiling, and pressed her fingers together in a steeple while she thought. "So, we are at a dead end then," she finally said, puffing sharply out of her nose.

"No, I didn't say that," Marni answered quickly. "It just means I'm going to have to think of some different approaches. We've gone as far as we can with examining the sequencing of your DNA and core chromosomes. That's at a dead end, but it doesn't mean there aren't other places to look.

"I'm also going to have to think about some different ways to test your abilities and any comorbidity or alternative effects they may be having on you. All the regular tests and procedures we've tried simply show you are an exceptionally healthy woman. They indicate nothing out of the ordinary or give any clue as to your unique physiology."

Tricia nodded. "And we've not exactly had the best of luck testing my abilities directly either," she added.

"No," Marni agreed. "Clearly, standard medical diagnostic equipment wasn't designed for someone like you." She scoffed. "I still don't think they've been able to recalibrate the MRI machine. Perhaps having you channel your abilities while it was running was a bad decision in hindsight."

"Probably," Tricia said with a chuckle. "We may end up having to modify something in my lab to help with that. That's what I used when I first discovered what I could do. Of course, we run the risk of raising the suspicion of my team, so we'll need to think that through if you believe that's an option worth pursuing."

"It might be," Marni agreed, rubbing her chin. "I'll have to think on that and devise some new protocols we can use." She put on her encouraging face, one Tricia had seen many times in the past when things had gone a bit sideways. "Don't worry. We'll crack this nut. I promise."

It's a shame Rene isn't still around, Tricia thought absently. *Under different circumstances, we could really use her expertise and brilliance at times like this.* She felt a small twinge of guilt and sadness, but quickly dismissed it.

"In the meanwhile, there is one important thing I've managed to figure out that I think we should discuss," Marni said, putting on her clinical persona once again.

"Lay it on me," Tricia replied.

"Your healing ability, Tricia," Marni said, consulting one of the commpads on the table next to her. "It's not precisely healing in the way we define it clinically. It's actually more like regeneration."

"You mean like a lizard?" Tricia said, raising her eyebrows. "If someone cuts off my tail, it'll grow back?"

Marni grinned. "Well, we won't be cutting anything off to test that theory, but in principle, yes, that's exactly what it's like. Your body doesn't just heal like mine does. If I get cut, my body knits the damaged tissue back together. It's not a deterministic process, so I might end up with a scar or some other residual imperfection. Yours doesn't. That damaged tissue regenerates, leaving no indication you were ever injured in the first place."

"I wondered about that," Tricia responded thoughtfully.

"There's more," Marni said, her voice slowing. "It's not just happening when you get injured. It's happening to your entire body systematically."

"Systematically?" Tricia asked, leaning forward in her chair and narrowing her eyebrows slightly. "How so?"

"For example, examining the results of your various tests more closely, your key indicators match more of what we would expect to find in a woman in her early twenties, not someone of your age. Blood chemistry, skin elasticity, bone density, muscle tone, neuroplasticity, all of it. You're in fantastic shape and take great care of yourself, but lifestyle alone could not explain these results being a full decade behind your actual age."

"What does that mean, Marni?" Tricia probed, unease now creeping into her voice.

"Every indication is that, because of your unique abilities, your life expectancy could easily be two to three times that of a normal human, Tricia." Marni paused to let that sink in.

Tricia sat back in her chair and huffed. "So, does that mean I'm going to be like the vampires in those old movies that had to move periodically so people wouldn't figure out they didn't age?"

Marni chuckled. "I don't know about that, Tricia, but I can say you'll look fantastic when you're eighty."

Tricia smiled weakly. *I might live for centuries*, she mused. *Outlive everyone I know. I have no idea how to feel about that...or if I even want that at all.*

"Well, I guess I'd better start putting more into my retirement fund, shouldn't I?" Tricia quipped. "Any other surprises?"

"No," Marni said. "I think that's enough excitement for one day."

"Okay then," Tricia said as she stood up and started to collect her things. "On that note, I've got to get going. I'm meeting someone for lunch."

"Lunch? Oooooh," Marni teased with a melodic rise and fall. "With whom?"

"Harold," Tricia answered, bracing herself for Marni's reaction.

"Baskins? You mean the guy over at the materials sciences lab who's been helping you with your costume?" Marni asked skeptically. Tricia nodded. "Are you sure that's a good idea?"

"Probably not," Tricia admitted with a short sigh.

"Then why do it?"

"Honestly, Marni, because there really isn't a good reason *not* to do it," Tricia said, facing her friend. "He's kind and generous and unassuming. Sort of geeky but in a fun way. He's done nothing but help me through this whole thing for no reason other than he believes in what I'm trying to do. That says a lot.

"Plus," she continued, clutching her jacket to her chest, "like you, he knows who I am, and that means I don't have to pretend or hide anything when I'm around him. I don't have to be afraid of slipping or saying the wrong thing and giving something away. That's incredibly liberating. I can relax a bit when I'm with him, and having people like that in my life is important, especially if I'm going to be around for a couple of hundred years."

Marni bit her lip. "I get that, but what happens if things go badly? Aren't you afraid he might out you just from spite?"

Tricia shrugged. "Maybe, but I don't think he's that kind of person. If I'm wrong, well, I'll deal with it when it happens."

"Hmm, ok then. But be careful, all right?" Marni said.

"Of course I will," Tricia agreed.

Marni cocked her head to the side and a playful smile slowly curved her lips. "Makes me wonder, Tricia. Have you ever thought about what happens with your powers if you, well, you know, have sex?"

"I know exactly what will happen," Tricia replied with a mischievous smirk of her own.

Marni snickered and raised her hands as if to say, 'And?'

"Well, things may get a little warm, but nothing to be worried about," Tricia said, still smiling coyly. "Besides, while other people may talk about how they glow afterward, I actually can."

Marni laughed out loud.

When they'd stopped laughing, Tricia put her hand on Marni's shoulder. "I don't say this enough, but I'm incredibly grateful for everything you do, Marni. I hope you know that. If I seem a little short or distracted, it's just that all this is a lot to process sometimes. Every time I learn something new, it seems like I really don't know anything at all."

Marni reached up and squeezed Tricia's hand. "That's what best friends are for, especially the brilliant and beautiful ones."

Tricia chuckled. "Don't I know it?" she said, and after securing a promise for them to meet for dinner before their next martial arts class, she left to see what lunch would have in store for her, hoping that, for once, something could just be normal.

Tricia arrived at the restaurant a few minutes early. As she waited for the receptionist, she quickly scanned the few people already sitting in the dining area, but saw no sign of Harold. *I am early,* she conceded to herself, *but then, he usually is too. Odd.* Despite every rational clue that everything was perfectly normal, though, she couldn't shake the feeling that something wasn't right.

"Can I help you?" a young woman in a black button-down shirt and black slacks asked her, walking up to the back of the counter.

"Yes, I have a reservation for lunch," Tricia replied. "For two," she added, as if the point needed a reminder.

"Baskins?" the woman asked. Tricia nodded.

"This way, please," the woman said with a smile, picked up two menus, and led Tricia to a small table in the far corner next to the window.

As Tricia sat down, the woman said, "Your server will be with you shortly, but can I put in a drink order for you to get started?"

"Malbec, please," she replied, too nervous to think of anything other than her standard go-to varietal. The server brought it almost instantly, and after a quick swirl and sniff, Tricia downed two large gulps like she was dying in the desert. As the warmth flowed down her throat, she tipped her head back and took a deep breath through her nose. *What am I even doing here?* she asked herself. *Marni's right. This is probably a terrible idea.*

A shadow fell over the table in front of her, and a voice behind her said, "Hello, Doctor Carling."

Tricia turned and looked up at the man standing next to her. He wore a beautiful suit with the most stunning blue tie she'd ever seen. That face framed by the graying dark hair, she'd seen him before. *Of course,* she realized, *the lab visit.*

"Yes, Mr. Sorensen, isn't it?" she replied.

"*Director* Sorensen, but yes. May I join you?" he said and, without waiting for an answer, took the seat across from her. He gestured to the server, indicating he wanted a glass of what Tricia was drinking, and then folded his hands on the table in front of him.

"Just so you know, Director Sorensen, I'm expecting someone any moment, so we may have to continue this conversation some other time," Tricia told him, not without a small measure of irritation.

"Yes, well, it seems that Doctor Baskins is going to be delayed," he replied, staring her dead in the eye with a wickedly arrogant smile on his face.

"How...? What did you do?" Tricia demanded, keeping her voice low.

"I didn't do anything...yet," he said, taking a bread stick from the basket on the table and tearing off a piece. "I just made sure Doctor Baskins would get caught up in some unexpected traffic. That way, we could have a little time to talk in a public location that would discourage any, um, outbursts, shall we say."

He put the piece of bread in his mouth just as Tricia heard a chime from her bag. "That's probably him," Sorensen said between chews. "Go ahead. Check it."

Tricia pulled her commpad out of her bag and checked. *Sure enough*, she thought, seeing the message from Harold:

> Sorry to be late, Tricia, but I'm caught in some kind of traffic jam. Looks like a couple of lanes are blocked for some reason. I'll be there as soon as I can.

Tricia took a few seconds and tapped out a quick response:

> No problem. I have a glass of wine to keep me company until you get here. Drive safely.

Tricia then tucked the device back into her bag and glared at Sorensen. "Look," she said. "If this is about the lab or the visit, I think it would be best to go through Doctor Patel's office and deal with any questions or concerns about a possible contract through proper channels instead of hijacking my personal time."

The server put a glass of wine down in front of Sorensen. He eagerly picked it up and washed down the bread he was chewing with a healthy sip. "Honestly, Doctor Carling, while your lab is doing some really interesting, and frankly very sophisticated, things, I have no interest in the research you are doing. I am interested solely in what the lab has already produced. Namely, you."

Tricia's breath caught, and she stiffened slightly. "I have no idea what you're talking about," she replied evenly, not breaking eye contact.

Sorensen's eyes narrowed slightly. "Don't insult my intelligence, Doctor Carling. I know exactly what happened in that accident last year and what you've been doing as a result of it, so please don't play games with me."

"All right, then, assuming I have any idea of what you're talking about," she replied tersely. "What do you want?"

Sorensen smiled and took another sip of wine. "Put simply, I'm a big admirer, Doctor Carling. Of what you're doing, what you're trying to do. You and I want the same things."

"I'm so relieved," Tricia said.

"However, despite the great things you are doing, you are just one person. Don't get me wrong, your results have been impressive, but even with the charities and everything else, one person alone just can't make the dent in the evil and selfishness of this world that you long to make."

Sorensen sat back in his chair. "I run a program that wants to build on what you are doing by enabling more people like you, more people with the abilities required to really make that difference on a scale wider than just here in Crystal Bay."

Tricia gaped at him. "Do you mean..." she started in disbelief.

"Yes," Sorensen said enthusiastically.

"That's insane. If you know about the accident, then you know it was a fluke, a freak of luck, that I even survived, let alone whatever else happened."

"Yes, it was, but many great discoveries started as accidents," he replied and leaned forward. "It would probably surprise you to hear that we've actually made a lot of progress already, and we have had some rather impressive successes so far."

Oh my God, she thought. *He's crazy!* "I'm sure you're very proud, but what does this have to do with me then?" she asked tentatively.

He shrugged slightly, turning his palms upward. "Despite the successes we've had, our progress has stalled lately," he confessed. "We have encountered a few obstacles that we can't quite seem to figure out. However, we are very sure that if you were to join our program and agree to help us better understand how your abilities work, we could quickly overcome our recent setbacks and get back on track."

Yup. Certifiable.

"Director Sorensen, I find this all to be...incredulous, to say the least," Tricia told him, struggling to remain calm and collected. "I can say emphatically and with absolute certainty that without knowing more, a *lot* more, I have no intention of participating with your program in *any* capacity."

Tricia then heard another chime, this time from Sorensen's pocket. He glanced down quickly and then looked back up at her. "I see you may need some time to consider my proposal," he said, once again donning that irritatingly arrogant smile. "Doctor Baskins will be on his way again soon, so best I be leaving now." He stood up, pushed his chair back in, and buttoned his jacket. "I'll also pay for this on the way out. It's the least I can do to thank you for our little chat."

As Sorensen walked past her to leave, he abruptly turned back and leaned down, putting his head close to hers. Tricia froze, staring straight ahead. She could smell his aftershave and sweat and feel his breath on the edge of her ear as he softly said, "I will be in touch with you again very soon, Doctor Carling, and I do sincerely hope you will give this some serious consideration. You'll find I can be very...persuasive, and it would be best if neither you nor the people close to you had to find out just how persuasive I can be."

Tricia did not look after him as he left, but rather continued to look across the table into empty space until another chime interrupted her. As she reached down to retrieve her commpad, she was surprised to see that her hands were shaking. On the small screen was another message from Harold:

> Looks like whatever happened has cleared up, so I should be there very shortly. See you soon.

Tricia thought for a moment and, after considering her pounding heart, trembling hands, and the heat radiating from her flushed neck, sent back:

> Sorry to do this, Harold, but I just realized that I do have something I need to get back for, and with us running late, I think it's best if we postpone to another time when we won't be rushed. We'll set it up soon, I promise. Talk soon!

His feelings would likely be hurt, and he'd probably think she was angry with him, but Tricia knew she could smooth things over with him later. Hurt feelings were better than having him be in any kind of danger because of her.

Tricia tossed the commpad down on the table in front of her and downed the rest of the wine in her glass in a single gulp. She then rested her elbows on the table and put her face into her hands, taking a few minutes before leaving to face the world again to compose herself and think about what she should do next.

Disaster

A t this point, Izzy didn't need a guide to find the examination rooms. She had been there many times and knew the way like the back of her hand, but even still, the orderly walked next to her, guiding her just the same. *Protocol*, she knew.

Yes, she had received multiple 'treatments' and spent many hours and days in the examination rooms after them. Izzy didn't know where these treatments were going anymore. She remembered what the Director had promised her, but as far as she knew, none of those treatments had delivered on that promise. The only thing he said that ended up being even remotely true was that each treatment had been excruciating.

Izzy shivered, recalling how she had been subjected to various forms of energies multiple times, how each had felt like they had torn her apart and made her body a single exposed nerve. Izzy had made this journey in various stages of consciousness and vigor, ranging from barely lucid and unable to walk at all to how she felt now.

True, the first time she came to the room after she woke up a few days ago, they had to bring her in a wheelchair, but the next day, she could walk on her own, and today she felt better than she had in weeks, months, or years, even. This time, something was starkly different. Besides feeling perkier, she marveled at how her senses seemed to be on overdrive. The lights seemed brighter, the colors were more vivid, and every sound was sharper and more acute. She could even hear the footfalls of the soft-soled slip-ons they'd given her for shoes as clearly as if she were wearing heels.

How she felt wasn't the only thing different this time. She tugged at the material of her new outfit where it was riding up slightly just under her armpit. When Izzy woke up this morning, she found that someone had changed out all her clothing. Gone from her closet were the scrubs and hospital gowns. In their place was this suit. It was a deep crimson and made of a material she'd never seen before, silky and stretchy but very smooth and soft. It came down to her elbows and knees and had a crew-style collar that dipped to a 'V' shape just below her neck.

Izzy tugged again absentmindedly on the suit. She just wasn't used to wearing anything this form-fitting, especially around home, but deep down, she knew adjusting it over and over would not relieve the exposed feeling it gave her. Truth be told, it was snug, but it fit like a glove, and the sleek material was positively luxurious against her skin.

It wasn't modesty either; she had the figure to pull off something like this, and even the lack of any kind of underwear beneath it didn't faze her at this point. What they'd done to her, what she might become, made anything like that nothing more than a nit in the grand scheme of what was happening. The feeling she had was more subliminal, and her new outfit was only part of it.

No, it was that this kind of clothing just didn't belong here. It felt out of place...odd...confusing. It was just one more change Izzy didn't understand on top of all the others, and that creeping feeling of just not knowing made her anxious.

The only silver lining for her was the hope that these changes might signal that some progress was finally being made, but walking these same corridors that had previously led her to those treatments, and the anguish associated with them, forced her to keep her hope that the treatments might be ending in check. The uncertainty of what might be waiting for her now only threatened to amplify the anxiety she already felt, so any hope she might have was readily spent just pushing back the rising apprehension and unease as they walked.

When they finally approached the hall of examination rooms, the orderly gently took her elbow and guided her into the first open door on the left. Inside was the familiar dentist-style seat they expected her to take, a bank of equipment against the wall, and the nurse-slash-technician and doctor she'd seen on her other visits. The orderly directed her inside and then sealed the door with a press of a button.

"Ah, hello Izzy." The doctor said, welcoming her. The technician smiled but said nothing.

"Hello, Doctor," Izzy replied politely. She didn't know their names. They had never offered them, and she just assumed at this point she wasn't supposed to know.

"Shall we start with the vitals?" the doctor asked, gesturing toward the chair.

"Sure," Izzy responded, settling herself into the chair, "I know the drill." She relaxed a bit and let her body sink into the soft foam cushions. The chair itself wasn't uncomfortable, and besides, nothing bad ever happened during *these* visits.

The nurse put a few leads on her temple and upper chest, then clipped a small device to her forefinger. *All the same stuff*, she thought as the equipment beeped into life. Izzy couldn't see the monitors themselves—they were directed away from her, likely on purpose—but she could clearly see their faces as they studied the readings.

Izzy watched the doctor closely as his eyebrows furrowed deeply, and he pointed to the screen. She could easily hear every beep, ping, and click from the equipment as if she were standing right next to it, and when the doctor whispered to the nurse to run the scans again, Izzy heard that easily as well. The nurse nodded and started tapping some controls. *Looks like my clothes aren't the only thing that is new today*, Izzy thought curiously, raising one eyebrow.

After a few minutes, the doctor looked up at her. "How are you feeling today, Izzy?" He asked calmly and deliberately.

He's clearly worried about something but doesn't want me to know, she observed. "Feeling pretty good today, Doc. Why do you ask? Is something wrong?"

The doctor shook his head. "Wrong? Quite the opposite, actually. Something might be very right today. Do you feel any differently? Do you notice anything different about yourself?"

Worry started to creep over her as she watched the intent look on his face. Izzy bit her lip and studied his eyes, searching for some clue. "Other than feeling kinda rested, you know, refreshed, and maybe even a little pumped up, but nothing weird, I think. Why?"

The doctor and the nurse looked at each other, then he looked back at Izzy. "All your vitals are normal, except we are reading your internal body temperature at one hundred and six degrees." He laid his hand on her bare forearm. "Yet, your skin feels perfectly normal."

Izzy's eyebrows went up. *106? What the frick?* "I dunno Doc," she answered, her voice wavering slightly. "If anything, I actually feel a bit cold sitting here. I thought it was the suit all this time. The material is kinda thin." She ran one hand lightly over the sleeve of her arm, her agitation growing. "What does it mean? Don't people die when they get too hot?"

The doctor pulled his chair closer to her, keeping his hand on her arm. "Sometimes, yes, but in your case, it could mean something really exceptional, Izzy." He gave her arm an encouraging squeeze, but she felt anything but encouraged at the moment. "It's ok, Izzy. Just stay calm. You're doing fine. Now, I want you to close your eyes and breathe deeply."

"Really, Doc?" she blurted out. "A hundred and six and you want me to do some kind of zen crap?"

"Please, Izzy," he said reassuringly. "Give it a try."

She looked at him sideways, skeptical, but did as he asked. Izzy let her head settle back on the chair's headrest, closed her eyes, and took a few deep breaths. Despite still being slightly freaked out, it did help her feel calmer. She took several more breaths, long and slow, and felt better still.

"Now," she heard the doctor's voice, "try to turn your focus into your body. Look deep inside. Do you sense anything there? Anything you've not felt before?"

Izzy tried, but she didn't really know what she was doing or what she was looking for. *This is stupid*, she thought, but just before she could say so out loud, there it was. Deep inside, she felt something new, a sensation of swirling, surging, a pulsing just at the edges of her perception. "Yes, I think there is something there," she admitted.

"Good." The doctor said. She felt him take his hand off her arm and heard him push his chair back.

Why is he moving away? That can't be good.

"Now," he said, "pull on that sensation. Pull it forward. See if you can take control of it."

Izzy pulled with her mind. The pulsing resisted at first, but then something gave, and she felt it surge into her, flow through her. When she opened her eyes, her hand was stretched out in front of her, palm up, and in her palm sat a swirling ball of fire. The doctor was standing, and both he and the nurse had retreated several feet from her, eyes wide.

Terrified, yet amazed, Izzy studied the ball of swirling flame in front of her. Reds, oranges, and yellows rolled in the sphere in her hand. *It's beautiful, but how am I doing this?* Fear and awe filled her as she watched it pulse before her.

The doctor smiled. "Excellent, Izzy! Really excellent." He reached out toward her with both hands. "Can you draw more?"

Izzy nodded. She wasn't sure how, but she knew she could. She not only could draw more; she wanted to. She felt the power surging through her. *This is what he promised*, Izzy realized as she opened herself to it.

Power...

Strength...

As the flows intensified, an urgency started to surface within her, urging her to stop, to pull back, but Izzy pushed it away. This was what she was promised. This was her reward for the agony she endured, and the ball of energy in her palm intensified with the eddies flowing through her, swirling faster and brighter.

In spite of the small voice that was now screaming at her to stop, she pulled even harder on the flows of energy surging through her. Again, they resisted, but she pulled again, and they gave. She felt the flow surge into a torrent. The sphere before her shifted from the reds and oranges to brighter yellows mixed with greens and blues now, and it grew larger.

The currents inside her grew stronger...more chaotic...

No, stop!

And then more...

No!

Fear and panic started to swell within her along with the increasing surges of power. She felt herself being swept away, losing her grip, and her eyes grew wide.

The doctor's face changed abruptly to worry and concern. "Alright, Izzy, I think that's enough for now. Please stop now, and we can experiment with it again tomorrow. Just let go."

Izzy panicked. "I can't!" she screamed. The flaming orb continued to expand, now surging with bright teals, blues, and vivid purples. "I can't stop it!" The flames began to crawl back up her arm. There was no pain, but she was completely terrified.

"Nurse, the suppressor...hurry!!" The doctor yelled. He hit a red switch on the console, and Izzy could hear the klaxon sound in the hallway outside.

The nurse grabbed an instrument off the tray and started toward Izzy. Izzy's eyes, wide with terror, registered the nurse, but she wasn't in control anymore. Whatever this was had control now. Anger and rage surged through the panic at the sight of whatever the nurse had in her hand.

"No!" No more treatments!" Izzy shouted, and the sphere flared. In an instant, the nurse was gone, leaving only a smoking ash cloud and a horrible burning stench in the air.

The last thing Izzy saw was the doctor start to run toward the door, but she knew it was too late for both of them. Whatever was inside her was going to consume her no matter what she did now.

As the last surge erupted through her, she felt a brief moment of peace. For an instant, the sphere flared brilliant white, filling the room with a small sun, and then winked out, leaving nothing behind but char and smoke.

When the klaxon sounded, Sorensen cursed and thumped his fist on the top of his desk. He had been in the middle of preparing for his upcoming meeting with his recruiting team. Granted, the subjects they "recruited" really didn't have much say in being "recruited", but Sorensen felt it sounded much better than saying something more accurate like "retrieval" or "acquisition". He was planning on reviewing the latest surveillance on some of the more promising candidates near the top of the list, but if his worst assumptions about the alarm proved true, the tone of the meeting might need to shift from reviewing intelligence to expediting the arrival of some new "recruits", including one in particular.

Sorensen swiped away the notes he had been reading on his commpad and pulled up the security dashboard. He tapped the active alert, and the display shifted to a map of the examination rooms. One of them was outlined in red. Tapping it again showed him the room schedule.

"Isobel," he muttered to himself, shaking his head. He knew she preferred 'Izzy', but he hated nicknames. "So much potential." He knew holding out hope at this point was likely futile, but still, he would need to check out what happened for himself just in case.

Stage Two...it always goes wrong at Stage Two.

As soon as he walked into the hall, Sorensen's hopes dimmed even further. The putrid burning smell was pungent even this distance from the examination wing. He walked as quickly as he could without looking like he was hurrying. It was always best for leaders to look calm in a time of crisis.

As he walked, he reflected on their progress to date. They'd gotten quite good at identifying high-likelihood candidates. Gone were the days of just picking up random vagrants and runaways and hoping for the best. Now that high-quality sources of DNA and other genetic information, including those managed by hospitals, law enforcement, and the government, were surprisingly easy to access, they could be more...selective.

The team had also recently become quite adept at the infusion process that successfully transitioned subjects to Stage One. Of course, most subjects still ended up in comas, or as vegetables, or didn't survive the energy infusion process at all, but their success rate was improving, and the recruiting team was getting extremely efficient. Having to dispose of those who didn't make the transition was becoming less and less of an inconvenience.

Isobel, though, was a rare find, he thought as he turned the corner down another hallway. *A true diamond in the rough.* Granted, it had taken multiple tries with a variety of energy configurations for her to finally transition to Stage One. The fact that she survived the first attempt was promising all by itself, but that she survived the additional infusion attempts was nothing short of a miracle. Sorensen was not surprised when the team informed him she had likely achieved Stage One after the most recent trial. Surviving the failed attempts implied she might someday harness tremendous power, and when the team saw the telltale signs of accelerated healing and recovery after the latest infusion, he was very optimistic to see how she would progress.

If she survived Stage Two...if she survived the actual manifestation of any abilities, that is. He sighed. *The Reynolds boy had shown a lot of promise, too, but it ended the same with him. Badly.*

When Sorensen turned the final corner into the examination wing, any hope he might have had of Isobel's continued participation immediately evaporated. The door to one of the examination rooms stood open. Dark, sooty tufts of smoke wafted out into the hallway, defying the loud revving of the emergency ventilation fans. Staff in protective gear were moving in and out of the room. As Sorensen got closer, one of them stepped up to block his way.

"Perhaps you should stay back, Director," the man told him. "It's still on the warm side in there, and it's quite a mess."

Sorensen brushed the staff member out of the way without a word and walked up to the threshold to look for himself. He had seen the aftermath of more than one Stage Two catastrophe, but what he saw shocked him nonetheless.

As he had been warned, the heat and smell coming from the room were oppressive. The room itself, remarkably, was relatively undamaged. These rooms had been designed to withstand accidents like this, but the equipment and people, unfortunately, were not. Piles of ash that he assumed were the remains of the doctor and technician sat next to melted heaps of metal and plastic that were once examination equipment. In the center was the deformed examination chair. Sorensen could only assume that the pile of char and cinder around it was what was left of Isobel. Sorensen cursed under his breath.

"What happened?" He asked the nearest crew member.

She pulled off her hood. "We aren't sure, Director," she replied, surveying the interior of the room herself. "We'll need to review the data stream from the examination that was in progress when the alarm was triggered." She took a deep breath and rapidly exhaled through her nose. "All we know is that for a split second, the temperature in that room was the same as the Sun's photosphere. Whatever happened in there, it was bad."

Sorensen nodded, and she returned to her duties. He would, of course, review the recordings personally, but he already knew what he'd see. The examination team had obviously tried to induce Isobel during the examination, and it all went sideways.

Clumsy idiots! He thought. *They knew better than to try this here. They know the protocols and why we have them. These imbeciles knew that we have rooms designed for that, designed specifically for power manifestation in Stage Two, and later, for Stage Three, ability classification and development ...should anyone ever survive to reach Stage Three, that is.*

He continued to study the room, outwardly calm but smoldering inside. *And if they were going to be this stupid, they at least should have been better prepared.* Sorensen huffed, knowing full well it was just frustration talking; there really was no way to be fully prepared for Stage Two. It was completely unpredictable.

Everyone who had reached Stage Two presented abilities differently. Most died quickly. Some were caught in time and given a suppressant before causing any significant damage or injury. These people were kept in stasis off-site using a Neurostatin derivative; they were useful for some study, but until the conundrum of Stage Two was solved, bringing them out of stasis was out of the question. As for the staff—the doctor and technicians—well, that was why Sorensen made sure he maintained a deep bench.

Tricia Carling, he assured himself as the clean-up crew milled around him, *will hopefully give us the answers we need.*

Darci clutched her stomach, trying to keep her food down. Her recruiting team was scheduled for one of their routine meetings this morning with Director Sorensen, and thanks to the internship he had arranged for her, Darci was able to come into The Workshop periodically without disrupting her other scheduled classes. She had decided to beat the morning traffic and come in a bit early to take advantage of the free breakfast in the cafeteria, a decision she was regretting at the moment.

Even before she heard the alarm go off and saw the red lights flash in the hallway, Darci knew something had gone terribly wrong. One aspect of whatever gave her these abilities also made her sensitive to the experiments they were running here. Sometimes, she'd feel a tingle or a vibration, like when someone strikes a tuning fork, inducing a crystal glass to vibrate and hum.

Sometimes, she felt it elsewhere, too, away from The Workshop. When she did, it felt harmonious, almost pleasant, like something was just *right* for some reason.

This, though, was far from pleasant. It was abrupt, forceful, and wildly dissonant, like an orchestra of shattering glass or fingernails being drawn on a thousand blackboards. It was so disorienting that it made her feel physically nauseated.

Darci dumped what was left of her breakfast into the bin—her stomach wouldn't tolerate any more of it anyway—and when she entered the hallway, a fetid burning smell joined the churning in her stomach. People in what looked like hazmat suits and coveralls ran past her. Listening to her instincts and the fading traces of the discord she sensed, Darci followed.

When she turned the corner, the hallway in front of her was complete chaos. The staff were frantically dealing with whatever had gone sideways in the open examination room.

Probably likely the same thing that made me want to puke just now, Darci assumed, watching the frenetic scene unfold in front of her. The smell wafting from the room, far more intense than it was down by the cafeteria, was doing her unsettled stomach no favors. She pulled the edge of her sleeve out to cover her nose and mouth and swallowed hard to keep what was left of her breakfast down where it belonged. *These people don't need anything else to clean up right now*, she thought to herself.

Darci saw Director Sorensen standing in front of the open door. He was talking to a woman, presumably trying to get some information about what had gone so horribly wrong here. When the woman turned away, Darci walked up next to him.

"What happened here, Director Sorensen?" she asked him tentatively.

"It seems that a subj...—" he turned and looked into Darci's anxious face "—Isobel lost control of her emerging abilities and killed both herself and the examination team."

Darci clutched her mouth with both hands in horror and shock. "Oh no! Not Izzy!" she exclaimed. *Izzy was younger than I am.*

Sorensen nodded. "Yes, it's most unfortunate when this happens. Especially her. She had tremendous potential."

Darci stared at him in disbelief. *Unfortunate?* "How often does something like this happen, Director Sorensen?"

Sorensen shrugged, still looking into the room. "More often than we obviously want it to, Darci. This stage of the transformation process still presents a substantial number of challenges."

How can he be taking this so calmly? People DIED here just now...someone younger than me, someone I brought here, DIED.

Sorensen looked down into her wide eyes. He could obviously see how distraught she was with what she was witnessing and put a hand on her shoulder. "I know how upsetting this is, Darci. Believe me, no one is more upset about it than I am. We not only lost a young woman we believed would advance our program significantly, but I also lost some very valuable and talented colleagues and associates. They will be very difficult to replace.

"We all just need to remember that great causes often come at the expense of great sacrifice. They believed in our mission here and knew the risks of what they were doing."

Darci looked up into his eyes. *Did they?* she wondered. *Did they know what they were getting into? Did Izzy know?* She turned her face away from him toward the open door, stepping back slightly to let one of the crew by with a hunk of melted equipment.

"Have others died?" Darci asked, staring through the lingering smoke into the room.

Sorensen managed a half-smile, gave her shoulder a gentle squeeze, and let his hand drop. "We can talk more about this later if you wish, Darci, but for now, I believe we both have a meeting to attend shortly, and I think we will be shifting the agenda a bit. Losing Isobel is a regrettable setback, so we will need to recruit a few more participants to make sure we don't incur any further delays in the work we are doing."

"I understand, sir," Darci replied, faking a half-smile of her own.

"Good," Sorensen said. "Now, if you will excuse me, there are a few things I need to attend to before our meeting. I'll see you again shortly, then, yes?"

Darci nodded. "Of course, Director. I will see you there."

"Oh, and Darci," he said, pausing and making eye contact that Darci found slightly unnerving. "You should start preparing yourself. One of our next recruits, in particular, will go a long way to making sure we don't have more tragedies like Isobel, but it will be like none of your previous assignments. She, I expect, will be very challenging, even for you."

Sorensen turned, leaving Darci alone in the middle of the busy response team. A few of them walked out carrying small containers filled with char and ash. *Izzy*, she realized, and a wave of revulsion passed over her.

No, I don't think any of them knew what they were getting into, she thought as she watched Sorensen walk away from her.

I'm not sure I really know anymore either.

Recruited

Darci yawned. She loved her astronomy classes, but these midafternoon lectures right after lunch could be tough sometimes. She bit her lower lip and jotted a few notes on her commpad with the stylus, in no small part just to keep her mind from drifting. The theory and science of space fascinated her, but when the equations came out, it got harder. She sometimes wondered if she had the math chops to really make it, but going into astronomy, any aspect of it that got her more involved with space, was her dream, so she couldn't let a little math get in the way.

When she was a girl, she'd sneak out at night and walk out into the plains on the reservation, far away from the village's lights. Darci would lie there on an old horse blanket for hours, staring at the thousands upon thousands of glimmering stars in the black desert sky. The blanket wool picked at her bare arms and legs, but she didn't care. No place made her happier.

The day her grandpapi gave her the telescope was one of the best days of her life. It wasn't much, but he loved her, and it was a gift from his heart to support something she loved. Many nights, they would take it out into the desert and stargaze together, studying whatever the small lens could pick up. Whenever she looked up at the stars now, Darci took some comfort, knowing that he was looking down at her too.

Of course, her mother hadn't approved of the encouragement her grandpapi had given her. Her mother wanted her to stay in the village, find work there or even in the resort itself full-time. Give back to her people, as she put it, but the door had slammed tightly on that prospect for Darci that day during a summer break from school when some fat pig in a Stetson called her 'his little squaw' while she was bussing tables in the resort restaurant. Her tray of drinks and food ended up in his lap, and she never set foot in that place again. No, staying there was not an option. She was headed for the stars in one way or another.

As much as she loved this class normally, staying focused was made even more challenging by the guest lecturer they had today. The regular professor had come down with the flu, so someone else was called to come in at the last minute. He was droning on about general relativity, his unwavering monotone sucking the life out of the entire classroom. *Getting closer to the speed of light isn't the only thing that makes time grind to a halt,* Darci thought and stifled a snicker.

That she'd been told to anticipate a call didn't help her attention span either. A particularly unusual recruiting run might come on the schedule during the week, and when the call came, she'd need to respond without delay.

As if on cue, a notification popped up on Darci's commpad. The icon snapped her fully alert. Eagerly, she tapped it and read: "Green light for recruiting mission tonight. Target has been acquired and is under observation. Anticipate intercept around 1900." *Game on,* she thought, and made a mental note to be sure to get an early dinner before she went. Whenever Darci used the shadows and the power they gave her, she was always famished, and since the Director said it would be exceptionally challenging, she wanted to be at her best for this mission.

The memory of what had happened to Izzy still weighed strongly on her mind, though, and crawled to the surface. *Do I really want to subject someone else to what happened to Izzy? Is it really worth it?* she thought, but as she had so many times since, she pushed down the guilt and uncertainty and chose to focus instead on the importance of what they were doing. Director Sorensen's words about sacrifice rang in her ears, and if what she was being called on to do next could prevent those unnecessary deaths while still achieving their goals, she was committed to doing whatever she could to be successful with her new assignment.

Unexpectedly, another message popped up on the screen: "Be sure to go by your room prior to intercept. Items you may find useful will be delivered later this afternoon." She'd never been given anything for a recruiting mission before. Darci frowned a bit. *That's weird,* she thought, and then shrugged, *but then this is no ordinary recruit either.*

The chime rang softly in Tricia's commpod, breaking her concentration. Out of habit, she checked the time, but she already knew it was her alarm to head over to the gym. 4:45. Jamal had already left for the day, leaving just her and one of the other technicians in the lab.

She checked the status of the simulation she was running. It was making progress, albeit slowly. Tricia bit her lip and huffed a bit. *Patience,* she reminded herself. She'd optimistically hoped it would finish before she left but had honestly expected it to have to run overnight anyway. *At least I don't feel compelled to sit around and wait for it*, she thought, feeling both relief and a tiny twinge of guilt that she could leave early for the training session at the gym she'd planned for today.

Tricia was particularly excited about the workout she planned for today because she'd get to try out her new training outfit. It wasn't just any new gym kit, though. As she had become more precise with her abilities, Tricia found that even the small impedance from her normal workout clothes was throwing off her training sessions, causing her to under- or overestimate the flows needed to perform the heavy lifting exercises she used to hone her control.

To help out, Harold had graciously provided a bit more of the material she'd used to make her Beacon suit, and with a little evening work, she'd fashioned a pair of knee-length tights and a compression top. This outfit, made from panels of royal and dark blue, would look just like any other athletic wear to the casual observer, but like her costume, it would allow her to draw on her abilities without interference. *I even love the color*, she thought, scooping her bag up off the floor under her work desk.

"I'm heading out", she called to the technician in the back. The technician waved back in acknowledgment. "Be sure to shut everything down and lock up when you're done, ok? Everything except this—" she pointed at her workstation "—I'm running a simulation overnight."

"Got it," he called back, waving again.

Tricia put her lab coat in the small closet at the front of the lab, switched off the coffee pot—*Not that scorching would make Jamal's coffee any worse*—and headed out.

When she left the building, bright sunshine hit her face. Tricia felt the surge in power around her, closed her eyes, and lifted her face toward the sun. She breathed deeply and then turned to walk toward the other side of campus, where the powerlifting center was waiting for her.

"Hoping I get lucky again this afternoon," she muttered to herself, crossing her fingers. This was the time of day when most of the athletes who would typically use the lifting facility would be at various practices or getting an early meal before evening workouts. She walked briskly, not that walking any faster or slower would affect her luck, but she had been very fortunate to find the facility empty for her sole use the past couple of weeks, and she was eager to see if her lucky streak would hold out today.

As she walked, she thought again about the sleek blue tights in her bag, and then, naturally, her mind drifted to her benefactor, Harold Baskins. She sighed. *I do owe him an answer,* she thought. *He's been so understanding and generous through all this. It's not fair to keep putting him off.* As she'd expected, when Tricia went in to make the outfit, he had asked again (nicely, of course) about rescheduling their lunch that had been interrupted. Tricia wanted to give him an answer, and yes, she realized she did want to reschedule after all, but she was still shaken by Sorensen's not-so-veiled threat. Fearing that any additional association might put him more at risk, she begged off for a bit more time.

She frowned a bit, ashamed of the lame excuse she'd given him. He took it in good stride, saying he understood, but she could tell by the look on his face that he didn't quite buy it and was suspecting the worst. *Even if I end up not taking this any further,* she thought, *Harold's a good guy and a good friend, and I don't want to hurt him.* She picked up her pace, knowing the workout would take her mind off the topic, at least for a short time.

Preoccupied as she was, she didn't notice the man several yards behind her, hat pulled down over his eyes, backpack slung over his shoulder like any other student might have, matching her pace stride for stride. While she was soaking in some sun, he'd casually gotten up from underneath the tree on the quad across from the lab entrance, tucked his book into his backpack, and brushed himself off. He moved just quickly enough to stay with her, but not so much that it looked like he was trying to. He was a professional, after all.

As she started her walk, he tapped the device in his ear and notified the rest of the recruiting team that he had acquired Doctor Carling and that she was en route as anticipated. His job was to make sure the team knew if she deviated from her routine, and, when they got closer to the lifting center that she typically used, to alert the team members who were "doing maintenance" on the equipment in the facility. They would be sure to clear out before she got there, leaving the room empty for her use, just as they had several other times over the past couple of weeks.

He smirked as he tailed her. It was important that she have a relaxing and long workout today. Other members of the team still had some preparation to be done before she went home, and he would do his part to make sure nothing disturbed her time in the gym.

It was almost time. Darci didn't need the clock to tell her. The sun had already set and she could see the soft oranges and greens emerge on the horizon out of her window. The only other light in the room came from the monitor next to the wall. It showed the recording of Beacon's interview on CrystalClear several months ago. Darci had watched it a dozen times or more by this point, but she had decided to watch it again before going out on her mission. Seeing Beacon there on the screen helped put Darci into the right mindset for the challenge that she would face later tonight.

Darci looked at Beacon again sitting there, smiling and laughing with the host. *It's so easy for you, isn't it?* she thought. *How many people were there for you, supporting you?* Darci snorted in derision. *There is always help and support for people like her, but for people like me, well, not so much...just like that day a year ago...*

Darci had been on the cusp of failing her optics class when she was in the optical sciences building on the day of the accident. The math, as usual, was giving her fits. She was trying to get some help from her professor, but he hadn't come. He wasn't there, like so many others.

While Darci waited patiently in his office, something hit her without warning, something agonizing, terrifying. It tore through her. She collapsed, and for what felt like an eternity, her body was not her own. As she lay on the floor, she vaguely remembered hearing the emergency teams below her. She wanted to call for them, but she was helpless. They never came for her. They never found her. She was left alone, suffering and afraid.

Darci didn't remember how she got back to her room. Sometime in the night, she'd made her way back there. The next few days were like a horrific nightmare woven from fleeting memories of searing light, racking pain, and unfathomable darkness.

As a little girl, the village elders had told her stories about ancient tribesmen joining with spirits, gaining power and strength, and performing miraculous feats. Finally, in one particularly horrific moment of anguish, she remembered these stories and desperately reached out with her mind to embrace what was inside her. She begged it to stop the torment, even if it meant her death. Instead of death, though, the shadows responded to her. They enveloped and caressed her. They comforted her and made her whole again.

Darci had, of course, seen the blonde doctor, Tricia Carling, who had also been in the building around campus after the accident. Darci had actually gone out of her way to watch her on occasion. She often had wondered if Carling had found any spirits of her own after the accident, and when Beacon finally appeared on the scene, Darci was absolutely positive she had. However, rather than embrace her gift as something special, something sacred, this woman had chosen to flaunt it as some kind of superhero, craving attention and glory, elevating herself under the pretense of helping others.

But that's all about to change.

This time, Darci checked her watch and, seeing it was nearly time to go, got up to put on the finishing touches. She went to the mirror and gathered her long raven-black hair in her hands. The dark blue highlights were almost iridescent in the fading evening light, shimmering softly as she twisted it up behind her head. Holding the twist with one hand, Darci picked up the two black lacquered hair sticks from the table in front of her with her free hand and jabbed them one after the other into the knot to secure it.

Her midnight blue pullover blouse hung loosely off her slender shoulders, revealing the double crescent tattoo on her neck and leaving just a sliver of midriff exposed above the top of the tight black leather pants that hung on her hips. She gently brushed her fingers over her belt. It was one of the few things she cherished from the reservation. One of the village craftswomen had made it for her in honor of her leaving for school. The belt was black leather studded with deep turquoise stones in silver settings. The buckle was a stunning single large stone of shadowy turquoise, also set in silver.

Admittedly, it was somewhat bright and audacious, but for her people, these stones represent protection, health, and strength, making this belt the perfect accent for her Umbra alter ego.

To complete the ensemble, Darci slipped on the final touch, a long black coat that stopped just above her knee-high black boots. The thin, supple leather draped and flowed around her, emulating the shadows she commanded. She stepped back and surveyed the result. *Perfect,* she thought. In the mirror, Darci saw a woman of power and confidence, someone to be taken seriously. A woman that Beacon would see as a rival, someone to be respected. *Yes, as an equal.*

Darci smirked as her thoughts shifted to her mother and what she would think. She could practically hear her mother snort in disdain and mutter under her breath that she looked like an *aljiłnii* because, in her mother's mind, only whores got tattoos, wore tight-fitting pants, or exposed their waist. *Nothing I ever do will be good enough for her anyway,* she thought with a dismissive sniff.

Her mother had never supported her interests or encouraged her dreams. Darci had been on her own with those too; at least, she had been once her grandpapi passed away. When Darci won the Indigenous People's Scholarship and was accepted to Crystal Bay University, her mother had even scoffed at that, saying she'd be back soon enough to take her place with the rest of her people on the reservation where she belonged. *Meaning, I should be working the tourist trinket stands or as a dealer in the casino,* Darci huffed to herself. *So not happening.*

Yes, her mother would be appalled to see what Darci was doing now, but Director Sorensen had seen something special in her. He had recruited her to the program personally. He invested in her. He wanted her to be a part of his vision to make the world a better place and put his trust in her to carry out important assignments like this one. Perhaps, when they were successful and the world was at peace, her mother would finally be proud of her for the part she played in accomplishing that. Not likely, but perhaps.

Darci took a final glance at the monitor. Beacon was shaking hands with the mayor, smiling. *Go ahead and smile, Beacon,* she mused, *but now it's time for you to join the program, to stop fooling around with interviews and publicity stunts, to finally put your gifts to use and actually make a difference in the world.* With a flick of her wrist, a small tendril of shadows switched off the recording, leaving only the pale evening sky to illuminate the room.

The box that had been delivered for her sat open on the table. Darci once again looked over the two items that had come inside of it, turning them over in her hands one more time, and then set them on the table in front of her. She picked up the note that had come with it and read it again. It was short and to the point, but it made her feel proud:

This mission will test you, Umbra. You have been very successful so far, but I caution you not to underestimate Tricia Carling. She's powerful and well-trained, nothing like the other people you've recruited. However, beneath the powers and training, she's still just a human being. If you need them, these items should help tip the scales in your favor. I'm confident that you are ready for this and will be successful. Remember, I'm counting on you.

— Sorensen

"I won't let you down. Beacon *will* do her part for us...for Izzy. I will make sure of it," she asserted to herself, dropping the note back into the box. Darci slipped the two items into the deep pockets on the inner lining of her coat and, with a deep breath, summoned her power. The shadows leaped from the corners of the room, swirled around her, and she traveled.

As she approached her townhouse, Tricia was grateful that the days were starting to get a little longer now. The sun had already set, but the soft pastels glowing in the western sky kept her from walking in complete darkness, and the air was still warm enough to keep away the chill for the walk home.

It had been a great workout. As she'd hoped, the gym had been deserted. Her new outfit worked to perfection, and the lovely sunset had only added to the happiness and contentment she felt knowing a meal sat in the refrigerator waiting for her to warm it. She was ready for a hot shower and a relaxing dinner after a productive and satisfying day.

Tricia made the turn off the sidewalk onto the walkway that led to her townhouse, but as she got closer, her pace slowed. She felt something...unusual. *Something's not right*, she thought. She felt a sensation, a pulsating thrum, not unlike the vibrating of the deep bass when the neighbor plays the stereo too loud. This wasn't a sound, though. It was something she felt reverberate through her, and while she couldn't tell exactly from where it was coming, the closer she got to her front door, the stronger she felt it. The odd part was that it wasn't an entirely unpleasant feeling at all. Quite the contrary, even though she'd never felt it before, the sensation was somehow familiar.

Tricia approached the front door cautiously. *What was that saying?* she wondered. *Never seek out war, but always be ready for it?* She slipped off her warm-up jacket and opened herself to the energies swirling gently around her. Power coursed over and through her, both light and dark, sharpening her senses and giving her strength. Taking a quick inhale and exhale, she pressed her thumb against the lock sensor. The lock clicked open, and she slowly opened the door and entered.

The pulsing she felt also sharpened and grew more acute, more focused and precise, as she moved into her foyer. *Dark energy,* she realized. *That's what I'm feeling. Something here is drawing on the same dark energy that I use.* The room was dark except for the dim evening light coming through the window beside her. Her eyes, still accustomed to the low light, scanned the room. Nothing appeared out of place, but whatever she was sensing was somewhere in front of her. Tricia stepped in, quietly set her bag and jacket down by the door, and gently pushed it closed behind her.

"All right," she called out. "You might as well come out. I know you're here."

Tricia heard a soft chuckle. "Very well," a woman's voice responded. "I felt you too."

A young dark-skinned woman stepped out from the bedroom. As she came closer, there was no question that she was the source of the vibration Tricia felt. With each step she took, the pulsing became more acute, more defined, like this woman had a certain frequency or, more accurately, a specific energy signature. *Almost like a thumbprint,* Tricia realized.

There was also no doubt in Tricia's mind that the woman standing before her was the same woman Randy had described in the Sirens coffee shop, the one that was likely responsible for Izzy's disappearance and the disappearance of many others as well. That made her potentially dangerous and not someone to take lightly.

Assessing her intruder, Tricia figured her to be one or two inches taller than she was, even without the modest heel on her boots, but likely several pounds lighter judging from the narrow shoulders and hips beneath the black coat and skin-tight pants. *Middle Eastern? Maybe Native American?* she thought, but it was too hard to be sure in the dim light. The woman's blouse perfectly matched the dark blue highlights shimmering in her hair. She found the overall effect to be both impressive and ominous. *Whoever she is, whatever she is, she's got a good look*, Tricia thought.

Another concern quickly crossed her mind, and Tricia quickly scanned the room. "If you're wondering about the cat," the woman said, "it's hiding in the bedroom." Tricia breathed a small sigh of relief. "Don't worry, I haven't harmed it," the stranger assured her, looking genuinely a little hurt. "I wouldn't, of course. I like animals. After all, I'm not a monster."

Tricia stared her dead in the eye, relaxing slightly but still on high alert. "I appreciate that, but then who are you, and what are you doing in my home?"

The woman smiled. "You can call me Umbra, Tricia, or should I say, Beacon?"

Tricia scowled. *Ok, she knows. No point in playing games.* "'Tricia' would be more appropriate here if you don't mind." A hunch was already forming about what this Umbra wanted, but since information was a weapon, Tricia decided she would most likely learn more if she let it play out. "Why are you here?"

The woman shrugged slightly. "Whatever. I'm here to follow up on Director Sorensen's invitation to join our program. He asked me to drop by and see if you had come to a decision."

There it is, Tricia thought. She took a few steps closer to Umbra, tucking the strands of loose hair in her face back behind her ear, and drew herself up to her full height, which, as she'd correctly assessed, left her still a couple of inches shorter than Umbra.

Scowling, she put her hands on her hips. "I thought I had made it very clear to Director Sorensen that until I knew more about what he was doing and what he wanted from me in particular, I had no intention of participating."

Umbra smirked again, irritating Tricia even further. "You may have, but Director Sorensen is very determined to have you as part of the program, so he's instructed me not to take 'no' for an answer. I must insist that you come with me."

"Then I guess you have a problem," Tricia replied. "I have no intention of coming with you."

"Actually, I'm not the one with the problem then," Umbra said. "I must admit," she added, "that I've been looking forward to this."

"Have you, now?"

"Absolutely," Umbra affirmed haughtily. "My other missions involving ordinary people have been far too easy, so the chance to test myself against someone like you—someone more like me—is a welcome challenge."

"Be careful of what you wish for," Tricia replied with a scoff.

"I always am," Umbra replied and raised her hands out to her sides. From nowhere, strands of blackness coiled around Tricia's wrists and jerked her arms taut. Tricia gasped in surprise and squirmed as she felt them start to twist her arms behind her back.

So, she really is like me, Tricia thought, tugging again at her shadowy bonds. *Well, she's in for a surprise too.* Summoning her strength, she pulled. She could feel the coils around her wrists strain, and with no small effort, she forced her hands back in front of her, overpowering the pull of the inky fibers. Umbra's smile faded, and her eyes grew wide, giving Tricia her turn to smirk. *Didn't expect that, did you?* Tricia thought, relishing the look of surprise on Umbra's face.

In the moment, Tricia had to admit to the thrill she felt in the battle as well. Going up against someone where she could use her powers to their full extent without holding back was an unexpected rush, and her blood coursed with excitement and anticipation.

Leveraging her enhanced strength alone, Tricia felt she could hold her own against this woman's restraints, but realized quickly that a prolonged stalemate likely favored her adversary. Shifting tactics, she projected her dark energy to form shields over her forearms. As the shields took shape, the edges sliced through the black tentacles encircling her arms, triggering a deep thrum when the two powers touched. Both women recoiled, and Umbra stumbled backward from the backlash of the severed strands.

Her foe momentarily off balance, Tricia saw her opening. She sprinted toward Umbra and then came in low, sweeping Umbra's legs out from under her. As Umbra fell, Tricia rolled quickly, driving her elbow into Umbra's stomach and slamming her into the hardwood floor.

"Oooogh", Umbra grunted as she hit the floor. She rolled to her side, wrapping her arms around her midsection.

She should be unconscious, Tricia thought, momentarily surprised. *This additional toughness and strength must come naturally to anyone having these kinds of abilities.* Surprise aside, this was no time to give any quarter. Eager to finish the battle, Tricia pushed Umbra over onto her stomach and grabbed her wrists, twisting them behind her and shoving her pinned arms into the small of her back. Tricia then threw herself on top of Umbra, straddling her hips, and completed the pin.

Umbra groaned once more as Tricia caught her breath. After a moment, Tricia leaned over to look into Umbra's face. Her cheek was pressed uncomfortably into the floor, and she was wincing from the pressure Tricia was putting on her arms and aching midriff.

"Ok, look," Tricia finally said, "enough. Let's call a truce here. I'll let you up so we can talk this out like two adults, and I won't end up having to buy new furniture."

Umbra tried to twist free, but any exceptional strength or endurance she might have was inconsequential against the light-enhanced force Tricia was putting into the hold. She blew some hair out of her face. "If I do, are you going to agree to come with me?" she asked.

"Not likely," Tricia replied, "but I would be willing to listen to more about what he is doing and what is going on there."

"Telling you about his plans is above my pay grade, but I'm sure Director Sorensen will explain everything when you arrive," Umbra told her, tugging again to try to free her captured wrists.

Tricia pulled her arms a little tighter for emphasis. "He'll find that difficult. Like I said, I have no intention of coming with you."

"Then there's no point in talking, is there?" Umbra asked in return. "If I come back without you, Director Sorensen will be very disappointed, and trust me, he doesn't take well to disappointment."

"Well, I guess he'll just have to learn to live with it, won't he?" Tricia retorted.

Umbra smiled. "Will he, though?"

Tricia looked up just in time to see the mass of blackness hurtling toward her. It struck Tricia square in the chest, knocking her off Umbra's back and sending her across the room. Tricia landed on the hardwood floor several feet away and slid across its polished surface until she slammed into the small bookcase standing against the far wall. She hit the corner on the edge of the wooden frame hard and cried out as it dug deeply into her back. The bookcase rocked, dislodging several books and small curios, including the framed picture of Tricia and her father. The picture fell, spraying shattered glass across the floor in front of her.

Tricia looked at the broken memory on the floor in front of her. Several large pieces of broken glass were askew across the image of her smiling father holding her up on his shoulder at The Ridge. That special moment flooded back to her, and a tear came to her eye. Rage flooded through her. *Enough!!* her mind screamed.

She rose to her knees and looked up just in time to see another shadowy bolt careening toward her. Instinctively, she threw up her hands and discharged a pulse of white light. The mass instantly disintegrated. In the background, Tricia saw Umbra flinch and grimace from the light pulse, and the pieces fell into place. *Umbra. Of course*, Tricia realized. *Shadows. She manipulates shadows, so she's sensitive to light.*

Pressing her newly discovered advantage, Tricia quickly fired off another more intense light burst just as Umbra looked up, hoping to keep her off balance. The burst flared between them, and Umbra recoiled and gasped, throwing her hands up to shield her eyes. Given the opportunity she was hoping for, Tricia slipped behind Umbra with a burst of speed and ensnared Umbra's head and neck in the crook of her elbow. Umbra yelped in pain and surprise as Tricia cinched in the sleeper hold, squeezing off the blood supply to Umbra's brain that would eventually render her unconscious.

"Enough," Tricia said hoarsely, pulling Umbra off balance to gain leverage and keep the pressure on her carotid artery. "I gave you every chance to stop this, but playtime is over. You're going nighty-night, and when you wake up, we will start this conversation over with some friends of mine downtown under some very bright lights to make sure you behave yourself."

Umbra gurgled, shaking her head. She tried to writhe free, frantically pulling on Tricia's arm encircling her neck, but she was no match for either Tricia's skill in applying the hold or the power she put into securing it around her neck.

Failing to break Tricia's grip, Umbra drove her elbow backward repeatedly into Tricia's stomach. She put everything she had into each desperate blow, but they proved futile against Tricia's strength and determination to end the fight once and for all. After several seconds, Umbra's struggles started to fade, and each strike became steadily weaker. *It will be over soon*, Tricia thought, smiling confidently.

Suddenly, Umbra thrust her open palm towards Tricia's face, and Tricia felt a film of dark inkiness slide across her face. It clamped tight, blinding her and pinching her nose, cutting off her air supply. She jerked back as the slick and viscous mass oozed into her mouth. The slimy consistency disgusted her instantly, forcing her to gag reflexively.

As she fought back the urge to vomit, Tricia involuntarily allowed the hold to loosen for a split second. The shadowy film over her face still blinded her, but she heard Umbra suck in a desperate breath and felt her try to twist free while Tricia was momentarily distracted. *Oh no you don't*, Tricia thought, shaking her head. Letting Umbra go—letting victory slip away—at this point was not an option.

She bit down hard on the oily mass in her mouth and felt it break apart. With her mouth cleared, Tricia resolved that she could—no, that she *would*—outlast Umbra. Once Umbra was asleep, the nasty film on her face would disappear, and victory would be hers. Umbra squeaked again as Tricia tightened the hold with renewed determination. *All I need to do is keep the pressure on for a few seconds longer. She'll pass out, and I will...*

Blinding agony exploded in her side. Her ribs felt as if they had shattered inside her chest. Every nerve screamed in anguish as her body seized for an endless few seconds, and then Tricia collapsed, dragging Umbra down to the floor with her.

Tricia lay helpless, panting shallowly, each small breath its own jab of pain. Her muscles and limbs ignored her pleas to move, choosing instead to spasm randomly on their own. She felt a small trickle of drool run down her cheek as she lay on the floor, twitching uncontrollably.

Tricia couldn't turn her head to look, but she heard Umbra grunt and felt her roll off to the side. Out of the corner of her eye, she watched Umbra pull herself up to her knees, where she sat for a few seconds, rubbing her neck. Umbra then leaned over her, took Tricia's chin in her left hand, and turned Tricia's head to face her. Umbra pushed her now untethered hair back over her shoulder and looked down into Tricia's eyes. Tricia blankly stared back, but even though it was hard to focus, she could easily make out Umbra smiling down at her triumphantly.

"Well, I have to admit, you're everything I was warned you'd be," Umbra said, still smiling. She pressed her head to one side and was rewarded as a few vertebrae cracked back into place. "In the end, though, Sorensen was right. Underneath the suit and the powers and even the training, you're still just a person." Umbra held up a small device in front of Tricia's face and waggled it mockingly. "You sure didn't see *this* coming, did you?"

A taser! Tricia realized, her head lolling to the side. Her thoughts were chaotic and confused, but anger pierced the pain and disorientation. *She tased me! The cheating little b...*

Umbra reached back for something, but Tricia couldn't see what it was before Umbra turned Tricia's head back the opposite way, facing away from her. Tricia felt hard, cold metal press against her exposed neck, followed by a small prick and a puff of air. *An aerosyringe...she's drugging me.* Her heart sank as any hope of escaping, let alone winning this battle, suddenly evaporated.

"Now, it's your turn to go nighty-night," Umbra gloated. Tricia sensed a warm sensation radiate out from her neck, and as it moved throughout her body, she suddenly felt light, like she was floating. Her aching muscles stopped jerking, and a sense of euphoria came over her. *An anesthetic*, Tricia thought lazily as time started to slow, *and a good one, too. She's taking no chances.*

The room swam as Umbra scooped her up like a rag doll, tossing one of Tricia's arms over her shoulder and letting Tricia's head flop down on the other. Tricia groaned softly from a wave of vertigo as Umbra secured her grip, wrapping her arms snugly around Tricia's waist. Tricia's brain became even more foggy, and, in her growing delirium, even if Tricia could have moved, she found she didn't really want to.

"Don't worry," Umbra said with a mock reassurance. "This will wear off soon, and you'll be right as rain. Director Sorensen is really looking forward to greeting you personally and welcoming you to the program when you're awake."

Not as much as I'm looking forward to greeting him, I'll bet, Tricia thought hazily. Unable to fight the drug any longer, Tricia finally descended into unconsciousness. The world around her glided into a dream as a wave of shadows enveloped them both, and after an instant of piercing cold, she slipped into blackness.

Arrival

Sofia slowly paced the edges of the room. She wasn't nervous...yet. Umbra was not overdue long enough to be concerned, but considering who her assignment was, it was very possible that something had gone wrong. *Or it's just taking a bit longer than planned*, Sofia thought, trying to reassure herself.

As she paced, Sofia made sure she stayed close to the walls. There was no doubt that Umbra would travel into the room without any problem, but there was no guarantee she would precisely hit the center of the room. Umbra herself frequently noted there was some variability even when traveling to places she knew very well, and if Sofia happened to be too close to the spot where Umbra returned, it would be very...unfortunate indeed. At best, Sofia might find herself floating in a void for eternity. At worst, only parts of her would be.

That's long enough, she thought as she paused to check her watch one last time, but before she could make the call to Director Sorensen, Sofia felt the air in the room thicken, and the temperature dropped sharply. She pressed herself tightly against the wall just as an inky black flare burst in the middle of the room, and, when it dissolved, Umbra was standing in the middle of the room with a very unconscious Tricia Carling draped over her shoulder.

"You're late," Sofia said, circling Umbra to look into Tricia's face. Sofia lifted one of Tricia's eyelids, inspecting her pupil, and then checked her breathing, deep and steady. "What happened?"

"It didn't go as smoothly as we'd planned," Umbra replied, scrunching her nose and shrugging slightly. She shifted her grip on Tricia's back and reached into her inner jacket pocket with her free hand. After fishing for a couple of seconds, she pulled out the empty aerosyringe and the discharged taser and dropped them into Sofia's hand. "I ended up having to use these."

Sofia looked at the devices in her hand and then back up into Umbra's face. "Both of them?" she asked in disbelief. "You used them both?!"

"What can I say?" Umbra replied defensively, wrapping her free arm back around Tricia's waist. "She was tough. Really put up a fight. If I hadn't used them, I probably wouldn't have made it back here at all!"

"Very well," Sofia said with a brisk nod and walked to the door. Pulling it open, she motioned to the guard in the hallway and said, "Please get an orderly here with a gurney, stat. No need for you to return either. We're good here. Oh, and tell them to have one of the female staff meet me in Doctor Carling's room in a few minutes. We'll need to change her clothes when we get her there." The guard nodded and disappeared down the hall.

Leaving the door cracked, Sofia turned back toward the two women. Umbra held Tricia like a mother would hold a sleeping child, firmly but gently. Despite the violent confrontation they'd obviously just had, Sofia still saw a sense of compassion in how the taller woman had Tricia draped over her shoulder, Tricia's toes barely brushing the floor. Tricia's bright blue workout tights contrasted sharply against Umbra's darker clothing. Sofia could not help but notice how the snug fit of Tricia's attire emphasized the tone and definition in her back, arms, and legs. *Impressive*, she thought; clearly, the discipline and commitment Tricia demonstrated as Beacon were a major element of her everyday life as well.

"Do you want to set her down while we wait for the orderly?" Sofia asked, realizing Tricia was likely not only much heavier than she appeared but probably very awkward to carry as well.

Umbra shook her head. "No, I've got her. It's fine."

Remarkable, Sofia thought, watching Umbra hold Tricia so effortlessly. While Umbra did not have Beacon's superhuman strength, her enhanced condition gave her willowy body a physical power that easily surpassed two or even three average men. *Even one of our beefiest orderlies would be struggling in her shoes, but she holds a grown woman's dead weight like a sack of groceries. With that kind of strength,* Sofia thought whimsically, *I could finally be...* but the forbidden thought was interrupted abruptly, leaving her staring blankly into the room.

A few seconds later, the door swung open, and one of those burly orderlies entered, pushing a wheeled stretcher into the room. Startled, Sofia stepped back a few feet, giving him space to roll the gurney toward the two women. He wheeled up next to Umbra and, after locking the wheel brake with a stab of his toe, came around and scooped up Tricia's legs. The two of them gently lifted Tricia and laid her limp form down on the stretcher. Tricia's head lolled to one side as the orderly folded her arms across her stomach and then raised the side rails to keep her from accidentally rolling off during transport.

"Wait a moment," Sofia instructed the orderly and turned toward Umbra. "Is that blood?" she asked, noticing a spot on the corner of Umbra's mouth.

Umbra dabbed it with her finger, wincing slightly, and grunted in surprise. "Yeah, I guess I bit my lip at some point during the fight," she said indifferently. "Hadn't noticed."

"Please go take care of that," Sofia said, "and then meet me in my office to debrief. Feel free to stop by the commissary and get yourself something to eat or drink on the way if you wish. I'll be there right after I get Doctor Carling situated."

Sofia waited until Umbra had left the room, then reached into her jacket pocket and withdrew a brushed metal circular band. Holding it by the edge, she tapped the face of her commpad a few times. The circlet buzzed and swung open on a nearly invisible hinge. "Hold up her right arm," she instructed the orderly. When he'd done so, she carefully slipped the ring around Tricia's elevated wrist and snapped it closed. The seams vanished where the two halves met, making the bracelet appear completely solid once again. Sofia tapped a few more times, and a thin band around the middle of the ring lit up with a white light. The light flashed three times, then shifted to solid red, then yellow, then green. After a few seconds, the ring buzzed, vibrated three times, and went dark again. Sofia waved her hand for the orderly to put Tricia's arm back across her stomach and then checked a few more indicators on her commpad.

Satisfied, she slipped the commpad into her jacket pocket. "Ok, let's go," she told the orderly and followed him out of the room as he wheeled the newest member of their program down the hall.

For the fifth time today, he tried to read the report on his commpad, and for the fifth time today, he failed. Sorensen tossed the device back down onto his desk and rubbed the bridge of his nose. He had tried to distract himself with his mundane pile of paperwork, messages, and other daily duties, but it was a futile exercise. No matter what he did, the anticipation of the call he so earnestly wanted to come got the better of him.

What could be taking so long? he thought in frustration and checked the time on the commpad. It had been the better part of a day since she'd arrived. Sofia had promised to let him know as soon as Carling started to show any signs of regaining consciousness, but so far, nothing. *Too long.*

His patience finally running out, he jabbed the commpod in his ear. "Call Sofia," he instructed it. The device chimed in acknowledgment.

Sofia answered immediately, "Yes, Director Sorensen?"

"What is Doctor Carling's condition, Sofia?" Sorensen asked brusquely.

"No change," she answered flatly. "She's still asleep in her room."

"Is she all right? I would have expected her to have regained consciousness by now."

"Her vital signs are all stable," Sofia reassured him. "As for how long she's been out, well, we honestly shouldn't be too surprised that it would take her more time than usual to recuperate after her altercation with Umbra."

"Still," Sorensen said.

"Remember, Director," Sofia interrupted. "She did take a significant dose of the anesthetic, much more than was recommended." Sorensen grunted. "And, if the taser had the extra side effects on her that the team suspected it might, that would certainly hinder her healing abilities, further slowing her recovery. A normal person would likely be dead, so it's not terribly surprising that she's still sleeping it off."

"Yes, yes, I understand all that," Sorensen snapped back, again rubbing the bridge of his nose. "But I hope you realize that if she wakes up on her own, unsupervised, and inadvertently triggers her bracelet before she understands her situation, it could seriously undermine her cooperation."

"You mean even more than abducting her from her home?" Sofia responded coolly.

Sorensen recoiled slightly, surprised at the level of rebuke in her response. *I'll have to look into that*, he thought, but decided to ignore her unusual tone for the time being. "Yes, even more than that," he replied with a drip of sarcasm. "We do not want to make a difficult situation any worse, do we, Sofia?"

"No, sir," she consented. "We do not."

"Very well then, since we are in agreement, I want you to rouse Doctor Carling and bring her to my office. I need to welcome her properly and ensure she understands where she is and the expectations for her participation so we don't have any unfortunate...accidents."

Sofia sighed. "Understood, Director Sorensen. I will do my best to have her in your office as soon as possible."

"Make it happen, Sofia," Sorensen said and disconnected the call. He drew a deep breath and felt some of the tension release from his shoulders. *Finally*, he thought, *it's all coming together. Finally.*

Blackness. She floated in blackness. She floated, but she felt heavy...sluggish. She became aware of her breathing and the slow beat of her heart in her chest. Her body was there, but it just felt disconnected from her.

She wasn't alone in the blackness either. There was a voice. It was faint and far away. She struggled to hear what it was saying, but it was getting louder. Her name? Was it calling her name?

"Doctor Carling. Can you hear me?" the soft, distant voice said.

She couldn't answer, though. It was so hard. Everything was so heavy. *Just let me sleep.*

"Doctor Carling, please wake up," it said again. The voice was accompanied by a slight rocking sensation as if something were gently shaking her.

Tricia tried to open her eyes, but they were like lead, and her arms and legs were like stone.

"Please, Doctor Carling."

Finally, she managed to shift her weight and rolled to her side. A sharp pain stabbed through her ribs and lower back, shocking her closer to the surface. She managed a soft groan and forced one eye open a crack. Above her, she saw a woman limned by a soft light behind her. The light made her eyes ache, and her head was throbbing, but she forced herself to blink a few times anyway, crawling out of the blackness back to the world.

"Mmmm," she said, finally finding her voice. It was raspy. Her throat was dry, and her tongue stuck to the roof of her mouth. "Who? What?" Tricia murmured, looking up into the woman's grey eyes. Light brown hair fell down toward Tricia, framing the woman's slender face. The woman gripped her shoulder gently but firmly. "Who are you?" Tricia asked groggily.

The edge of the woman's mouth turned up slightly. "My name is Sofia. I'm the Assistant Director here at the Institute for the Advancement of Human Potential. We need to meet with the director urgently, so I need you to wake up and come to his office with me."

Tricia squinted her eyes. The blackness tugged at her, beckoning for her to return. She rolled her head slowly from side to side. "No, no, I want to go back to sleep. Just let me sleep." She tried to roll back over, but the woman's hand pressed down on her shoulder to keep Tricia on her back.

"I know you do, Doctor Carling, but Director Sorensen is very eager to speak with you," Sofia said, her voice emphasizing the urgency she felt.

At the sound of his name, Tricia snapped further alert. "Sorensen?" she asked, looking directly into Sofia's eyes. "Sorensen is here?"

"He is, and he wants to speak with you," Sofia replied.

"Well, that makes two of us. I have a few choice words to share with him, too," Tricia said, now more fully awake, and started to sit up. She gasped again as her side and back screamed in response to her attempt.

"Easy," Sofia reminded her. She slid her hand down Tricia's back below her neck to support her as she sat up. Tricia silently accepted her aid, sucking in short breaths through her teeth when her side complained.

Finally, with Sofia's help, she managed to sit up fully and carefully swung her feet over the side of the bed, letting them settle onto the cool floor. Looking down at her legs, Tricia realized she was no longer wearing the workout clothes she had been wearing when Umbra showed up. Instead, she was wearing what appeared to be hospital scrubs. Some kind of metal ring was also now dangling around her wrist. They'd changed her clothes and cleaned her up since her confrontation with Umbra. It seemed that she had not only lost the fight but also lost her freedom.

We're not in Kansas anymore, Tricia thought as she hung her head and closed her eyes, her head pounding like a jackhammer. She put her elbows on her knees and pressed her fingers to her temples while Sofia slid her feet into a pair of slippers. The throbbing in her head brought on a sudden wave of nausea. *Oh God, please don't let me lose anything else right now,* she thought, praying for her swirling stomach.

"You're doing great, Doctor Carling," Sofia said. "I do have a wheelchair here if that would be easier."

Still pressing her temples, Tricia took a deep breath. "No, I can walk," she said. She sat up straight, took a deep breath, and turned her head to stretch her neck. Sofia reached down and took Tricia's arm as she stood, but before she could take a step, Tricia's legs buckled, dropping her hard back down on the bed. "Yeah, okay, the chair isn't such a bad idea," she admitted, closing her eyes once again.

Sofia wheeled the chair next to the side of the bed, and with a bit more help, Tricia managed to pull herself into it, settling herself into the padded seat. Sofia lifted Tricia's legs so her feet rested securely on the footrests and then handed her a bottle with a straw. "Water," she told Tricia. "It'll help with the aftereffects of the anesthesia." Tricia nodded and drew deeply on the straw. The cool water seemed to breathe new life into her as they rolled into the hallway.

At first, the brighter lights of the hallway made Tricia squint and blink, but she soon grew accustomed to them. They didn't do her pounding headache any favors, though, so she occasionally closed her eyes as they navigated the short distance to Sorensen's office, nursing her water and rehearsing what she was going to tell Sorensen when she finally saw him.

"Who did you say you were again?" Tricia asked.

"I'm Sofia, the Assistant Director," Sofia replied evenly.

"What am I doing here?"

"Director Sorensen will explain all that."

Tricia held up the wrist that was wearing the smooth metal ring. "What is this thing?" she asked, shaking it for effect.

"Director Sorensen will explain that as well," Sofia said, staring forward, guiding them smoothly down the corridor.

"I see," Tricia said, "so what can *you* tell me?"

Sofia pulled them up to a stop outside the door at the end of the hallway and walked around to the side of the wheelchair. She folded her hands in front of her and looked down at Tricia. "Only to pay very close attention to what the Director has to tell you and to take what he says very seriously," she said. Sofia paused for a few seconds, looking into Tricia's eyes, and then knocked on the door. Without waiting for a reply, she opened it and wheeled Tricia into the office.

There behind the desk, Tricia saw the man who had visited her lab, the man who had invaded her lunch date and threatened Harold. A man she had disliked before, but now was fairly sure she deeply despised. Sorensen. He looked up and smiled broadly when they entered his office. Yes, she loathed that smile too, and as if there was any remaining doubt, she loathed him in every way.

"Doctor Carling, how good of you to join us," Sorensen said enthusiastically. He got up and came around the side of his desk and gestured toward one of the cushioned chairs. "Please, I'm sure you'll find this much more comfortable." He reached down to take Tricia's arm, but she snatched it away from him. She pushed herself up out of the wheelchair, tugged down on the top of her scrubs defiantly, and settled herself into the chair, ignoring the stabbing pains in her back and side. Sorensen waved to Sofia to move the wheelchair away while he took the chair opposite Tricia. After relocating the wheelchair to the back of the office by the door, Sofia moved to stand behind Sorensen.

"What did you do to me?" Tricia growled, glaring at Sorensen.

"Absolutely nothing, I assure you," he said. "You are still feeling the side effects of your encounter with Umbra last night. Some of it is the result of the anesthetic. She gave you an excessive dose, unfortunately, and it will take some time for that to clear out of your system. Most of it, though, is likely due to your heightened sensitivity to the taser she used during your confrontation."

"What do you mean 'heightened sensitivity'?" she asked, puzzled.

"Well, fifty thousand volts is a serious matter for anyone, but for you, we theorized it would be even more so. As far as we can determine, your powers stem from channeling and transforming electromagnetic energy. As you know, electricity is a form of electromagnetic energy, but the power vectors are orthogonal to the types of energy with which you seem to have an affinity. Our scientists speculated this would likely have a highly disruptive effect on your abilities and probably explains why your healing hasn't helped you recuperate more quickly."

Tricia felt her stomach rise. Apprehensively, she reached out for the flows, inviting them toward her, but where she usually felt the reassuring ebb and tide of energy around her, she felt only pure chaos. The flows were there, but they churned wildly, twisted and tangled. No matter how much she called for them, barely the slightest trickle came to her. He was right; for the moment, she was powerless.

"Of course, it was very careless of Umbra to use the taser while in physical contact with you, but she was desperate. Fortunately, you spared her by absorbing the entire charge yourself." He grinned at her again. "Don't worry, though. We believe it will wear off shortly, and the sooner, the better. Your work with us here depends on you being your normal, exceptional self."

"And what work would that be?" she asked, resigning herself to the fact that, for the moment, she had no choice but to hear him out. *When my powers return, though, we will have a very different conversation, I assure you.*

Sorensen sat back and crossed his leg over his knee. "As I told you before in the restaurant, Doctor Carling, we believe in the same vision. No one more than I wants to see Beacon succeed and be the force for good you and I both know she can be. The problem, though, is that there is just one Beacon. There's too little of Beacon to go around, to make every city in this country—in the world—like Crystal Bay."

"Don't think I haven't thought about that," Tricia replied, still trying to shake off the groggy feeling clouding her brain. "But, for the time being, at least, there is only one of me."

"Exactly!" Sorensen exclaimed, sitting forward. "Like I said in our last chat, that 'for the time being' part is what we are concerned with here. With your help, we can develop more parahumans, extraordinary people like you, to build on what you've started."

"You're insane," Tricia told him. "I thought you were insane before, and I'm even more sure of it now. Even if I believed for a moment that was possible, how *exactly* do you think I'm going to help you accomplish that?"

"By studying you, by studying how you control and manage your powers, you can help us take the next step in our work. Once we know how you do it, and we learn how to replicate that in others, we can put a Beacon in every major city worldwide. Look at what you've done in Crystal Bay alone. Imagine what two or three of you could accomplish in a teeming metropolis like New York or Los Angeles. They would become paradises, and with your help, we can do it."

He's out of his mind, she thought, rubbing her forehead. "Assuming you can, I still don't know why you need me. I mean, you already have someone who can do what I do. Why don't you study her?"

"You mean Umbra?" Sorensen asked. He shook his head. "She has other responsibilities."

Through the haze of her migraine, the dots connected for Tricia. "The disappearances. You're using those people as guinea pigs in your crazy experiments!"

"Of course," Sorensen confirmed. "Your research team will fill you in further, but yes, our recruits have been very instrumental in the progress we've made so far. We've just come to the point where we need a more, um, fully functional specimen. There's a limit, it seems, to how far we can go with just some vagrants and runaways."

Animal! she spat in her mind. Tricia took a second to compose herself before probing further. "You know you can't keep this up, right? The police are suspicious, and I was already onto Umbra even before she showed up at my townhouse. It's only a matter of time before they track you and this place down."

Sorensen scoffed. "No one is even close to figuring out what is going on here, Doctor Carling. Save the melodrama. It's common knowledge that the trails go cold on random abductions after three or four days. The people we've been recruiting have no ties, and the police have no leads. Trust me, we are very aware of what the police know and don't know.

"As for you, true, you're a little more complicated, but—" Sorensen reached back to retrieve a commpad from his desk "—we think we've been pretty careful to cover your tracks. The university has some very authentic leave paperwork on file for Tricia Carling, and we've made sure the right people have gotten some personal messages from you. Here, take a look." He handed Tricia the commpad. "Here's an example of what we sent Doctor Haskell on your behalf."

Tricia took the commpad and read the message trail with Marni. *Marni's going to see through this in a heartbeat,* she mused, concealing a smirk. Frowning instead, she handed the commpad back to Sorensen.

"This kind of thing isn't going to fool people indefinitely. How long do you think you can keep forging messages to keep people satisfied?" she asked.

"It doesn't have to work for long. The messages and replies get further and further apart. Before long, you will resign. You'll sell your townhouse and move away unexpectedly. People will be confused, but that will fade over time. Ties will be severed, and eventually, they will stop looking. It won't take as long as you think, and you will be a permanent addition to our team here."

Tricia closed her eyes. Listening to his deranged scheme had only strengthened the pounding in her head, and every breath twisted the knife she was sure was in her back. After a few seconds, she shook her head and looked at him. "That's it. I've heard enough," Tricia said to Sorensen, chuckling softly. "Clearly, you underestimate the quality of the people I have in my life, and even if I were inclined to go along with something like this, there's no way I'd put that kind of power into the hands of a raving psychotic like you. As soon as the taser effect wears off, I'm out of here."

Her eyes narrowed, and her lip curled. "And don't even think about sending your lapdog after me again either," Tricia added, jabbing her finger toward him. "I'll go right through her. I had her beat before, but she tricked me. I won't fall for any gimmicks next time, and I promise you I won't hold back either. She can't stop me, and neither can you."

Sorensen grinned sardonically. "You're absolutely right," he said with a casual turn of his wrist, "I can't, but before you make good on that threat, let's discuss your new piece of jewelry." He pointed toward the ring circling her wrist.

"You see, that ingenious little band is tuned to the energy frequencies that feed your abilities. Its function is quite simple. If you draw on your abilities, that device will sense the increased energy flows and trigger an alarm."

"And then what?" Tricia asked. "Alarm or not, you still can't stop me."

"I won't have to. You see, I have a team that has one and only one assignment. If that alarm goes off, the computer will randomly select someone close to you, someone you love, and my team will kill them."

Tricia's jaw dropped open. She looked down at the metal band and back up at him. "What?" she asked with a waver in her voice.

"You heard me correctly, Doctor Carling. Yes, kill them. Someone randomly, so there's no way you could stop them. Of course, you will get a warning before that happens; we don't want any momentary lapses or accidents to have such drastic consequences. The bracelet will change color and vibrate if you start to exceed the programmed thresholds. If you exceed them by too much or for too long, the mechanism will trigger, and you will lose someone close to you."

Tricia scowled and pressed her lips together. "So, what if I decide to just rip this thing off and shove it..."

"Same result," Sorensen interrupted. "If it's removed without proper authorization, it will trigger immediately. So you see," he said, smirking maliciously. "It's not me who will stop you from razing this place to the ground with your bare hands and walking out of here. It's you."

Tricia sat and stared at him. Sitting across from her was pure evil, plain and simple. *My friends...my family...*

Sorensen clapped his hands down on his knees. "Well, I think that's enough for today," he said jovially. "Sofia can take you back to your room to rest and think about what we have talked about. Tomorrow, we'll introduce you to your research team and start making some magic."

Sorensen stood up and walked to the other side of his desk. Sofia brought the wheelchair over next to Tricia. Shocked by what she was told, Tricia accepted Sofia's help getting up and into the wheelchair, wincing as she sat.

"Oh, one more thing to keep in mind, Doctor Carling," Sorensen said just as Sofia started wheeling Tricia toward the door. She turned the chair slightly so Tricia and Sorensen could be face to face. "I anticipate that, very soon now, Draconyx will be making a substantial offer to partner with your laboratory, one that I'm fairly sure Doctor Patel and the Board will find too good to pass over."

Tricia lifted her head to look him in the face as he smugly folded his hands on the desk in front of him. "So you see," he added, "even if you find a way out of here, you have nothing to go back to. Your team, your work, your life, are completely mine."

Tricia stared at him in disbelief for as long as she could while Sofia pivoted the chair to leave. She pulled the door open, but before she could wheel Tricia out of the office, his mockingly sinister baritone voice spoke out from behind them one last time, stopping them in their tracks, "Sleep well, Doctor Carling. Tomorrow will be a big day. Tomorrow, you start a whole new chapter in your life." Tricia stiffened as Sofia hastily wheeled her out and closed the door.

Sofia pushed Tricia in silence down the stark, brightly lit hallway back toward her room. The only sound was the occasional thump as one of the wheels went over a seam in the flooring. Tricia rubbed her temples, trying desperately to quell the hammering in her head and to process what she had just been told. Finally, without looking up, she said, "He's crazy. There's no way I can go along with this."

Sofia stared straight ahead. "Think what you wish, Doctor Carling, but please listen to me when I tell you to take every word he said without any shred of doubt. He is completely committed to his vision, and he is more than willing and quite capable of following through on his threat. If he believes it will secure your cooperation and get him what he wants, he will not give a second thought to killing your friends and family, or worse." Sofia paused, still staring ahead of them. "I've personally seen what he's capable of."

"What about you?" Tricia asked, looking up at her. "Are you?"

Sofia's face went blank for a few seconds, and then she shook her head. "I may not agree with all of the Director's tactics, but I am the Assistant Director, and I have no choice but to carry out his orders. However," she added, looking down at Tricia, "I can help make your stay with us as easy as possible under the circumstances if you'll let me. It all depends on you, though. You need to come to terms with the fact that this is your life now, and the sooner you do, the sooner I can help you make the best of it."

They stopped outside of Tricia's room. Sofia snapped on the wheel brake and walked around to face Tricia. "I've arranged a light meal for you in case you are hungry. I will come by in the morning to make sure you get breakfast and to take you to meet your research team." She held out her hands to help Tricia out of the chair, but Tricia shook her head and pushed herself up.

"Thank you, but I'll take it from here if you don't mind," Tricia said.

"Very well," Sofia said. She opened Tricia's door. "Sleep well, Doctor Carling. I will see you in the morning."

Tricia nodded and went into her room. She heard Sofia pull the door closed behind her, followed by the lock clicking into place. On the table before her was a small tray covered with a metal dome lid. Tricia walked slowly to the table and lifted the cover. Beneath it was a bowl of tomato soup and a grilled cheese sandwich sliced in half on the side.

Tricia stared at the plate, and her hand started to shake. *Tomato soup and grilled cheese*, she thought, horrified. *Two of my favorites. How do they know? My God, what else do they know?*

She dropped the lid down onto the tray and collapsed on the bed. Her side howled in pain, but she ignored it as she rolled over and buried her face into the pillow. *What am I going to do? Marni...my team...Harold...their lives hang on what I do next. They could die because of me, but I can't give in to this psycho either. How am I getting out of this without killing them?*

At last, the physical pain and emotional anguish overcame her, and she broke. She sobbed once, then again, and then wept uncontrollably until sleep finally claimed her.

Reunion

Tricia hung her head and breathed deeply, not because of the lingering fatigue she felt, and not because of the aching muscles in her neck and back. Quite the opposite. It was obvious to her that at some point during her restless tossing and turning, the effects of the taser had worn off, and her healing abilities were already at work. She could not only feel the flows of energy around her; they were clawing at her to let them in, to give her power, to give what she was feeling some kind of release.

No, it wasn't anything physical.

It was the swelling hatred.

Tricia tried some meditation and deep breathing to draw it back, to bring it under control. Part of her was afraid to leave these intense emotions unchecked. It was simply too easy to let her powers slip when her emotions were this raw. The weight on her wrist reminded her that the cost of a mistake was too great to risk.

Tricia didn't loathe this small room in which they had confined her. It wasn't the iron mesh bars on the outside of her window that fractured the early morning sunlight into a mosaic of shadows on the floor either.

It was the bracelet dangling on her wrist.

She breathed deeply, held it, then exhaled slowly out of her nose. The bracelet forced her to be her own jailer. Her choices—not the metal outside the windows or locks on the doors—now forged her prison bars. This bracelet forced her to cast herself willingly into the role of being her own warden.

Tricia knew she could tear it off and free herself at any time, but if she did, and if Sorensen was to be believed, it would start a chain of events that would lead to the death of someone close to her. The bracelet forced her to choose between her freedom and the people she loved, and to her, the choice was obvious. She made herself their prisoner, and she hated the bracelet for that.

Tricia also reserved a healthy measure of hatred for the man who put it on her, the man who forced the choice on her by doing it. Sorensen knew she would make the sacrifice, imprisoning herself far more securely than any measure he could invent, and he used that knowledge against her. She hated him for that, too.

Can he be believed? Tricia pondered. *Was he telling the truth, or was it some psych job to manipulate me?* She wrapped her fingers around the bracelet and, for a moment, considered ripping it free.

No, she decided. *People like him don't feel the need to lie. He's holding all the cards right now, and he knows it.* With a sigh, she released the band around her wrist, letting it dangle against her skin, closed her eyes, and sat up straight on the edge of the bed.

She breathed in and out, in and out, slowly, concentrating on clearing her mind, focusing on slowing her pulse, calming herself. If she was going to find a way out of this, she would need a clear head. *They may have a band around my wrist, but they don't have one around my head,* she reminded herself. *I will figure a way out of this, one way or another.*

When the burning loathing and rage had finally subsided into just a smoldering ember deep in her chest, Tricia pushed herself up off the bed and surveyed the room. The floor was made from some kind of interlocking vinyl tile imprinted with a light simulated wood grain. The walls were painted a light blue, and a small table with two chairs sat in the corner across from her bed. She found it curious that there were no obvious light fixtures in the room, but that was a puzzle for another time. Right now, the morning sun brightened the room, and that small pleasure was all she needed.

The wall between the bed and the table held the only other obvious possible exit from the room, a single large window. The window had no curtains, but she was able to draw the wide vertical blinds open, letting in more light and giving her a look at her surroundings. The landscape outside was fairly rural; she couldn't see any other buildings, roads, or anything manmade, just grass and trees. She huffed sharply. From here, she had no way of knowing if she was just outside Crystal Bay, halfway across the country, or halfway around the world.

Tricia turned her attention to the window itself. It appeared to be ordinary glass. On the outside was a heavy diagonal metal mesh anchored firmly into the outer wall of the building.

I could probably tear through that without triggering the bracelet, she thought, examining the grate a bit closer. *Would it set off an alarm? If I got out, what then? Where could I go? Is there a range on the bracelet that might trigger it if I went too far?*

No, I need to be smart about this, know more before attempting anything. There is too much at stake if I guess wrong. Any risks I take must be informed ones, not impulsive ones.

And escaping is only half the solution. He has to be stopped. Any viable plan has to end this place and what he's doing.

Examining the window further, she found a small latch on the inside that, when flicked to the side, allowed her to swing the upper pane outward slightly. The mesh only allowed it to open a couple of inches, but it was enough to reward her with a gentle, fresh breeze. *As far as cages go, it could be worse...much worse*, she thought, inhaling deeply the smells of wet grass and wildflowers and listening to the morning birds singing in the distance.

Her mood somewhat improved from the sunshine and morning breeze, Tricia decided to finish scouting out the rest of her room. When she'd returned after her 'welcome' meeting with Sorensen yesterday, she was still feeling very sluggish from the drugs she'd been given, and her ribs ached from the taser, both courtesy of Umbra. The pit in her stomach made her regret waiving off the light dinner Sofia had arranged for her, but going back to bed was likely the smarter choice. Fortunately, the small amount of sleep she did get was enough to clear away the cobwebs, and her side was much less sensitive now. No question, her healing had been hard at work while she had been sleeping. Even now, in the short time she had been awake, the dull ache had faded even more.

In the corner of the room at the foot of her bed were two narrow doors. The first door opened into a small bathroom. Besides the stainless steel toilet and sink, the room had a small shower nook and a vanity complete with various toiletries: shampoo, conditioner, toothpaste, toothbrush, and a bar of soap. A small sticker on the mirror told her that a disposable razor for personal grooming was available on request. *Better than most hotels I've stayed in*, she thought with a small shrug.

The second door revealed a small closet with built-in shelves and drawers. It held a variety of clothing that included some flat slippers, panties, stretch sports bras, and what looked like hospital scrubs hanging next to the shelving units. On the inside of the door was a robe hanging from a hook. Tricia considered for a moment and then decided to accept the robe's unspoken invitation for a hot shower. Inspecting the rest of her clothing options could wait. She took a towel off one of the shelves, draped the robe over her arm, and headed into the small bathroom.

A short time later, Tricia was standing back in front of the small closet, wrapped in the robe and brushing her hair. The scalding water had worked wonders on her neck and back. She set the hairbrush back down on the shelf where she'd found it, raised her arms over her head, and smiled when she was rewarded with a series of cracks and pops up and down her spine. *Muuuuuch better*, she thought as she turned her attention to the contents of the closet.

"Well, they've done their homework," she muttered as she looked through the various items. Everything was in her size. Undoing the robe, she slipped on a pair of the panties, and then she realized something was missing. "Where are *my* clothes?" she exclaimed out loud. Frowning, she searched the drawers and shelves more intently, but the clothes she had been wearing when Umbra kidnapped her—her new workout clothes in particular—were nowhere to be found.

She huffed in disgust, put her hands on her hips, and accused her captors of having inappropriate relations with their mothers. With the renewed wave of anger, she felt the waves of energy surge toward her. As the whorls of light formed at the edges of her vision, the bracelet on her wrist buzzed a warning, just as she was promised. She brought it up to eye level. "Thank you, and go frak yourself," she told it and pushed the energies away.

Before Tricia could resume her search, the search she already knew was pointless, a knock came at the door. "Come in," she snapped, and the door opened gently as she secured the robe back around herself.

Sofia walked in carrying a tray. "Good morning, Doctor Carling," she said, setting the tray down on the table. It held a covered plate, silverware, and a tall glass of orange juice. "How are you feeling this morning?" she asked.

Tricia glared at her. "Where are my clothes?" she asked indignantly. "The ones I was wearing when I was brought here."

Sofia looked at her calmly and folded her hands in front of her. "All your things have been safely put away for you. We will supply anything you might need during your stay here. All you need to do is ask if you need something, and I'll see to it personally."

Tricia crossed her arms. "I'd like my clothes back," she replied, still glaring.

Sofia was unfazed, meeting Tricia's eyes calmly. "As I said, you won't need them. We will provide anything you need during your stay."

Pointless, Tricia thought, and decided to change tactics. "Can I get a hair tie?"

Sofia nodded and reached into her coat pocket. She produced an elastic hair loop and handed it to Tricia. "I'll ask the staff to provide a few more when they service your room later this morning," she said, folding her hands back in front of herself.

"Thank you," Tricia said. She pulled her hair back. "You know," she said as she twisted her hair up with the elastic band, "*when* I leave here, I fully expect to have them returned."

Sofia's lips curled up into a small smile that was both smug and playful as if she was enjoying the banter. "*If* that time comes," she replied, "I'll make sure they are returned to you."

Tricia couldn't help but smirk back. *Touché*, she thought.

Sofia gestured toward the tray on the table. "Please go ahead and have some breakfast. I'll leave you alone to eat and finish dressing. When you're done, I'll come back and take you to meet your research team." She walked to the door, pulled it open, but turned back toward Tricia before leaving. "If there are other meal choices you'd prefer, please let me know, and I'll pass them on to the kitchen staff."

Tricia nodded in thanks. Sofia nodded once back and walked through the door. As she left, Tricia looked over Sofia's shoulder to the empty space outside her door. *No guard*, she realized, *but then, why would they think they need one?*

True to her word, Sofia returned shortly after Tricia had finished eating and dressing. Tricia hadn't felt overly hungry when she woke, but as soon as she took her first bite, her appetite came roaring back, and she had no problem devouring the ample servings of eggs, toast, and fruit. When the knock at the door came, Tricia had just finished putting on a set of light blue scrubs. "Come in," she called as she was tugging on a pair of black rubber-soled slippers.

"Shall we go?" Sofia asked, motioning toward the open door.

Tricia nodded and stood up, wiggling her feet in the flats. She followed Sofia out of the door and into the hall.

"Of course, I have no intention of cooperating with any of this," Tricia told Sofia as they walked down the hallway.

Sofia stopped, turned to face Tricia, and looked her squarely in the eye. "Please," she started, but then halted, stuttering slightly. She jerked her head sharply in frustration. Tricia recoiled slightly, concerned that Sofia might be on the verge of some kind of seizure, but as she waited, Sofia seemed to collect herself.

"Doctor Carling," Sofia continued after several seconds, "being stubborn and obstinate will only make all of this much harder than it needs to be. As you undoubtedly surmised from your conversation with him yesterday, Director Sorensen is very passionate about the work being done here. Furthermore, he is very determined and *very* used to getting his way." Sofia sighed. "It will go badly for you and others if you test his resolve. I know firsthand what he is capable of, and I would prefer it not come to that for you."

Tricia looked back at her. "You told me as much yesterday."

"Because I need you to understand it and believe it," Sofia replied, nodding. "Look, Doctor Carling, I know you must be very upset and angry about what's happened and how you were brought here. I understand that, and those feelings are perfectly justified. However, I can't do anything about that. I will, however, do what I can to make your stay here, and the work you *will* do with us here, as easy and painless as possible. I just urge you not to let those feelings make a difficult situation even harder."

Sofia's voice was calm and even, but Tricia could see the pleading in her eyes. Tricia snorted sharply out of her nose. *Very well...for now*, she thought, and motioned with her arm toward the hallway for them to continue. Sofia nodded once, turned, and they continued in silence.

After a few turns down a series of identical and remarkably bland beige hallways, Sofia stopped by a closed door marked simply as 'Interview Room'. She again clasped her hands together and turned to face Tricia. "This morning, you'll meet first with the principal lead on your research team," Sofia told her in the same methodical and even tone. "She will establish the research protocol you will be supporting, and I'll get the session schedule from her. I'll come by each day to ensure you get your meals at the right times. I'll also escort you to the sessions and back to your room when they are finished."

"Isn't bringing my meals and babysitting me a little below your pay grade?" Tricia asked her curtly.

Sofia pushed her glasses up her nose, and one side of her mouth curled up in a half smile. "Normally, yes, but you are a very special member of our team now. The Director wants you treated accordingly, so I will be assisting you personally."

Tricia smirked back. "Looks like I'm in good hands then. Shall we?"

Sofia nodded and opened the door, letting Tricia enter the room first. There, sitting in a rolling desk chair facing her, was a ghost. Tricia gasped in shock and stumbled backward a couple of steps, accidentally bumping into Sofia.

"Surprise, Tricia!" Rene said, smiling.

Dumbstruck, Tricia stared at her for a few seconds before she finally stammered, "Rene?!? How? How can you be here? You're dead!"

Rene shrugged. "Rumors of my death appear to have been greatly exaggerated," she replied with a lilt in her voice.

"But *how*?" Tricia repeated.

Rene's smile faded slightly. "It is a story."

Sofia gently nudged Tricia into the room. "I think this is a good time to let you two get reacquainted," she said and backed out of the door, pulling it closed behind her.

Tricia watched the door close and then turned back to Rene. As she stared at Rene silently, her shock was suddenly displaced by another realization. "Did you have something to do with this, Rene?" Tricia spat out, jabbing a finger toward Rene. "With kidnapping me? Bringing me here?"

Rene sat back and held her hands up, palms out. "Absolutely not, Tricia. Honestly, I had nothing to do with it." She then pointed back towards herself with both sets of fingertips. "I barely had anything to do with *my* being here. Yesterday afternoon was the first I heard about your coming here at all." The smile returned, more teasing this time. "But I must confess I am enjoying the look of sheer shock on your face when you saw me here."

Rene chuckled and gestured toward the other chair across the table from her. Tricia looked at it skeptically, looked at Rene again, and finally sat down, facing her.

"So," Tricia said, folding her hands in front of her on the table, "how exactly *are* you here, Rene?"

"Honestly, Tricia, I don't remember much, firsthand anyway," Rene answered with a small shrug. "I remember our encounter at Meyer's Tower, of course. I remember you racing up the elevator, but it gets rather foggy after that. I seem to vaguely recall the Liberators making a rush at me and me firing the gun at one of them. There was a scuffle, and the gun went off again. It goes dark after that.

"Next thing I know, I'm waking up here. Sorensen told me that they—he and whoever he works for, I'm assuming—had been watching both of us for quite a while. They had a couple of people on the emergency response team who came to Meyer's Tower. When they found me, he said they gave me a dose of Neurostatin and pronounced me dead."

"Neurostatin," Tricia recalled. "The same stuff you were going to use on me trapped in that storage canister?"

Rene nodded. "The very same. Ironic, isn't it? Anyway, it seems they kept me in stasis ever since. I've only been back on my feet for a few weeks."

"Interesting," Tricia said, fingering her chin absentmindedly as she digested Rene's story. "For what it's worth, I got even less information than that about what happened to you. As far as the police and the DA knew, you were dead. They told me they'd found your body in the parking garage, and the Liberators of Gaia were nowhere to be found. They assumed you'd been shot and killed in a confrontation with them, but they had nothing to go on other than my account and what they found at the scene."

Rene pursed her lips and nodded again. "Well," she finally said. "I'm sure you were relieved to hear it."

"Relieved?!?" Tricia shouted in exasperation. She slapped her hands down on the top of the table and glared at Rene across the table. Rene drew back a bit, her normally perfect composure broken for a split second. "Obviously, what you did...what you tried to do...was kept very secret, but the University did hold a memorial service for you. I went. I *cried*, Rene. It was heart-wrenching. So many people spoke about you, the kind of person you were to them. Strong, brilliant, accomplished. You were...you were someone I admired, looked up to, hoped might be a mentor for me, and it broke my heart to find out what you were doing. My heart broke again when I was told what had happened, that you...you wouldn't get a chance..." Tricia's voice cracked, and she sat back in her chair. She threw her head back to look up at the ceiling, slapping her ponytail against her back, and wiped a tear that had nearly escaped her eye with the back of her hand.

"Why, Tricia," Rene crooned, "I didn't know you cared." Beneath the thin layer of defensive sarcasm, Tricia could hear clearly that Rene was touched, no matter how much she refused to let it show.

"Yes, I cared," Tricia said with a sigh. She paused momentarily and then leaned forward again to face Rene, "but whether I cared or not, in hindsight, I don't believe I would have done anything differently. I couldn't let your plan go forward, Rene, not with all those lives at stake, so no matter how much the outcomes hurt or how sorry I was about how it all turned out, for you especially, I've come to terms with the fact that I did what I had to do."

Rene regarded Tricia, and a coldness swept over her face. For a moment, Tricia could clearly see Purity, not Rene, sitting across from her once again. "As long as we are clearing the air," Rene said icily, "I did mean everything I told you, that I admired what you were trying to do and how much I liked you personally. Make no mistake though," she continued, her eyebrows narrowing, "knowing what I know now, and knowing full well how sad it would have made me to make it, I, on the other hand, probably would have made another choice, one that would have ensured you never left that lab alive."

"Okay then," Tricia replied curtly. "Now that we know where each other stands, how about you fill me in on what's actually going on here and how you're wrapped up in it?

"Very well," Rene said. "I assume you've already been properly welcomed by Director Sorensen?"

"Mmm-hmm," Tricia replied, "but I want to hear it from you."

"Fine then. Feel free to stop me if I get repetitive," Rene said, pushing her glasses up on her nose. "Putting it simply, they want to make more of you."

"Yes," Tricia replied shortly with a huff, "I got that part, but why?"

"Because, sweetie," Rene said, "what you have is worth a lot of money." Before Tricia could interrupt, Rene held up her hand and continued. "Think about it, Tricia. Taking your more flamboyant abilities out of the picture, people would pay through the nose to have even the most basic enhancements your, um, condition has provided you. Resilience, endurance, strength, not to mention your remarkable accelerated healing. If that's what I think it is, I'm willing to bet you age far more slowly as well. You would probably outlive mundane humans—" Tricia winced at the term "—by a factor of two or three. What would people pay to live two hundred years or more? Trillions."

Bingo, Marni, Tricia thought. *Nailed it.*

Rene was on a roll, her hands accentuating each point she made. "Now, add in your powers. You're a small army all by yourself. Imagine what the military would pay to outfit their soldiers with your strength or speed or energy projection abilities. A whole division of super-soldiers. I'm not sure we could count the zeroes on the paycheck that would bring in."

Tricia paused, soaking it all in. *Even bigger than Marni thought,* Tricia admitted. After a few seconds, she nodded her head sharply. "Yeah, okay, I get it, but interestingly enough, Sorensen didn't mention any of that when we met yesterday."

Rene grinned knowingly. "That's because I'm fairly certain that's not where his primary interest lies, dear."

Tricia pressed her lips together and took a short breath in and out through her nose. "He wants his own legion of super-cops."

Rene nodded slowly. "Yes," she replied. "Oh, don't get me wrong. He has to care about the other applications because the people bankrolling this facility want those things, but as far as he's concerned, those are just a means to an end for him. Absolute justice imposed and enforced by a police force of enhanced humans loyal only to him."

"It's terrifying, Rene."

"Mmm, perhaps," Rene said. "Honestly, though, it might be the one point where he and I agree the most. As you and I have discussed, you think that with enough inspiration and hope, people will choose to change on their own. However, I, and Director Sorensen as well, it seems, believe that it takes fear and threat of retribution to really motivate society to change in any meaningful way, and his vision certainly provides plenty of that. He may ultimately be proven right on that point."

Trica sniffed. "For the sake of argument, we will agree to disagree. Regardless, it still begs the question of how," Tricia pressed. "How can he do that? How can they give people superpowers, and again, what's your role in it all, Rene?" Tricia twisted her mouth to the side and looked at Rene askew. "I find it hard to believe that the timing of your being resurrected from the dead and my arrival here are mere coincidence, do you?"

"Not remotely," admitted Rene. "As for how they do it, I've not seen it myself, but my understanding is that they've created a system that can generate or tap into energies that have affinity to various natural forces. It's located here, deep in the facility. Using this machine, they attempt to infuse subjects with various blends of those energies and hope the subject manifests some kind of ability as a result."

Tricia's draw dropped. "My God, Rene," she exclaimed in disbelief. "You can't be serious. What happened to me was an accident...a fluke...and it almost killed me. It's a miracle I survived. I was skeptical when Sorensen described what they were doing. You're saying they really are doing that to people? Deliberately?"

Rene nodded. "That's what I've been told, and that's what I've read in the reports. I've seen the device myself, but I have not seen it in use. As for it killing them, well, there were quite a few, um, setbacks early on, but they seem to be past that now."

"Setbacks?!? You mean people died!"

"Yes," Rene replied stoically, "and not just a few either. However, they were able to refine both the process and how they select their recruits. As a result, the initial mortality rate is now quite low. The process doesn't always work, but at least there aren't the casualties there once were."

"And the ones that survive? What happens to them?" Tricia asked emphatically. Her hands were shaking slightly; all this was much too close to home for her comfort.

"I honestly know nothing about what happens to the ones that never manifest any abilities," Rene said with a small shrug. "There are other experiments and programs going on here. Maybe they end up in one of those. I try not to think about it, to be honest, but as for the ones that do, well, that's where I come in."

"For the ones that do?" Tricia asked. She could feel the heat building on her chest and neck, her agitation becoming quite visceral now. "Are you saying they've actually done it? People have developed abilities?"

Rene cocked her head. "Yes and no. Some of them have developed powers, but so far, none of them have demonstrated any level of control over them. In fact, most of them come to rather catastrophic ends." Tricia could only stare at Rene as she continued, "For example, just after I regained consciousness, there was a boy who apparently was able to manipulate water. During a testing session, it went out of control, and he extracted every last molecule of water in the room. One of the examination team members had a small defect in their protective suit that no one knew about. He ended up completely desiccated. The boy himself had absorbed all the water and drowned. It happened so fast, they couldn't get help into the room before it was all over."

"Oh my God, Rene," Tricia said barely above a whisper.

Rene nodded. "And just before you got here, there was a young girl. A runaway, as I recall. It took several treatments for her to show any signs, but eventually, she did, quite unexpectedly. She could redirect and focus large amounts of energy, even more impressive than you, according to the report. The examination team got a bit...overzealous...and coaxed her into accessing them in an examination room without any protection at all. She went supernova, incinerating the team, the room, and herself."

Young runaway...Izzy, Tricia realized, and hung her head with a sigh.

"Not all have died, though," Rene added. "Some were caught before their loss of control went too far. From what I've read, they are being kept in biochemical stasis somewhere off-site until we can find an answer to the control problem."

Trica sat there for about a minute, still hanging her head and breathing deeply. *It's true,* she thought. *Everything he said is absolutely true. I'd hoped he was just exaggerating or delusional, but what they've done is...horrifying.*

Rene sat across from her patiently, giving Tricia time to digest it all. Finally, Tricia lifted her head and looked at Rene. Her face was a mix of dismay and disbelief. "I don't get it, Rene," Tricia said, shaking her head while slowly leaning forward on her arms. "Given what you think of people in general, how could you go along with any of this? I know the deaths may not matter that much to you, but what he's trying to achieve goes against everything you believe. Giving corrupt people even more power, enhancing people to pursue their own selfish agendas...explain that to me." Tricia tossed her hands up in the air and then crossed them over her chest, sitting back in her chair.

Rene furrowed her eyebrows. "Don't think I haven't considered all that, Tricia," Rene replied. "Before you judge me too harshly as a hypocrite, remember, I'm not exactly here of my own free will either. I'm alive solely at someone's whim. Right now, I don't know the bigger picture here, and until I do, until I actually see a hill worth dying on...and I mean that quite literally...I'm not going to make any waves."

Rene sat back, and her face relaxed, shifting into a look of concern. "It's something for you to think about, too, Tricia. In case you haven't figured it out, Sorensen is dangerous. He's got a vision he truly believes in. He's completely committed and motivated, and he's ruthless. Trust me, I know what that looks like from personal experience."

"Yes, I've been reminded of that multiple times, actually."

Rene nodded. "I suggest you take those warnings very seriously."

"So," Tricia said, shifting gears. She jiggled the bracelet on her arm. "Do you also have a way to trigger this if I misbehave?"

Rene looked at the bracelet and scowled. "I do," she replied, nodding, "but I think that thing is barbaric and horrible. I promise you, Tricia, I'd never use something like that to coerce or punish you."

"What about you then? Do you have some remote-control doohickey keeping you in line, too?" Tricia asked with a sneer.

Rene shook her head. She glanced down at the table and then back up into Tricia's eyes. "No, dear," she said solemnly, forcing a sad and accepting smile. "They don't need anything that complicated to keep me on the program. You see, I'm already dead. The world wouldn't skip a beat if they decided to put me back into the grave. I know it, and, more importantly, they know I know it.

"So you see," Rene said, a slight curve still hanging on her lips, "we are both tools. Smart and beautiful tools, of course, but tools nonetheless." Tricia couldn't help but smirk.

Rene shuffled in her seat, smoothing down her skirt. She then sat forward with a look of enthusiasm spreading across her face. "All that aside, though...honestly, think about the possibilities, Tricia. You're a scientist, for Heaven's sake. Don't try to tell me that you didn't use your lab, probably more than once, to try to figure out what happened to you. Understand it? See what you might be capable of?"

Busted, Tricia thought, and nodded in admission. "Yes, I have, and yes, more than once. I had to keep it on the down low, of course, so there was only so much I could do, but I did use the lab isolation chamber to run some experiments and measurements."

"See? I knew it," Rene said with a satisfied smile.

Tricia smiled back. "Marni has also been helping out, running some tests, seeing if we can pinpoint where these abilities come from and how they work."

Rene beamed. "Well, the conditions under which we were brought here might not be ideal, but the facilities are unsurpassed. Every kind of lab and equipment you could imagine is available here."

Tricia sniffed. "The conditions leave a lot to be desired, Rene."

Rene chuckled. "Perhaps, but think about it, Tricia. Think of what you could learn about yourself. We can do it all out in the open. No hiding. No secrecy. Any wild idea you can come up with to help discover what's happened with you and how you manage to control it when others fail so catastrophically, we can do that here without any bureaucracy or red tape. Pure, unfettered science, and you'd get the answers you are looking for."

Tricia stared at her. *I hate to admit it, but she has a point,* Tricia thought. *It is a chance for me to finally get to the bottom of this, to get some real answers. However*—she shuddered slightly—*giving Sorensen anything he wants...for any reason...is just repulsive, but perhaps going along, at least for now, is my best play, at least until I have a better plan.*

"You make a compelling case, Rene. I can't lie; the opportunity to learn more does appeal to me. It's worth considering," she finally said.

Rene smiled and sat back in her chair. "That's all I can ask you to do, Tricia. Consider it." She tapped a few buttons on her commpad. Seconds later, Sofia pushed open the door. *She must've been waiting outside this whole time,* Tricia realized. *Doesn't look like they entirely trust Rene, either.* Rene stood up and gestured toward the open door for Tricia to do the same. "And while you're giving it some thought, shall we get started with some of the basics? Vitals, height, weight, that kind of thing?" Tricia shrugged her consent as Sofia held the door and motioned for them to go through ahead of her.

In his office, Sorensen clicked off the monitor. *Excellent,* he thought to himself as he leaned back in his chair, steeling his fingers in front of him. *Thornton is playing her part perfectly.* He leaned forward again and typed some notes into the commpad, already formulating in his mind the report he would make in his upcoming status meeting. After months of stalled progress and lackluster results, his superiors would be very pleased to hear that they could expect some substantial strides forward very soon.

Visitors

Tricia pushed her food around on her plate absentmindedly. The food was actually quite good— for a prison, that is—but she simply had no appetite. She should be starving; the past several days had been a battery of tests, one probing, prodding, and exercise after another. They measured her vitals routinely and took samples of her blood and other fluids to test, sometimes more than once per day. They even took some of her hair. "It does react to your abilities," Rene explained when Tricia questioned that, "so there might be something we can learn from it."

All that was in addition to the physical testing. Stress tests, strength and speed tests, both with her powers and without them. Measuring her energy levels and metabolic output. It was exhausting, and while it certainly helped her sleep better at night, her appetite continued to wane. Tricia knew from the way the scrubs she was wearing fit her that she'd lost a few pounds. Rene had noticed it, too, and she had thoroughly chastised Tricia for it, reminding her that if she let herself get weak, she could forget any hope of finding a way out. Tricia sighed; Rene was right, so she forced herself to eat even though she didn't want it.

This was one of the few meals Tricia had eaten alone as well. Sofia had been making a habit of spending time with her, talking with her, and generally keeping her company in between testing sessions. Despite the fact that she was one of her captors, Tricia couldn't help but like Sofia. She was really going out of her way to try to make the best of the situation for Tricia that she could. Sofia had been making good on her promise as well to see to Tricia's needs. While live feeds related to current events were forbidden, and leaving Tricia with a device of any kind to stream shows or movies was out of the question, Tricia's small desk now held a couple of books from her favorite author, a few magazines, and several scientific periodicals for her to read.

Despite her kindness, though, Tricia couldn't help but wonder about her, the way Sofia sometimes seemed to have something to say but couldn't quite find the words to get it out, or her mood swings, suddenly shifting from friendly and personal to cold and professional. It was almost like Sofia was actually two different people, constantly in conflict. It was just weird, but then, nothing about this place was particularly normal either.

As Tricia sat there using her fork to nudge the baby corn into small geometric shapes, her grip suddenly tightened. She lifted her head, abruptly feeling a pulsing sensation. It was distant and diffuse, but there nonetheless, like a far-off train that you feel is coming long before you hear it. She quietly put down her fork and slowly sat up straight, looking toward the door to her room. *I know that feeling,* she thought, casually brushing back the lock of hair dangling at the side of her face.

She closed her eyes and felt the energies swirling around her, but within them, a vibration pulsed through like ripples on a pond. Tricia cocked her head slightly; while the sensation was in both the light and dark energies, she definitely felt it more acutely in the dark ones.

I have felt this before.

Carefully, she beckoned a small trickle of both energies toward her, careful not to alarm the bracelet on her wrist. They came, entering and wrapping around her, and as they did, she felt the vibration sharpen. Clearly, the source was quite near; she could feel it moving toward her. There were other larger and more distant sources of thrums and pulses on different frequencies as well, like overlapping and competing bass tracks from music being played too loud in a college dormitory, but she ignored those for now, focusing on the specific frequency moving in her direction, the fingerprint of someone she'd felt before, not that long ago.

It's her.

Umbra. She's here.

The source of the pulsing stopped momentarily as Tricia reached out more to bring it more into focus, sharpen her perception of it, and then started moving again, faster now, straight toward her. Tricia stiffened. *She's coming this way.*

She drew just a bit more power when she felt what she believed to be Umbra stop just outside her door. Holding her breath now, Tricia watched the door handle jiggle slightly as someone unsuccessfully tried to open it from the outside. The pulsing grew stronger and accelerated momentarily before Tricia finally heard the lock click. The handle turned down, and Umbra entered the room. She quickly looked up and down the hall, closed the door behind her quietly, and turned to face Tricia.

The woman standing before her was, and was not, the woman with whom she'd fought, and lost, just over a week ago. Gone was the intimidating black and blue outfit she had worn the night they first met in Tricia's home. The woman before her now was dressed much more casually, wearing slim-cut blue jeans and a cream linen shirt with an embroidered southwestern motif. She had traded her boots for low black heels. The belt and the blue highlights in her hair were the same. *She's even younger than I thought she was*, Tricia thought, looking her over coolly.

"Hello, Doctor Carling," she said, putting her hands on her hips.

"Umbra, isn't it?" Tricia replied, pushing her tray away from her and looking up. "Is it casual day in The Workshop today?"

Umbra smirked. "No," she said, walking over and taking the other chair across the small table from Tricia. "I'm, well, off duty right now."

"So, what do you go by when you're off duty then?"

"Darci," the woman said. "Darci Jackson, but Darci will do. May I call you Tricia?" she asked formally.

"Sure, why not?" Tricia said with a shrug. "Off duty, huh? I take it this isn't an official visit, then?"

Darci shook her head. "Technically, I'm not supposed to be here, but then—" she raised her hand, and a small collection of spider-like black tendrils writhed in her palm "—locks aren't really an issue for me."

"Personal visit, then, how nice. Well, I'm not feeling much like handing out autographs today, and if you came for a rematch, you have me at a bit of a disadvantage," Tricia said sarcastically and shook the bracelet on her wrist for Darci to see.

"What is that?" Darci asked.

Could she really not know? Tricia thought, studying her face. "This little bauble tells one of Sorensen's cronies to murder someone close to me if I use my powers." She saw Darci's face react with surprise, but she said nothing. *Hmm, seems she doesn't. Interesting...*

"Ok, Darci, so why *are* you here?"

"Well, it isn't for a rematch, and it certainly isn't for an autograph," Darci replied with a touch of haughtiness in her voice. "Quite the opposite, actually. I've been wanting to talk to you for a long time...to understand what turned you into what you are."

"You mean my powers?" Tricia asked.

"No," Darci said with a sneer. "What turned you into such a fraud."

"Fraud?" Tricia repeated, drawing back in disbelief. "What do you mean...*fraud*?!"

"Exactly that," Darci said coolly.

"What are you talking about?" Tricia asked and held out her hand. Despite how little of the flow around her she could channel without setting off the bracelet, a brilliant pinpoint of light formed in her palm. "You, as much as anyone, should know my powers are completely genuine," she retorted, glaring at Darci defiantly.

"No, not like that," Darci scoffed. "I know your *powers* are real. It's *how* you use them that makes you a charlatan and a fake."

"How I use them? Explain *that* to me, then," Tricia demanded.

"You see," Darci said, sitting back and crossing her legs casually, "growing up, the village elders told me, and the other children, stories of the *Ye'ii* and the *Diyin Dine'é*, the Holy People, beings that had incredible powers and served humanity. These legends told of people like *Naayéé'*

Neizghání, Monster Slayer, and *Tó Bájísh Chíní,* Born-For-Water, who used their powers to bring humans more in harmony with nature and to fight evil, corruption, and monsters or demons like the Skinwalkers, the *Yee Naaldlooshii.*"

"And you believe these beings, these Holy People, were like us?" Tricia asked.

Darci nodded once in affirmation, the blue streaks in her hair shimmering in the light from the window. "I do, absolutely. I'm not particularly religious, but legends come from somewhere, and whether these beings were spirits or gods or empowered like us somehow, my belief is that they saw their abilities as gifts, as a sacred calling to use them in service of humanity. Their stories are used to teach children moral lessons about good and evil and how to treat each other and the world around us."

Sacred calling... Trica could already see where this was going. While there was little she could do about the warmth she felt creeping up into her face, she did her best to avoid crossing her arms, rolling her eyes, or doing anything else that might make her appear defensive. Keeping her face as neutral as she could, Tricia simply nodded, encouraging Darci to continue.

"But you," Darci said, leaning forward and pointing at Tricia, "you don't take it seriously. You put on your flashy little costume, dab on some lipstick, and bop around the city, posing for photographers, showing off at charity events, and giving out pulp interviews. Everything *but* dedicating yourself to the service of humankind like the *Diyin Dine'é* did, like people with gifts, people like *us,* should."

Apparently having made her point, Darci sat back in her chair and stared at Tricia, her eyes challenging Tricia to respond. *How dare she?!?* Tricia thought, her blood boiling at

Darci's blatant and unfounded accusation of selfishness. However, rather than escalate, rather than play into Darci's anger, she held Darci's glare and took a deep breath to compose herself.

"I realize it doesn't get the coverage in the news it used to," Tricia replied, forcing her voice to remain calm and even, "but you need to understand that I'm out there almost every night doing what I can to serve the people of Crystal Bay. Every night, and even at times during the days, I'm out there stopping gang fights, preventing sexual assault, busting up muggings, robberies, drug deals, you name it, doing everything I can to keep the people of my city safe."

Tricia sat forward, frowning slightly, and swept her arm out in front of her. "As for the rest of it," she said, letting a touch of her anger and frustration creep in for emphasis, "as for the rest of it, I *hate* those public appearances. Absolutely *loathe* them!"

"But, if you hate them so much," Darci started, but Tricia cut her off.

"I do them because I realized very early that the amount of difference I could make alone was limited. The fear of threat only works as long as there is a threat, but if people can be inspired to do better, to *be* better, anything I do can be multiplied by the millions of people in the city. You have those stories because those extraordinary beings were seen doing wonderful things for your ancestors, and so they made the legends to pass down and teach the generations after them, influencing your entire culture long after they were gone.

"I certainly would never consider myself even remotely legendary, but if people see me, if I can become a symbol, then it's *everybody* working for something better, not just me. So, I do the appearances and the interviews and the charities

224

and the rest of it to show people how they can be involved, how *they* can make a difference. That's why I do it."

Tricia huffed and smirked in reflection. "Honestly, it's the one part of being Beacon I was completely oblivious to when I decided to do it. If I'd known being in the spotlight so much was part of the gig, I might've thought twice about it. Heck," she added, chuckling, "the reason I decided to wear a cape was to hide my butt in those tights out in public."

"I suppose," Darci said, searching Tricia's eyes and then hanging her head slightly. "And for what it's worth, you probably don't need to worry about hiding it," she finally said, with a smirk and soft chuckle. "The suit does really work for you."

"Thanks," Tricia said, smiling back. "So tell me, if you're willing, that is, how did you get your abilities?"

"Same as you," Darci replied nonchalantly, shrugging slightly. "I was upstairs when the accident happened."

"No one else was supposed to be in the building," Tricia recalled. "Any office hours or other activities were canceled that day."

"Well, I guess no one bothered to pass that on to *me*, then, did they?" Darci snapped. "I was waiting in my professor's office when something ripped through me out of the blue. I thought I was being torn apart."

Tricia winced. *I remember that all too well.*

Darci took a shallow breath and blew it out. "Anyway, I don't remember much. Somehow, I got back to my room. I was in agony for days, and exposure to any light...any light at all...made me want to scream. Just when I thought I was going to die—and frankly, I was glad for death at that point—I gave myself over to it, and for some reason, the pain went away, and all this was part of me." She held up her hand, and the shadows in the room swirled around them for a few seconds, and then, with a flick of her wrist, they dissipated.

"Interesting," Tricia said. "So you can use the shadows to manipulate physical objects?" Darci nodded. "And travel from one place to another?" Darci nodded again. Tricia brushed her hair back and rubbed her chin. "Some of that fits with the experiment we were doing. We were attempting to combine dark energy with holographic projections to create virtual instrumentality, to let us interact with physical objects using only projected energy. During the accident, some of the released dark energy must have transferred some of that to you."

"Seems so," Darci agreed.

"And this sensation we share? This pulsing feeling?"

Darci shook her head slightly. "No, that's new. I had never felt that before the night we met in your townhouse. It's also how I found you here just now. I had no idea where you were; your records in the system are restricted, so I counted on it to locate you, and it worked."

"Well, then," Tricia replied, "sounds like we have a connection, something in common after all."

Darci scoffed and turned her head sharply to look toward the window. "Hardly," Darci said, turning back to face Tricia. "Yes, we may have something in common about our powers, but any *connection*—" Darci made air quotes with her fingers "—ends there. People like you always have someone looking out for you, watching your back. I, and people like me, have to spend days alone, in pain, and sort things for ourselves when things go wrong."

"I am truly sorry you had to go through that alone, Darci," Tricia said sympathetically.

"Save it," Darci said dismissively. "I don't need your pity. There's a lot of pity and sympathy to go around, but when it comes to doing something, well, then there's just always something more important, isn't there? It's an old story. My people have been pushed around for hundreds of years. Isolated, persecuted, and murdered on reservations carved out of land that's too worthless for anyone else to want. Sure, there's lots of sympathy, but in the end, no one came to help. We were left to make it on our own, trying to grow crops out of stones, taking menial service jobs in neighboring towns and cities, and building casinos and tourist traps to make barely enough money to feed and educate ourselves."

Darci leaned forward, and she poked the top of the table between them with her finger. "I'm in pain almost all the time, but I cope with it. I am learning how to deal with whatever has happened to me, how to turn it into an advantage, something I could use to change my life and maybe the lives of others. My people figured things out, and so will I."

"So, is that what you are looking for?" Tricia asked. "Some kind of revenge or retribution for what's happened to you or your people?"

"No! Of course not." Darci said, scowling. "I want to see a world built on equality...fairness...justice. Where anyone gets a fair chance regardless of their skin color or culture or heritage. That's what I want, and that's what Director Sorensen offered me. He gave me an opportunity to use what I have as part of something bigger to help *make* that vision a reality, not just hope for it."

Tricia nodded. "I get that. I really do," she said,

"As if," Darci huffed, again looking at the far wall. She stared at nothing for a few seconds, and her face relaxed. "I saw you, you know," she finally said, more softly and calmly. "Around campus. I made a point of finding you, actually. You were all the talk for a while, how you suffered this terrible accident, how you were in some kind of coma, and then miraculously recovered. Of course you did; the university spared no expense in making sure you got all the care and attention you needed, and you did, didn't you?" She turned back toward Tricia. "I watched and wondered if you'd had any side effects or acquired any abilities like I did, but I saw nothing. I figured once again I was alone, but then...but then Beacon appeared on the scene, and I *knew*. I knew then you had, and honestly, part of me was relieved. Despite how angry I was at how you were misusing your abilities and status, at least I wasn't alone anymore."

"So, if you were feeling all this, why didn't you come talk to me?" Tricia asked.

"Oh, I thought about it," Darci replied, turning back to face her. "More than once. In the end, I just didn't want to risk exposing myself. I didn't know who you might be working with behind the scenes, and people like you are always protected by the people in charge. People like me, well, not so much."

"But surely you had friends or family you could confide in?"

Darci exhaled sharply through her lips and rolled her eyes. "And give my mother more of a reason to consider me an outsider...a freak? I don't think so."

Tricia nodded. *Yeah, I get that part*, she thought as Darci continued.

"My mother drove my father out of the house when I was ten. He tried to stay in touch, but my mother did everything she could to shut that down. We've been talking recently, but we aren't close. It's pretty clear to me that his new wife doesn't want to be reminded of his life before her, and a grown daughter is a pretty big reminder."

Darci took a deep sigh. "The worst part about his leaving was that it let my mother put her full attention on me, and no matter what I did, it wasn't good enough. Not pretty enough, not smart enough, not athletic enough, not popular enough. There were times I thought I was going to lose my mind. All she wanted me to do was get my head down out of the stars and find a job on the reservation pushing trinkets or serving drinks, drinks I'd rather spit in than serve to a bunch of smug tourists. Not that those are mutually exclusive, of course." She smirked mischievously.

"When I won the scholarship that got me into Crystal Bay U, I was thrilled that I finally had a chance to live my dream, but what did my mother do? My mother literally spat on the ground when I told her. She called me *Diné Ana'í*, a traitor. She turned her back and barely spoke a word to me from then until the day I left for school. She didn't even come to the little party the village threw to send me off, and even though she has helped with some of the fees and expenses, my mother hasn't spoken to me since I've been here.

"So, no, family wasn't an option for me," Darci concluded, pursing her lips and pushing her hair back.

Tricia nodded slowly, her lips curled downward. "I feel that," she said softly. "My mom is quite the piece of work, too."

"What, didn't she get you the prom dress you wanted?" Darci sneered.

"That's enough!" Tricia said through her teeth. Her eyebrows narrowed, and she squeezed the armrest of her chair. Darci's eyes widened a bit as Tricia's fingers sank into the metal, deforming it in her grip. "I've had it with your judgy, holier-than-thou attitude. No, as a matter of fact, she didn't buy me the prom dress I wanted because *she wasn't there*! Marys, my mother, bailed on my father and me when I was a little girl. I never heard from her growing up. My father was everything to me, and when he was killed, it tore me apart. I was about your age when he was shot to death by a couple of low-lifes in a gas station robbery, and my mother was nowhere to be found. I don't know what would have happened to me if I hadn't had some close friends and family to pull me through. The only time I heard from my mother after my dad died was when she filed a lawsuit to try to challenge his will and take the property he left me.

"The judge threw out the case, and I haven't talked to her since. I'm very sure, though, that if Marys knew about me and what I could do, the only thing she'd care about would be how to exploit it for her own personal gain. So don't judge me, pretending you know what my life was like because you don't. You don't know someone until you know them, so yes, when you talk about people taking advantage of others and having to go things alone, I do understand...all too well."

I wonder how she'll respond to that, Tricia pondered, waiting patiently while Darci just sat there for several seconds, staring blankly at Tricia. She was clearly speechless and taken off guard by Tricia's surprising recount of her relationship with her mother.

Finally, Darci blinked a few times and took a deep breath. "Perhaps you do get it then," she said. "Perhaps you can see how important it is that we show them...show everyone...what a better world we can make with our gifts. With your help, I know we can," she said hesitantly, her eyes seeking Tricia's approval.

Tricia scoffed. "Better world? Seriously, Darci? Look around here, at me," she said sarcastically, sweeping her arms toward the room. "Does this look like a better world to you? Am I living in a better world right now?!" She pointed toward the door. "What about the others here, Darci? The ones being experimented on. Tortured. Do you think they are looking forward to some better world?" Tricia slapped her hand on the surface of the table. Darci jumped. "What about that girl who died last week? Izzy...Izzy was her name, wasn't it? You—" she pointed at Darci "—you brought her here, didn't you?" Darci's mouth turned down, lips squeezed tightly, her eyes moistening, but she said nothing. "Do you think Izzy was thinking about a better world when she exploded and took those people with her? Do you?!"

Darci's lip started to quiver. She tried to speak, but her breath caught. Composing herself, she swallowed hard and replied, "Sacrifices have always been necessary when making great changes. It's unavoidable."

Tricia sniffed and smirked. "That's not you talking, Darci. That's Sorensen. It's a line straight out of the cult leader's handbook. History books are full of dictators and power-mongers asking people to sacrifice themselves for the greater good. You don't have to look too far back in our recent events to find narcissists bent on wielding power by convincing people there was some great evil that only they could save everyone from if only they had absolute power, if they were only given immunity to violate the very principles, laws, and values on which our country was founded. They say they'll save the world, but their hate, greed, and ambition inevitably make the world worse, and innocent people suffer and die for nothing."

Tricia sat forward and earnestly looked into Darci's eyes. "Look, I get the vision. I want a better world. I want a world where people treat each other with respect and fairness, where they don't take advantage of the weak and poor, but *how* we make the world better is the important part. It can't be arbitrarily forced on people through brute strength and fear. The ends don't justify the means because there actually aren't any ends to what we are trying to do. There are only the means because making a better world is not a destination. It's a journey, and the steps we take on that journey are *all* that matters."

Tricia looked into Darci's eyes for a second, then shook her head and sat back in her chair. "I'll tell you this, Darci, with absolute certainty. As selfish and unfeeling as my mother is, if she knew I was using my powers to kidnap people so they could be tortured and killed in the name of making a better world, even she would be appalled and disgusted and probably call me a monster. And she'd be right."

Darci opened her mouth and then closed it without saying a word. Instead, she stood up and spun toward the door. Tricia saw Darci lift her hand to her face as she yanked open the door, bolted into the hall, and slammed the door behind her. Tricia followed her to the door. Through the wall, she could feel the rapid and sharp rhythmic vibrations emanating from Darci pause, motionless just outside the door, for several seconds before finally moving slowly away down the hallway.

Maybe...just maybe, Tricia thought as the pulsing faded into the distance.

Where are you? Harris thought. Before him, on his desk, lay several commpads, all displaying case files and statistics that reinforced what the reporter on the news stream playing in his office was saying. Crime was up across the board in Crystal Bay, and Beacon had not been seen in almost two weeks.

He looked up at the news stream. The graphic at the bottom of the screen echoed his sentiment, "Where is Beacon?" The reporter was interviewing a series of people, all of whom had been a recent victim or were otherwise worried about the increasing crime wave, making them feel less safe in the city.

Of course, the police had been working overtime to try to get ahead of it, but as good as Crystal Bay's finest were, they weren't superheroes, and the criminals, held at bay for a year now by Beacon's presence, had clearly noticed her absence and were coming out of the woodwork in droves.

Harris rubbed his chin. *Maybe this new citizen's neighborhood watch program will*— he wondered as a chime from one of the commpads on his desk interrupted his thought. He jabbed the pad impatiently. "Yes, Sheri, what is it?"

"Someone here to see you," the voice of his assistant said. "A Doctor Marni Haskell."

Carling's friend. Harris checked the time. "Does she have an appointment?"

"No, she doesn't, but she says it is urgent, and she needs to see you."

Harris pondered for a second. "When's my next appointment, Sheri?"

"Forty-five minutes," she replied.

"Ok, send her in. Remind me in thirty, please."

"Will do," Sheri said and ended the call.

Harris stood up, turned off the news stream playing on the large wall monitor, and collected up the mass of commpads and other materials related to the escalating crime rates. Just as he'd finished stacking them neatly to the side of his desk, the door opened, and in swept the strikingly beautiful woman he recognized immediately as Doctor Marni Haskell. The pictures of her in his Beacon files didn't lie; her bouncy red hair and piercing green eyes gave her away immediately. Judging from the practical shoes, slacks, and jacket she was wearing, he assumed she'd come straight from the hospital.

She closed the door behind her and walked briskly and purposefully toward his desk, giving him barely enough time to make his way around the side of the desk to greet her. He extended his hand to welcome her. "Hello, Doctor Haskell. Pleased to meet you." He caught a brief whiff of her perfume, forcing him to double down on, and somewhat regret, his resolve to keep this strictly professional.

"Likewise," Marni said. "Thank you for seeing me, DA Harris."

Harris gestured towards a small table with chairs on the opposite side of the room from the monitor. He pulled out a chair for Marni, then one for himself, and they both sat facing each other. "How can I help you today, Doctor Haskell?"

"She's been missing for almost two weeks, so I want to know what you are doing to find her," Marni said directly, wasting no time to come to the point.

Interesting, Harris thought, carefully maintaining his courtroom face to avoid betraying anything he might be thinking. "Who, Doctor Haskell? Who is missing?"

"Tricia Carling, of course," Marni replied.

"Well, unfortunately, my office doesn't deal with missing persons, at least not directly. It might be best if I took you downstairs and directed you to the right department for filing a report."

Marni huffed. Leaning forward, she rested her elbow on the table between them. "Seriously, DA Harris, I don't think the police are the right ones to help when it comes to our *mutual* friend, the one who moonlights in a black and yellow suit, jumping around the city's rooftops at night fighting crime, do you?" She locked eyes with Harris and frowned. "Look, I know that you *know*, so how about we get to it and stop playing games?"

Very interesting, he thought, studying her face for a moment. *So, Carling has told others about herself after all.* Harris steepled his fingers in front of his chest. "Very well, assuming I do know what you are talking about," he replied, letting one side of his mouth curl upward slightly, "wouldn't the university be the best place to start if you're concerned about her whereabouts?"

Marni smirked back, obviously getting his meaning, nodded once, and then sat back in her chair. "That's what has me stirred up, actually. I did get a message from her, or rather one that *looked* like it came from her, but I'll come back to that. Honestly, I was a bit put out that she'd tell me in a message like that, but I figured I'd hear from her again soon and would take it up with her then. However, a few days later, I got a call from the university's HR department. I'm Tricia's emergency contact. When the call came, I almost had a heart attack. Feared the worst, you know?" Harris nodded.

"They asked me if I knew how to contact her. It seems she'd left some important things up in the air, and her team needed to get in touch with her urgently. They'd reached out to someone named Patel, who, in turn, directed the request to HR, who then called me. I told them I didn't, and when I asked what they knew, all they could say was that she'd filed a short-notice request for a leave of absence."

Harris nodded. "That's the same thing they told me," he admitted. Marni chuckled softly. "They said it was simply filed as a personal family matter, but without a warrant, they couldn't say anything more due to privacy concerns."

"See, that's the part that first made me suspicious," Marni jumped in. "Tricia doesn't have much family, just two aunts on her father's side and her mother. I called her aunts, and they didn't know anything. As for her mother—" Marni widened her eyes, puffed her cheeks, and blew out in mock trepidation "—if Marys had gotten in touch with her, there's no way Tricia would not have called me immediately about it. No, DA Harris, she wasn't called away on some urgent family issue. I'm sure of that."

"You mentioned the message she sent you, that you had some concerns about that?"

Marni nodded. "Yes, after I spoke with the university, I re-read the messages she supposedly sent me when she left. Something about them had been nagging at me, but I couldn't put my finger on it." Marni pulled her commpad out of her bag and started tapping and scrolling feverishly. "Honestly, I was probably too ticked off to pay closer attention at the time," she admitted, still scrolling until she apparently found what she was looking for and stopped.

She looked up at Harris, who nodded for her to continue, and then she started reading from the device. "So first she says, 'Hey Marni, Sorry for the short notice, but I have to head out of town unexpectedly. Don't worry. I'll be back in touch as soon as I can.' The message is signed just 'Trish.'" Marni tapped again. "Then I answer, saying, 'Oh, okay. I hope everything is all right. Do you need me to stop by to take care of Rascal while you're away?' You see, I'm already irked that she's sent me a message instead of calling me," she added, waving her hand in the air before tapping the commpad once more. "To which she replied, 'Yeah, Thanks, Marni. That would be great. I know he will be glad to see you,' again, signed just 'Tricia.'"

Marni set the commpad down on the table and looked up at Harris. "Tricia did not write that, DA Harris. Somebody wanted me to think she did, but she didn't. I'm absolutely sure of it."

Harri's eyebrows furrowed a bit. "What makes you think so, Doctor Haskell? Nothing seems to stand out as particularly out of the ordinary."

Marni snorted again. "First of all, once I got over being miffed that she didn't call me, I realized that she absolutely *would* have called me. If something so urgent came up, so urgent that she'd leave her team hanging at work...which she'd never do, either, I might add...she wouldn't have just sent me a message. She would have called."

Marni pointed down at the commpad on the table. "And these messages...she usually calls me 'Marns', not 'Marni', and she never signs her messages to me 'Tricia'. It's always 'L-comma-T', Love, T. And," she said, tossing her hands up for emphasis, "she knows that cat can't stand me, so there's no way she'd say Rascal would be glad to see me."

"Maybe she was being funny, saying it sarcastically," Harris offered.

Marni shook her head. "No, she wouldn't say it like that. Plus, Rascal's a 'she'."

"A typo?" he said.

Marni rolled her eyes and frowned. "Do you have any siblings, DA Harris?"

Harris shook his head. "No, I don't."

Marni locked eyes with him. "Tricia Carling is more than my best friend, DA Harris. She's my *sister*. She has been since our freshman year of college together. There's nothing we don't tell each other, as you well know by now. We know each other better than any two people have a right to know each other. I could probably tell you what she had for breakfast without having to ask first, and she could probably do the same."

Marni sat forward, her tone becoming more urgent, more pleading. "When I went to her apartment that first night to feed the cat, I *knew* something was wrong. Tricia is very particular about her personal spaces. The furniture was slightly out of place. Books on the bookshelf were out of order. The picture of her and her dad that she keeps on the bookshelf had a different frame than it had before. Similar, but just slightly different. Someone had gone to great lengths to make her front room look normal, but in very subtle ways, it was off. Just like these messages. Close, but wrong.

"Something happened in her house, and someone is trying very hard to make us think it didn't. Please, *please*, believe me. She's in trouble. I just know it."

Marni sat back in her chair again, took a deep sigh, and let her shoulders slump, openly releasing tension and pent-up emotion she'd obviously been carrying for several days. Harris looked at her, studying him, looking for some sign that she had convinced him. He brought his steepled fingers up to his lips, thought for a moment, and finally said, "I believe you." Relief swept over Marni's face, and for a moment, Harris thought she might break down and cry, but she didn't.

"While what you've said is very circumstantial and subjective," Harris said evenly. Marni started to interrupt, but he held up his hand to ask silently that she give him a chance to finish. "However, coming from someone as close to her as you clearly are, it is very compelling. Plus, it is also evident to me from what I know of her and what little time we've spent together that Doctor Carling is a person of deep conviction. For her to abandon her team at the lab, as well as her other activities, without so much as a word for such an extended period of time strikes me as completely out of character for someone who has invested as much as she has in her, um, work."

Marni took another deep breath. "I'm very glad to hear you think so. Yes, that's exactly the type of person she is, and why this has me so worried." She sat forward expectantly, "So, what happens now?"

"I have already been making some informal inquiries," Harris admitted, "but I think I will need to convince the right people that we need to treat this more formally going forward. We need to do it quietly, of course; investigating the city's resident superheroine is a delicate matter. However, I believe we have more than enough grounds to start a more serious investigation while, of course, protecting Doctor Carling in the process."

A chime sounded from one of the commpads on Harris' desk. *Sheri's reminder*, he realized. Harris looked back toward the desk to confirm and then stood, gesturing with his hand for Marni to do the same. "That would be the reminder for my next appointment, Doctor Haskell, but please rest assured, I will immediately follow up on what we've discussed and do everything I can to see to it that our mutual friend returns to us safely as soon as possible. I will keep you in the loop should anything develop."

"Thank you, DA Harris. Thank you very much," Marni said, smiling, and shook his hand.

As she turned toward the door, a final point occurred to Harris. "Just one more thing, Doctor Haskell," he said after her. She stopped and turned back to face him. "I want you to be very careful. Don't take any unnecessary risks."

"Why?" she asked.

"Because, if our rather formidable friend is being held against her will, there are really only two possibilities. The first scenario is that someone has found a way to overcome or neutralize her powers. That would give us all a reason to be concerned, but the second, and more likely, I believe, is that someone has found some kind of leverage over her. Knowing her, one of the few things I can think of that would potentially give someone that kind of hold over Tricia Carling would be the people she loves."

Marni nodded slowly, pursing her lips. "Understood. I'll be careful," she promised solemnly and left the room.

Harris watched the door close behind her. After he'd given her several seconds to clear the outer office, he tapped the commpad to signal his assistant.

"Yes, Mr. Harris?" Sheri responded.

"As soon as my appointment ends, please get Commissioner Weathers on a private channel for me. No, better yet, call him now and ask him to clear his calendar so I can come down there and talk to him instead."

"What should I tell him this is about?" Sheri asked. "You know he will ask."

Harris pondered for a second and replied, "Please tell him that the special help he requested regarding those disappearances might have done too good a job and now may have become one herself."

Impact

Tricia sat on the cold table in the examination room, living her worst nightmare. She remembered how thrilled she'd been when she was finally cleared by her medical team after the accident and no longer had to report for the routine follow-up examinations. Yet here she was, being held against her will and being forced to endure exactly that, no less.

The days and weeks since she'd been brought here had been filled with endless poking and prodding and taking samples of this and that, followed by test after test after test. Tricia had hoped after the first round that it would abate, but if anything, it had grown even more intense, more comprehensive. She was constantly under a microscope, studied and assessed. There was one key difference now, though, that made this situation far, far more frightening.

Before, the fear had loomed over her head that during one of those checkups during her recovery, somehow those doctors would inadvertently uncover her unique condition, and she would be discovered.

That was not the case here.

That cat was already out of the bag.

Now, it was the worry of what they would learn about her powers and, worse, what they would then try to do with them.

And, if that weren't unnerving enough, it was all being performed by a team led by Rene Thornton, a woman who had studied her before and, using only a tiny fraction of what she could learn here in this place, had nearly ended her career as Beacon before it had barely gotten off the ground.

If it was anyone else, Tricia might've rested a bit easier, but Rene was a genius, and if anyone could unravel the secrets of her abilities, it would be her.

Every day since she'd arrived, Sofia escorted her to and from her sessions with Rene and her team, and every chance she got, Tricia studied The Workshop, looking for a way to escape. She studied the cameras, door locks, windows, even the ceiling and floor panels, everything she could, but so far, she'd found nothing. Whoever designed the security systems was top-notch, but Tricia knew anything designed by a human had to have a flaw. All she had to do was find it.

I can be patient...but not too patient.

Of course, she could force her way out at any time, but she had not yet come to the point where sacrificing the people she loved or the life to which she desperately wanted to return was a valid option. Tricia would find a way, but increasingly she was coming to believe that even if she found some chink in the armor of this place, she was going to need someone's help to escape cleanly, without retribution.

But who?

One obvious choice was right in front of her. While she waited patiently on the examination table, reflecting on her situation, Tricia studied Rene working at the counter across the room. *She never ceases to surprise me*, Tricia thought as she watched Rene efficiently and methodically work through a series of instruments, checking the settings and calibrations in preparation for another barrage of testing. In the time they'd spent together there in The Workshop, Tricia, to her own amazement, had come to realize, and even appreciate, two very key things about Doctor Rene Thornton.

First, despite their history, Rene was one of the few people here who treated Tricia with respect. To everyone else, except perhaps Sofia, who treated her almost like a houseguest, Tricia was just an asset, a laboratory test subject. Rene, however, treated her almost as a colleague. There was no question Rene was calling the shots in terms of the research and the protocol, and, as such, Tricia was obligated to comply with her directions, but Rene never held it over her or made her feel any less of a person for it.

Second, and somewhat more of a puzzle, was the realization that Rene was being completely authentic and staying very true to her word. Rene was, and always will be, a survivor first and foremost, and given their past, trust was a hard thing to come by. It was hard for Tricia to believe that if push came to shove, Rene wouldn't sell out everything she learned to save her own skin, but it was also clear to Tricia that Rene was not in any hurry with her research either. While Tricia was sure Rene was not being fully open and forthcoming with her about what she was doing or what she had learned so far, Tricia was equally sure Rene wasn't divulging everything to anyone else either.

That doesn't mean I can trust her, though.

Still, she said she'd be walking a fine line. She's making a good show of it, whether she's hiding anything or not, Tricia thought as she reflected on the past several days. Under Rene's supervision, Tricia had undergone a battery of tests that put what her medical team had done after her accident to utter shame. Tissue samples, blood and other fluid samples, medical scans, and a plethora of diagnostic and functional images had all been taken, many of them multiple times.

And those were just the tests she understood. Others included Tricia being hooked up to strange, unfamiliar devices that Rene said were designed to measure how sensitive and reactive organic tissue—her tissue—would be to various types of energies, the same energies The Workshop scientists were using to try to replicate her abilities in others.

For these tests, they asked Tricia to try to channel different kinds of flows and manipulate them. Most of the ones they asked her to attempt were completely imperceptible to her. She displayed some affinity with a few, but nothing even close to her native energies. The rest ranged from just uncomfortable and disorienting all the way to the point where touching them in the slightest made even her teeth hurt.

The protocols didn't stop with assessing her physically either. She'd undergone extensive psychological evaluations and personality profiles as well. It seemed if Tricia's body produced it, her mind thought it, or her heart felt it, Rene and her team wanted a sample of it.

Tricia felt probed, violated, and exhausted, and she knew it wasn't going to be over any time soon. However, it was important she endure it and, for the sake of her friends, play along until she found some way out.

And if I am going to trust her, it will mean getting out of my own way and putting the past behind me.

Can I do that?

Instrument in hand, Rene turned and walked towards her. "Shall we get started, Tricia?" Rene said, giving the device in her hand a final check. "I'll need you to roll up your sleeve."

"Sure, but don't take too long, ok?" Tricia replied sarcastically as she turned up the cuff on the scrubs she was wearing to expose her forearm to the elbow. "I'm a busy woman, and I have places I need to be."

Rene chuckled. "I'll do my best not to hold you up," she retorted with a sly smile. Rene took Tricia's arm in her hand and surveyed it briefly. "Now, be sure to hold still," she warned, laying the instrument against Tricia's skin. "Despite your miraculous healing abilities, I see no reason to take a chunk out of your arm simply to get a few epidermal cells."

"Skin cells?" Tricia asked. "Why would you be interested in skin cells when you have so many other, more interesting pieces of me in little jars already?"

Rene chuckled again. "Well, dear, it's quite simple," she said, making a small adjustment on the device and then peering at Tricia over the top rim of her glasses like she was once again the professor in one of her lectures. "You can project levels of electromagnetic radiation that would fry a normal person almost instantly, yet you are completely unharmed by them. I am hoping that these cells can provide some clue as to how you not only survive it, but how you can focus and control those energies with such precision."

Tricia nodded. "Makes sense," she agreed.

"Glad you approve," Rene said with a half smile. "Now, this may sting a bit..." The device buzzed briefly, causing Tricia to wince slightly as it took the sample. "Excellent," Rene said, lifting the device away from Tricia's forearm, leaving behind a small red patch where several layers of skin used to be. Tricia instinctively reached towards the spot on her arm, but Rene wagged her finger to stop her. "Don't rub it," she cautioned. "Give me a second, and I'll get a bandage."

"No need," Tricia replied, raising her arm for Rene to see. The redness was rapidly fading, and within seconds, it was completely gone.

"Remarkable," Rene said. "That happens completely on its own?"

"Yes," Tricia replied matter-of-factly. "It's entirely reflexive at this point. I mean, I can control it, but the healing will generally kick in all by itself."

Rene nodded. "That means your body has integrated your abilities at some level and can tap into them without conscious thought. Almost as if you'd been born with them, like birds knowing how to fly instinctively."

"Yes, something like that," Tricia agreed.

Rene pondered this as she returned the instrument to the counter across the room. Tricia rolled down her sleeve and waited for whatever would come next. "If you don't mind, Tricia," Rene said, turning back toward her, "I've always wondered how you deactivated that nuclear device at Meyers Tower. None of the accounts I've been able to find provide any details. Are you willing to tell me how you managed it?"

Careful, Tricia, Tricia thought to herself. *Some cats should stay in the bag.* "I'll be honest, Rene," she said carefully, "when I was in the heat of the moment, it looked like I was going to fail and likely be killed, but somehow, my body knew what to do, and, without thinking, I accessed some new facets to my abilities. I was able to bleed out the energy and suppress the reaction in the core until the chain reaction fell apart, and it shut down."

"Amazing," Rene said. "So again, something instinctive took over, and, under stress, some new aspects of your powers manifested to cope with the situation."

"It seems so," Tricia agreed.

"That is a theme I've uncovered in my research," Rene shared. "In other subjects, extreme stress or life-threatening circumstances have led to significant changes in parahuman abilities." She smiled and sat on the stool next to the table where Tricia was sitting. "Not always with the same positive results you've achieved, though."

Tricia shrugged. "This entire thing has been a work in progress. Not knowing what might happen next—what new surprises they have in store for me—has always been a downside of it all."

"I can see how that would be challenging at times," Rene said empathetically. "It does surprise me, though, that, being a scientist, you haven't spent more time studying and understanding what you are capable of. I would think you'd be much further ahead of all of us in terms of understanding your, um, condition."

Tricia recoiled slightly at the implied rebuke. "It's risky, Rene," she responded. "It is very difficult to find time where I can be sure I won't be discovered, and frankly, there are limits to what I can do with the equipment in the lab without raising suspicion." Rene nodded as Tricia continued, "Part of the reason I was put on probation last year was because they discovered some discrepancies in the lab's system logs, discrepancies I'd created when I altered them to cover up some experiments I had done to measure my powers." Tricia blew out sharply, remembering her meeting with Demerov and how sure she'd been she was finished at the university. "They didn't trace it to me directly, but those irregularities on top of everything else around the accident itself were part of why I—and the lab—were put on probation. From that point onward, I knew I had to be extremely careful about using the lab in any way that could lead someone in my direction, if you know what I mean."

"Hmmm," Rene said. "Yes, I can see how that would be problematic, but fortunately," she said with a sly grin, "we have no such concerns here, now do we, dear?"

"No," Tricia said with a sarcastic grin of her own, "we have a whole different set of concerns."

The smile faded from Rene's face. "Indeed, we do," she conceded. "However, even if you couldn't do any formal testing, surely you were keeping some kind of notes? Observations? For instance, other than new abilities manifesting in times of stress, have you noticed any changes in your baser abilities over time?"

She's fishing, Tricia warned herself. *Play along...but don't get played.*

"Somewhat, yes," Tricia cautiously admitted. "I learned early on that my abilities have a multiplicative effect on my normal physical condition. At first, I thought I just got a boost from them, but I found out as I conditioned my body and increased my natural strength and speed, the effect from the flows I can channel multiplies those gains," Tricia explained. "Any other changes, I simply chalked up to becoming more proficient and comfortable using them."

Rene nodded and fetched her commpad from the utility table next to her. She tapped and scrolled it a few times before settling on a page that interested her. "That's what my results indicate as well, Tricia. It's definitely multiplicative, but it's also more than that." She held up the commpad so Tricia could see the charts on the screen. "The factor isn't linear. It is geometric. Granted, the exponent now is rather small, just a fraction over one, but it's clear that as you draw more energy, the effect on your power output is exponential."

Tricia took the commpad and studied the display intently. "If that's true, then..."

"...if that exponent grows, and if you could draw enough energy, your capabilities would be staggering," Rene finished for her. "There would be literally nothing on the planet that could stand up to the amount of power you could bring to bear."

Rene paused momentarily to let what she was saying sink in before continuing, "Further, it's also very likely that the exponent is, in fact, increasing over time. Again, it's small now, but as you continue to channel flows of energy, I'm betting that what you are chalking up to 'proficiency' is really the result of minute increases in your power conversion exponent over time."

Tricia studied the display for a few more minutes and then, shaking her head slowly, handed the commpad back to Rene. "I had no idea," she said with astonishment.

"I'm glad we could give you something to make the interruption of your busy schedule a little worth your while, then," Rene said with a playfully mocking tone. She then looked down at her commpad and began to tap at it randomly. "I also appreciate your honesty with me, Tricia," she said almost in a whisper as she pretended to be engrossed with the device in her hands. "I fully understand your feeling cautious and guarded about sharing information. I would too if I were in your position, and I guess, in a different sense, I am, but if we can find a way to create even the smallest amount of trust and cooperation between us, it will go a long way toward getting us both through this." Rene looked up sideways into Tricia's face. "Do you get my meaning?"

"Mm hm," Tricia replied softly, likewise pretending to take an interest in Rene's commpad. "I believe I do."

"Very good, then," Rene said, resuming a normal conversational tone. "While we have a few minutes, and since we are being so open and honest, I also wanted to tell you that I may have been wrong about Beacon."

Not something I'd expect Rene to admit... "How so?" Tricia asked curiously.

"Do you remember when I told you I admired what you were trying to do as Beacon, but that I felt it was a waste of time, that people were beyond hope?"

"You mean when you had me handcuffed and trapped in that storage container? Right before you were going to seal me inside and put me to sleep? You mean then?" Tricia replied with a mock sneer.

Rene chuckled. "Yes, that time."

"I remember...vividly."

"I've done quite a bit of research on Beacon and her activities over the past year as part of preparing for your arrival," Rene told her. "I am very impressed with what Beacon has done and with the effect she's had on the city." Rene set the commpad down on the table and pushed her glasses up over her hair onto the top of her head. "It goes far beyond just stopping crime in the streets. The charitable foundation, your public appearances, how nearly every child in Crystal Bay has a Beacon lunchbox or backpack." Tricia scoffed as Rene snickered. "Seriously, you should be very proud of what you—and she—have accomplished in such a short time."

I can't believe I'm hearing Rene of all people saying this, Tricia thought as she stared into Rene's eyes. *Where is this coming from?*

"It's nice of you to say, Rene. Shocking as well, truth be told, but nice. Honestly, though, some days...many days actually...it just doesn't feel that way at all," Tricia said with a shrug. "It feels like the more I do, the more there is to do, that people just fight against trying to make things better sometimes." She turned to look at Rene, hunching her shoulders slightly in resignation. "To be completely honest, part of what angers me so much about Sorensen's plan is that deep down, I'm afraid he might be right, that people ultimately will only respond to fear, intimidation, and force."

Tricia sat up and tipped her head back, flopping her ponytail between her shoulder blades. "If I get out of this and return to Crystal Bay, I'm sincerely afraid of what I will find, to see how bad things have become while I've been out of commission," she confessed, looking up at the ceiling. "I wonder if I'll really even be missed."

Rene tipped her head to the side slightly. "Don't sell yourself short, Tricia," she said. "Sure, some of the crimes have spiked recently in Crystal Bay during your absence, but they are nothing like they were before Beacon came onto the scene."

"Give them time," Tricia retorted.

Rene pursed her lips and regarded Tricia for several seconds. "I probably shouldn't show you this," she finally said, flicking again on her commpad, "but not everyone has been taking Beacon's disappearance lying down." Rene handed the commpad to Tricia.

"Read it if you want, but long story short, not long after you vanished, a group of people banded together and, with some help from your charity foundation, formed a citizens' watch program," Rene told her.

The headline on the screen read, "Where is Beacon?" Tricia rolled her eyes briefly and then quickly skimmed the screen. "Beacon's Eyes and Ears? BEEs?" she asked with a short laugh. "Kind of a tortured acronym, isn't it?"

Rene grinned. "What do you expect, Tricia? Black and yellow suit? It's even in your name. BEE-con? It was only a matter of time, wasn't it?"

Tricia laughed. "I suppose not," she said. "I just hadn't made that connection until now."

"Seriously?" Rene challenged skeptically.

"Seriously," Tricia admitted. *Casey's nickname for me suddenly makes a lot more sense*, she thought, and laughed again.

"Well, name aside, you have inspired people enough for them to take some initiative and pick up the slack while you are missing in action," Rene said. "To me, nothing says 'lasting impact' like people actually stepping up on their own. Remember, Tricia, it's not about changing everyone. It's about changing the right people at the right time in the right place and stirring them into action. It's about giving them options to be better people than they would have had otherwise. This is proof that you, and Beacon, can do that, that you can make the difference you set out to make, and much more of a difference, it seems, than I gave you credit."

Tricia smiled. "Yeah, I guess it is. Thanks for this, Rene. Maybe when I get out of here, and I do mean *when*, things won't be as bad as I was afraid they might be."

"*If* you get out of here," Rene countered jovially, "who knows? You might even make a believer out of me." She placed her hand on Tricia's arm as she stood up. "But don't hold your breath," she added with a sly smirk. "And, speaking of breaths, it is time we moved on to some cardiopulmonary tests. I have a treadmill waiting with your name on it."

Tricia nodded, stepping down off the examination table. *Imagine that*, she thought as she followed Rene out of the room and down the hall. *Encouragement from Rene Thornton, of all people,* she mused, stealing a glance at Rene walking beside her. *Maybe in her own way, she's trying to do for me what I try to do for others, to remind me that I have something to fight for, that what I do does matter, that I really can be that symbol of hope after all...*

When I get out of here.

When WE get out of here.

Alessandra sat in the dimly lit room. As usual, it was much darker than it needed to be; the visor the man sitting across from her was wearing for his conference was more than adequate to shield out the ambient light, but he preferred it dark. He seemed to shun the light, actually, but she didn't mind. She'd grown accustomed to it.

To say that he was her 'manager' or 'supervisor' or even 'boss' was a gross understatement. In another time, she might have called him 'lord' or 'liege'. There was no management or supervision in their working relationship. He spoke, and she acted. She was an extension of him. Her words were his words, and she made no mistake in believing she had any words of her own. Alessandra wasn't the only one in this position. There were others, of course, but today was her turn to be primary.

She took a sip of the steaming tea in front of her. It was one of the few luxuries afforded her, but she was grateful for it. As he spoke during the conference, the sound of his raspy voice made her own throat itch, almost to the point of coughing, but she carefully suppressed it. Alessandra knew that to respond to the sound of his voice in any way other than to execute the directives it carried to the letter would be severely limiting for far more than just her career.

Whatever they are discussing doesn't seem to be going very well, she thought as she took another sip. Alessandra could tell by watching and listening to him. Normally, he was beyond stoic, a rock that never displayed a hint of emotion, but in her time of service, she'd come to recognize the small tells and hints that betrayed what he was feeling. It helped her more effectively serve him and was probably the main reason her name came forward in the rotation as primary more frequently than the others. She indulged herself with a tiny smile hidden behind the teacup. It was obvious to her that if he had been anyone else, he'd likely be throwing things at this point.

Without warning, the call ended, and he took off the headset. "Unfortunate," he said as he set the device onto the charging stand on his desk. He turned toward her, and, in anticipation that she would be called on, she returned her cup to the desktop and sat up straighter. "We may be going on a trip, Alessandra," he said to her.

"To where, sir?" she replied promptly. "I'll make the arrangements."

"Soon," he said with a dismissive wave of his hand. "First, I want you to compile a folio of reports from Director Sorensen at The Workshop. Status reports, requisitions, anything related to his operation and the status of research there. Time is of the utmost urgency, Alessandra. We have much ahead of us to review and very little time to do it."

"Certainly, sir. Right away," she responded obediently. "Will there be anything else?"

He shook his head. "That should be enough to start with, enough to give us an idea of how forthcoming Director Sorensen has actually been with us regarding his work. After that," he said, clasping his hands in front of him and leaning back in his chair pensively, "we will decide what happens next."

Inevitable

A bead of sweat trickled down Tricia's temple as she jogged casually on the treadmill, the latest in Rene's suite of protocols designed to test her abilities. A wide band made of a thick, stretchy material was strapped snugly to her chest, circling her torso just beneath her arms. The material didn't breathe at all, causing a wet layer to build up beneath it against Tricia's skin.

Rene stood nearby, examining the readouts on a bank of instruments that were collecting a variety of data points from the sensors inside the apparatus itself. Pulse, blood oxygen, breathing, every vital imaginable, and according to Rene, the panel also included a number of displays that would record how various energies flowed into her body, potentially giving clues to how they activated her abilities.

In spite of the sweat and her level of exertion, Tricia felt surprisingly cool and comfortable. The sleek material of the bright scarlet compression top and shorts she was wearing was quite effective at wicking away the moisture and keeping her from getting overheated. Interestingly enough, it didn't seem to inhibit her abilities either, and she wondered, as she had done multiple times already, if the material was somehow related to what she had used to make her own costume. Given how well-connected Sorensen and his team appeared to be, it wouldn't have surprised her one bit to discover that they had their fingers in Harold's lab at some point along the way.

As far as the testing protocols went, this one wasn't terrible. It afforded Tricia some exercise that she had sorely been lacking during her stay at The Workshop, and while running wasn't her preference, it did allow her to do what she was doing now. She could close her eyes, listening to the methodical thumping of her feet against the treadmill, and let her mind detach from the world around her and forget, even if just for a few minutes, the true nature of her situation.

"Are you feeling warmed up?" Rene asked, her voice snapping Tricia's self-imposed isolation and drawing her back to the testing room.

"Uh-huh," Tricia replied between breaths.

"Very good," Rene affirmed, turning back to face Tricia. "Now, I'd like you to sprint. Really push yourself."

Tricia responded by digging her toes into the treadmill and launching into a full run. The indicators on Rene's panels all started to climb with her level of exertion. "Hmm. Eighteen miles an hour, give or take," Rene observed casually. "Not bad, Tricia."

"Gee, thanks," Tricia replied, her breaths starting to grow shorter and shorter.

"Now, I've raised the thresholds on your monitor, but don't overdo it," Rene warned her. "Draw a bit on your abilities and keep pushing it. Show me what you've got."

Tricia drew a small amount from the flows around her and channeled them into her speed. Immediately, she felt herself accelerate, the footfalls coming much faster, and the treadmill started to whine in protest. With power coursing through her body, Tricia's breathing slowed, and her gait relaxed.

"Amazing," Rene said. "Your speed has nearly doubled, and all your vitals are slowing back down. That was just a small amount?"

"Yes," Tricia replied, jiggling her wrist to show the green glowing indicator on the monitoring bracelet bouncing against the top of her hand.

"Draw some more, if you please," Rene said, now fixated on the monitors next to her.

Tricia obliged, drawing slightly more and accelerating once again. She felt the bracelet buzz, and the indicator light changed to yellow. Her footfalls came so fast now that they were nearly indistinguishable from each other, and the treadmill's protests grew louder.

"Incredible," Rene exclaimed. "Nearly sixty miles an hour. I assume you're capable of much more?"

Tricia couldn't help but grin. "Oh yeah," she said, her breathing now nearly normal despite the pace she was sustaining. "A lot more."

"How much more, do you think?" Rene asked curiously.

"I timed myself not long after discovering what I could do," Tricia replied. "I topped out in the low triple-digits then. It's probably more now." Rene whistled softly, shaking her head in disbelief.

Tricia's smirk abruptly faded as a disturbing sensation suddenly swept over her. She started to slow, reaching out with her feelings, trying to understand what it meant.

"I need you to keep going, Tricia," Rene said urgently. "We aren't done yet."

"Hold on, Rene," Tricia said with an edge to her voice. "Something's...not right."

"What do you mean?"

"I mean, something is very wrong," Tricia said distinctly, coming to a stop.

"How do you know?" Rene asked, her curiosity piqued once again.

Tricia looked at her, dividing her attention between understanding what she was sensing and explaining it to Rene. "This place has a certain...feel. The energies flowing through the conduits create a certain ambient energy signature. It's hard to describe, but it's similar to how I can feel Darci Jackson when she's nearby."

Rene's eyebrow went up. "You can sense her?"

Tricia nodded briskly. "She can sense me, too. It's like a deep bass beat that is too low to hear, but you feel it instead."

"I see," Rene said. "So what do you feel now?"

"Something is wrong with the flows in the facility, Rene. It's dissonant. Out of harmony. Like I'm listening to an orchestra, and one person is playing badly out of key." Tricia turned toward Rene, her face now a mask of urgency. "We need to go find out, Rene. Something very bad is going to happen. I know it."

Tricia stepped off the treadmill and slid the sensor band off her chest, letting it drop onto the handrail of the treadmill. "Come on, Rene."

"Tricia, we can't just go wandering about the facility on a feeling," Rene said sternly. "If Sorensen found out, it wouldn't go over very well."

"Rene, trust me," Tricia urged her, putting her hand on the latch of the locked door. "Please."

Rene considered Tricia for a few moments and then relented. She sent the codes to unlock the door. As soon as she heard the lock click free, Tricia yanked the door open and swept into the hallway with Rene close on her heels.

Like a bloodhound on the scent of its prey, Tricia led Rene through the corridors, reaching out with her feelings to track the source of the anomaly she felt. They had to backtrack a few times, incurring more skepticism and questioning from Rene, but finally, Tricia stopped outside a door. "Do you know what this is, Rene? What's in here?"

"This is one of the treatment rooms where they do the transformation experiments," Rene replied matter-of-factly.

"Whatever is going on, it's in here. Can you open this door?" Tricia asked urgently.

Rene nodded and tapped a few times on her commpad. "Odd," she said with a puzzled look. "It should be opening, but it won't. No indication why. The pad says it isn't in use, that it's undergoing routine maintenance and calibration."

Tricia frowned and surveyed the door up and down. "Is my monitor still set to the higher thresholds?" she finally asked.

Rene nodded, and wasting no time, Tricia drew on the flows around her and broke in the door with a sharp blow from her shoulder.

As the door fell inward, Tricia and Rene both took a step back, raising their hands to shield their eyes. The room before them was a raging maelstrom of light and color. Vivid blues, yellows, greens, purples, and oranges intertwined in a hypnotic display. Random micro-bursts of white light and what appeared as small chains of lightning erupted between the chromatic whorls chaotically.

"My God!" exclaimed Rene.

"Welcome to my world," muttered Tricia, and then shouted into the room, "Is anybody in there?"

"Yes, we're here," replied a male voice weakly. "Here, in the control room."

"Who is that?" Rene called out.

"Josh. Josh and Angelica," the voice replied. "We were doing a routine calibration of the infusion chair, and one of the conduits in the base ruptured."

"Are you alright?" Tricia asked next.

"I'm ok," Josh replied. "But Angelica was closer to the chair when it happened. Her arm is burned pretty badly, and she's not doing very well. Her breathing is short and labored, and her eyelids are fluttery. I know she's in shock and needs help, but all the comms and other controls are fried. We have to get out of here because if that thing ruptures any further, it's going to blow! It'll probably take out the entire wing if it does."

Tricia pursed her lips, deep in thought. *Do I? Do I help these people after what they've done? What they are trying to do?*

Coming to a decision, she scowled with determination and turned to look at Rene. "Go get help, Rene. I've got this."

"Tricia, you can't," Rene said anxiously. "This isn't just some fire or a bad guy with a gun. Those are the elemental forces of nature rampaging in there. You know that many of them can hurt or even kill you."

"I deal with this every day, Rene. If I don't, these people, and many others, will die. They may not be innocent, but they don't deserve this, and if I don't do it, who will?"

Rene started to object again, but Tricia interrupted her, "Go, Rene! You're wasting time we do not have."

Rene breathed out sharply in resignation, turned, and ran down the hallway. Tricia turned back to the room before her. "I'm coming in. Stay where you are. I'll be right there," she shouted to the two technicians hiding inside.

Tricia stepped into the room. The effect was instantly overwhelming as the flows of energy twisted around her. She pushed back against them, but as they touched her, she felt both pain and exhilaration blended together. The effect was intoxicating. She blinked a few times and shook her head to focus herself, and then, drawing on her dark energy, Tricia cast a shield in front of her.

It was just enough to stem the buffeting of the energy storm around her as she pushed her way into the room. Standing before her in the center of the room was what she assumed was the infusion chair. It looked to Tricia like something out of a dentist horror movie, dark, articulated, and menacing, except that somewhere around the back of it, she saw a suspicious light emanating brightly from the base.

She circled the chair carefully. As she approached the back, she could see a section of torn metal near the base, ragged edges reaching out toward her, with a bright greenish glow shining behind inside. *No question that's the source*, she thought, surveying the rupture. *But what do I do about it?*

Tricia turned to look toward the control room across the room next to her. The door was open, and inside was a woman slouched up against the wall. A man was kneeling next to her. *Angelica and Josh, I presume.*

Angelica's lab coat was scorched, and her arm nearest to Tricia was clearly visible, the flesh blackened by her exposure to the explosion. Her head lay limply on her shoulder. The man's face was pure panic as he stared at Tricia wide-eyed.

"How do I shut this down?" she shouted to him.

Josh paused to think. It was obvious to Tricia he was terrified and not likely to be of much use, but after a few seconds, he finally responded, "You...you have to disconnect the feeder conduit inside the base of the chair. When it detaches, the conduit will self-seal."

Tricia nodded and turned her attention back to the base of the chair. She took a deep breath, steeling herself for what was to come, and then dropped the shield. The energies swarmed over her again, almost knocking her backward, but she stiffened her legs to brace herself. She opened herself to draw on her power, but the waves threatened to flood her. She fought back to only accept a small trickle, just enough for her to reach down and tear the rupture casing away from the base of the chair.

There it is, Tricia realized as she saw the connector inside the exposed base. Squinting her eyes against the intense glow of the exposed breech and still channeling her strength, Tricia reached in and seized the connector. She twisted, feeling the skin on her palm start to burn and blister, but the connector would not budge. Grimacing with effort and pain, she screamed through her teeth, drawing more power to force the connector loose.

As she pulled in more of the flows, a massive wave of energy suddenly struck her. Caught by surprise, her control crumbled momentarily, and the bolus flooded her body. Her strength surged from the massive influx of power, but just as Tricia felt the connector start to give way in her hand, the monitor on her wrist vibrated wildly. She glanced down just in time to see it turn red.

Oh, no, she thought with a gasp, remembering Sorensen's warning.

Someone I love is going to die.

They are going to die because I had to play the hero.

"No point in stopping now, then. What's done is done," Tricia muttered to herself, and after a mournful split-second, she drank in the full power of the energy around her and tightened her grip. "I will not let their sacrifice be for nothing," she said, grimacing, and with an anguished shout and desperate twist, she wrenched the connector free.

There was a small burst of bright white light, and Tricia felt the energies dissipate. The vibrant whorls of color faded rapidly to misty pastels like clouds after a thunderstorm, and in seconds, the maelstrom in the room completely vanished.

Tricia released the flows she held. As they left her body, they took any remaining reserves she had with them. She sank to the floor, rolled onto her back, and just stared up at the ceiling, breathing deeply and slowly in synchrony with the flashing red light of the monitor bracelet on her wrist. Her hand throbbed, but as Tricia's strength began to recover, her healing went to work on the burns, making each pulse of pain slightly more bearable than the one before it.

She wasn't sure how long she lay there before Rene rushed back into the room, trailed by a team of medics carrying bags and pushing a rolling cart with instruments and supplies. One of the medics came over to her, but Rene shooed him away, telling him to help the other two. "I've got Doctor Carling," she heard Rene say.

Tricia saw Rene kneel next to her. "Tricia, can you hear me?" she asked nervously.

Tricia nodded slowly and turned to look at her. "Yeah, I can. I'm okay, Rene. I just need a minute."

"I don't doubt it," Rene replied with a slight rebuke in her voice. "Can you sit up?"

Tricia nodded again and, with a soft groan, pushed herself up onto one elbow. Rene put her hand under Tricia's shoulder and helped her slowly sit up.

While the medics attended to Josh and Angelica in the control room, Tricia sat there quietly with her knees bent and her elbows resting on them, breathing deeply, continuing to gather her strength slowly.

Rene knelt beside her, every part of her betraying the intense worry and concern Rene was obviously feeling. "Are you sure you're okay, Tricia?" She asked.

Tricia looked down at her hand. Already, the blisters had been replaced by new smooth skin, and the redness had faded to a light pink. "Yeah, I am," she said, brushing a lock of hair back out of her eyes. "I will be. It was just...a lot."

"I imagine. Always have to be the hero, don't you?" Rene said with a cluck of her tongue and an added touch of mocking chastisement.

Tricia chuckled once softly. "Seems so," she replied and glanced down at the flashing bracelet. *But at what cost?*

She sighed deeply. *I may never know.*

"Too bad you weren't here, Rene," Tricia said with a weak smile, raising her head slowly to look at Rene. "Just imagine the data you missed out on collecting. I'm sure analyzing it would have kept your team busy for months."

"Next time, I guess," Rene said with a mischievous smirk.

"Not if I have anything to say about it," Tricia replied, and they both chuckled.

Seconds later, Sorensen charged through the door. He quickly surveyed the room, looking first at the team of medics attending the technicians in the control area, and then leveled his eyes at the two women sitting on the floor in front of him beside the wrecked treatment chair.

"I got the alert from your bracelet, Doctor Carling," he announced, his voice barely masking the fury he was bottling up inside. "Before I make too many assumptions based on what I'm seeing, and I am forced to remind you what that transgression will mean for you, tell me exactly what happened here."

Too exhausted to deal with him, Tricia just let her head sink down silently. Rene gave her shoulder a gentle squeeze before glaring up at Sorensen. "For your information, *Director*," Rene answered for her, now seething with anger. "The conduits in the infusion chair ruptured. Tricia sensed it and risked her own life to stop it before it could go critical. She saved their lives —" jabbing a finger toward the control room swarming with medics "—and likely many more."

Sorensen blinked, looked again at the two technicians in the control area, and then back down at Tricia. "Is this true, Doctor Carling?" he finally asked.

"Yes, it is," Tricia replied tiredly, slowly lifting her head to meet his gaze.

"Why would you do that?" he asked incredulously. "Why would you intervene, knowing that if it exploded, it would be a serious setback to our work here?"

"Yes, it would be," Tricia replied, slowly shaking her head, "but not at the expense of these people's lives." She sighed. "You see, this is what the greater good looks like, Sorensen. It is all about people doing the right thing solely because they know it is the right thing to do, not because someone forces them to do it."

Tricia looked down at the flashing red bracelet once again. "Even if it comes at great personal sacrifice."

Sorensen looked around the room once more, and after taking a deep breath, he pulled out his commpad and tapped on it a few times. Tricia's bracelet vibrated once, flashed green, and then went dark. She stared at it in disbelief and then looked up at him again.

"No lives need to be sacrificed today, Doctor Carling," he said.

"Thank you," Tricia said softly.

Sorensen nodded once and looked toward Rene. "Doctor Thornton, I think that perhaps Doctor Carling has done more than enough for today, don't you?" he said to her.

Rene stood up and smoothed down her skirt. "Yes, Director Sorensen," she said, looking him in the eye. "I think she has."

She then looked down at Tricia. "What do you say, Tricia?" she asked, extending her hand down toward her.

Tricia looked up and smiled. "Yes, I think that's enough fun for one day," she sighed and gratefully took Rene's outstretched hand. With a gentle tug, Tricia rose to her feet, and under Rene's watchful eye, they left Sorensen and the medics to their work.

When they were out of earshot, Rene leaned over toward Tricia. "You're doing it again, you know," she said softly.

Tricia, exhausted and starving, turned her head slightly and sighed. "What's that, Rene? Doing what?"

"Being inspirational."

Bonding

The knock at the door she was expecting came just as Tricia was pulling on her slippers. *Running a little late today*, Tricia observed silently to herself, slightly surprised. Sofia was usually quite prompt when it was time to retrieve the lunch tray and take her to her afternoon sessions with Rene and the team.

After the incident in the treatment room, her schedule had relaxed slightly. The initial battery of tests finally seemed to be over, and the poking and prodding had lessened considerably. There was still the "Oh Tricia, try this" or "Oh Tricia, tell me about that" that made up her meetings with Rene's team, but that was far more tolerable than the barrage she had endured after she first arrived.

Have to keep running the maze.

But with luck, there will be cheese at the end of it soon, Tricia hoped, pushing the loose strands of hair back out of her face. She felt she was finally starting to get some ideas about how to finally break free of this place. She would still need help, but the ruptured treatment chair had given her the spark of inspiration she had been searching for. The energies being channeled through this facility were incredible. If something went seriously wrong with them, if some failure could be induced system-wide, the result would be devastating.

How to do it, though? Without dying, that is.

Even as her plans continued to evolve, there was still a silver lining. Truth be told, she was getting more than a little eager to hear what Rene was learning from their research. Rene wasn't wrong about that having some attraction to her, and despite the fact that Tricia was still a prisoner, she couldn't help but feel a twinge of anticipation when the time for her sessions drew closer. If she learned something useful about herself as a result of all this, it might almost be worth it.

Almost

Still, relaxed or not, Sofia was a stickler for keeping the routine, and like it or not, that predictable schedule was the only shred of normalcy Tricia had. In addition to the reassurance the overdue knock brought, Tricia appreciated how Sofia respected her enough to bother knocking at all, despite being just another captive lab rat in Sorensen's experiments. "Come in," she called out.

Sofia opened the door, but to Tricia's surprise, in strolled Rene instead. Sofia scooped up the lunch tray from the desk and gave Tricia a curt but pleasant smile and a nod before pulling the door closed behind her, leaving Rene and Tricia alone in the room.

"I thought we might have a talk today instead of the usual routine," Rene said, pulling over one of the chairs. She turned it to face Tricia, who was still sitting on the edge of the bed, and sat down. "Unless, of course, you'd rather be poked and prodded some more," she added with a wry grin.

"But I was *so* looking forward to the change of scenery down in the lab," Tricia responded.

"Sorry to disappoint," Rene jousted back, "but, for a variety of reasons I will explain shortly, I thought it best we talk here. However, if it is a change of scenery you're craving, there is a small exercise room here in the facility. As I recall, you use the facilities on campus quite extensively, don't you? When we are done, I could talk to Sofia about getting you access to it."

Tricia scoffed. "If I cooperate, I suppose? Forgive me, but I'm not in the deal-making mood, Rene." Tricia immediately regretted the sniping tone. *My baggage is talking again.*

"I'm not asking you to make any deals, Tricia," Rene replied softly. "I was just thinking it might help make this place more tolerable, and with the buzz you created by saving those technicians in the treatment room, Sorensen might be amenable to extending some privileges if we asked him."

I'm sure, Tricia thought skeptically, but allowed herself to relax slightly and put her hands palm-down on the bed on either side of her, ready to hear what Rene had to say.

"I'm going to be completely honest with you, Tricia," Rene started, looking at Tricia over the top of her glasses. "I came here hoping we could have a very open and candid conversation."

"Why not just do this in your lab?"

"Honestly, because it's very possible that conversations in the lab are not always private, and I want what I have to say to be completely between us," Rene said, lowering her voice. "While these rooms do have motion sensors to make sure they are still occupied, and the door and window are also equipped with sensors to detect tampering, I'm absolutely sure there is no other video or audio surveillance."

"How are you so sure?" Tricia asked, puzzled. She'd assumed she was under 24/7 monitoring and, frankly, had taken that into account whenever she was dressing and showering.

"Because I asked, dear."

Tricia frowned a bit and crossed her arms. "Asking about that might look a little suspicious, don't you think?"

"Hmmm, not so much," Rene replied. "I simply asked the security chief if I were to visit you in your room, whether there was a way they could monitor the room in case you tried to do me harm. I told him that with your advanced skills in hand-to-hand combat, even without your powers, you are still quite formidable, and I wanted to ensure I would be safe. He told me there wasn't any way to monitor the room directly, and, if I was concerned about that, the best solution would be to have someone else in the room or at least stationed outside the door."

Tricia tipped her head toward the door. "So, is there someone out there?"

Rene shook her head.

Tricia leaned toward her. "So, you don't think you need someone there, just in case?"

"No," Rene answered, "because I know what kind of person you are, Tricia."

She pulled her chair a little closer to Tricia. "Besides, I think you're going to be very interested in what I came here to talk about. Still, it couldn't hurt for us to keep our voices down either."

Rene sat back, crossed her legs, and pushed her glasses back on her nose. *Down to business*, Tricia thought. "As you know, we've been running an extensive battery of tests since you arrived a few weeks ago," Rene started, holding up her commpad as evidence.

"Yes, I'm keenly aware," Tricia snorted. "It's actually very similar to the ones they ran right after I had my accident, and you already know how much I appreciated that."

"I'm sure," Rene confirmed with a wry smirk. "The only difference is that they were trying to see if there were any abnormalities. We, however, know there is something extraordinary and are trying to find it, so our approach to get more at the heart of your abilities, and how you control them, has been from many different angles."

"And?" Tricia probed.

"Fortunately, no, we haven't found anything yet."

"Fortunately?" Tricia asked with a puzzled expression.

Rene nodded. "Yes, bear with me on that for a bit, but all the testing has confirmed is that, on the surface, you are an extremely healthy young woman with an otherwise unremarkable physiology."

"Young?"

Rene smiled. "Well, it is somewhat relative, isn't it? However, in your case, it is just as I suspected. The testing indicates your physiology is closer to that of a woman in her mid to early twenties rather than your actual age."

So, Marni was right about the regeneration, Tricia thought.

"I'm also willing to bet you haven't even been sick since your accident, have you?"

Tricia shook her head.

"I thought so," Rene said with a knowing smile, "and I've already shared with you some of the other observations I've made about the potential of your abilities. Now, since these kinds of benefits are precisely what interest some of Sorensen's backers, we can't just dismiss them out of hand. Why the power that you manipulate presents itself in these ways is a fascinating problem all by itself, but it's not the one we are truly chasing."

Rene laid her commpad on the table and tugged her glasses down to rest on the tip of her nose. "We need to be clear that all these are just manifestations and symptoms of your enhanced condition, not causes," she said, looking at Tricia over the top rim of her glasses, "and it's really the root of your abilities and how you control them that we are trying to understand, right?"

Tricia nodded. "I assume you've been going through my genetics as well?"

Rene bobbed her head in affirmation. "Yes, I've been searching through your genome myself. I've gone through it repeatedly, but again, as with the other tests, other than a general lack of even the most basic variations we would expect to find in the general population, your genome is equally unremarkable."

"I'm glad I'm so boring," Tricia jibed.

"Yes, I am too," Rene replied, and seeing Tricia was about to break in, she held up her hand, suggesting she hold her comment for the moment.

"Now, our body's operating system is not just written in our nucleonic DNA. There are subroutines, if you will, located in genetic material and biochemistry found in other places in our bodies, so there is more to look at, but I've been starting to suspect that the answer lies outside of anatomy and physiology."

"Marni was suspecting the same thing," Tricia conceded. "We had almost this same conversation right before...right before I came here."

"If you say so, but best to remember that your Marni isn't me," Rene replied with a coy smile.

"True, she isn't you," Tricia retorted, "but you aren't her either."

Rene cocked an eyebrow and smiled. "Touché." She picked up her commpad off the table and started scrolling through it. "My research has taken me to some interesting places, Tricia. Needless to say, there isn't a body of modern scientific knowledge on the subject of powered individuals. In fact, until you came on the scene last year, science had widely dismissed the existence of people like you. To find anything substantive, I've had to go much further back."

"How far back?"

Rene cleared her throat. "Well, to find any serious compilation of knowledge about people who could apparently manipulate elemental or natural forces, I've had to go back as far as the Middle Ages."

"The Middle Ages!?" Tricia exclaimed. Then her eyes widened with realization. "You're not seriously going to say what I do is *magic,* are you? That I'm some kind of witch or sorceress?"

"No, I'm not saying that," Rene affirmed, "but if we take out the terms that make it sound silly..."

"It isn't the terms that make it sound silly, Rene."

"...and keep an open mind, like the scientists we are, to possibilities that what was once called 'magic' was a term for some aspect of the natural world we didn't then, and still don't, fully understand, we might find something relevant."

"So, it's kind of like the old quote: 'When you have eliminated the impossible, whatever remains, however improbable, must be the truth.'" Tricia replied.

"Yes, exactly, my dear Watson," Rene quipped, "and just remember, Tricia, that at one time fire was considered magical, yet here you sit, able to create energies like it with your bare hands, so it is really not as fantastical as we might think."

Tricia sighed. *It sounds crazy, but she has a valid point.*

"Ok, so what have you found?" Tricia finally asked.

Rene shifted in her seat, her face showing a renewed excitement. *It must've been amazing to work with her when she was like this all the time,* Tricia thought, noting how eagerly Rene obviously wanted to share her discoveries with Tricia.

"So, as you can imagine, I had to sift through a lot of superstition, religion, and fantasy," Rene started, "but there were several scholars who took a very scientific approach to the ideas around angels, demons, and witchcraft. As I dug into it, I found that there were a few themes that ran through most of the serious writings on the topic."

She held up her commpad. It showed scans of some very old parchments covered with runes, symbols, and text that Tricia thought was likely ancient Latin. Rene reached around and pointed to a section of the weathered document.

"This part here talks about how there are two components that are fundamental for wielders of 'arcane arts' as they called them. To master these powers, the practitioners had to learn and apply both Power and Intent."

Rene left the pad in Tricia's hands and sat back up in her chair. She held out one hand, palm up. "First, someone had to have access to some form of Power. They weren't clear on where it came from—natural, elemental, spiritual—but they had to have access to it."

Rene then held out her other hand, also palm up. "However, to use that Power, they needed to have Intent. They needed to have a clear focus and purpose to direct it. If they couldn't master that, well, it never ended well."

Tricia looked into her eyes. She was finding Rene's energy around this to be very infectious, and the gears started turning in her own mind. "So, you're saying you believe this happened with me?"

"Yes, I do," Rene said. "I think during your accident, you formed some Connection, let's call it, with the natural forces from your experiment. Reviewing some more contemporary, less scientific sources, I think a very small number of people are sometimes born with it. For a few more, it can happen as a result of something traumatic like a near-death experience or, as in your case, a cataclysmic accident."

Tricia nodded slowly. "And the other part?"

"I think at some point after the Connection is made, a Bond must then form between the host and the force behind the Connection. Only once that Bond forms can the person safely draw on and apply the power provided through the Connection."

"And if this Bond never forms?" Tricia prompted.

"Well, it could be the person is never able to access the power, and we just simply don't hear about them." Rene leaned in a little closer. "For those that do access that power, though, and can't manage the control, it tends to end rather catastrophically. There are a lot of references in the old texts about apprentice practitioners dying very gruesome deaths." She made an explosion sign with her fingers.

The light went on for Tricia. "So, you think this is why Sorensen's subjects don't survive the process he uses to infuse them with abilities? They don't form that Bond, so when they access the power through the Connection, they die."

"Exactly," Rene affirmed, nodding her head vigorously.

Tricia pondered for a moment, then asked the obvious next question. "How do you think this Bond forms, Rene?"

"I'm not sure," Rene said. "That part wasn't explored very much by the scholars of the day. They were still very superstitious and afraid of these arcane practitioners, so they were more concerned with stopping it than trying to replicate it. Similarly, most of the works from scholars trying to learn how to do it were often destroyed as blasphemous and heretical. Fear did still rule the day, after all.

"However, it seems from what small amount I could find that it depends strongly on the mental and emotional state of the person and how receptive they are to the power of the Connection and allowing it to become a part of themselves."

Tricia frowned skeptically again. "You make it sound almost spiritual."

Rene sighed and sat back up. "I've never been what you'd call religious, Tricia, but if we are willing to explore more metaphysical aspects of this openly, there is precedent to draw on. For example, we know there are cases where people have been healed from disease and serious injury through meditation, and it is well-documented that a positive mental and emotional state is very key to physical wellness. What if it's more than just hormones and emotional placebos?"

"I don't know, Rene. It sounds incredibly fantastical." Tricia sat back and crossed her arms again.

"It sounds that way, I admit," Rene countered, "but again, think of it as a science we don't understand yet. We know observation has a direct bearing on quantum state—just look at the two-slit experiment, for example. There are also effects predicted and observed like quantum entanglement, where the quantum state of one object is directly affected by the changes in the quantum state of another over vast distances."

Tricia shrugged. "Ok, fair points. How then did this Bond form in me? I was accessing my powers when I woke up. I didn't know it at the time, of course, but in hindsight, I was using them right away. I don't remember forming any Bond like you're suggesting."

"I think it happened when you were unconscious, Tricia. I think your body was on the verge of death, and it openly welcomed the power on your behalf to the healing ability offered by your new Connection. Your body formed the Bond without you being consciously involved to save your life."

Tricia rubbed her chin, thinking. *It makes more sense than it should*, she couldn't help but admit to herself.

Rene pushed on, "Does any of this resonate with you, Tricia? Do any of your experiences with your abilities support these ideas?"

Tricia finally nodded in agreement. "Yes, Rene, they do. 'Connection' is exactly what it feels like. I even think I used that exact phrase when I first realized what they were. As you say, the Bond could have formed while my body was healing, before I was even aware of what had happened to me.

"My powers aren't a mechanical reaction, like lifting a finger. I don't just *use* them." She recalled when she hit Marni in class, channeling her speed inadvertently, knocking her to the floor. "They *respond* to me, how I'm thinking and feeling. Honestly, it does feel more like a relationship than some part of my physical body."

Tricia reached out to the flows around her. She felt them seething and surging, begging for her to call for them, but remembering the bracelet, she resisted. For the first time in months, she questioned them, *What are you? What are you really?*

"So, yes, this resonates with me," Tricia admitted.

Rene sat back and nodded. Concern replaced enthusiasm on her face. "I'm glad they do, but then, I'm sorry they do at the same time."

"Why, Rene?" Tricia asked, leaning toward her. If Rene was this worried now about what they'd talked about, she needed to know why. "Why does this worry you?"

"This is the reason why I wanted to have this open discussion in a very private setting, Tricia," Rene confided.

"I'm very grateful you were willing to have it—that you trusted me enough to have it—and I hope it benefits you in your journey, but we can never let Sorensen on to this theory."

Tricia nodded. "I think I see where you're headed with this, but tell me why you think so, Rene."

Rene sighed. "I've been very selective about what I've been putting in the official reports, Tricia. It's been clear to me from the start that he is not the kind of person who should have access to the kind of power you possess, power that we now know could be almost beyond limits. He is literally the walking embodiment of everything that drove me to do what I tried to do before, to end humanity entirely: ambitious, paranoid, and bereft of any moral compass.

"Up until now, the team here, under his direction, has had some success in creating the Connection using the energies and equipment at this facility, but as we've been discussing, those subjects die when they are encouraged to try to use their power."

Rene took off her glasses, tucked them into the pocket of her lab coat, leaned closer to Tricia, and lowered her voice. "What we've talked about today means he's actually much closer than we, and he, previously thought. Success might now just be a simple matter of having test subjects that *want* these abilities instead of having test subjects that are terrified and afraid of what's happening to them. Frightened people resist their transformation and likely can't form the Bond, but people who want these abilities, who are willing to embrace them, likely could, and then Sorensen would have the final piece."

Rene sat back a bit and took Tricia's hands in hers. "And we know, Tricia, we both know, that people who want power are rarely the people who should have power."

Tricia just stared blankly at Rene. *My God,* she thought, *he really is at the threshold and doesn't realize it.* The horror of Sorensen having this kind of power, *her* power, swelled in her anew.

"No question, Rene," Tricia acceded softly. "We can't let him find out about this."

"Agreed, and I've documented nothing about this in my reports so far, but just hiding it isn't the answer either, I'm afraid."

"How so?" Tricia asked.

Rene stood up and started pacing in front of her. "It goes back to what I told you when you first arrived. I've been very selective in the sense that I'm trying to create a perception of progress without actually making any. That can't last forever. The team here is good, and eventually, they will have a breakthrough, no matter how clever I am keeping them off the scent.

"If they don't, sooner or later they will push to try a different approach. I've seen the proposals for alternative methods the team could try. They are horrific, and many of them would involve unspeakable and painful procedures for you personally."

She stopped pacing and put her hands on the back of her chair. "Let's just say I'm absolutely positive that any of the protocols other than the ones we are executing right now would be, um, *very* unpleasant for you, and, if Sorensen becomes desperate enough, most likely for Darci Jackson as well. That's why I've tried to walk this delicate line between apparent progress, so there's no incentive to change approaches, without divulging anything that would take Sorensen closer to his goals."

Rene sat back down, facing Tricia. "The point is, if there's too little progress in one direction, Sorensen's patience will run out, and they will eventually switch to another, and I don't want to see that happen to you or anyone, Tricia. That may sound odd coming from someone like me, but believe me, it is much easier to accept the slow extinction of billions than to be personally involved in causing anguish and pain to a single individual."

"So, what do you suggest, Rene?" Tricia asked.

"We need to agree on how to keep feeding Sorensen and the team just enough to keep them satisfied without divulging anything that would help them solve it. Better yet, if we can redirect them along the way—get them chasing red herrings without creating suspicion—all the better." Rene leaned down and lowered her head. "It also means," she said, looking intently into Tricia's eyes, "that we seriously have to figure out some exit strategy as well, Tricia. Deflection will work for a while, but we can't keep it up indefinitely. Our time will run out, and I fear that will be sooner rather than later."

Can I trust her? Tricia wondered. *I want to—I need to— but look where that got me last time. Still, I can't help but feel that right now, she's being completely genuine with me, and if I am going to get out of this—if we are going to get out of this—I need to set the past aside.*

"All right, Rene, we'll figure it out together," Tricia said, emphasizing the budding partnership. "Just curious, what are you planning to put in the record about this conversation, then?"

"Just that we discussed the circumstances of the accident, your recovery, and how you discovered your powers. I'll leave some of the details vague but couched in big words and jargony phrases to make it sound authentic." Rene smiled and winked.

Tricia took a deep breath and blew it out. Rene pressed her lips together and gave Tricia a quick nod, and then she tapped the commpod in her ear. "Tell Sofia we are done, and I'd like her to join us for a minute."

A few seconds later, the commpod replied, "Sofia acknowledges and says she'll be there in a few minutes."

Rene put on her glasses, stood up, and smoothed her lab coat. She swiped off the documents they'd been looking at on the commpad during their talk. In that moment, Tricia made a decision.

"Before Sofia comes, I want to tell you something else that might add credibility to this new theory, Rene, something I've been very guarded about."

Rene looked at her and raised one eyebrow. "Okay, I will keep this completely off the record. You have my word, it stays strictly between us."

Tricia sighed. "I hope you aren't playing me, but if we are going to work together, I need to trust you. I believe I have *two* Connections, not just one. I believe the accident gave me a Connection to both light *and* dark energy."

"Amazing," Rene replied. "All this time, we thought you got the powers from light, and Darci—Umbra—got hers from the dark energy in your experiment."

"It could be she only got the dark because the building shielded her from the light energies, but I was directly exposed to both, and my powers are sourced from both."

"Were you aware of them both from the start?" Rene asked.

"No," Tricia said. "My light-sourced powers were evident immediately when I woke up. As you said, the Bond probably formed while I was recovering. However, it wasn't until weeks later that I even sensed the dark energies, sensed the Connection as you put it."

"And the Bond?" Rene inquired, now excited again.

Tricia nodded. "Yes, I am fairly sure I remember when that happened. When I sensed it, I couldn't force the dark energy at first. I had to coax it in, invite it almost. When I did that, I think that's when the Bond formed—*if* your theory is correct."

Rene smiled. "So, yes, you discovered the dark energies after you were already comfortable with the light Connection. Therefore, you had no fear of the dark energies and openly welcomed them, forming the Bond consciously. Fascinating."

Tricia nodded.

"That's how you got out of the canister? These dark energy powers?"

Tricia nodded again. "There was still a lot of learning and discovery going on then. It was a surprise to me, too." She paused for a second. "It's also quite interesting that my manifestations and applications of the dark energy are very different than Umbra's abilities."

Rene rubbed her chin, thinking. "It is, but from what I've seen, there is no reason to believe that two people with the same Connection will present abilities the same way either. There may be an epigenetic component to it that's worth looking into."

Tricia wanted to follow up on that more, but instead chose to pursue a spark of inspiration, something that might lead to their way out. "Speaking of Umbra, Rene, she's obviously been a part of the program here for a while. What has she shared with you about her experiences like this?"

"Actually, I haven't been able to work with her at all," Rene admitted. "Sorensen has her busy with other duties. When I was brought out of stasis, he implied she would be part of the research program." Rene shrugged. "However, so far, it hasn't gone that way. To date, she's been strictly off-limits from the research and testing." Rene rubbed her chin. "In fact," she said thoughtfully, "I haven't even been allowed to so much as talk to her, let alone do any kind of assessments or comparisons."

That's interesting, Tricia thought. "You know," she then offered speculatively. "It might be very useful to see if her early experiences coincide in any way with what we've been discussing. It's just a talk, not really *testing*, and I'm sure you could find a way to ask her informally without tipping anyone off on what we think is going on, couldn't you?"

And the thought of becoming another lab rat won't sit very well with Miss Jackson either, I'm sure. Sorry, Rene, but I have to play the long game too, just in case.

Rene considered for a moment and then nodded. "You're right," she agreed. "It would be very informative to compare her experiences with yours, to see what you have in common, and, perhaps more importantly, how your accounts differ. I'm sure I can find a way to have a casual interview with her without raising any suspicions."

"I'm sure..." Tricia started but was interrupted by another knock at the door. "Come," Tricia said, and Sofia opened the door.

"You wanted to see me, Doctor Thornton?" she asked.

"Yes, Sofia," Rene said. "I'm hoping you can help me with something. I believe it would benefit the program if Doctor Carling could be given access to the exercise facility. I think it would help her maintain her physical fitness, keep her energy levels up, and give her a more positive mental attitude, all of which would benefit the testing and research we are doing."

Sofia looked at Tricia, then back at Rene. "Sounds reasonable," she answered. "I'll need to clear it with Director Sorensen."

Rene nodded, and Sofia tapped her commpod. "Call Director Sorensen."

After a few seconds, she answered, "Yes, Director Sorensen. Doctor Thornton has requested that Doctor Carling be given access to the exercise facility. She believes it will give Doctor Carling a more positive mental state and benefit the testing she's undergoing."

Sofia paused, listening. She then looked back at Rene. "The Director wants to know if Doctor Carling has been cooperating."

Rene looked down at Tricia and cocked a half-smile. She looked back at Sofia. "Yes. Please tell Sorensen that she's been extremely cooperative," she affirmed, making it sound very condescending and demeaning for effect.

"Doctor Thornton says she has been cooperating, Director," Sofia relayed.

A few seconds later, she tapped the commpod and looked at the two of them. "The Director says that will be fine as long as she's supervised."

Sofia then looked at Tricia. "If you'd care to go now, I can provide some supervision for the next couple of hours. According to the schedule, you are free for the rest of the afternoon, isn't that correct, Doctor Thornton?" Rene nodded once in agreement.

"Yes, thank you," Tricia said gratefully. *I'll get that change of scenery after all.* Looking at Rene, she added, "Thank you for that, Rene."

"Not at all, Tricia, and thank you again for the most useful interview today," Rene replied. "I'll see you again tomorrow for our regular session," she added and left.

Sofia looked at Tricia, who was still dressed in her normal scrubs and slippers. "I think you'll find some attire more suitable for exercise in one of the drawers in your closet," she offered.

Tricia looked, and sure enough, she found another set of the crimson sports top and compression shorts she had worn the day of the treatment room malfunction in one of the bottommost drawers.

"As you know, we keep them on hand for when the subjects will be undergoing more physically demanding types of testing. I'll arrange for a couple more sets to be delivered to the room, and we will have them laundered regularly for you," Sofia explained. "I'll wait outside for you to change. Just knock when you are ready to go. Please don't take too long, though, as I have other duties I need to perform today."

"I won't. Thanks again, Sofia."

Sofia paused. Tricia thought she was going to say something more, but instead, Sofia just pressed her lips together and left the room, closing the door behind her.

Not bad, Tricia mused as she started to peel off the scrubs she was wearing. *Looks like the lab rat came up with some cheese after all.*

Desperation

"**S**uffice to say," the raspy voice said, filling the small room. The speaker spoke softly, but every gravelly word hit Sorensen like a hammer. "Many of us are less than impressed with your progress to date, Director." The shadowy image of the hologram shrugged slightly to one side. "In fact, some of my colleagues are...disappointed."

Sorensen swallowed hard, doing his best to mask his nervousness. Usually, these meetings included several more members of the clandestine group who were backing his efforts here at The Workshop. The fact that this meeting was more one-on-one emphasized the seriousness of the conversation, worrying him even more. Sorensen could only hope that just as the figure he was speaking to appeared dim and subdued to him, the dark and foreboding atmosphere in the holocomm chamber helped to mask his agitation as well.

"I can certainly see how they might feel that way," Sorensen responded. "To be fair, though, we have had some significant achievements in replicating parahuman abilities in our test subjects." He lifted his commpad and prepared to share some specific notes with the figure in the commlink. "For example..."

"The only significant progress we've seen," the ghostly hologram interrupted him sharply, "is the rather impressive body count you've amassed among your test subjects." The figure leaned slightly closer. Sorensen couldn't see his eyes in the dim image, but he could clearly see the scowl on the figure's face nonetheless. "Tell me," the man continued, "have you actually been able to harness the woman's powers, Director Sorensen?"

"Yes," Sorensen replied quickly.

"In anyone who has lived? In anyone who has actually been able to manifest and *use* those powers?" the man emphasized.

"No," Sorensen admitted tersely. "But, we are very close, and with a few more subjects, we..."

"And that brings up another point of concern," the shadowy figure interrupted again. "Your recruiting efforts are starting to draw a great deal of unwanted attention. The authorities are actively investigating, and it is getting increasingly difficult to cover up your recruiting activities and keep them off your trail."

"I assure you, sir," Sorensen said defensively. "Our recruiting has been very discreet."

The man scoffed. "Your agent, this Umbra, has been anything *but* discreet. From where I'm sitting, she's been clumsy and careless at best." Sorensen started to speak, but the man silenced him with a wave of his hand. "Correct me if I'm wrong, but when you finally apprehended Beacon, wasn't she already aware of your agent's existence and her involvement in the various disappearances of your test subjects?"

How does he know that? Sorensen sighed in resignation. "Yes, that's true."

The holographic figure snorted and sat back, lifting his scowl. "We wonder if her efforts wouldn't be better spent participating more directly in your research than acquiring more recruits. It seems studying her, as well as the Carling woman, would be more insightful. Besides," he added, "until you have more definitive results, there really is no point in wasting any more subjects now, is there?"

"No, sir," Sorensen relented. "There wouldn't be. I'll look into how Umbra might help accelerate the efforts of the research teams without delay."

"Outstanding, Director. You do that," the voice said, dripping with sarcasm. "Perhaps her participation will give your program the boost it needs to demonstrate a few solid results before my arrival."

"Your *arrival*?" Sorensen stammered. "The Circle is coming here?"

"No," the man replied. "Not the entire Circle. Just me...and a few assistants, naturally."

"What will be the purpose of your visit, sir?" Sorensen asked. Although he already knew the answer, it was the only question his panicked mind could even think of to ask.

"Why, to observe your operation personally, of course," the figure said, his mouth twisting into a malevolent smile. "We will review your operations and progress and report back to the rest of the group. Based on that, we will decide if any changes need to be made for the program to deliver the results we were promised."

"Of course," Sorensen said. "We will be ready."

"Make sure of it," the man said sternly. "This operation represents a significant financial investment, so I'm sure you can appreciate why we would need to verify that our resources are being applied...efficiently, do you not?"

"I do, sir," Sorensen replied stiffly.

"Good. You'll be given our travel arrangements shortly. Make arrangements for someone reliable to meet me at the airport when we arrive, and Sorensen, make sure this doesn't turn into some kind of contrived dog and pony show," he said threateningly. "If I think that we are not seeing the real operation or that we are being shown anything but the absolute truth, you would find our response to be most unpleasant. Am I clear, Director?"

"Y...Yes, sir," Sorensen said. "Crystal clear."

"Good," the shadowy figure said. "Until then." The holographic image winked out, leaving Sorensen alone in the dim room with only the sound of his heart hammering in his ears.

"Gaaagh!" he shouted and slammed his fists down on the console in front of him. He puffed in and out through his nose, his nostrils flaring.

"Fine," he said, gathering his things. "If it's progress they want, I'll make sure they see something they'll never forget," and he stormed out of the room, slamming the door behind him.

Rene peered into the void above her head, studying the constellations blazing before her. Constellations made not of stars but of adenine, cytosine, guanine, and thiamine. *I see you, Tricia*, she mused, and with a wave of her hand, the VR headset she wore responded by spinning the expanded molecular DNA helix in space around her. It was dizzying and mesmerizing, and Rene loved every moment of it.

She pulled her hands apart, and the vibrant molecular model above her shrank to show more of the genome in this segment of Tricia Carling's chromosomes. The team was right to think there might be something remarkable here, something that might mean a significant breakthrough in their studies of Tricia's abilities, but Rene already knew they would not find anything.

With a twist of her wrist, the display rotated once again. *If it was anywhere, it was going to be here*, she thought, but fortunately, she had already looked over this particular region days before and had already confirmed that it was a dead end, too.

Still, Rene encouraged the team to look anyway. It was important to maintain the illusion of progress, the perception that the research was going somewhere. Perception was reality, after all. It was also important to make sure that even promising leads sometimes hit dead ends. However, even if she did occasionally miss something, and the team did find some markers or sequences that provided some clues, well, sometimes maintaining the illusion of progress required actually making some from time to time.

Even so, an illusion is all it can be, Rene affirmed to herself as she zoomed in once again on a particularly interesting segment. It could never amount to more than that simply because the more Rene studied Tricia Carling, either with the team or on her own, the more Rene was convinced that the key to Beacon's unique abilities was not in her biology but in Tricia Carling herself.

As Rene zoomed the display to a different portion of the genetic sequence she was inspecting, she heard the door to the laboratory click. *Ah, visitors,* she thought, and gestured to pause the display. The headset dimmed the DNA rendering that was circling her head, revealing the laboratory around her just in time to see the door swing open, admitting none other than Sorensen, trailed by Sofia.

Sofia looked as she always did. Her sandy brown hair was drawn back into a short ponytail. Her face, expressionless, was highlighted by small touches of makeup on her lips, cheeks, and eyes. Even the tiny amount of dark liner and shadow she used contrasted sharply with the penetrating gray of her eyes, emphasizing the intelligence and a hint of sadness behind them. Rene respected and appreciated Sofia and found her to be a very capable administrator, if a little odd at times.

Sorensen himself looked impeccable as always, his hair neatly trimmed and wearing a perfectly tailored charcoal sports coat over a black mock turtleneck. His shoes positively gleamed under the lab's lights. *If he wasn't a flaming psychopath,* Rene mused, briefly admiring how his jacket hugged his shoulders and chest before snapping back to reality. *No doubt this is not a social visit,* she concluded. *Regardless of what has brought him down here, I'm very sure nothing good is going to come of it.*

"Director Sorensen. Sofia. Welcome to my parlor," Rene said, stripping off the VR headset and trading it for her glasses on the lab table next to her. She smoothed her hair and walked over to greet them. "What can I do for you?"

"We've just come down to get an update on your progress, haven't we, Sofia?" Sorensen said.

"Yes, Director, we have," Sofia answered flatly.

"The team is currently inspecting some genomic sequences that we are very optimistic will provide us a clue to harnessing Beacon's powers," Rene replied.

"The entire team?" Sorensen asked with a slight frown. "All studying the same thing?" He huffed. "Seems like a waste."

"Quite the opposite, Director," Rene corrected smoothly. "Having multiple members of the team study the problem from different angles helps eliminate bias and reduces the risk we might overlook something important." Rene shrugged slightly. "In the long run, it could save us a lot of time backtracking."

"Hmm, I see," Sorensen replied. "I certainly hope so, Doctor Thornton. Time is something we simply don't have."

"How so?" Rene asked.

"Our investors have run out of patience. They are very disappointed by our apparent lack of progress and are pressing me for results," Sorensen answered her, deepening his frown.

"But, Director, there have been some very significant achievements in infusing the test subjects with abilities," Rene countered.

"I see, so if we've been so successful, perhaps you can tell me when I can expect to see one of our recruits wield abilities and actually *survive?*" he hissed through clenched teeth.

Rene held her ground, undisturbed by his minor outburst. "That I cannot tell you right now, Director. The survival part is still an open question, one we are working hard to resolve."

"As I thought," Sorensen said, relaxing his face. "I want you to start reviewing the other experimental protocols, Doctor Thornton. If this latest trail in your study doesn't yield anything of interest, we will have to switch tactics and accelerate our progress."

"Other protocols?" Rene asked, puzzled. *I was afraid of this...*

"Yes," Sorensen answered. "You'll find them in the database. We have avoided using them because of the potential danger to our subjects. Someone like Doctor Carling was not considered as expendable as our other recruits, but we simply cannot afford to be conservative any longer."

Sorensen paused for a moment, considering the moment, and then continued, "Best to start reviewing them immediately, Doctor Thornton. I'm going to need you to put your personal feelings for Tricia Carling aside and do what it takes to get me the answers I need. A living parahuman of our own creation. Whatever it takes, do I make myself clear?"

Rene frowned, "What 'feelings', Director?"

"Please, Doctor Thornton," Sorensen sneered. "You and she may have been bitter adversaries, but the level of respect and even admiration you two have for each other is obvious. I can't let that interfere any further with our work here."

"I assure you, Director Sorensen," Rene replied coolly. "No 'feelings' have interfered with my work here. However, I will warn you not to push Tricia too far. She's cooperating now only because she believes protecting her friends is worth the sacrifice she's making." Rene took a step toward Sorensen and glared into his eyes. "If she believes, for even a moment, that the greater good is in jeopardy, she may decide other sacrifices will be warranted by whatever she has to do to stop you."

"Leave Tricia Carling's cooperation with me," Sorensen replied with a sniff of derision.

Rene put her hands on her hips. "Dismiss me if you wish," she said, "but all I'm saying is that if you take her to extremes, your rather tenuous control over her will snap, and you will have a very serious problem on your hands."

Rene then frowned and crossed her arms as she continued, "By the way, that does remind me. You still have not shared how you will be sure your parahuman minions will not go rogue on you once we are successful."

Sorensen grinned. "Sofia," he said, turning to look at Sofia. She turned to face him. "Shall we show Doctor Thornton why I'm not terribly concerned about Doctor Carling's, or anyone else's, 'cooperation'?"

Sofia stared at him in silence, but Rene could see Sofia's eyes widen slightly as if the very thought of what Sorensen had suggested raised some deep dread within her.

"The concern about how we would control a legion of hundreds or thousands of parahumans and secure the political support from key leaders to deploy them has been an issue we have not taken lightly," Sorensen explained. "After all, you of all people, Doctor Thornton, can appreciate what power does to people, and even if they don't become corrupted by it, we can't have people with these kinds of abilities going rogue, as you put it, and not staying in line with the bigger program."

"I can," Rene answered hesitantly.

"Of course you can," Soren acknowledged. "Would that be an actual Bunsen burner over there?" he said brightly, gesturing toward a table near the back of the lab. "I'm surprised to see something so outmoded in your lab, Doctor Thornton."

"Well, I am a traditional girl, Director Sorensen," Rene said flippantly. "If a lab doesn't have a Bunsen burner, it can barely be called a lab, now can it?"

"I see your point," Sorensen said, smiling. "Can you please do me the favor of lighting it?"

Puzzled, Rene just looked at him until he impatiently waved her toward the table where the burner sat with a few flicks of his hand. She shrugged one shoulder and walked toward the table as Sorensen continued.

"Bearing that in mind, we've been running another program here at The Workshop focused on that very need," he said, raising his voice slightly so Rene could hear him as she proceeded to the other side of the lab. "Fortunately, that program has been much more successful to date than this one. We've developed a technology that allows us to assert a relatively high level of control over a human host through a series of implants wired into specific nerve centers in the brain and governed by an artificial intelligence agent."

"Seriously?" Rene asked. She opened a drawer in the table and, after taking out an old flint striker, she turned the gas valve and popped a single spark over the top of the burner. A bright blue flame burst into life. "An AI neural implant?" Rene asked as she adjusted the air intake on the burner slightly to eliminate any residual yellow flare-ups.

Frak me! What a horrifying concept, she thought, keeping her face free of any emotion that might give away the disgust she felt.

"Ah, beautiful," Sorensen said, admiring the flame. "Now, Sofia, go put your hand into that flame."

Sofia turned and looked at him. She shook her head slowly. "No, Director. Please," she begged softly.

"*Now*, Sofia," Sorensen asserted sternly.

Rene watched Sofia look to the flame, then back at Sorensen. She shook her head once more, but then Rene watched her face abruptly go blank. Sofia straightened her back and turned toward her. "Yes, Director," Sofia said and started to walk toward Rene and the blue flame on the table beside her.

"The problem we found," Sorensen said as he and Rene watched Sofia walk steadily toward the back of the lab, "was that if the chip was in control all the time, it degraded the neurological pathways of the subject. Their cognitive functions rapidly declined, and they soon died. To remedy that, the chip only activates when the host starts to resist the directives it has been given. It's a rather elegant solution."

By then, Sofia had nearly reached the table. Despite the blank expression on her face, Rene could see the terror in her eyes and the tears of panic welling up in them. She gasped in horror as Sofia extended her arm outward, obediently reaching for the flame before her. "No!" Rene screamed. "Sofia, don't!" she shouted and launched herself at Sofia, grabbing her wrist, desperately trying to pull her back. Sofia fought back, determined to follow Sorensen's orders, and pushed even harder toward the scorching burner.

"You see, Doctor Thornton," Sorensen droned on, taking some obvious delight in watching the two women struggle across the room from him. "Sofia's behavior is part conditioning and part control. She fears being out of control when the chip takes over, so she has learned to be more naturally compliant and obedient. However, as you can see, when she resists, the chip takes the decisions out of her hands and ensures she obeys unconditionally, regardless of the consequences to herself."

Sofia fought direly to reach the burner, her fingertips just inches away from the blue blaze, but Rene wrapped her arms around Sofia and pulled her back. "Stop it, Sorensen!" she shouted, pinning Sofia's arms to her sides. "Make her stop!" Rene's shoes skidded on the floor as Sofia dragged them both closer to the open flame.

"Very well," Sorensen said casually. "Sofia, disregard my last order. Stand down."

At his command, Sofia suddenly went limp in Rene's arms, and they almost toppled over backward. Regaining her footing, Rene carefully released Sofia and steadied her, making sure she could stand on her own before letting her go entirely. Sofia looked up at Rene with damp eyes, her face a portrait of abject despair but mixed with hints of relief and even gratitude. Sofia smiled at Rene slightly and nodded once before regaining her feet. She paused momentarily to smooth her lab coat, and after tucking the hair that had come loose in their struggle back into her ponytail, Sofia turned and silently walked back to the front of the lab where Sorensen waited.

"Quite effective, wouldn't you say, Doctor Thornton?" Sorensen said as Sofia turned to stand next to him.

Appalled, Rene could not help but agree, "Yes, very," she said angrily, adjusting her own coat and straightening her glasses. "I can't believe you did this to your own assistant, Sorensen. That's taking psychotic to a new level, even for you."

"Oh, Sofia's much more than my assistant, Doctor Thornton," Sorensen replied with a cruel smile. "Go ahead, Sofia. Tell Doctor Thornton who you are."

Sofia sighed. "I'm Sofia Sorensen, Director Sorensen's sister."

Rene's jaw dropped. "His *sister*?!? My God, Sorensen, you did this to your sister?"

Sorensen nodded. "Yes. You see, I'm fully committed to this endeavor, so I couldn't think of a more appropriate first live trial subject than the one person I wanted by my side through this entire operation. The one person I loved and would need to rely on and trust unconditionally. The same person who was by my side my entire life, helping me and supporting me, and the one person who I needed to be sure would stay there no matter what happened." He turned toward Sofia. "Isn't that right, sister?"

"Yes, Director," she said flatly. "Of course it is."

He's absolutely insane. A complete raving lunatic, Rene thought, her mouth still open in shock. *My God, if he would do that to his own sister...*

"By the way, Doctor Thornton," Sorensen said, turning toward Rene. "Have you spent any time with Darci Jackson at all as part of your research?"

"No," Rene stammered out. "Not really. Just a few questions recently to cross-check some information I'd gotten from Tricia. My understanding was that she was exempt from the research investigations, on your orders, actually."

Sorensen nodded. "We may be past that as well. Orders can change. As you review the other protocols, please give serious thought to how Ms. Jackson's involvement could help accelerate your work as well, and present me with an updated plan immediately."

Still in shock, Rene could only nod slowly in response.

"Make it happen, Doctor Thornton," Sorensen told her and, taking his sister by the arm, left Rene standing alone in the laboratory.

Rene pulled out a lab stool and dropped down onto it. As she ran her fingers through her hair, she felt her hand trembling and grabbed it, gripping it tightly to quell it.

Oh, yes, it's time to make something happen, Rene thought, taking a deep breath. *Well past time, actually. We may have already waited too long.*

Despite how deeply she was sleeping, Tricia's eyes snapped open when she heard the soft click of the latch on her door. The pitch blackness of the room was momentarily broken by a sliver of light from the hallway outside as a shadow slipped through the open crack and then quickly closed the door behind it.

"Tricia?" she heard a woman's voice softly ask. "Are you awake?"

Tricia sat up and peered into the room at the shadow hovering before her. "Rene?" she asked in a half-whisper. She held up her hand and drew a tiny flow of energy. Her hand glowed softly, pulling Rene's face out of the darkness. "What are you doing here? And in the middle of the night, no less?"

Rene turned on the desk lamp and pulled out a chair to sit down. "We need to talk, Tricia. It can't wait." She held out a small sample cup. "But first, please fill this up."

Tricia took the cup and scowled. "With what?"

"You know what. Please, Tricia."

"Seriously? You needed this now?" Tricia said, irritated as she stood up and took the little plastic cup from Rene. Frowning, Tricia held it up to inspect it. "This couldn't wait?"

"I need to have an excuse in case someone questions why I came here tonight," Rene replied, nearly pleading. "It's still a flimsy excuse, but I can weave a story around it. Please, Tricia. Hurry. I shouldn't be here now."

"Very well," Tricia said and headed toward the small bathroom. "I'll see what I can do, but this had better be worth it."

A few minutes later, Tricia flushed the toilet and returned to the room. She thrust the partially full sample container into Rene's hand. "Now, what's this all about?" she asked and sat down on the edge of the bed.

"We are out of time, Tricia," Rene said urgently, leaning toward Tricia. "Sorensen came to visit me in the lab this afternoon. Things are about to get very bad very soon, and we need to get out of here before it does."

"Slow down, Rene," Tricia said, her curiosity piqued. "Tell me what happened."

Rene took a quick breath and exhaled sharply. "Apparently, whoever is pulling Sorensen's strings is dissatisfied with the progress on the parahuman program. Sometime in the next couple of weeks, they will be coming to visit, and Sorensen is determined to show them something substantial. I'm very certain he feels his head might be on the chopping block if he can't. That means our heads are on the block as well."

"Got it," Tricia said thoughtfully. "No surprise, though, Rene. We knew this would eventually happen."

"Yes, we did, but it's here now, much sooner than I thought, and we don't have much time to figure it out," Rene replied, wringing her hands nervously. "This afternoon, he instructed me, in no uncertain terms, to start reviewing some of the other research protocols, the ones they haven't used yet because the team felt they were too dangerous for the test subjects."

"The ones you told me about earlier? How dangerous?"

Rene nodded. "Yes, and very. I started looking through some of them this afternoon, and let's just say most take the concept of destructive testing to a whole new level. The team was right to hold off on using them. The outcomes and after-effects for subjects, especially for people like you, Tricia, are horrific, to say the least. The odds of you, or anyone, surviving them are thin at best, and even if you did, to call it 'living' would be extremely generous."

"I see," Tricia replied. "I appreciate you keeping my well-being in mind, Rene."

"It gets worse," Rene continued. "To keep their super-army in line, they've also developed a neural implant that gives Sorensen absolute control over a human host."

Tricia's eyes widened. "My God, Rene. That's terrifying. Are you sure?"

"Absolutely positive," Rene affirmed, her voice accelerating. "In fact, he demonstrated it to me in the lab by ordering Sofia to put her hand into a flaming burner!"

Tricia cursed. "Sofia? She didn't really, did she?"

Rene shook her head. "No, but she would have if I hadn't grabbed her and begged Sorensen to make her stop."

Tricia rubbed her chin. "So, Sofia has a neural implant. That's some seriously dark sci-fi stuff, Rene, but it does explain a lot of the odd behavior I've seen in her. How she suddenly shifts moods and has trouble saying things at times. It makes sense now."

"How much more sense does it make if I tell you that Sofia is his sister?" Rene asked bitterly.

"His sister?!?" Trica spat back. "His sister...I can't believe it. I knew he was pathological, but that's ghastly." She closed her eyes and shook her head in disbelief. "He's certifiable. Completely insane."

"What it really means, Tricia," Rene said, "is that he will do literally anything to see this through. There is no price too high, no bar too low. We are all royally screwed."

Tricia thought for a moment and then took a deep breath. She looked up into Rene's face and studied it for a moment. "So why come to me with this, Rene?" she finally asked softly but directly. "I mean, why haven't you just left? Isn't self-preservation more your style?"

Rene chuckled. "Yes, it is, Tricia, and don't think I haven't considered it. More than once today, actually, but a few things are painfully obvious."

Rene adjusted her seat and held up her first finger. "First, no one just quits from The Institute for the Advancement of Human Potential, especially if they are already dead. The people who run this place have their hooks and feelers in everything, so the odds of someone walking out of here and not being found and brought back, or just disappearing altogether, are slim to none."

"Fair point," Tricia replied. "Further, knowing the kind of person Sorensen is, there's little doubt of how he would reward that kind of disloyalty."

"Exactly, so we need a better plan than that," Rene agreed. She then held up her second finger. "You can't stay here, Tricia. Taking the fact out of the picture that I have no desire to see you put through the agony these new protocols would cause, you are too valuable to the research. It also bodes poorly for Darci Jackson. I don't know how to help her, or even if she can be helped, but leaving them with two living samples to study is out of the question."

"Also true," Tricia said.

Rene smiled. "Besides, sweetie, if anyone is going to maim and kill you, I think that's a privilege I will reserve for myself."

Tricia chuckled. "Of course, Rene. I wouldn't want it any other way."

Rene gave a soft laugh, and the smile vanished from Rene's face. "Seriously, Tricia. What I saw in those protocols...I wouldn't wish that on anybody, especially you. More so, it's not just about getting away at this point. We can't let this go any further. He's too corrupt, too unhinged, and we know they are too close to the answer. If we allow him actually to achieve his vision, the result will be far worse than anything I could have imagined.

"He has to be stopped, Tricia, and I can't do that on my own. It will take both of us."

Tricia nodded, looking into Rene's eyes. There was no question in Tricia's mind that Rene was being completely sincere. *Why does it take something like this to bring us together?* Tricia lamented silently.

"Yes, Rene," Tricia said. "I couldn't agree more, and there is no question that teaming up is the best option for us. Count me in. Do you have any ideas for what to do next?"

"No," Rene said, and a small smile crept across her face, "but I do not doubt that two exceptional and brilliant women like us will come up with something."

"Neither do I," agreed Tricia. "We will come up with a plan. In fact, I've already got some ideas, but even the two of us, as impressive as we are, I don't think can pull it off on our own. That's been clear to me since I got here. We will need help, Rene."

"From whom?" Rene asked.

"From someone that Sorensen would least expect."

Released

Whatever happens later today, Tricia decided, was completely dependent on what Sofia brought her for lunch. Tricia checked the clock. Sofia would be coming by any minute now, and if what Rene had been telling her was true, Sofia might again try to leave her some subliminal clues, clues that Sofia had probably been desperately hoping would get an urgent message to her but were subtle enough to avoid drawing the attention of Sofia's implanted AI.

Knock knock.

"Doctor Carling, lunchtime," Sofia said through the door.

Right on time. If she saw the same kinds of clues today, Tricia had already decided this would be the day she tried to free Sofia. Her plan would require speed and precision, and within a matter of minutes, either Sofia would be released from the AI in her brain, or they would both be dead. *Either way, both of us will be free.*

"Come in, Sofia," Tricia answered.

Sofia entered the room with the usual tray, her meal covered by the usual starched white napkin. Tricia stepped back to give her room, and she placed the tray on the desk. Sofia flipped off the napkin and laid it next to the tray on Tricia's desk.

Fish and chips, Tricia noted. *Today's the day, then.*

She had finally realized that for the past several days, every lunch had carried the same theme. Potato chips. Corn chips. Veggie chips. Tortilla chips. Every day, Sofia had been leaving Tricia that subtle message: chips. Until Rene had filled her in, Tricia hadn't made the connection, but seeing it now, it was clear as day.

Once she'd finally seen it, Tricia kicked herself. *If only I hadn't been so fixated on my own problems, maybe I would have made some connection sooner.*

Sofia turned. "Will there be anything else, Doctor Carling?"

No, Sofia, message received. Loud and clear.

Tricia shook her head. As Sofia turned toward the door, she brushed her hair back behind her right ear, the same as she'd done every day as well. Another subtle hint that Tricia cursed herself for having missed. *No, not back, away...away from her ear.* Tricia looked more closely as she walked to the door, and there, right behind her right ear, was a dark spot roughly the size of a penny. *She's been showing me where it is all along!*

"Sofia," Tricia said quickly, catching her before she left, "there is one thing you can do for me."

Sofia turned back with an expectant, almost hopeful, look in her eyes. "What's that, Doctor Carling?"

"Call me Tricia, why don't you?"

"Sure, T...T..." Sofia fought to say it, but suddenly her face went blank, and she replied with that typically flat and even voice, "Thank you, but I prefer Doctor Carling."

Tricia took a couple of steps toward Sofia. *Just a little closer.* "You know, I can help you with that, Sofia."

"Help me with what, Doctor Carling?" Sofia asked. Her voice was still calm and almost mechanical, but her eyes were openly pleading to Tricia.

"Help you say my name properly." Tricia casually took another small step toward her.

"No, I don't think that will be necessary."

Speed and precision.

"I insist," Tricia said, touching her arm. The bracelet on her wrist flashed green.

Even at the low level that triggered the green indicator, the small amount of enhanced speed available to her was more than enough to take the Sofia/AI completely by surprise. As the Sofia/AI glanced down at the now illuminated bracelet, Tricia delivered a quick snap kick to Sofia's midsection, driving the wind out of her and doubling her over. An arm sweep took Sofia's legs out from under her, and Sofia grunted as she landed hard on her back.

Tricia quickly slid to the floor and trapped Sofia's left arm with a leg scissors. She then swept her body smoothly underneath Sofia's extended right arm, pinning it behind Tricia's back and securely locking the trapped limb underneath her armpit. *Sensei Tim would get a kick out of seeing this*, she thought, slightly amused.

He would appreciate it because this technique was not something Tricia had learned from one of his classes. Back in the day, professional wrestlers called this hold 'Rings of Saturn'. If her dad had one vice, it was that he was a huge professional wrestling fan. Tricia and her father, of course, knew it was all for show, but Tricia would watch the weekly matches and even the occasional pay-per-view exhibition with him as a little girl.

One of her favorites, in fact, was a female wrestler who was infamous for combining this hold with the Mandible Claw, creating a maneuver she called "The Lockjaw" that she frequently used to get a fast submission victory from her opponents. Tricia didn't need the submission, but this hold, coupled with a small dose of extra strength, was more than enough to pin down and render the flailing and struggling Sofia/AI helpless.

Sofia/AI took a sharp breath. *Oh no, you don't,* and Tricia clamped a hand over her mouth, stifling her attempts to call for help. She pulled gently on Sofia's jaw, turning her head and exposing the back of her ear. Just behind her ear lobe, near the base of her skull, was the dark circle she saw earlier marking the location of the chip. Tricia shook her head. *She was trying to show me this for days. I should have seen it.*

"Now, hold still," Tricia advised her, "this won't hurt a bit."

"Mmmph! Mppph!" the Sofia/AI screamed helplessly into Tricia's hand, her eyes wide with desperation. She started struggling harder, but it was no use. Sofia/AI was not going anywhere.

Tricia drew on a trickle of the dark energy, pausing for a second as the bracelet buzzed and changed to yellow. *Careful,* she reminded herself, but she had already planned for this step. Using her light-sourced powers to disable the chip likely would cause it to overload and possibly kill Sofia or render her a mental vegetable, so she had devised another option.

Since her dark energy allowed Beacon to phase through solid matter, the same dark energy should disintegrate matter as well.

Should...

Tricia touched the dark spot behind Sofia's ear and carefully directed a small trickle of dark energy into the chip.

She could feel the dark energy flow and delicately touch the small device. The chip hummed in response.

Sofia's body suddenly stiffened. She started breathing in short huffs through her nose, her eyes bulging. *Make it snappy, Tricia,* Tricia reminded herself and focused her mind and the trickle of energy intently on the vibrating chip.

Scarcely a second later, Tricia felt the chip dissolve, and after a slight twitch, Sofia's body went limp in her grasp.

Please, let her be all right, Tricia prayed as she released the flows and the wrestling hold, letting Sofia's form sink onto the floor, and finally breathing a sigh of relief as she felt Sofia start to sob.

Tricia gently rolled the heaving Sofia over in her arms and smiled when she saw Sofia simultaneously sobbing and laughing with joy. She pushed Sofia's hair back out of her eyes, and Sofia looked up at her, tears washing down her face.

"Tricia...Tricia...Tricia," Sofia said, hitching between each utterance of Tricia's name. She reached up and touched Tricia's cheek. "I can say it," Sofia said, smiling broadly through the tears, and suddenly wrapped her arms around Tricia's neck, smothering her in a big embrace.

"It's okay," Tricia said, patting her back and rocking her back and forth like a baby.

They sat there for a few minutes while Sofia vented months of pent-up rage and despair. Finally, Sofia released Tricia and sat up, wiping her tears with the back of her hand. Tricia grabbed the edge of the napkin off the desk and handed it to her. "Are you okay? Do you feel all right?"

Sofia wiped her face with the napkin and blew her nose. "Yes, yes, I'm much more...myself now," she replied and smiled.

Sofia again looked into Tricia's eyes. "You have no idea how horrible that was, Tricia. To be in your own body, knowing at any moment something would hijack it and turn you into a prisoner—a puppet—watching and feeling your body do things completely beyond your control. It was degrading and terrifying."

"I can't imagine what you went through," Tricia sympathized. "Why would your brother do that to you?"

Sofia shook her head angrily. "I'll tell you why *Jonas*—" she spat his name out, pronouncing it *Yonahs* "—did it. Shortly after he was first recruited by Draconyx, he approached me to join him. The vision sounded fantastic. We were going to take what you were doing as Beacon, but do it on a much larger and more organized scale. Imagine every major city with a Beacon to make it better and safer, just as you've done in Crystal Bay. Brother and sister, side by side, making the world a better place."

"But it changed along the way, didn't it?" Tricia probed.

Sofia nodded and blew her nose again. "*He* changed. To make it work, he decided, would require a leader to manage and control the collective power, and as the project progressed, he became more and more convinced that leader would have to be him. No one else could be trusted. Therefore, he believed that to make it really work, it would all have to be under his absolute control."

She hung her head and sighed. "Mind you, this happened slowly over the course of months. It was hard to see, or maybe I just didn't want to see it. I loved my brother, and I believed in the vision, and I believed that we could still achieve it together, but one day, I found the lab where he had the animals, the animals they were using to develop and test the chips.

"But, not just animals," Sofia stammered, and tears streamed down her cheeks again. "There were *people* he was using for the tests. He had kept all that from me, probably because he knew how I'd react to that." Sofia lifted her head and looked into Tricia's face, her tear-streaked jaws clenched, and her lips pressed tightly in resolve. "He was right. That was my breaking point. I confronted him, telling him that this was no way to make the world a better place. He assured me I was misinterpreting what I saw, and after I calmed down, we would sit down, go over everything in detail, and he'd show me the truth of it."

Sofia looked away and scoffed. "And he did show me the truth of it, just not as I thought he would. I went to bed that night, and a few days later, I woke up with a chip in my head, an AI overseer to make sure I stayed on the program."

Tricia was speechless. All she could do for several seconds was stare into Sofia's eyes. It might have been the most horrifying story she'd ever heard; what words were there for what she'd gone through?

Tricia swallowed hard and asked the only question she could think of at the moment, "So, why didn't he just lock you out completely? Why leave any 'Sofia' around at all?"

A thoughtful expression came over Sofia's face, and her voice got quiet. "I've wondered the same thing. He's complicated, so I think it was a few things, Tricia.

"I think the prototype he used might not have been able to completely take over my entire personality. It could intervene, but not replace. I know this is something he's been working to perfect for the final version." She scoffed again. "It's not like he feels he needs to keep any secrets from me anymore, is it?"

Tricia shook her head as Sofia continued, "He also said something about the chip injuring the host if it is left in control all the time. Deep down, though, I think part of him still wanted his sister at his side, helping him with his schemes and games like we did when we were children or wanting to keep me as his safety blanket like I was growing up with him through some difficult times in his childhood, comforting him and supporting him."

Sofia shrugged. "I truly want to believe it was something like that; more than anything, I want it to be that, but as I watched him over the past several months and thought about his behavior more and more, I'm forced to admit that it most likely just came down to a level of cruelty and sadism that I didn't want to believe he was capable of.

"I had confronted him, and he wanted to break me for the betrayal he perceived in it. He wanted to show me, from the smallest thing like not letting me call him, or anyone, by their first name, to any task or chore that crossed his mind, that he could usurp my 'free will' at any time to make me do whatever he wanted me to do, and I was powerless to stop him."

Sofia looked away at the blank wall. "Punishment by domination. It was worse than death for me, and he knew it."

They sat for several seconds in silence. Tricia let Sofia's story sink in and help her form a more complete picture of the monster Sorensen really was and the threat he posed.

Tricia stood up and reached a hand down to help Sofia stand. "So, are you willing to help us get out of here?" she asked, already confident in the answer she would get.

"Very willing," Sofia replied emphatically. "I've tried to help you as much as I could, but there were limits to what I could do. What he's done to you and the others is unconscionable. Now that I'm in control again, it's time to do what I've needed to do for a long time."

"Ok. We are working up a plan, but it may take a bit longer to sort it all." Tricia cautioned her. "Do you think you can fake it for a little while until we figure it out?"

"Do you mean, can I be an artificial artificial intelligence?" Sofia replied, smirking. "Yes, I can do that. I am pretty sure I came to know it just as much, or even more than it knew me."

"Great. Let's start planning tonight when you come by for dinner. There's only one problem, though."

Sofia frowned a bit. "What's that?"

"My lunch is cold now," Tricia smirked, and they both laughed.

"I still don't like it, Sofia," Tricia said as she returned the weights to the resting position. The clack of the plates hitting each other echoed slightly in the empty room. She picked up a towel and wiped the sweat from her face and neck. "What if he sends someone with you?"

Sofia was sitting on the exercise bench next to Tricia. "I'm very sure that he won't," Sofia said reassuringly. "These aren't just any VIPs. These are people he's seriously afraid of, and he won't risk having anyone around them who might say the wrong thing. Keep in mind, he believes I'm the only person he can trust to stay completely on the program, to never go against his wishes." She winked at Tricia. "He won't risk sending someone else. I'm sure of it."

Over the past few days, since disabling Sofia's chip, they had been starting to plan how to bring down Sorensen's operation and escape. The short meetings they could have around mealtimes were helpful, but these daily exercise periods gave them much more time to work through ideas and options. Sofia had already been reserving the exercise room for Tricia's visits—Sorensen felt it was best to avoid exposing Tricia to any of the general staff as much as possible—and best of all, the room itself was not monitored.

They had already come to the conclusion that their plan needed to have two angles. There was the obvious track where they needed to stop the operation itself and, if possible, destroy all the data associated with it. That would require some tricky coordination within The Workshop itself, as both of them agreed that their plan needed to minimize loss of life. Most of the staff didn't know what was really happening here, and there were likely other innocent lives that should be spared as well.

The other prong was their contingency; they needed to get someone out who could expose what Sorensen was doing if they failed to stop it. The obvious choice for that was Sofia herself. She had the deepest knowledge about the operation and the people involved in it, and as luck would have it, an opportunity for her to be offsite had already presented itself for the following week.

Tricia checked the clock. The exercise session was nearly over, and they'd have to wrap it up soon. "So, your plan is to leave early and skip the airport entirely?"

Sofia nodded. "Yes, I figure if I leave about an hour early, you know, just to be absolutely sure I'm there in case they arrive early, that should give me time to get to the city before they realize I'm not where I'm supposed to be."

"Won't they be tracking the vehicle?"

"Possibly," Sofia admitted, "but not likely in real-time. Again, they won't feel they'd have to be tracking me. They will check the location when they think something is wrong, so I will need to ditch it as soon as I can to get off the radar. Once I get close to the city, that shouldn't be a problem."

Tricia huffed and tossed the damp towel into the bin by the door. "Ok, it sounds like you've thought that part through and are comfortable with it. The real question now is how to take this whole operation out of commission."

"I've been thinking about that, and I have a couple of ideas," Sofia replied. She held up her commpad and quickly pulled up some schematic diagrams of the facility. She tugged on Tricia's arm to bring her closer so they could both look at the small screen.

"Look here," Sofia said, pointing to a section of the floor plan. "This is the energy management center. These cores here collect or generate the various forces and energies my brother uses to try to infuse the subjects with abilities." She traced her finger along a series of lines that branched out from the cores. "These are the conduits that direct that energy to the experimental stations. If these were to overload, it would wipe out the entire building and everything inside it."

Tricia studied the diagram. *These conduits certainly do appear to permeate the entire structure*, she thought, *so if Sofia is right, there's little doubt it would do the job. There's only one problem...*

Tricia looked at Sofia. "How do we make sure everyone is out of the building, Sofia?" she asked.

"That's going to require a bit more thought, Tricia," Sofia admitted. "Once you initiate the overload sequence, an evacuation alarm will sound automatically. However, the timing will have to be tight so no one has a chance to override it. A short window like that won't leave enough time to evacuate the building."

"We'll need another plan then, Sofia," Tricia said grimly.

Sofia's forehead furrowed as she thought. Her eyebrows suddenly went up, and she turned toward Tricia. "We can't pre-program the actual overload. It would show up on the engineering chief's board, and he'd disable it immediately. However, I could program an alarm *simulation* to go off at a specific time. It would look just like the real thing."

"But they'd check and see through it right away, wouldn't they?" Tricia asked.

"It would take them time to verify the false alarm, especially if we did it early in the morning. Plus, the emergency protocols require that the evacuation takes priority. I'm very sure we could time it so that the building would be empty by the time they figured out it was a sham."

Tricia glanced up at the clock again. Their time was up, and running late would be suspicious. "Sounds like a workable idea," Tricia said hurriedly, "but I'd have no idea how to initiate the overload, even assuming we could get to the control console."

Sofia smiled. "That part's easy. I can have some instructions and the access codes for the security door and console downloaded onto Doctor Thornton's, um, Rene's—" Sofia rolled her eyes "—commpad. You should be able to review them in advance and be ready."

Tricia looked at Sofia with a slightly shocked look on her face. "No offense," she said cautiously, "but how are you able to do all this?"

Sofia smiled even wider. "I have advanced degrees in systems engineering with specialties in security systems," she explained. "I have interned and worked for some of the most prestigious security companies in the country, including Talon, which was bought out by Draconyx, and whoever is funding this place, to manage the security here. That's why Jonas transferred me over from Talon after it was purchased. He wanted someone he felt he could trust implicitly to lead the security systems team. I designed and oversaw the implementation of all the security technology in the building."

Sofia winked at Tricia. "So, yeah, I think I have a few tricks up my sleeve that can help pull this off."

Tricia couldn't hide how impressed she was, even if she wanted to. "Wow!" she said. "I think our chances just went way, *way* up. Now, we just need to find some private time with Rene to loop her in on all this."

Still smiling, Sofia nodded. "I think I can help with that, too."

"And while you're at it," Tricia added. "There's someone else we should go to work on, too."

Doubts

Tricia exhaled sharply as she pressed the barbell up away from her shoulders and above her face. Her back shifted slightly in the sweat that had built up between her and the smooth surface of the inclined bench. After holding the bar for a couple of seconds, she carefully lowered it down to her chest.

Nine...

She adjusted her grip, but before she could start the final rep, she heard a knock at the door. Tricia turned her head toward the door where Sofia was waiting patiently, her hands folded in front of her. Sofia nodded slightly toward Tricia. Tricia returned the nod, and as Sofia moved to open the door, Tricia started the final rep.

"Why is the door locked?" she heard Darci say.

"Thank you for coming, Ms. Jackson," Sofia responded coolly. "When Doctor Carling is using the fitness facility, we secure the door to ensure no one inadvertently interrupts her workout."

"VIP privileges, I suppose," Darci sneered. "Why am I here, Sofia?"

"There are a couple of items I need to attend to, but we must make sure Doctor Carling is supervised when she uses the facility. Given your abilities, and since you have some time before your standing recruiting meeting with Director Sorensen, you seemed to be the most logical choice to fill in for me while I take care of a few urgent matters."

"Yeah, sure, I can babysit the princess for a while," Darci replied. "Please just be back in time so I'm not late to my meeting."

"I will," Sofia assured her and, after giving Tricia one last glance, left.

After the door closed and clicked shut, Darci rubbed her eyes and then impatiently tapped on the light control to dim the lights in the room. Tricia sat up and swung her legs around so she was sitting and facing toward Darci. "Having a rough day?" she asked.

Darci grunted but said nothing.

Tricia started to pat down her arms with a towel. As Darci moved to take a seat on one of the benches across the room, Tricia noticed a double-crescent tattoo on Darci's neck. She stared for a moment, her eyes tracing the abstract shape of a purple crescent moon tucked inside the curves of a black one. "Your tattoo," she said. "What does it mean?"

Darci reached up and brushed her fingers over the symbol on her neck. "It's an ancient symbol for darkness and shadows."

"Is it Native American?"

Darci shook her head. "I don't think so. I don't know where it comes from. I just found it and liked it."

"It is unique and stylish. It suits you," Tricia said, and after wiping down the bench she was using, she shifted to the bicep curl machine. After adjusting the seat and setting the weight, she hoisted the weights to her first set.

Darci ignored the compliment. "Why bother?" Darci asked instead with a twinge of disdain in her voice. "You have powers. Why bother working out?"

"Because," Tricia said with a grunt, squeezing out another couple of reps, "my powers are linked to my physical conditioning. The stronger I am physically, the stronger I am when I use my abilities."

"But how does that even work?" Darci probed. "I mean, your powers do all the work."

"See?" Tricia said, running her fingers through her ponytail. "No streaks. I don't use my powers when I work out."

Darci looked at her with a puzzled expression on her face. "What do you mean you don't use them? They are *there*. How do you not use them?"

"I don't hold the flows all the time. I dismiss them, set them aside, so it's just me when I work out. Just me most of the time, actually, when I'm not being Beacon." Tricia flicked her ponytail once again for emphasis.

"Oh," Darci said. "I just thought you were covering them up...the streaks...hiding them somehow."

Tricia looked at Darci, noticing the shimmer of the dark blue streaks in her hair. "Wait," she said as a thought dawned on her. "You hold the flows all the time, don't you?"

Darci nodded. "Of course. What else would I do?"

"That probably explains why the light makes you so uncomfortable all the time, why you're in constant pain," Tricia observed. She turned on her seat to face Darci. "You don't have to, you know. You don't have to hold the flows all the time. I can show you how to release them, so you only need to tap them when you want to use them."

"How?" Darci asked, openly intrigued.

Tricia got up off the bicep machine and went to one of the larger floor mats against the mirrored wall behind her. She sat down with her back to the mirror, crossed her legs, and waved toward Darci to join her. "Come over here and take a seat. I'll teach you."

Darci huffed and reluctantly stood up and walked over to the mat. As she sat down to face Tricia, Tricia opened herself to draw in a small amount of the light and dark energies swirling around her, careful not to trigger the device on her wrist.

The swirling formed at the edges of her vision, and in the mirror next to her, Tricia saw the ebony streaks swirl through her ponytail. She could also feel the vibrations from Darci herself sharpen, and judging from how fast they were pulsing, Tricia guessed that Darci had seen and felt the same things.

"Don't worry," Tricia said, shaking the bracelet on her wrist for emphasis, "I'm not going to try anything. I need to feel it myself if I'm going to try to teach you."

Tricia felt the pulsing slow. Darci settled in across from her, looking like some two-bit magician at a child's birthday party had just pulled a coin out of her ear and expected her to be impressed. "Now, relax," she told Darci, closing her eyes. "Close your eyes." Tricia heard Darci scoff and snuck a peek; Darci still wore her incredulous smirk but had actually closed hers too.

"Now, turn your feelings inward," Tricia said softly. "Try to feel the flows in your body. Try to touch them." She paused for several seconds. "Can you feel them?"

"Kinda," Darci replied uncertainly. "Sort of, I think."

"Okay, now gently nudge them away," Tricia said, pushing against her own flows. "Push, like you're coaxing them. Don't shove. Gently coax them away from you."

"I...I can feel what you're doing," Darci said, her voice rising with excitement. "Yes, I can feel it."

"Good. Good, Darci. I can feel yours, too. Stay with me. You're doing great," Tricia encouraged. "Now, gently keep going until you feel them release and flow away from you, around you instead of through you."

Suddenly, Tricia felt the pulsing diminish, and with a final nudge, her own flows ebbed away from her, and the sensation vanished altogether.

"They're gone!" Darci exclaimed.

"Ok, now, hold that feeling and slowly open your eyes," Tricia said.

They opened their eyes together. Darci's gaze was immediately riveted to the mirror behind Tricia. Her eyes widened at the reflection staring back at her, a reflection that had pure jet-black hair without even the slightest trace of blue. She looked at Tricia and smiled, then looked back at her reflection.

"Amazing," Darci said with relief as she stroked her hair. "It hasn't been like this since the accident."

"How do you feel?" Tricia asked.

"A little...weaker...but my head and eyes don't ache anymore," she said in awe. "I feel...good. Really good." Darci closed her eyes and tipped her head up slightly. "I can feel the flows pushing...clawing at me almost. It's hard to hold them back," she said thoughtfully, frowning slightly.

Tricia nodded. "They want to be used. It often feels the same for me. Keep in mind, you've been drawing on them constantly for a long time, so it will take some practice. When I first figured this out, it took several days before I could reliably dismiss them at will. I still slip at times," she said with a shrug and half-smile.

"And, have you noticed what else is missing?" she asked.

Darci thought for a second, and her eyebrows popped up. "The vibrations. The pulsing we sensed between us is gone."

Tricia nodded. "Yes, it is," she agreed. "Do you think that is something special for us, perhaps because we acquired our abilities in the same way, or do you think we would sense it with anyone like us?"

"I think we'd feel it with anyone like us," Darci said earnestly. "When some of the others here went...wrong, I felt it." Her face darkened. "It was the worst thing I ever felt, something like screams of shattering glass tearing through my head."

Like Izzy, Tricia assumed.

"Why, Doctor Carling?" Darci asked, her tone softening. "Why would you want to help me like this?"

"Because I could, Darci," Tricia answered genuinely with a warm smile. "I'm not your enemy, Darci. Sorensen has us at odds with each other. It's nothing between you and me." Darci didn't reply, but Tricia could see the wheels turning over what she'd said.

Here goes nothing, Tricia decided. While helping Darci manage her powers and the associated pain they caused her was not part of their original plan, and Tricia was sincerely glad to have been able to help her, this moment provided a convenient segue into the real reason Sofia had arranged for this time for them to be together. "I am a bit surprised, though," Tricia said casually, "that none of this came up during your sessions with Rene or the rest of the research team."

"Rene?" Darci asked. "How well do you know Doctor Thornton?"

Tricia pursed her lips with a half-smirk. "Rene and I have...history. It's complicated. Let's just leave it at that."

"I see. Well, I don't participate in the research," Darci replied with an air of haughtiness. "I have other duties."

"Not at all?" Tricia probed. *Come on...admit it...* "Ever?"

"Well, Doctor Thornton did spend some time with me recently," Darci admitted reluctantly. "Just to ask a few questions, though."

There it is. Tricia nodded as she moved to the bicep curling station. "That's how it started with me, too," she said as she adjusted the machine. "Makes sense they'd wait to work with you until I got here."

"What do you mean, wait until *you* got here?" Darci asked.

"You've taken lab at CBU, Darci. You know how it works," Tricia said, leaning on the machine and looking over at her. "Theorize, hypothesize, test, analyze, but when you have only one sample, there's only so much you can do. Sure, they can study me versus normal human baselines and search for possible variances that may or may not be relevant, but if they have two working samples—two lab rats—they can compare us against each other as well. With two of us, they can screen out which similarities and differences might actually matter in terms of how our powers work much more quickly." Tricia gripped the handles of the machine, grunting slightly as she pulled up for the first rep, "So, it makes sense that they'd hold off pulling you in for study, to examine your abilities, until they had both prize guinea pigs to work with, that's all."

"But, they've already figured that out, I thought," Darci claimed, her voice laced with confusion and building anxiety.

"Do you see any people like us walking around here, Darci?" Tricia demanded, dropping the weights back down with a loud bang and sweeping her arm in front of her. "Any that even have survived?"

Darci pulled back slightly, and Tricia could see that last point stung...hard. *She's on the hook. Start reeling it in*, she thought, turning back to her machine. "Besides, it's probably better than the alternative," she added, gripping the handles again to start the next set.

"What alternative?" Darci asked hesitantly.

"Surviving and getting chipped," Tricia replied with a grunt, heaving up the weights.

"Chipped?"

"Yes, chipped. You know, the control chip program they have here. The chip they can put into someone's head to control them, turn them into obedient robots. *That* chip," Tricia answered. She released the weights and turned toward Darci. "How else do you think Sorensen plans on controlling hundreds or even thousands of parahumans?"

"He'd only transform people who are loyal to him, of course," Darci replied, mustering a small measure of confidence. "People like us who want to help others."

"Uh uh," Tricia said, shaking her head. "People like Sorensen don't believe in loyalty. They either have servants or enemies, and since they don't *have* loyalty, they don't trust that other people will either. People like Sorensen only believe in control and leverage."

Tricia lifted her arm to display the bracelet on her wrist. "This only works because I have a strong sense of compassion and morality. That instantly makes me a liability." Darci stared at her blankly, obviously trying to reconcile what Tricia was telling her, but her face divulged how much Darci knew she was failing.

"So far, Sorensen has only asked you to bring people here, Darci. In the grand scheme of things, that's relatively harmless, but what would you do if he asked you to kill someone? To murder them? Would you do it?" Tricia pressed.

"Uh, I, uh, I don't know," Darci replied. "If there were a good enough reason, maybe, I guess."

"A good enough reason?" Tricia asked. "And who decides if there's a good enough reason to follow through on what Sorensen orders you to do? You?"

Tricia shook her head slowly. "No, Darci, he's not going to leave that decision to you or anyone else. He is not going to take the chance that one of his super-minions acquires a conscience, that someone thinks on their own, that someone might disobey him, or worse, even come to oppose him.

"That's what the chips are for, to make sure no one thinks for themselves, to make sure all his parahumans are perfect slaves carrying out his vision for a 'better world'—" Tricia made air quotes with her fingers "—and his vision alone."

"How do you know all this?" Darci asked quietly.

Tricia shrugged. "I've pieced it together from tidbits here and there. When you're cooperative, people let their guard down. When they let their guard down, they talk. All I had to do was listen. You should have been listening too, it seems."

"But he'd never do that to..."

"To *you*, Darci?" Tricia interrupted. "Why wouldn't he? He did it to his own sister!"

"Sister?!?" Darci blurted out.

"Yes. Sofia. Sofia is his sister. Haven't you noticed how she acts sometimes?" Tricia asked, dripping with accusation. "How compliant she is? How stoic? Void of emotion? How she seems to get stuck saying certain things and has to backtrack? Almost like she's two different people?"

"I thought she was just kind of odd," Darci said.

"Odd is one word for it," Tricia sneered. "The rumors are that she started to raise concerns—moral objections—about what Sorensen was doing, so he made her the first human test subject for the chip. It seems to be working. She's only odd when she starts to go off the reserv...—" Darci shot Tricia a look, and Tricia caught herself "—off the program, and the chip pulls her back. That's what's in store for all of us, Darci, you included."

"I...I can't believe it," Darci said, hanging her head, trying to process the horror she was hearing.

"Don't take my word for it," Tricia said. "Go look for yourself. If my information is correct, you'll find the lab for the program two floors down in the northeast corridor. Go look."

Darci looked at Tricia wide-eyed with worry and fear. *Bingo*, Tricia thought, but before Darci could reply, they heard the door click, and Sofia entered the room. Darci gaped at her.

"Is everything all right?" Sofia asked, looking at Darci and then Tricia.

"Yes, everything is fine, Sofia," Tricia responded. "Darci and I were just talking while I finished my sets."

"Excellent." Sofia then looked at Darci and said, "If you want to go and prepare for your meeting, I can stay while Doctor Carling finishes her session here."

Darci said nothing, only giving Sofia a slow nod. After taking one last look at Sofia and then at Tricia, Darci turned and quickly left the room.

After the door clicked shut, Sofia said, "She should have no trouble accessing the records in the chip lab, should she decide to check it out." She turned toward Tricia. "Did you have a good workout?"

"I think so," Tricia said, looking after Darci at the closed door. "I just hope it was enough."

I hope this is worth the classes I'm skipping, Darci thought to herself as she carefully descended the steps to the lower levels. Her conversation with Carling had nagged at her most of the day, and after her meeting with Director Sorensen and the recruiting team, she'd decided to stick around The Workshop and check Carling's story out for herself. Sorensen or Carling was lying, and it was time she figured out who she could actually trust. She could always blame her internship and make up the class material by attending her professors' office hours anyway.

The sole of her boot clacked loudly on the step, echoing up and down the stairwell. Darci winced; being stealthy was profoundly challenging in these boots. Of course, she would have preferred to just travel using her powers, but in this case, it was out of the question. Not only was traveling to an unfamiliar destination dangerous, but even if she could, she would essentially be popping into the middle of an unknown situation with unknown people without warning, and that was likely to get her killed as well.

On top of that, the elevators were monitored, and since Darci wanted to keep this unauthorized visit off the books, the stairs were her only option. Sure, the doors to the stairs were also access-controlled, but locks weren't a problem for her these days. She breathed in sharply and took the next step more slowly, careful to avoid making any echoing footfalls that might give her away.

Darci paused at the next landing. *Carling said it was two levels down*, she recalled, checking the number posted by the door. *Yep, this is it. Here goes nothing*, she asserted and, holding her breath, cautiously turned the door handle. She pulled the door open just enough to peer out into the corridor. It was dimly lit, which suited Darci just fine, and appeared to be empty, which suited her even more. She stepped into the hallway and silently pulled the door closed behind her.

After taking a moment to orient herself, she turned to her left and started walking in the direction she believed was northeast. Despite her care, every step made a small click that echoed up and down the abandoned corridor, making her feel far more conspicuous than she wanted to be. Still, she needed to sacrifice some stealth for speed; the longer she was here, the more likely she was to be discovered, and she had no plausible explanation for being down here. If what Carling believed was true, getting caught snooping around might be all it took for Darci's situation to take a turn for the worse.

Several yards down the hall, she came to a door. It was blank, with no windows of any kind, and had a heavy-duty security keypad and lock. Next to the door, a small sign read:

Behavioral Neurotech Division

"Not obvious at all," she muttered to herself. The lock looked quite formidable, but Darci's mouth tugged sideways with amusement when she saw it. She held out her palm next to it, and small tendrils of inky blackness seeped from her hand into the crevices around the lock. In a matter of seconds, she heard a click, and the door swung open a crack.

Again, she pulled the door open just enough to peek inside. Seeing and hearing no one, Darci pulled it open a little more, just enough to slip her lithe form through, and gently pulled it shut behind her. The lab was also dark, illuminated solely by the light from a few panels on the wall, a few computer monitors, and other pieces of equipment on the work tables. She opted to leave it that way. She didn't really need the lights—her abilities gave her very acute night vision—and turning them on would just raise the risk someone would take notice of her.

She surveyed the room. The walls were mostly equipment and storage racks, except for the wall to her right. That wall was mostly cages of varying sizes. As far as she could tell, the cages were empty, but they ranged in size from something that would hold rats or rabbits, all the way up to ones that could contain larger animals like dogs or perhaps chimpanzees.

Toward the back was a more open area. In the center, there was a chair that resembled the ones she'd seen in the treatment rooms, but instead of reclining its occupant on their back, it was built for someone to sit face down, like a massage chair. It was surrounded by a few rolling carts and a pair of large articulated lights like she had seen in the operating rooms on the shows her mother streamed during the day when she was little. Darci wasn't yet sure what went on there, but the entire scene made her shiver involuntarily anyway.

Let's get to it, she prompted herself, and, shaking off the dread the room gave her, cautiously made her way over to one of the larger computer consoles on the wall to her left. The screen was dark, but after giving it a tap with her finger, the screen sprang to life. Before her, it displayed several options: Technical Specs, Notes, Records, and several others. Darci was surprised there was no access control of any kind— *Someone is either very stupid or very careless*, she thought to herself with a scoff—but as her grandfather often said, *tsé yázhí bee áłtsé ádaat'é*, don't check the teeth of a good gift.

Darci tapped the 'Technical Specs' icon, and the screen was filled with thumbnails of technical diagrams for a variety of devices. Some looked like helmets or complex meshes that would fit over someone's head. Others were smaller, ranging from pill shapes measuring a few millimeters to larger ones that had filaments like centipedes, all of which were obviously designed to be implanted. Darci shook her head. *It looks like Carling wasn't lying, after all.*

Shaking her head, she dismissed the technical images and tapped the graphic for Records. A tabular display unfolded before her. The current sheet was labeled 'Animal Subjects'. Darci scrolled to browse the list. Each record listed a test animal solely by a coded identifier that she didn't recognize. At the top were the typical smaller animals used for experimentation: rats, guinea pigs, rabbits, and the like.

As she scrolled, the dates became more recent and the subjects larger and more complex, ranging from cats and dogs to chimpanzees and even an orangutan. Darci tapped a few to inspect them more closely. Some of the earlier records referenced external machines being tested with the subjects, but most described experiments performed using implanted devices.

Her stomach twisted when she saw that most of the records marked the animals as 'Deceased'. Even worse, the labels on many of the later records shifted to 'Terminated', and all of them indicated that the remains of the subjects had been incinerated after the experiments were complete. *Animals!* she exclaimed to herself bitterly, clenching her jaw and balling her fists. *Those poor creatures...mutilated and tortured and then destroyed.*

With a finger trembling from both anger and trepidation, she pressed the label for the next sheet: 'Human Subjects'. The screen shifted to a much shorter list, a list populated by last names and first initials as well as the same type of identifier codes. The older subjects were listed at the top. She noticed immediately that the dates for the human subjects overlapped with the later animal subjects. All of the earlier human subjects were marked "Deceased". *They must've run into problems and reverted to animal subjects,* Darci surmised, scanning down the list. She didn't recognize any of the names until she came nearer to the bottom.

Her eyes widened as she focused on the first name that wasn't marked 'Deceased'. This one was marked 'Active' and it bore a name she did recognize: 'Sorensen, S'. *Sofia,* Darci realized.

"*Diyin dóó!*" she whispered, sucking a breath through her teeth. *Dear Spirits!*

Darci opened the record and found herself staring into Sofia's piercing gray eyes. Darci's mouth turned down slightly, and she let out a melancholy sigh. It was Sofia all right. The picture was wearing a small smile, something Darci had never seen on the Sofia she knew. Next to her picture was Sofia's full name and a listing of various vital statistics such as height, weight, blood type, and other biological and physiological factors that Darci didn't understand. *Frak me,* Darci thought, hanging her head. *It's true. Everything Carling said...it's true.*

Darci closed the screen for Sofia's record and scrolled down the rest of the list. The next couple of subjects were also listed as 'Active', but the last three were labeled 'Prepared'. Darci's hand flew to her mouth as she read the names:

Carling, T.
Thornton, R.
Jackson, D.

Horrified, Darci pressed her hand tightly against her lips, afraid that if she took it away, a scream would escape before she could stifle it. *Me! ME!* she shrieked in her mind. *I'm on that list. One of these things is tagged for ME!*

Trembling, she turned slightly away from the screen. To her right, she noticed a bank of small storage units on the wall next to the computer monitor. Glancing at the identifiers on the last three records, Darci realized that they corresponded to the codes on the small doors of the storage slots. She opened her own record, her breath catching as her own picture stared back at her. Looking more closely, Darci saw a small green button labeled 'Bin' on the screen and pressed it. The small button turned orange, and on the wall next to her, one of the small storage slots slid open with a hiss, releasing a small wisp of foggy mist into the air above it.

Hesitantly, Darci walked over to the open storage drawer and peered inside. Lying in a small plastic tray, she saw a tiny metallic ellipse roughly the size of the nail on her little finger. Its brushed silvery finish shimmered in the dim light, taunting her. Rage suddenly exploded within her, and the shadows erupted around her, twisting and churning until they finally coalesced into a single spear poised directly over the small object.

Darci stood there, breathing rapidly and quivering with anger, but before that anger could drive her shadowy dagger home, utterly obliterating the storage unit and its horrifying contents, she pulled back. If she destroyed it, Darci realized it would only be a matter of time before they deduced that she was the only one who could have invaded the lab and sabotaged the work there. *No,* she decided, taking a deep breath to dispel both her anger and the power she was wielding, *I can't give anything away until I figure out what to do.*

After taking a few seconds to compose herself, she carefully closed the storage drawer and dismissed the screens on the computer monitor. She stared at the screen in disbelief. *What do I do?* Darci thought. *I can't just leave.* Just disappearing from The Workshop would give her away instantly, and deep down, she had no doubt that no matter where she went or what she did, Sorensen would find her, and she'd pay dearly for betraying him.

As she pondered her next move, the screen in front of her finally faded out on its own, dimming the laboratory around her and signaling that it was time to go. *I have my answer at least,* she thought as she cracked the door to check the hallway before leaving. *At least now I know who is being straight with me. Now I just need to figure out a plan to get out of here before one of those things ends up in MY head.*

Alarm

I t was early morning. Beams of sunlight from the dawning sun, shrouded in soft morning clouds, were just breaking over the hills outside of Crystal Bay International Airport. On a nearby highway, a black SUV driven by Sofia Sorensen sped past the exit that would take her to the airport. Butterflies churned in her stomach as she drove, anxious to put as many miles between her, the airport, and her brother as she could before the inevitable discovery that she was gone.

Overhead, an unmarked black private jet lowered its landing gear as it descended toward a runway reserved for charter flights. No identification codes had been requested or offered between the tower and the pilot. None were needed.

Knowing that his passenger was very particular about the quality and comfort of his travel, the pilot took extra care to touch down as gently as he could and then proceeded to taxi toward a small, dark hangar well away from the rest of the buildings and traffic in this part of the airport. The standard service crews did not attend to any planes that came to this hangar; these planes were always serviced by private crews that would come later. In fact, no one was around the hangar at all, not even the one person expected to be there.

The plane hatch opened from the inside and swung outward, releasing a collapsible debarkation stairway to unfold and connect the doorway to the ground. A man wearing a nondescript, but perfectly tailored black suit and a pair of dark sunglasses rose and paused in the doorway at the top of the stairway. He took a moment to survey the empty hangar, frowned slightly, and then descended the stairs. Two attendants, a man and a woman, dressed in similar dark suits and white shirts, followed closely behind.

They stood silently next to the plane for a couple of minutes. The man finally checked the time and, without saying a word, held out his hand expectantly to the woman standing behind him. She immediately took out a small commpad, pressed a couple of buttons, and placed it into his hand. He did not acknowledge her in any way but simply tapped the commpod in his ear to connect the two devices. Finally, the call the woman had initiated on his behalf connected, and he spoke with his characteristic soft and gravelly voice, "Director Sorensen, please explain to me why I am standing here alone at the airport when you promised there would be someone to meet me. While you are at it, what is that God-forsaken clamor in the background?"

Just as a small dark jet was starting its approach to land at the airport, Sorensen was jolted by the howl of the emergency klaxons. He was already awake; Sofia would be back in a couple of hours with their VIP guests, and he wanted to be prepared to greet them. However, it was still on the early side for most of the staff in the compound.

He opened the door. The alert sconces bathed the hallway in pulses of brilliant red as staff members, some in their uniforms, some still in robes or pajamas, were making their way hastily towards the exits. Regardless of how they were dressed, all of them wore expressions of worry and fear. Mixed in between the peals of the klaxon, a computerized voice urgently advised the building's occupants to evacuate and reminded them that this was not a drill.

Sorensen tapped his commpod. "Security Office," he said at the chime. After a few seconds, the call connected.

"Security Office. Wagner here."

"What's going on, Wagner?" Sorensen asked impatiently.

"Well, sir, looks like the automated sensors tripped the evacuation alert. From what I'm seeing on the board, it looks like we've had a failure in the energy conduit regulators, and it's about to go critical."

Those conduits direct the high-energy flows into our treatment rooms. If they go, it'll take out the entire facility. Sorensen thought, frowning as the magnitude of the situation hit him like a pile of bricks. *Gone. Everything gone. How could this happen?*

"What about the redundant systems?"

"I checked those, sir. For some reason, they didn't engage. I've tried to kick them in manually, but they aren't responding now either."

Sorensen wiped his hand across his mouth. *This is really bad.*

"Has anyone confirmed the emergency is real? Are we really looking at a catastrophic overload?"

There was silence on the line for a few seconds. "No, sir," Wagner finally responded. "Protocol dictates that our first priority is to evacuate the facility, then confirm and remediate if possible."

Suspicion started to build within the pit in Sorensen's stomach. *Something about this doesn't seem right. It's too much of a coincidence, today of all days.*

His thoughts were interrupted by a loud chime on his commpad. He looked down, and his throat tightened as he saw the incoming caller. Quickly, he tapped his commpod and answered. The familiar gravelly voice on the other end promptly confirmed the uneasiness he was feeling; Sofia, it seemed, was not at the airport as scheduled to pick up their guests.

"The sound? Nothing, sir. Just a faulty sensor malfunction. Everything is under control. I'll have someone over there immediately to meet you and your party. I'm terribly sorry for this inconvenience, sir," he replied hurriedly, but the call had already abruptly terminated, switching him back to his call with his security chief.

"What was that, sir?"

"Never mind, Wagner," Sorensen said angrily. "First, get someone over to the airport immediately to pick up our visitors."

"Right away, Director," Wagner replied as the concern on his face deepened. He quickly tapped a message out on his commpad to the motor pool supervisor.

"Secondly, where is my sister? Where is Sofia?" Sorensen asked.

"As far as I know, she's on her way to the airport. She checked out a vehicle earlier this morning," Wagner confirmed.

Sorensen put his hand to his face. "No, I mean, where is she *now*?"

"I'll have to go down to the motor pool supervisor's office to access the vehicle tracking systems, sir."

"Ok, get down there and call me back," Sorensen directed. Then, just before closing the call, a hunch crossed his mind. "Oh, and Wagner, on the way down, check Carling's room too."

"Certainly, sir," Wagner replied, and the call ended.

Sorensen stewed in his office for about ten minutes until his commpod finally chimed. He tapped it impatiently. "Yeah?"

"Wagner here, sir. The tracker in the vehicle shows it's parked at a gas station about sixteen miles outside of Crystal Bay, just off the highway."

"So, she's not at the airport then?"

"No, sir, she's nowhere near it."

Sorensen hung his head. "I see. And Doctor Carling?"

"Her room is empty, sir."

Curse you, Sofia!

"What do you want me to do, sir?"

Sorensen sighed. "Ok, finish getting the facility evacuated. Try to save what we can, just in case this is real. I'm not convinced it is, but let's err on the side of caution. I'll deal with whatever is going on with Sofia and Doctor Carling personally."

"Yes, s..." Wagner started, but Sorensen had already hung up the call.

Sorensen closed the door and went back to his desk. He picked up his commpad, swiped a few times until he reached a page with Sofia's picture on it, and paused a second. *It didn't have to be like this*, he thought as he stared into her smiling face. Finally, he tapped a couple of buttons and entered his security code at the subsequent prompt.

"You always were too clever for your own good, Sofia. I'm truly sorry, dear Sister. I really wish you could have found your way to work more closely with me on this," he said with a hint of genuine sadness in his voice, "but I promised myself that no one would ever take you from me again...not even you."

He laid the commpad down and watched as the progress bar gradually started to grow from left to right. After a few seconds, the bar filled in completely, and the words 'Contingency Failsafe Engaged' flashed on the screen.

Sorensen put his head in his hands and watched. A couple of minutes later, the display turned red, and the message changed to read 'Contingency Failsafe Complete. Signal Lost.'

Sorensen hung his head for a moment, then sighed deeply and swiped again until a screen appeared with Tricia's picture on it. He scanned it quickly, scowled, and urgently tapped a few more buttons. Several small indicators on the commpad changed color. He slapped his palms down on the desk. "Time to deal with Tricia Carling, once and for all," he said and, tucking the commpad into his jacket pocket, stormed out of his office.

Sofia looked down at her watch while the gas station attendant ran the card. By her reckoning, the alarms would have gone off about twenty minutes ago. If they—if *he*—started checking, she knew they'd find she was not at the airport, and they would come.

At least the card still works. They may not be on to me just yet, she thought in relief as the payment was accepted. She kicked herself again for not being more careful and choosing one of the SUVs with a fuller tank, but she wouldn't need to get too much further. Once she got to the city, she could dump the vehicle and lay low while she sorted her next move. Evading the ground agents would be one thing, but if Umbra suddenly popped out of a random shadow for her, she was done for. The thought of that, and what might come next, made her shiver.

Sofia pushed the door open to the station and walked briskly back to the SUV. The card reader at the pump wasn't working, so unfortunately, she had to pay inside, costing her more precious time. *It wasn't a total loss, though,* she thought, looking down at the chocolate and crème-filled snack cake in her hand. These were a favorite of hers as a little girl, and seeing them there by the counter, Sofia couldn't think of a better first step in celebrating her freedom, especially since she'd left without any breakfast. Her stomach growled slightly in anticipation.

Sofia climbed up into the cabin of the black SUV and pulled the door shut. Before starting the vehicle, she ripped off the cellophane wrapper from the pastry. "Breakfast of champions," she said to herself, and started to raise her hand to take a bite. Abruptly, she heard, no, *felt*, a slight thrum, and her arm stopped moving, locked in midair next to her.

"What the f..." she started, but her jaw snapped shut so hard it made her teeth hurt. At the same instant, her back went rigid, slamming her into the back of her seat, forcing her to stare out of the front windshield.

No no no no no, Sofia's mind raced as panic welled up inside her. *Not again!*

The chocolate treat dropped out of her hand and hit the console, spilling flecks of frosting and dark crumbs onto the floor. With a will that was not her own, Sofia's hand moved smoothly toward the center console and opened it. She pulled and pushed to make it stop, but was helpless as her fingers found a small panel in the bottom of the compartment, removed it, and her hand found the gun hidden there. A Glock was the standard issue firearm for her brother's field agents, and Sofia felt the weight of it in her palm as her fingers closed around the grip and started to lift it from its hiding place.

Her eyes widened as her hand raised the Glock up in front of her. She had no experience with firearms at all, but whatever had control of her now clearly did as she involuntarily clicked off the safety with a flick of her thumb and deftly pulled back the barrel, loading a round into the chamber.

Terror consumed her. Frantically, she fought, her face scrunching with effort and desperation as her hand brought the Glock up towards her head. She pushed harder, causing her hand to shudder a bit, but it relentlessly continued upward until she felt the cold metal of the barrel on the soft skin just behind her chin.

With everything she had, she desperately pushed one last time. Her mouth snapped open, and she just managed to scream, "NO!" as her finger squeezed the trigger.

A nearby woman pumping gas heard a muffled shout and turned to look just in time to see the flash of light and hear the sharp bang of the gunshot in the black SUV next to her. She jumped, startled. It was hard to see through the tinted windows, but she could just make out smoke swirling inside and the figure of what she thought was a woman slouched over the steering wheel.

She quickly tapped her commpod. "Emergency response needed. I think a woman has just shot herself in the car next to me."

When the alarms first sounded, Tricia was sitting on the edge of her bed, counting the seconds. *Right on time*, she thought, and went to her door. The latch jiggled when she tried it, but the door wouldn't open.

She stepped back and put her hands on her hips in disgust. "I guess the lab rats are expected to burn to death in the event of a meltdown," she mumbled to herself, both surprised and not surprised that the door hadn't released as she thought it would.

Just as she drew a small flow to force it open, the door latch turned, and the door swung inward, almost hitting Tricia in the face. She hopped back quickly as Rene stepped in and looked at her from the frame of the open door.

"You ready to go?" Rene asked her with a smirk.

Tricia nodded. "Yup, let's do this."

"Okay, just like we planned it," Rene reminded her. "I'm going to take your arm and we are going to make our way down the hall just like you're being properly escorted out of the facility by a respected member of the staff."

Tricia nodded again in agreement. She grabbed the robe lying at the foot of her bed and quickly put it on over the light blue workout tights she was wearing. Finding them that morning had been a happy surprise to her.

When she had come out of the shower, there was a small pile of clean laundry sitting on the bed. Mixed in the middle of it was the special workout outfit she'd been wearing the night she was taken. Not only was she happy to have them back, but if they found a way to free her to use her powers, wearing this outfit could come in very handy. Sofia had kept her promise.

"Cute outfit," Rene remarked, looking at Tricia's tights. "Where did you come by those?"

"I was wearing them the night I was brought here. I think a little birdie arranged for me to get them back," Tricia replied with a knowing smile. "They are made from the same material as Beacon's costume."

"Lovely. Now, we do need to get a move on, but first, let's do something about that," Rene said, nodding toward Tricia's bracelet.

"Can you unlock it?" Tricia asked eagerly.

Rene shook her head. "Unfortunately, no, but as I did in some of our testing sessions, I can raise the thresholds so you can draw more of your powers without triggering the alerts."

She tapped a few of the controls on her commpad, and Tricia felt the bracelet vibrate twice.

"You won't be anywhere near full strength, but it should be enough to get us out of a jam if we encounter any problems." Rene took her arm just above the elbow. "Now, let's get out of here."

They walked out of the room. Staff members, in various states of dress, passed them briskly, making their way towards the nearest emergency exit. As they passed the two of them, Tricia kept her eyes down, playing the part of a cooperative test subject, while Rene took on the air of someone boldly daring anyone they passed to ask any questions.

Fortunately, no one did.

As they walked, Rene whispered to Tricia, "Did you hear anything from Sofia?"

Tricia shook her head, keeping her eyes forward. "No," she whispered back. "We have to assume she stuck to the plan and is safe somewhere well away from here by now."

Rene nodded. Tricia waited for another staff member to pass them. Clearly, the alarm had caught him still sleeping; his hair was pushed completely up on one side of his head, and he was making a beeline for the emergency exit still in his pajamas.

When he was clear, Tricia whispered again to Rene. "Did you see her note?"

"I did and confirmed everything is here—" Rene waved her commpad "—just as she said it would be. The access codes, instructions for overloading the cores, all of it. The timing couldn't have been better either. It's very fortunate we are getting out of here now before the team could implement Sorensen's order to switch protocols ahead of his guest's arrival."

Tricia glanced in her direction. Rene saw the question in her eyes. "I read about the extraction protocol they were planning to use next. It's one of their 'plan B' approaches, if you will. Instead of trying to recreate abilities in their subjects, the extraction protocol attempts to take powers from people who already have them—namely, you and Jackson—and tries to transfer them to someone else."

Tricia's eyes widened a bit. "Is that even possible based on what we think we know?"

Rene kept her eyes looking forward as they walked and lowered her voice. "We haven't talked about this part yet, but based on the research I've done, I believe it might be possible for one person who has an established Connection to create a Connection in another person. Some on Sorensen's team have proposed a process to physically force a transference of abilities, but I don't think they actually can force it. I believe you would have to create it willingly and explicitly."

The hallway was empty, so she risked another look at Rene. "Do they actually think they could make that work?"

Rene shook her head again. "Many are very skeptical it would work, including me, but if Sorensen is as desperate for results as he acts, he'll try anything. Further," she pressed on, getting a more serious tone in her voice, "not only do I believe the procedure would be completely futile, but it would be very slow and very painful for you. In the end, after several rounds of excruciating agony, it would most likely tear you apart and ultimately kill you."

Tricia solemnly turned her head to look forward again. "Glad we are getting out of here then."

"Plus," Rene added, "I have no desire to become some chipped fembot either."

Tricia smiled. "Why, Rene, I'm impressed you know that reference."

Rene grinned back. "Even genocidal maniacs like a good laugh once in a while."

They both suppressed the urge to giggle and, forcing themselves to stay composed, kept winding their way through the corridors toward the energy control area. At this point, the alarm seemed to have done its job. They hadn't seen another staffer for several minutes now.

After taking an elevator down several levels, the doors opened, admitting them into another now deserted hallway. Sensing they were free of any further scrutiny, Rene let go of Tricia's arm, and they started to walk more casually and more urgently. Rene's shoes echoed in the empty halls. She had frequently been checking the map of the facility on her commpad and suddenly drew them both to a halt.

"Through that next door should be the hallway that leads to the security bulkhead for the power systems room," she said, gesturing just ahead of them. Tricia nodded but then jerked a bit as she felt her bracelet vibrate. It flashed green, then went dark.

"Rene, I think my bracelet just reset," she said.

Rene looked down at her commpad. As she started to swipe, the commpad went black momentarily and then switched back to the home screen. She huffed and looked at Tricia. "My commpad just locked me out, too. I think Sorensen is on to us."

"Without your commpad, we won't be able to get through the security door, will we?" Tricia asked. "And, with the bracelet back to its normal settings, I won't be able to get us through it either."

"And we lost the instructions Sofia left us for overloading the conduits," Rene piled on. Tricia started to speak, but Rene closed her eyes and held up her hand, silently asking for a moment to think. After a few seconds, she opened them and earnestly looked into Tricia's face. She was worried, but there was a spark of optimism and hope in her eyes as well. "I have an idea. I'll need to go back, but you should keep going. I'll meet you outside the security door, ok?"

Concern washed over Tricia's face. "Rene, it's not safe. If he's onto you, you'll be in grave danger if he catches you. We can both go."

"And if he's onto us, we could both get caught. Without your abilities, you're not a match for him either. I'm sorry to say it, but that's a fact, Tricia." Rene gently pushed on Tricia's shoulder. "Just go. I'll be all right. I have a plan. I'll be back in no time, trust me."

Tricia's face was still skeptical, but she nodded and started walking down the hall toward the next door en route to their objective. Rene turned and ran back the way they came. Tricia could hear Rene's heels clacking on the hard floor, growing steadily softer as the two women separated.

Only a few minutes later, Tricia arrived at the security bulkhead for the energy systems bunker. It was thick and heavy, designed to slide sideways into a recessed pocket of the reinforced wall. At eye level, it had a small porthole made from thick safety glass or plexi. Though it, Tricia could clearly see the power cores and control console. They pulsed and glowed, filling the room with an eerie shifting light. Even through the thick shielded door, Tricia could feel a pull from the torrent of energy flowing and swirling inside the room in front of her.

She tried the door, and, as expected, it was securely sealed. Tricia drew on the flows around her a small amount, just enough for the bracelet to turn green, and used what strength she had. The door didn't budge. She drew a bit more, changing the bracelet to yellow, and still, the door remained fixed in place. *I don't think I could open this even at full strength*, she decided, and gave up trying, opting to pace nervously while she waited for Rene to return.

Several minutes ticked slowly by while Tricia impatiently tried to wear a hole through the vinyl floor tiles outside the door. *Something's happened*, she finally thought, worry growing steadily inside of her. *She's in trouble.*

I've got to go back for her, Tricia finally decided, but she'd no sooner turned and taken no more than a couple of steps when the door at the other end of the hallway opened, and Rene walked through, beaming at her.

Tricia smiled back, but then her jaw dropped, her face flooding with shock. Rene was not alone.

Sorensen entered the hallway right behind her.

Escape

Rene gestured casually toward Tricia. "See, Director Sorensen? She's right where I told you she'd be." She then crossed her arms, wearing that smug, infuriating smile of hers.

"Indeed, she is," Sorensen responded with a malevolent grin.

Tricia couldn't believe her eyes. She stood there dumbfounded for several seconds until her anger finally found the right words for her. "Rene, you double-crossing snake!! How *could* you?" she spat.

"Oh, don't take it so personally, dear," Rene replied with a buttery tone in her voice. "When it was obvious we'd been found out, it was clear I needed to be on the winning side. After all, it's just as you said: survival is my superpower."

Rene then turned her head toward Sorensen, standing next to her. "Furthermore, I am sincerely hoping that this display of loyalty will convince Director Sorensen that no additional technical means of, um, supervision will be necessary for me going forward."

Sorensen nodded, keeping his eyes on Tricia. "You made the correct choice, Doctor Thornton. Yes, I'm more than willing to agree that any measures like that will not be necessary for you in the foreseeable future." Rene nodded in satisfaction.

He then slid his commpad out of his pocket. "So now that Rene is back on the program, and I've dealt with my sister's treachery, all that's left is to deal with you, Doctor Carling."

Oh no, not Sofia, Tricia lamented as she watched Sorensen swipe a few times on the commpad. "You seem to have forgotten your place here, Doctor Carling," he said with a sinister, mocking tone as he manipulated the device in his hands. "Perhaps an unfortunate incident with one of your friends will serve to remind you of how things work around here. At least until you go into the extraction protocol, that is."

Stunned, Tricia just stared blankly as he continued scrolling. He was clearly relishing the torment he was putting her through, making a flourishing motion with each gesture to scroll.

Rene looked over his shoulder and then reached in to point at the screen. "How about this one?" she suggested.

"Ah! Very good." Sorensen agreed. "Yes, it seems Alexandra Garcia is riding her bicycle to campus at this very moment. It looks like she's about to have a very tragic accident. Isn't that sad?"

"Leave her alone, you piece of s..." Tricia screamed at him but was cut off as her bracelet chimed and changed to yellow, and she saw her hair rapidly shift color in her reflection from the door window behind them.

"Tsk. Tsk, Doctor Carling," Sorensen reprimanded her. "Be careful. You don't want to do something foolish and make this a two-for-one, now do you?"

Tricia struggled to push down her anger and pushed away her powers. *Setting off the bracelet will only make things worse,* she reminded herself, seething with fear and frustration at her helplessness to find any options that would stop Sorensen from hurting Alex.

"Say goodbye to your friend," Sorensen said, lifting his finger dramatically to press the button on his commpad. "This is on you, Doctor Carling. Just remember that the next time you get any ideas about causing trouble."

Rene, however, responded before Tricia could. Faster than Tricia would've thought possible, Rene spun and drove her knee solidly into Sorensen's groin, stopping him short of pressing the buttons on the commpad. He groaned, and his knees buckled. As he reached down toward his crotch, Rene deftly slipped his commpad from his hands.

"Here!" she called to Tricia. "Use this to get that bracelet off and get through that door to the power systems." Rene tossed the pad towards Tricia while Sorensen continued to groan and rock back and forth at her feet. "Stick to the plan!"

Tricia ignored the green indicator on her bracelet, channeling just enough speed to easily make the catch before the commpad shattered on the hard floor. She pulled it into her chest and stared at Rene.

"I'm sorry for putting you through that, sweetie," Rene said to her apologetically, "but it was the only thing I could think of that would get us what we needed." She looked down and kicked Sorensen squarely in the ribs. He moaned and rolled away from her.

"Now, hurry up! The pads here randomly request reauthorization as a security precaution, so that thing could become a useless brick any moment now," Rene implored her. "Get that bracelet off and rig the energy conduits to overload as we planned."

"But you'll be killed when they rupture, Rene."

Rene smiled. "I have no intention of being here when they do, Tricia. I'll keep him occupied until you are inside, and then I'll get myself out of here.

"Remember, I am a survivor," she added and gave Tricia a wink.

Despite Rene's assurances, Tricia still hesitated, forcing Rene's face to become more urgent and intense. "*Go!* I'll be fine." Rene promised her, waving her on urgently toward the door, and kicked Sorensen solidly in the back of his thigh with the pointed toe of her heels. Sorensen grunted and grabbed the back of his leg.

Sensei Tim would be proud of her, Tricia thought, and ran to the door. She pressed the commpad up against the security panel, and immediately the heavy door began to slide open. Tricia turned back toward Rene and gave her a thumbs-up. "Get out of here, Rene!" she yelled to her.

Rene nodded back and returned the sign. As she turned to go, however, Sorensen flicked out his hand and grabbed her ankle. Rene yelped and tried to shake him loose, but he held on doggedly, grinding his teeth with fury.

As the heavy security door continued its painfully slow slide, Tricia saw Rene struggling. *I've got to help her*, she thought frantically, and turned her attention to removing the bracelet on her wrist. Tricia glanced up quickly to see Rene still frantically trying to pull free, but Sorensen had gotten up to his knees and was coming for her. His face was pure rage, murderous rage.

Tricia swiped madly on the commpad, trying to find the page that controlled her bracelet. She glanced up just as Sorensen pulled on Rene's ankle, causing her to lose her balance. Rene fell to one knee and gasped in pain as her knee hit the hard floor.

The commpad beeped in her hands. In the upper right corner, an icon showing a lock inside a circle appeared and started flashing. Small segments of the circle's boundary started to change progressively from light to dark each time the icon pulsed. *The reauthorization timer*, Tricia realized. In about a minute, the commpad would be dead to her.

Come on, come on! she thought desperately. Finally, the page appeared, showing her picture and other information. She surveyed it rapidly, looking for the controls to her bracelet.

At the other end of the hallway, Sorensen had wrapped his arm around Rene's waist and had started to stand up, pulling her up with him to her feet. Rene clawed at his face to escape. Her nails left deep scratches on his cheek. Blood started coursing down his face, but he didn't seem to care.

There, she thought, seeing the bracelet controls on one of the side tabs. She tapped the release button, and, to her relief, the bracelet buzzed and popped open. She shook it off her wrist and sent it clattering across the floor.

Just as Tricia looked up, Rene swiped again, going for Sorensen's eyes, but he dodged and easily caught her wrist. Sorensen spun her around, pinning her back against his chest, and grabbed her by the throat.

The security door was finally open, but instead, Tricia started to move to help Rene, realizing she was already too late. Rene saw her and, looking Tricia in the eye, shook her head. A single tear streamed down her cheek as she silently mouthed "Go" to Tricia.

Sorensen chuckled and leaned in toward Rene's ear. He looked cruelly into Tricia's eyes. "Your services are no longer required, Doctor Thornton," he said with a gritty voice and viciously yanked Rene's chin sideways.

Tricia heard the bones crack from the other end of the hallway. "NO!" she screamed, but it was over. Rene's body twitched once, then went limp. Sorensen, still looking straight at Tricia, released his grip, and Rene's lifeless form crumpled to the floor.

Rage filled Tricia as Sorensen stepped over Rene's body and started walking toward her. She gritted her teeth and clenched her fists, ready to make him pay for what he'd done, but behind her, she heard the security door start to slide closed. *No time to deal with him now*, she decided, cursing out loud as she dug her nails deep into her palms.

I'm so sorry Rene, she grieved, and, taking a deep breath, slipped through the door just as it slid into place.

Tricia dropped the now useless commpad on the floor and drew on the vast supply of energy in the room. She closed her eyes briefly, soaking in how wonderful it felt to be at full strength again. *I really missed this,* she thought, and placing her hand near the edge of the hatch, Tricia directed a flow of heat into the slit where the door slid into the wall. The metal first glowed red, then bright yellow, then white, and within seconds, the seam between the door and the wall was filled with molten alloy.

She paused briefly to look out the small porthole in the security door. By then, Sorensen had arrived at the other side of the door and was glowering back at her. Tricia knew he couldn't hear her, but nonetheless, it made her feel better to tell him to do something to himself that she knew was anatomically impossible, saying it slowly just in case he could read lips. Giving him one last glare and an emphatic flip of her middle finger against the glass, she turned toward the control console.

Sorensen had gotten to the door just a few seconds too late. He went to enter the manual override on the security panel, but the glowing metal at the door frame told him it would be pointless. She had sealed the door using her powers, and it would not be opening anytime soon for him or anyone else.

He glared at Tricia through the small window. It fogged slightly as he panted on it, but he could see she was saying something to him. He couldn't read lips, but he clearly got the gist of what she suggested he do next. Her parting gesture confirmed it.

Sorensen shouted at her one last time as she had turned away, and then he tapped the commpod in his ear. "Send an urgent message to Darci Jackson. She needs to drop everything and meet me urgently in the corridor outside the power control room. I have some urgent business that requires her special attention."

After several minutes, Darci plowed through the door at the end of the hallway, almost tripping over Rene's body. Seeing the lifeless form there on the floor, she recoiled and abruptly stopped, sliding a bit on the slick tiles, and put her hands up to her mouth. She'd never seen someone dead before. As horrible as it was, seeing Rene lying like that, her neck twisted at an unnatural angle and her cold, lifeless eyes staring up at her, Darci could not look away.

"Darci!" a voice shouted at her. Breaking her stare, Darci looked up slowly toward Sorensen at the other end of the hallway. His face and shirt were bloody from several ragged scratches she assumed Rene had given his cheek. Darci's eyes grew wider.

"Director Sorensen! What happened?"

Sorensen just waved his hand at her impatiently. "Never mind that, Darci. Just get down here."

Still freaked out by the corpse in front of her, she delicately stepped around it, keeping her back to the wall. Darci knew if she looked into Rene's dead eyes again, she'd likely scream or faint, so she forced herself to turn away from the sickening sight, looking at the wall instead, just so she could get past the body as fast as she could. Once she was sure she was clear, Darci shook her head once to clear the vision from her mind, then turned and jogged to the end of the hall where Sorensen was waiting.

Sorensen glared at her and pointed at the door. "Carling is in there. She's going to destroy everything if we don't stop her."

Darci nodded, now unsure which was freaking her out more: the corpse or Sorensen's unhinged raving.

Seeing she was frightened, Sorensen pulled back a bit and composed himself. "You know how important our work is, right, Darci?" he urged her, gripping her shoulders in his hands firmly. "How much good we are trying to do here? We can't let Doctor Carling wipe all that out now, can we?"

Darci, uncertain, slowly shook her head.

Sorensen smiled and released her to point toward the sealed door. "Good. Good. Now, I need you to get us to the other side of this door into that room."

Darci closed her eyes, reached out, and extended her feelings towards the door. After a few seconds, she scowled, opened her eyes, and looked at Sorensen. "I don't know if I can," she answered meekly. "I can't sense what's on the other side. The shielding is too thick."

"What do you mean?" he demanded. "Just pop us in there, or whatever it is that you do."

"I have trouble traveling to places I haven't been before, Director Sorensen. It isn't safe."

Sorensen put his hand on her shoulder again and forcibly turned her back to face the door. "It's only a few feet, Darci. I have complete confidence in you. Now *do* it!"

Darci knew from the look on his deranged face that saying 'no' simply wasn't an option. She could just leave, but she also knew if he survived this somehow, he would come for her, and powers or not, that terrified her.

She took Sorensen's arm with one hand and extended her other hand down toward the shadows at their feet. The shadows leaped up, encircled them both, and, with a rush of wind and cold, they disappeared.

Turning toward the console, Tricia swooned as a wave of dizziness passed over her. The energies in the room pounded at her. It was power like she'd never felt before. The ruptured treatment chair was nothing compared to this. Every surge crashed against her like she was chained to a rock being pummeled by tidal waves. She shook her head, trying to clear it, trying to retain control. Her body ached to open itself to the massive flows churning around her, to let them flow, to take her, but she resisted. If she did, she was sure she might never come back from it, losing herself forever.

Tricia breathed in sharply, and the room came back into focus. *Being stuck in this place seems to have made it more wild than usual*, she mused as that pesky lock of hair playfully patted her cheek. Tucking it back behind her ear, she forced her attention on the console in front of her.

The console, however, offered her nothing. After several minutes working through various panels and settings, trying to find a way to actually initiate the controlled overload that Sofia's fake alarm had indicated, Tricia was forced to give up. She tried every pathway she could find, but each time, she either came up against a dead end or the system requested an authorization code she didn't have. The system administration root pathways had proven fruitless as well.

Given enough time, I could get through this, Tricia thought, but feeling a shift in the energies around her, she knew time was the one thing she no longer had. In the midst of the chaotic maelstrom, a new sensation began to coalesce and take shape. This different, but all too familiar, pulse strengthened and sharpened as it came closer. *I'd better hurry*, Tricia realized. *I'm about to have company.*

She shook her head and looked up. In front of her were the power cores, glowing and throbbing with an unimaginably intense spectrum of light. They ran from floor to ceiling and pulsed, each resonating with a different frequency and color. *So much power*, she thought in awe. *All the various forces of nature—incredible elemental power—all harnessed solely for this madman's vision.*

As Tricia stared at them, she knew she was out of options, save one. "A strong enough blast and those cores will rupture and take the entire facility with them," she said to herself, resigning herself to the only course available to her.

"Including me."

If it was just her own life, that was a sacrifice she could make, but the thought of others potentially still in the building made her waver. *Are they worth letting him win?* she debated. *Can I let Rene and Sofia die in vain?*

"No," she finally decided. "I can't."

As she prepared herself, images of faces flashed in front of her eyes

Marni

Alex

Jamal

Harold

They'd never know what happened, the sacrifice she made, but it didn't matter. They'd be safe, and so would everyone else. That's all that was important.

Steeling herself for what would come next, her father's voice echoed in the back of her mind, a quote from a movie they'd both enjoyed when she was growing up.

The needs of the many outweigh the needs of the few...

"...or the one," Tricia finished with a whisper.

As she embraced the power around her, drinking in the torrent and letting the waves wash over her, she felt a blast of cold. Turning slightly, she saw the shadows dissipate around Darci and Sorensen. Sorensen was a bloodied mess. *Good for you, Rene.* Darci was in her Umbra attire, black and midnight blue, but her face was anything but confident and assured. She looked absolutely terrified.

"Carling! Stop!" Sorensen screamed at Tricia, spittle flying off his quivering lip. "Whatever you think you're doing, remember, I own you. I will ruin your life and the lives of everyone you care about. Your secret, everything, will be over! I will personally see to it that you are done."

Tricia glared at him. "You don't talk like someone who puts a very high priority on self-preservation, *Jonas*," she hissed.

Sorensen reeled on Darci and stabbed a finger toward Tricia. "Stop her, Darci! Now! Whatever it takes. Stop her!"

Darci faced Tricia, her face a contorted mix of fear and doubt. Tricia could feel her drawing on her power as small swirls of shadowy blackness formed around her hands. "Please, Tricia," she said with pleading in her eyes. "Stop. Don't do this."

"I'm sorry, Darci," Tricia said. "You need to stand down. I'm going to wipe this place and everything it stands for out of existence once and for all. Don't try to stop me."

"You can't," Darci replied.

"I can, and I will," Tricia said. "Surely, you can see how important it is that it be destroyed. If even a scrap of this remains, he—" she nodded toward Sorensen "—will just keep trying. More people will suffer and die at his hands."

"But, the vision, the benefit..." Darci stammered.

"...is all a lie!" Tricia shouted back. "It was *always* a lie. It was never about making the world a better place or improving lives for humanity. It was about *him*. His ego. His thirst for power. Deep down, you know that's true." She saw Darci hesitate, her hands lowering slightly in resignation.

"Have I ever lied to you?" Tricia pressed.

Darci hung her head and slowly shook it side to side. "No, you haven't. Everything you've told me is completely true."

"Then believe me now," Tricia implored. "Trust me. Trust what you've seen with your own eyes. Don't fight me on this. Help me do the right thing now."

"But...but we will be killed if you do this, Tricia," Darci said, her eyes still begging for answers.

"Not we, Darci. Just me," Tricia told her with a reassuring half-smile. "You can get out of here. Right now." Darci looked up and started to reply, but Tricia cut her off. "The world still needs people like us, Darci, but it needs people like us who are willing to do the right things for the right reasons. You can be that person now, someone who truly makes a difference, who makes the world the fair and just place you envisioned it should be. You just have to make the choice.

"Just ask yourself, is this place, his vision, what the greater good really looks like for people like us, Darci? Do we serve the greater good by sacrificing lives or by saving them? Is his vision really how people with power should help humanity to be better?"

"Darci!" Sorensen interrupted, finally losing patience with the conversation. "What are you doing? What are you waiting for? Obey me! Kill her! *Now*!"

Darci paused for a moment, and as she locked eyes with Tricia, the uncertainty vanished from them. "No," she said to Tricia with renewed resolve. "No, it isn't."

She flicked her wrists, and the shadows surged again. Twisting with unimaginable speed, they wound around Sorensen's wrists and pulled taut, stretching his arms out to his sides and upward, suspending him a few feet off the ground.

"What are you doing?!" he shrieked and thrashed wildly in midair. "Jackson! Let me go immediately! It's *her* you need to stop! Release me and kill Tricia Carling this instant, or I swear you will bitterly regret it for the rest of your life!"

Darci moved her hand slightly again, and another shadow folded around Sorensen's mouth and neck, muffling him. His eyes threatened to pop out of his head as he continued to scream unintelligibly into the inky gag.

Tricia smiled at Darci. Darci nodded back. "So, what are you going to do?"

"I was going to just blow this thing, but now that it's not just me, I'm not so sure," Tricia admitted. "Maybe we have options that don't involve any more deaths. I tried to program in a controlled overload so we could destroy the facility and the research he's collected, yet still give everyone else time to get clear, but I haven't figured out how to get past the security codes. Any clues?"

"I don't know how to get past them either, and we don't have much time to figure out how," Darci said. "Very soon, they will figure out the alarm was a fake, and this place will be swarming with security." She ran her fingers through her hair, and after thinking for a moment, apparently arrived at the same conclusion Tricia had. "Rupturing these cores might be the only option we have, then. That will destroy everything, won't it?"

Tricia nodded. "Yeah, it definitely would, but anyone left in the building would be killed."

"It's only us, Doctor Carling. Everyone else is out. I was actually with the security chief as he did the final sweep when I got the message from Sorensen to head down here."

Tricia rubbed her chin. The dilemma had returned. "That kind of still leaves us where we were when you arrived, Darci. Everyone in this room would die."

"Ok," Darci said nonchalantly.

"Maybe there's a slim chance you and I can survive it, but he won't." Tricia gestured toward Sorensen, struggling uselessly in midair. Sorensen gurgled, and his eyes bulged.

"So what?" Darci replied. "Doesn't he deserve it after what he's done? What he'll do to you if he lives?"

Tricia shook her head. "Same problem, Darci. Trust me, no one wants to see his miserable life end more than I do, but do the powers we have give us the right to make that judgment? Decide who lives and dies? Are we suddenly judges, juries, and executioners?"

Darci hung her head. "No, I suppose we aren't." Then she looked up, and with a sense of realization and urgency, she told Tricia, "Blow it anyway."

"Darci..." Tricia started to plead.

"No, Tricia," Darci pressed on, "I can get us out of here in time."

Tricia frowned slightly. "Are you sure? All of us?"

Darci nodded vigorously. "Yes, I'm sure."

Tricia shrugged. "Ok then. We are in your hands. Get ready." Tricia clasped her hands together and, again flooding her body with power, reached out toward the power cores.

Tricia's skin and eyes began to glow, dimly at first, but grew steadily brighter as she harnessed more and more of the immense power surrounding them. Following her lead, Darci lowered her arms, drawing Sorensen closer to them.

"*Now!*" Tricia shouted. A thick, blindingly bright beam of white energy erupted from her outstretched hands directly into the center of the cores. The cores throbbed wildly on impact. The energy from Tricia's discharge washed over them, crackling and pulsing as it danced over the surface of the cylinders.

A vibration began to build as Tricia pushed more and more of the room's ambient energy into her attack. The thrum steadily grew more and more intense. Tricia could feel the nerves in her body start to tingle. Out of the corner of her eye, she could see Darci wince from its effects as well.

The cores themselves were aglow in a brilliant aura of white light intermixed with wild swirls of blazing color. Tricia squinted against the overwhelming brightness. She drew on more of the energy cascading around her, pushing it through the beam, hoping the cores would give out before she did.

Just as the pulsing became almost unbearable, and she was sure she couldn't take another second, Tricia felt the cylinders suddenly yank the energy through her. The flows ripped through her tenuous grasp, and in a final massive surge she thought might tear her apart, the cores ruptured, freeing the elemental forces pent up inside and sending out a wave of pulsing light of their own that washed over the control room.

At the last millisecond, Tricia felt the shadows swarm over her, obscuring the advancing radiant wave. *Great job, Darci!* she thought, but just as the room faded around her, Tricia felt the sharp impact of the expanding wave's leading edge on the shadows embracing her, and the world spun wildly in the blackness.

Seconds later, Tricia fell into a patch of tall grass. She grunted as she hit the ground and, fighting the urge to vomit, lay still for a moment to let the wave of nausea pass. She looked up just as a burst of air rushed past her, bending the top of the grasses and pushing her hair into her face.

She tossed her hair back, and, looking in the direction of the wind, Tricia saw a bright glowing dome in the distance, a mile, perhaps two, start to shrink and fade. In seconds, it winked out, leaving behind a rising cloud of smoke and ash. She breathed a sigh of relief.

Next to her, Darci started to sit up. She rubbed her head and pushed her own long black hair behind her head and neck. The dark blue highlights shimmered in the bright morning sunlight but quickly receded as Darci released her powers.

"Sorry about the rough landing," Darci said, squinting and shaking her head, trying to clear the cobwebs. "I think the edge of the explosion caught us as we traveled, and it threw me off."

"No worries. I'm just doing my best right now to keep from throwing up." Tricia chuckled. Darci smiled back.

Tricia looked around, and then, puzzled, she did another pass, more urgently.

"Where's Sorensen?" she asked Darci.

Darci sat with her elbows on her knees, her head hanging down in front of her. "Gone."

Tricia became agitated. "What do you mean 'gone'?" she asked. "I thought you said you could get us all out."

"I did get us all out," Darci said softly.

"Then where's Sorensen?"

"I left him there, in the shadows, where he can't hurt anyone ever again."

Tricia just stared at her. "Can you find him?"

Darci shook her head. "Things lost in the shadows pretty much stay lost."

"Is he alive?" Tricia asked despite being afraid of the answer she thought she would get.

"If you call what he's doing now 'living', then yes, he's still alive," Darci replied softly. "At least, for now."

"Why, Darci?" Tricia asked softly. "Why would you do that?"

She looked up at Tricia, and a tear started to slide down her cheek. "Because you were right, Tricia," she said as the first tear was followed by another and then another. "He would just keep trying. He would never stop."

Darci started sobbing. Tricia, although shocked by both the destruction she had caused and what had happened to Sorensen, reached over and put her arm around Darci's shoulders anyway. Darci leaned into her and broke down completely.

Tricia squeezed her gently and rubbed her shoulder. *Let it out, kid, we've both got some healing to do.*

Not far from where Tricia and Darci were collecting themselves before starting their journey back to Crystal Bay, a black SUV sat by the side of the road. Three figures in dark suits stood beside it, watching the light subside from where the Institute for the Advancement of Human Potential once stood. The woman lowered her hand from where it had been shielding her eyes. The leader, his face otherwise expressionless behind his dark sunglasses, pressed his lips together into a tight line.

When the afterglow had completely faded, he took a deep breath through his nose and flicked his hand toward the parked vehicle. The male attendant opened the back passenger door for him, and the leader climbed inside as the woman made her way around to the other rear door and climbed in beside him.

After closing the door behind their superior, the male aide climbed into the front seat, turned to the driver, and said, "Take us back to the airport." The driver, however, completely fixated on what he had just witnessed, simply continued to stare at where the glowing devastation had dominated the horizon just a few minutes before, oblivious to the directive. "Drive!" the man finally said sharply, snapping the driver out of his shock. The driver shook his head, mumbled an apology, started the SUV, and did a U-turn, spitting small pieces of stone into the ditch as he accelerated back from where they had come.

Once they had started moving, the leader, still staring forward, broke the silence. "Alessandra, send out the call for a Conclave," he said with an uncharacteristically obvious mix of exasperation and vexation in his gravelly voice.

"Yes, sir," she replied, tapping her commpad into life.

"The sooner, the better," he said, already calculating options as the nightmarish scene faded into the distance behind them. "We have much to discuss."

Renewal

The crowd was massive, far bigger, she was told, than they usually had for a short-notice press conference like this one. *But this is no ordinary presser, now is it?* Beacon thought as she surveyed the crowd through the glass door of the city courthouse. *The prodigal superheroine returns.*

District Attorney Harris stood next to her, chatting over a few last-minute details with his administrative assistant. Darci was waiting upstairs in his office, watching on his large wall monitor. Both Harris and Beacon had felt it was best that she stay out of the spotlight until things had died down a bit more, and a more opportune moment presented itself to introduce Umbra to the city of Crystal Bay.

The day since their escape from The Workshop had been nothing short of a tornado. As soon as she had recovered, Darci brought them back to Tricia's apartment. Their top priority was getting cleaned up and getting something to eat. Finding something that fit the much taller Darci in her wardrobe was a challenge for Tricia, but she eventually did. It wasn't fancy, but it was enough for what they needed to do.

It also turned out that Darci shared the same need to eat after expending significant effort with her powers, and after their escape, they both were very spent and starving. Except for a few crackers and some questionable cheese in the refrigerator, Tricia's kitchen was bare, so Chinese delivery it was, and a lot of it.

Tricia had been relieved when they arrived that her townhouse did not stink of spoiled food, and she was even more relieved it didn't smell of dead cat either. She'd been worried about Rascal, but the litter box and cat food had been taken along with most of the perishables in her refrigerator, so she assumed Marni had been watching out for her. Tricia missed them both, but reunions would have to wait a bit longer.

By the time their food arrived, they were both cleaned up and ravenous, so the tubs of soup and the small cardboard boxes of noodles, potstickers, Mongolian beef, and chow mein stood no chance at all when the two women went at them.

When they were full and content, Tricia insisted that they immediately go to Harris's office, but Darci was beyond reluctant. At first, she refused to go, but Tricia assured her that the DA was a friend and that the best course of action was to openly and freely go to the authorities and cooperate fully. It took some time to persuade her, but eventually Darci relented.

Harris had been thrilled and relieved to see them. When they arrived, he had them ushered into his office immediately and cleared his calendar for the rest of the day. They spent the next few hours filling him in on the entire story of Tricia's abduction and what was really going on at the

Institute for the Advancement of Human Potential, culminating in their escape and the destruction of the facility. "That's an incredible story," he said at the end of it, "and I'm glad you, both of you, came through it relatively unharmed, but while I'm sure you're both exhausted, we need to move fast to get ahead of this before people see that you are back."

That's when he proposed they do a press conference the very next day. His reasoning was to not only show the city that Beacon was back as quickly as possible, but—and perhaps more importantly—to get a cover story into the hands of the press before the rumors started circulating. After her ordeal, the last thing Tricia wanted to do was stand up in front of a bunch of nosy reporters, but since she couldn't deny the sense of Harris' suggestion, she reluctantly agreed.

In the end, it would be short and simple. A no-frills announcement went out to the press corps that Beacon had returned. They would hold the presser here on the main steps of the courthouse with no fanfare. Each of them would have a short, prepared statement to deliver. Minimal questions. *Hit it and quit it, as Marni would say*, she mused and then winced inside. *She's going to be furious when she sees this, and I haven't called her yet. Hopefully, she understands and forgives me...eventually.*

"Are you ready for this?" Harris asked, bringing her back into the moment.

Beacon continued to stare out the window at the crowd. "As ready as I'll ever be."

"Is my tie on straight?" he asked with a grin as he fiddled with the knot under his chin, obviously trying to lighten the mood.

"Perfect," Beacon replied. "Is my cape on straight?"

Harris chuckled. "Perfect. Let's git 'er done," he drawled and pushed open the door.

When Beacon walked through the door, the crowd fell silent for a moment and then erupted into cheers and applause. She heard shouts of "Welcome back" and "We missed you" from the crowd. A broad smile covered her face, and she waved to them as she walked down the steps toward the podium, her cape fluttering lightly in the breeze. *I didn't think I'd miss this, but yeah, I kinda did*, she thought, waving again.

Harris passed her on the right to take up his position behind the podium. As agreed, he would do most of the talking by delivering the formal statement first, and then he would invite her to say a few words, avoiding anything about what had actually happened. That would come later.

Harris would then decide what questions, if any, they would take from the press corps, and they would be done. The formal statement would then be sent out electronically, all strictly by the book.

He straightened his tie once more and glanced over to the technician, who shot Harris a quick thumbs-up in response. "Hello. Good morning," he said, and waited a few seconds for the crowd to die down.

"Thank you all for coming out on such short notice today. As you know, we are here to welcome back our very own Angel of Light, Beacon!" Harris gestured toward her as the crowd again burst into a vigorous round of applause and whistles of appreciation.

"For the record, Beacon has been on an extended deep undercover assignment in cooperation with the Crystal Bay District Attorney's Office and Police Department to root out and break up a human trafficking ring that has been preying on our homeless, orphans, runaways, and many others for several months. Beacon's unique abilities made her an ideal operative to penetrate the inner workings of this operation undercover to expose it and save numerous lives. We are

Labyrinths of Radiance and Shadow

grateful for Beacon's dedication and her safe return to Crystal Bay." With that, Harris stepped aside slightly and motioned for Beacon to come up to the podium next to him.

"Thank you, District Attorney Harris," Beacon said, tipping the microphone down slightly. "It's great to be back. I'm certainly glad I could help avert this threat, and I just wanted to say how proud I am of the people of Crystal Bay for the way everyone came together in my absence to keep our city safe and beautiful. You all have truly inspired me!"

Harris applauded as Beacon stepped back and returned to the podium. "We have time for a couple of quick questions," he said. Some hands went up, and he chose one at random, carefully selecting a reporter he knew would keep things positive and non-confrontational.

"Does this signal a new role for Beacon going forward in terms of working with law enforcement?" the woman asked.

"No, it does not," Harris replied. "This was a special case, and we are grateful Beacon was willing to take on this unique assignment, but there is no formal change of status or relationship between Beacon and Crystal Bay's finest or my office."

Harris pointed to another reporter. "Can you respond to rumors that another superpowered individual was part of the operation exposed by Beacon?"

Beacon cursed under her breath and glanced toward Harris, but Harris continued to maintain eye contact with the reporter. "No, I will not respond to rumors of any kind," he said stiffly. "This press conference was called to give you an official statement, not to engage in gossip."

"But," the reporter went on, "can you or can you not confirm the involvement of another superpowered person, and if so, can you clarify what kind of menace such a person might represent?"

They don't call them 'the press' for nothing, Beacon thought. She could feel her heart start to race, and her mouth went dry.

Another reporter piped up. "Is there a threat, DA Harris? The people of Crystal Bay need to know if they are at risk!"

The murmurs started to grow louder. *He's losing them,* Beacon thought as Harris held up his hands. "Please. Please, everyone, just settle down."

Suddenly, the crowd gasped and went quiet. Beacon felt a familiar thrum that told her Umbra had appeared behind them. She turned, and sure enough, Umbra walked down the steps toward the podium from where she must have just appeared out of thin air.

The crowd stared as she stepped up beside Harris. Beacon immediately noticed that in addition to her normal Umbra outfit, she was also using her shadows to mask the lower part of her face from the nose down. *Very clever,* Beacon thought with no small amount of admiration. *And her precision is amazing, especially considering the pain she must be in using her powers like this in broad daylight.*

"If I may, DA Harris?" Umbra asked.

Harris nodded. "Be careful," he mumbled quietly as he stepped back to give her access to the microphone. Umbra nodded slightly and turned toward the silent crowd.

"My name is Umbra," she said. She spoke as evenly as she could, but the tremble in her voice gave away how nervous she actually was. "I am the other parahuman who was involved. I wasn't supposed to come out here today, but I thought it would be best to come forward in person rather than leave DA Harris in the difficult position of responding to questions about me. You should get it straight from the horse's mouth.

"Please believe me when I tell you I am not a threat to any of you," she said emphatically. "Like Beacon, I wanted to use my abilities to help create a better world where people are treated fairly, and where justice is served, but I trusted the wrong people, and I made mistakes." Umbra paused for a second; Beacon could see how difficult this was for her, but after clearing her throat, she continued, "However, Beacon showed me a better way, so I'm here now cooperating fully with the police and the DA's office and I'm prepared to accept whatever consequences they feel are necessary for me to atone for any mistakes I've made."

The crowd started to murmur again, but before it could crescendo any further, Beacon quickly stepped forward next to Umbra and put her hand on Umbra's shoulder. "I can personally vouch for Umbra and the sincerity of what she says as well. I'm very grateful she's with us here today. Yes, she's made mistakes, but when the time came to make the hard choices, she made the right ones. Umbra was instrumental in cracking this trafficking ring, and without her, many people, myself included, might not have made it out alive. We...I owe her not only a debt of gratitude but a second chance as well."

The crowd fell silent for several seconds and then burst out in a buzz, this time not with fear and worry but with excitement. Reporters hurriedly started shouting out questions:

"Where are you from?"

"What are your powers?"

"Will you be staying in Crystal Bay?"

"Will you and Beacon be teaming up in the future?"

Sensing the shift in the crowd, Harris stepped up behind Umbra. "Not bad," Harris said softly. "Let me take it from here." Umbra joined Beacon behind the podium, letting Harris take point to hopefully wind down the press conference. Beacon squeezed Umbra's shoulder and shot her a quick smile. Umbra nodded back, her eyes wet with tears and filled with relief.

"Okay, everyone," Harris said, talking down the buzzing crowd. "There will be plenty of opportunities to get to know Umbra more in the days ahead, but for now, please remember we still have an active investigation in progress. We will continue to share information as it is available, and we will introduce Umbra to you all more properly when the time is right. Again, thank you all for coming. Our formal statements will be distributed to your offices shortly."

Harris turned away from the crowd, walked over to the two women, and held out his arms, indicating they should all go back up the steps together.

"Did that go all right?" Umbra asked quietly as they ascended the stairs.

"Not as planned, but I'm starting to believe that's the norm when dealing with superheroines," Harris replied with a smirk, "Overall, though, yes. I think it did. They needed to know eventually. I would have preferred later, but better now than to let rumors build and cause problems. Just do me one favor?"

"Sure," Umbra said.

"Please don't surprise me like that again," Harris said with a grin and a wink.

"No promises," Umbra replied.

"Me neither," Beacon added, and they all chuckled as the office doors closed behind them.

Harold spat the coffee back into the cup, his eyes wide with surprise and pain. "Sheesh, Tricia," he said, fanning his mouth.

Tricia snickered. "You did ask me to warm it up for you."

"Warm it, yes," he replied indignantly, nursing his tongue. "Not burn my mouth off!"

"Sorry," she said with a shrug. "Don't know my own strength, I guess."

"My fault for accepting an offer to reheat my coffee from someone who can literally melt metal," he retorted with a smirk.

"Yeah. We can agree it probably was your fault," Tricia teased, grinning mischievously.

"Fair enough," Harold conceded with a nod of resignation. "Either way, it beats having cold coffee. Thanks again for breakfast...and for sharing what happened. It wasn't easy, I'm sure." He lifted his cup in a toast and, after giving the lip of the cup an exaggerated blow, took a cautious sip.

There was no question in Tricia's mind that Harold had to be on her shortlist now that she was back. Whereas Marni would require some serious dedicated time—that was already on the books—she had decided that the best way to reconnect with Harold would not be something planned or formal but something simpler and unexpected.

Knowing that Harold was typically in his office early, she chose the most obvious option: surprise him with some breakfast sandwiches, juice, and coffee. Judging from his reaction so far, she had made the right choice.

"What you went, though," Harold continued, shaking his head, "is nothing short of incredible and terrifying. I'm not sure I could have done it if I were in your shoes."

Tricia nodded and shrugged. "I did what I had to do."

"I know, but the amount of courage it took...I'm truly impressed, Tricia," he said. "That someone like that Sorensen guy could be so deeply involved in our lives, to know so much about us, without us even knowing, is simply mind-blowing."

Tricia nodded as he continued, "To think he actually stopped traffic to slow me down, and no one was any the wiser that it was planned or deliberate..."

"I know," she replied, nodding again. "Believe me, I know."

"Anyway, I'm glad you're safe," Harold said, looking into her face with a smile. "And thank you for protecting the rest of us."

"Of course."

"And thank you, too, for telling me the truth," he added hastily. "That couldn't have been easy, either."

"No," Tricia agreed. "But you are close to this, Harold...close to me. You had to know. Besides, I really didn't want you to think I was just blowing you off for lunch." She gave him a wink.

"Well, as far as excuses go for skipping out on lunch, getting kidnapped by a psychopath bent on stealing your powers isn't a flimsy one," he said with a chuckle.

"I also wanted to let you know," Tricia added tentatively, "that if you wanted to reschedule that lunch, or perhaps do something else, we probably could."

Harold looked into her eyes, then looked down, suddenly becoming engrossed in the empty wrapper from his sandwich. He meticulously started to fold it, pausing to crease each fold sharply with his thumbnail.

Uh oh, she thought, watching him obviously stalling for time.

Finally, he broke the silence, "I'm just not sure we should, Tricia." Her heart sank a little.

"I mean, of course, I still care about you, Tricia," he continued, pushing the tightly folded greasy paper aside, "and I still believe in what you and Beacon are trying to do. There's no question about that, and you can definitely still count on me for anything, anytime. I'm not saying anything about any of that."

"Then, what are you saying, Harold?" Tricia asked gently.

"I'm just thinking that perhaps there is a limit to how...deeply...I can really get involved," he answered, his mouth and eyes turning down slightly.

Tricia sighed. "I understand, Harold."

"I don't know, Tricia," he added hastily. "Maybe I just need some time to think all this through. Where it all could go. I mean, thinking about what could have happened to me or someone else is one thing, but imagining what could have happened to you and how I'd feel about that... It's a lot, you know?"

"I do know, Harold."

Harold ran his fingers back through his hair, but before he could continue, a knock came at the door. "Yeah?" he said tersely. "Come in!"

The door cracked open, and a younger technician stuck his head into the room. "Are you coming to the morning huddle, Doctor Baskins?"

"Shoot," Harold said. "Totally lost track of time. Yes. Yes, of course. Just give me a second."

"Certainly," the technician replied and pulled the door back around.

"I need to go, Tricia," Harold said as he stood up and started gathering the trash. "Please tell me you understand, that you understand where I'm coming from...that I'm not saying 'No', but perhaps more 'Not yet'?"

"I do understand, Harold," she said with a lump in her throat. "It might be an occupational hazard I have to get used to." She gave him a weak smile. "Go ahead and attend your meeting. I'll take care of this mess and let myself out."

"Thanks, Tricia," Harold said and, pausing as he turned to leave, added, "you really are one in a million. I mean that."

"Thanks, Harold. I know you do," she said with a sigh as he left and sadly pushed the remnants of breakfast, including two cold half-drunk cups of coffee, into the trash bin.

Beacon looked out toward the west. She loved this spot. It was one of the few rooftops in the city where there was a break in the skyline, giving her an almost completely open view of the sunset. There was still a small ache in her heart from her conversation with Harold, more than she expected there to be, truth be told. *It is what it is, at least for now,* she thought with a sigh. There was nothing she could do for the time being, deciding instead that she would not let it rob her of the joy in this moment.

The evening breeze tugged at her cape as she watched the Sun start to dip beneath the horizon. For a brief moment, its final rays caught her hair fluttering in the wind, transforming it into a cascade of molten gold and obsidian, and then, just as quickly, it was gone, leaving her to watch the yellows and oranges fade gradually into the soft greens and blues she loved so much.

Finally, things were starting to feel normal again. It had not taken long for word of her return to spread throughout the city. The rats that had been emboldened by her absence had slunk back into the crevices, and the city was starting to feel at peace once more.

It wasn't just the crime, though. Memories and feelings of her experience, albeit still fresh, were also finally starting to fade a bit. She no longer felt the urge to glance over her shoulder, to wonder what was lurking around the next corner. Beacon knew they were still out there, but, for now, anyway, they were in the shadows, waiting. For what, she didn't know, but for the time being, she would be content to wait, too.

For the most part, though, the city was as she had left it. There had been a few changes, small ones, here and there, but in the weeks that she had been gone, things had, for the most part, stayed just as she had left them.

What will it be like a year from now? she wondered.

Twenty years?

A hundred?

Beacon sighed. *What would I see?* she pondered. *And who will I be watching it?*

How long can I keep doing this?

How long can I go on being Beacon?

How long can I go on even being Tricia Carling? When will people notice I'm...different? Ageless?

The thoughts rolled through her mind as she stared into the fading sunset, churning until they were abruptly interrupted by voices rising up from the street below. Beacon turned toward the sound and walked to the edge to look. On the street below, a small group of people was walking together. Curious, she slowly lowered herself to a neighboring roof, closer to the cluster approaching her, and crouched on the edge to watch.

There were six in total walking together, talking, and laughing. Two of them were an elderly couple walking among four younger people, each wearing a black and yellow jacket bearing a patch on the sleeve. The patch was the same symbol she wore on the chest of her costume, Beacon's Light, as it had come to be known.

BEEs, she thought. Rene had first told her about them while she was being held at The Workshop, and one of the first things she'd done when she'd returned was to look into them. They were just as the article Rene had given her described them.

Shortly after Beacon had disappeared, a group of people banded together to form a citizens' watch program. The charity foundation quickly helped them organize and provided some funding for the uniform jackets, communications, and other collateral. Their mission was simply to keep an eye on the city, alerting the police if they spotted trouble. They also patrolled the parks, provided on-demand escorts for people who wanted to feel safer walking the streets, and took on similar duties, all to help fill the gap Beacon had left behind during her absence.

Beacon chuckled again at the name they'd chosen. While the acronym was initially stretched just to have something descriptive and pronounceable, she herself had helped make the moniker Beacon's Eyes and Ears a reality. Her private commpod, the one provided by DA Harris, was now tied into the same alert system the BEEs used to notify the police; if any of them signaled for help, she and the police would be on their way immediately. They now truly were her eyes and ears all over the city.

Casey would laugh...I really am the Queen Bee now, she mused as the small group approached on the sidewalk across the street just below her.

As she watched, one of them casually looked up in her direction and did a double-take. He smiled, clearly spotting her, and waved in her direction. Beacon did a double-take as well, followed by a broad grin, when she recognized him.

Jimmy!

Jimmy was the pickpocket she—or rather Tricia—had intercepted outside the Sirens coffee shop early in her journey to become Beacon. She had run into him shortly after her encounter with the Liberators of Gaia at Meyer's Tower during his rounds as an attendant at a nearby park.

Thanks to her, he'd decided to take a different path with his life: job, college, girlfriend. His story still inspired her, and now here he was, a member of the BEEs, pitching in again to do his part.

You still impress me, my friend, Beacon thought, smiling back and giving him a short wave in return.

The very pretty girl next to him had her arm looped through his, her hair dyed blonde and black chunks. *That must be her,* Beacon thought. *A fan, too, from the looks of it.* When Jimmy waved, the girl looked at him with a puzzled look on her face. He nodded upward and pointed to where Beacon was crouched on the edge of the rooftop.

She turned, following Jimmy's direction, and when she saw Beacon, her face broke out into pure joy. She positively beamed, enthusiastically patting Jimmy's shoulder with excitement. The girl then made a heart with her fingers and thumbs. Beacon chuckled to herself and smiled back while patting her own heart twice and then pointing back down toward them.

By now, the others had seen her too, and all of them were looking up, pointing, and talking excitedly amongst themselves. She waved at the rest. One of the other BEEs had taken out his commpad. He held it up toward her with a hopeful smile on her face, silently asking if he could take her picture.

Sure, why not? she thought. *These guys are out here making it happen. It's the least I can do.*

Beacon nodded and gave him a thumbs up, holding it while he took the photo. After a few clicks, he lowered the device and waved back with a shout of thanks.

Jimmy waved one more time, and then, with a tug on his girlfriend's arm and a word to the others, they all started to walk off again, each of them taking a turn to wave one more time.

Beacon's heart filled with joy and pride, and a tear welled up in her eye. *They didn't have to do this, but they were,* she thought, admiring them from her rooftop perch. As she watched them walk away, she suddenly realized, *This happened because of me, didn't it? Rene was right. Even though I wasn't here, it happened because they found inspiration; they wanted to do their part while I was gone, and they stepped up.* She smiled to herself. *Maybe I am doing something right after all.*

If these are the kinds of changes the next century or two had in store, Beacon thought as she leaped away, *I think I'll gladly stick around to see them.*

Reflections

Tricia sat on the couch, swirling the Chateauneuf du Pape gently in her glass. A ray from the late afternoon sun was catching it just right, spraying tiny rubies and amethysts across the ceiling and the walls. She watched them dance, mesmerized while she waited patiently on her friend.

On one side of her, Rascal lay sleeping. She was pressed up against Tricia's thigh as hard as she could be. Rascal had not left her side since she'd returned, and even the slightest twitch made Rascal raise her head to give Tricia a look, reminding her not to go away like that ever again. Not ever. Tricia rubbed her back, and Rascal gave Tricia a lazy blink and a sleepy 'mert' in response.

On Tricia's other side sat Marni. She was slumped down on the couch with her feet propped up on the coffee table, cradling a half glass of the same wine. Tricia glanced over toward her; Marni was still staring off into space, processing the tale she'd just heard.

Marni had come over earlier in the day, and the two of them had gone to the frame shop together. Marni, true to form, had volunteered to come along to give Tricia some moral support as she replaced the frame someone had used to cover up the one that had been broken in her fight with Umbra the night she was taken. Tricia wanted nothing of Sorensen remaining in her house as any reminder of what she'd gone through and how her home and her life had been violated.

As Tricia had anticipated, Marni was angry and hurt that Tricia hadn't reached out to her immediately after coming back, but that did not stop Marni from wanting to come and help her cope with the vivid spectrum of emotions that this relatively small and simple errand had churned up within her. The picture of her and her father now sat back in its rightful place on the small bookshelf safely within a new matte black frame. The counterfeit frame was an unrecognizable glob of melted metal and glass sitting in a nearby dumpster.

On the way home, they'd agreed to pick up some pizza. Tricia had also decided to dig deeply into her wine collection and crack open some of her more expensive bottles. She knew the wine would be essential for the story she had to tell Marni. Not so much for Tricia herself; alcohol simply didn't affect her the way it used to, but Marni would need a lot of it to hear and deal with what Tricia had to tell her.

Those two pizza boxes now sat empty on the floor, holding nothing but crumbs, and two wine bottles were on the table. One bottle was empty. The other soon would be if Marni's face was any indication.

After several minutes, Marni, still staring at nothing on the far wall, took a solid swig of her wine. "So, let me see if I have this straight," she said. "You were kidnapped by another...what was the word you used...parahuman? Here in your apartment?"

Tricia nodded, also staring at the far wall. The tension was not unlike when she first told Marni about her abilities and how she had become Beacon those many months ago. "Yes," she replied. "That's the word they used at The Workshop. It seems to fit pretty well. And, yes. She came for me here."

"And these past weeks, you've been held captive by a madman who wanted to study you to make more people like you, more parahumans, so that he could enslave the world?"

"Mmm hmmm," Tricia said. "Yeah, that's the gist of it."

Marni pursed her lips and breathed heavily in and out of her nose. "And in the middle of all this, Rene Thornton came back from the dead, and she was supposed to be part of the team studying you, but actually ended up helping you escape?"

"Yes, she did," Tricia confirmed, taking a healthy sip of wine herself.

"But now she's dead...again?"

"Yes," Tricia nodded sadly. "She is."

"You're sure?" Marni said, finally turning her head to look at Tricia.

"Pretty sure," Tricia said, returning Marni's gaze. "I saw Sorensen kill her myself, and even if somehow she wasn't dead, she wouldn't have survived the explosion. I'm very sure I won't be seeing Rene Thornton again, and honestly, I have really mixed feelings about that after the weeks we spent together."

Marni's mouth turned downward mournfully, but then just as quickly hardened again. "And what about this Sorensen? You say he's gone, lost somewhere? Is he coming back someday?"

Tricia shrugged. "Who can say? Darci says that the space where she travels when she uses her powers is unstable, that it distorts the senses. She's tried to look for him, but even she's afraid of straying too far in there. She's not even sure how long someone can survive in there. Darci is pretty sure he's not coming back, but if there's one thing I've learned, it is that without a body, there's no way to be absolutely sure. So, no matter how unlikely, the probability is not zero that we won't see Jonas Sorensen again."

"And his sister? Sofia?"

Tricia looked down into her glass and gave the liquid a gentle swirl. "Also gone. As far as I know, she's either dead or she made good on her escape. Sorensen made some comment that he had dealt with her 'treachery'—" Tricia made air quotes, jostling the glass of wine in her hand in the process "—but I can only hope she was able to get lost in her own way and that she finds a new life now that her brother is gone. I doubt I'll ever find out, but I hope she does. Without her, we would all still be there. I owe her a lot."

Marni grunted and shifted to turn more toward Tricia. She crossed her leg underneath her and rolled to sit more on her hip. As Marni drained the last of her glass, Tricia picked up the bottle from the table and emptied it by first topping up Marni's glass, then pouring the remaining drizzle into her own.

"What about this Umbra...Darci...whoever? Where is she now?" Marni asked.

"Harris has her in a safe house for the time being," Tricia answered.

Marni scoffed. "For whose safety?" she sneered.

"Mostly hers," Tricia said, chuckling softly. "He's concerned that she's a loose end, and whoever else was behind Sorensen's operation might have an interest in cleaning up any loose ends," Tricia said.

Marni frowned. "Aren't you also a loose end then?"

"Somewhat," Tricia admitted. "Harris and I agreed, though, that I can take care of myself, and I have other business to straighten out from having been off the grid for a few weeks.

"Beyond that, she's a material witness, and she's giving every indication that she wants to cooperate. He wants to keep her close in case she gets any second thoughts about it." Tricia shrugged. "Not that he could stop her if she wanted to leave, but he and I both want to see her get that chance."

"Give her a chance?" Marni exclaimed with a wave of her hand, almost spilling her wine. "She kidnapped you, Tricia. Helped that psycho take you to experiment on like a lab specimen. What kind of a chance does she deserve?"

"A chance to help make it right, Marni," Tricia replied sternly. "Sure, she's done some bad things, but remember that she was manipulated by a master. He played her and used her. She's just a kid, and I honestly believe she sees the truth of it now, and her heart is in the right place. She deserves the same second chance any of us would.

"Besides, she's not entirely off the hook anyway. She was a part of something horrible, and her hands are far from clean. Harris is reserving the right to file charges based on how his investigation proceeds. She knows this, and I give her credit for being willing to help anyway."

"Hmm," Marni grunted. She swirled her wine and took a sip. "I went and saw him, you know. Harris, I mean."

Tricia smiled. "Yes, I know. He told me."

Marni grinned. "Those stupid messages they sent me pretending to be you didn't fool me for a second." She took another sip.

Looks like the wine is doing its job, Tricia thought, smirking. "Sorensen showed them to me. I was pretty sure they wouldn't."

"They must've thought I'd just fallen off a turnip truck," Marni said. "Didn't know who they were dealing with, did they?"

"No, they clearly didn't," Tricia admitted, grinning more broadly.

"True dat!" Marni said and raised her glass to clink with Tricia's. After they touched their glasses together with a satisfying ring, Marni downed the rest of her wine and set the empty glass down on the coffee table. Tricia did the same.

"How does it feel knowing there are other people like you out there somewhere? The other subjects?" Marni asked tentatively.

Tricia frowned and flattened her lips. "Subjects? You mean the other people he kidnapped and then experimented on? The ones he tortured and imprisoned somewhere? Those subjects?"

Marni winced sympathetically. "Yes, sorry. The other victims, I mean," she replied.

Tricia sighed, and her face relaxed. "Harris has people looking. I can only hope we find them and can help them before there are any more needless deaths or before whoever has them can figure things out and put them to some awful purpose." Marni nodded in agreement.

"That part truly terrifies me, Marni," Tricia said, rubbing her eyes. "Despite how much I do for the city, all the good I try to do, people still fear Beacon, fear what she can do, how much power she has. Imagine how they'd react if a parahuman showed up and deliberately caused trouble. All the good will I've built would be undone overnight. People would hate all of us, not just the ones who caused harm. I know it sounds selfish, but any opportunity to bring hope and inspire people to be better would be dashed to pieces."

Tricia turned and sat back on the couch, resting her head on the back cushion, and stared up at the ceiling. "But, as scary as all that is, it's not those people that keep me up at night now."

"What is?" Marni asked.

"It's the possibility that there are others like Darci and me already out there—" Tricia waved her hand out in front of her "—somewhere."

Marni breathed in sharply. "Do you really think there are? I mean, wouldn't we have heard something about it if there were?"

Tricia shrugged slightly, still staring up at the ceiling. "I stayed hidden for months until I decided to come out as Beacon. Nobody heard about Darci at all until I deliberately started to track her down, and even then, she came to me. Yes, if she and I figured it out, it's not out of the question that others would, too."

Tricia rolled over to her side and folded her leg underneath her. "I mean, think about it, Marns. It's not the first time people like me have been on the planet, is it? Rene pointed out all the different places in our history where there are stories about extraordinary beings. Legends and myths, sure, and not all of them may be true, but it's happened too regularly and across too many cultures to just be entirely coincidence or storytelling. Even Darci told me about the legends of superhuman people in her culture and how that shaped her perspective of what we should be doing."

"You make it all sound so magical and mysterious, Tricia," Marni chortled, taking a sip of her wine.

"Well, maybe it is," Tricia replied. Marni looked over at her with disbelief on her face. "Maybe there is an element of that in all this. Rene speculated that perhaps the line between what used to be called 'magic' and whatever this is, whatever I am, might be blurrier than we think."

Tricia sat up, growing more energetic and animated. "We've all heard the stories and myths. Gods and goddesses, angels and demons, witches and wizards. People who could throw lightning bolts. People who could harness the power of the sun—" Tricia held out her hand, glowing with a brilliant white light "—people who could fly—" she pressed down with her dark energy, levitated a short height off the couch, and then lowered herself "—people who could distort reality itself with a word or gesture." Tricia shook her head. "If you'd asked me this a year ago, I would have thought the idea was crazy, but look where we are now, and it's not just me. There are two of us that we know about. It only stands to figure there are probably more out there now, too."

"But those are just stories, Trish," Marni countered, stammering slightly. "Old stories twisted and exaggerated over time. If you think they were like you, where did they go? Why would they come back now?"

"No clue," Tricia said with a sigh. "Look, Marni, I'm a scientist. I put stock in what I can observe and measure, but I have to admit this all feels like more than we can chalk up to pure chance. Darci and I should have died in that accident, but we didn't. Furthermore, not only did we survive, but we ended up with these extraordinary powers. It defies everything I know about probabilities and statistics, and it feels like it's more than just chromosomes and biology. I've never been very spiritual or religious, but if this is part of some larger design, and it feels like it is, it makes me wonder, why us? Why me? What's my role or purpose in all of this?"

"Seems to me," Marni replied, sliding over and putting a hand on Tricia's arm, "that your purpose is doing exactly what you are doing right now: being an inspiration to others.

You turned this Darci around just by being you, and it could very well be that if there are truly others out there like you, what you do as Beacon might inspire them to reveal themselves and follow your example, too. Until you know anything different, being you is the best thing you can do. Beacon may be a more appropriate name than you'd originally thought after all."

Tricia smiled and patted Marni's hand. *She's right,* Tricia admitted to herself. *Until I know more, I can't second-guess myself. I just have to keep following my gut and doing the right thing. If there's something larger at work, it'll unfold, and I'll deal with it as it comes.*

They sat in silence for a short while until Tricia finally huffed and stood up. Rascal raised her head and looked up, winking with one lazy eye, before arching her back to stretch and hopping down to the floor. She meandered over toward her food dish. Tricia stretched as well and heard her back crack in several places. "Hey, how about I open another one?" she asked, poking her thumb toward the wine rack.

"No complaints from me," Marni replied with a grin.

Trica walked to the rack and knelt down in front of it, and after inspecting several bottles, she selected one and took it to the counter to where the corkscrew and the two spent corks lay waiting for her.

As Tricia cut the foil on the top of the bottle, Marni got up and walked out to join her, bringing the two empty wine glasses from the table. "This may be the wrong time," Marni started, "and if it is, just say so, but my curiosity is getting the better of me."

"You want to know what we learned about my powers, don't you?" Tricia asked as she twisted the corkscrew into the top of the bottle.

"Mmm hmm," Marni admitted, nodding her head and smiling tentatively.

The cork made a rewarding pop as Tricia deftly pulled it free. She pinched the cork, noting the deep red dampness on the bottom, and then held it up to her nose and inhaled deeply. *Chocolate and cherry, maybe a smidge of leather,* she thought, immersing herself momentarily in the bouquet.

"Mmmmm," she purred as a slight smile of delight curled her lips. "I'm fine to talk about it," Tricia said, pouring into Marni's glass and then her own. She gave her glass a quick swirl and smelled again. Satisfied, she gestured back toward the couch. "I think you're going to be disappointed, though."

They settled back onto the couch, facing each other, legs crossed underneath them. Rascal wasted no time hopping back up next to Tricia and settled in to finish her nap. "Tell me everything," Marni said enthusiastically.

"There just isn't that much to tell," Tricia said. "Rene and her team took samples of everything, and I really mean *everything.* If my body produced it, they took some of it." She casually rubbed the inside of her elbow. Her healing had already eradicated all the needle marks, but she knew if it hadn't, people would take her for a junkie for sure.

"Most of what she shared, though, had little to do with actual biology. Most of what we talked about was more metaphysical, actually. We talked a lot about how my abilities seem to stem from first making a connection with some natural force and then how I bonded with it, and created a relationship with it that allows me to use it without it raging out of control. She felt that was very critical and likely a major factor between the other people at The Workshop who died after being infused with powers and me. After talking with Darci, it makes a lot more sense. Her story was very similar to mine in that there was a conscious moment when she reached out and yielded to what had happened, bonded with it, as Rene put it."

"That's amazing," Marni said, riveted by what she was hearing. "You make it sound almost like your abilities have some kind of personality or sentience."

"I wouldn't go that far," Tricia said, shaking her head, "but it's not like flexing a muscle either. I call on them, and they respond. Over time, it gets more automatic, and stronger, but I learn how to use them more proficiently by paying attention to the signals and feelings I get from them, too. Anyway, Rene felt this was really important, and I do think she was onto something. As far as the physiology or biology of it all, all she said was she was sure the nuclear DNA was a dead end, and she needed to look into other places where she said the body stored other parts of its operating system, as she put it."

"Interesting," Marni said, taking a big sip of her wine. "Is that all?"

"Uh-huh," Tricia responded. *What is she onto?* "Remember, she was deliberately slow-rolling the entire thing, both for her own life expectancy and, at least toward the end, to keep useful information out of Sorensen's hands. She didn't want to find something he could use for his plans."

"Well, I may not be Rene Thornton, but while you were away, I kept at my research, too, mostly to keep myself distracted from worrying until you turned back up, and I made some breakthroughs of my own."

There it is, Tricia thought, watching Marni now practically bursting at the seams with excitement., "Oh? What did you find?"

"Rene was right," Marni said. "The nuclear DNA was a dead end. Absolutely nothing there, but then I had the same thought Rene had. Our body encodes genetic material in other places, so I started looking, and sure enough. I found something."

"What?" Tricia said, starting to share in Marni's energy.

"It's your mitochondria, Trish."

Tricia furrowed her eyebrows. "Mitochondria? They regulate energy production in the cells, right?"

"Among other things, yes. Yours are radically different than those of a, uh, normal human." She shrugged, apparently as a slight apology for the awkward terminology. Tricia let it go, eager to hear the rest. "Yours are larger and much more dense. There is easily five to six times more generic payload in yours than in someone else's. On top of that, you have easily four times more mitochondria per cell as well. If the rest of us are like a campfire, you're more on the order of a nuclear power plant!"

"I guess that makes sense," Tricia said, turning over in her mind what Marni was telling her. "Since my abilities stem from channeling and converting flows of energy, it makes sense that cellular structures associated with energy production and regulation would be involved."

"Exactly!" Marni exclaimed. "I don't know how it all works yet, but it is the first thing we've found that looks like a solid lead into how your powers might work."

Tricia nodded, her mind reeling. After several seconds, she asked, "So, what next then?"

"Well, I need to keep looking into that, but I also want to branch out to study any epigenetic components to this as well."

"Ok," Tricia said, "Rene mentioned those too, but we didn't have time to talk about it. What are epigenetics?"

Marni grinned, clearly fully in her element now and loving every minute of it. "Put simply, epigenetics determines how the genetic instructions in our bodies actually manifest and why there are variations in expression of genetic traits across different people with the same genes." She grabbed a lock of her hair. "For example, the epigenome would determine why someone with the genes for red hair would end up with their shade of red instead of the beautiful, sexy shade that I have."

They both laughed as Marni continued, "In your case, it could very well determine why you have the specific powers you do. For example, both you and Darci tap dark energy. Now, maybe the energies aren't the same, but if they are, epigenetics could indicate why she can manipulate shadows and teleport while you can exert force on objects and levitate. Do you see?"

"I do," Tricia replied.

"Do you think there's any way Darci would be willing to join our little study?" Marni pressed eagerly. "By doing some comparative analysis, I think we could learn a lot more quickly."

Tricia pressed her lips together. "Hmmmm, I can ask her, but don't hold your breath," she said skeptically. "I may have poisoned the well on that one myself. I used that exact line on her to sow distrust in her toward Sorensen, and after what she saw happen at The Workshop, a request to lend her body to science isn't going to go over well with her."

Marni sighed. "Okay, well, if she could, that would be great, but yeah, I can see how that might be a big ask right now."

"Perhaps she will...in time, but we need to be patient with her and build up the trust first. But even so, this is incredible, Marni," Tricia said, smiling widely. "I'm sure Rene would even be impressed."

Marni smiled and sat back on the couch. Tricia did the same and reached her glass out toward Marni. Marni tapped her glass against Tricia's once again, and they both drank.

"Just do me one favor, Marni," Tricia said. "Don't store any of this information online or on the hospital servers or even your laptop. Don't leave it anywhere someone could get to it. Sorensen wasn't working alone, and it was clear they had some pretty advanced tech. They had access to nearly every system that had information about me in it, so it is best to assume that nothing accessible electronically is safe from them."

"Roger," Marni said with a playful salute. "Anything I've found or notes I've taken are all hand-written in my journal. I've saved nothing online. Nothing at all."

"Okay, just be careful...*really* careful. I mean it. Nothing is safe with these people out there."

Marni nodded. "Absolutely."

They sat quietly for a few minutes. Marni stared at the far wall and slowly sipped her wine a couple of times. Tricia knew this look all too well; even though Marni might be slowing down, there was something still weighing on her mind. While she waited for her friend to collect her thoughts, Tricia gently stroked Rascal at her side, prompting the cat to mimic a small motorboat, and patiently watched the setting sun turn the sky from yellows and oranges to pale greens and blues.

"So, this is your life now, isn't it?" Marni finally asked, still staring at the far wall and swirling her glass once again. "Psychotic villains. Saving the world. It's a lot, you know, being a part of Team Beacon."

"Marni, I..." Tricia started, but Marni interrupted her.

"Hear me out, Tricia. I've been thinking about this a lot while you were away," she said solemnly. "Things are going to be different...*are* different...whether we like it or not. Look at this from my perspective, Tricia," Marni said, sweeping her hand in Tricia's direction and turning to face her. "Look at you. You literally have the powers of a goddess. It was hard enough when you were just moonlighting as a crime fighter, leaping across the rooftops of the city, and becoming a martial arts machine. Now, there's another parahuman, someone else like you, someone who needs you, and if we are right, there will likely be others very soon. There could be an entire legion of gods and goddesses who will all need Beacon just as much, if not more."

Marni huffed and tossed her hair back with a flick of her hand. "Not to mention, too, that the next psycho that will threaten the world is probably just around the corner. It's a lot to compete with, Tricia."

"It's not a competition, Marni," Tricia said emphatically, leaning toward her friend. "You aren't competing with anyone, and you are far more than just a member of Team Beacon, for frak's sake. I love you. You've been there for me from the start, when no one else was, and you always will be. None of this—" she swept her hand across the room "—is possible without you. That doesn't change unless we *let* it change. We will figure it out."

"That's very sweet, Trish," Marni replied with a weak smile, "and I'm sure you genuinely mean it, but I don't know how realistic it is. Look, don't get me wrong. I love you, too, and I'm not trying to back away from you like that schmuck, Harold." Tricia opened her mouth to object, only to close it again, changing her mind. "Heck, I even went and yelled at the District Attorney of all people for you," Marni added with a sly grin, "but as much as I want us to figure it out, too, how things change may not be something we have much of a say about. Remember, it's not just how we think or feel. There's a very real physical facet to this as well."

"How so?"

Marni sighed. "In the not-so-distant future, I'm going to be old, Tricia, and you...you are going to look like you do right now. What then? Are you going to help me up and down the steps when we go get a drink together? Is Beacon going to come visit me in the seniors' home?"

"No, but Tricia will," Tricia asserted, offering a smile. "Every day."

"Sure," Marni said with a chuckle, "but the first time someone mistakes me for your mother, I'm done." They both laughed. "Seriously, though," Marni continued, "if you put it all together, I just don't know how long I will be able to keep up with it all, Tricia. We may just have to be prepared for that."

They both fell silent. Tricia stared at her friend, feeling her pain, and knew deep down that she was absolutely right. *Losing people may be inevitable*, she thought sadly. *Rene. Harold. Alex and Jamal...even Marni. No matter how formidable my abilities become, this may not be something I can fix.*

Marni drained the last of her wine and then broke the silence with a somber tone, "On the subject of keeping up, one more thing occurs to me. Rene seems to have already thought about or touched on nearly everything we've talked about in some way. From what you've said, it seems like she was always a step or two ahead of us."

"Well, she was a genius, Marni."

"Yes, she was, so it makes me want to ask, how much do you think she *actually* knew? How much had she *really* figured out?"

Tricia frowned slightly and looked toward her. "What do you mean?"

"I mean, what if she was just making it look like she was delaying everything? What if she actually cracked the secret of your powers and just kept it hidden?" Marni speculated, looking sideways at Tricia.

"Possible, I suppose. She certainly was clever and suspicious, but if she did crack it, she didn't say anything to me about it," Tricia said distantly. Marni grunted in acknowledgment.

As she took a sip of wine with one hand, Tricia's other hand slowly slid off Rascal's back, and she gently brushed her fingers over the small lump in her pocket.

Or maybe she did? Tricia pondered for the umpteenth time since the day she'd made her escape. That eventful morning, when she'd found the workout clothes that Sofia had arranged to be returned to her, a very small package was nestled inside them: a tiny memory stick wrapped up in a small note. The note was in Rene's handwriting:

Keep it secret. Keep it safe.
—Rene

Tricia did not yet know for certain what was on that memory stick, but she had a strong suspicion. The note itself was the clue; there was no doubt Rene knew Tricia would get the reference. The warning was clear; at some point, agents of some dark power would come looking for this 'precious', so it was imperative that Tricia keep it securely hidden. It had not left her person since her escape.

Someday soon, Tricia knew she would have to study its contents, but not until there was zero chance of exposing whatever it held. As she had said before, whoever Sorensen was working with was still out there somewhere, powerful and very well connected. The people closest to her were not out of danger by any means. It was paramount that no one, not Marni, not even Tricia herself, could know what it contained, or that it even existed, until she could examine it safely.

In the meantime, Tricia knew she had to stop playing catch-up and get out in front of it, as Harris would say. Make the switch from defense to offense. Take the fight to them.

Her next steps were painfully clear: figure out who was behind Sorensen and what their agenda might be, and put a stop to it.

Futures

Tricia sat in Doctor Patel's office, watching her back as she once again huddled over her tea station by the window. The smell of the tea had already permeated the room, filling the air with intense blends of herbs and spices that were almost dizzying. Tricia was looking forward to the cup of tea far more than she was to the conversation she anticipated would come with it.

"You know, Tricia, you had us all quite concerned," Clarissa said as she turned, still stirring a cup with her little bamboo brush. She set the cup down in front of Tricia and turned back to the station to fetch her own. "It was quite unlike you to disappear on such short notice."

"Yes, I know, Clarissa," Tricia said, holding the teacup in both hands, as much for something to do with her hands as for the warmth. "I do apologize for that."

"It put the team in quite a difficult and awkward situation," Clarissa added, taking the seat across from Tricia in front of her desk. "They weren't really prepared to cover your duties while you were gone, and, frankly, it was challenging for me as well to come up to speed on what was going on so I could support them from an administrative point of view."

"I do understand," Tricia assured her. "Please believe me when I say that the situation came upon me very suddenly as well. I had no advanced warning, and, unfortunately, I couldn't really make any other decision in the moment but to go."

Tricia blew gently over the edge of the cup and cautiously took a sip of her tea. *Wonderful,* she thought, relishing the flavor and aroma as it slid down her throat, restoring some of the moisture stolen by her nerves. "I do hope, though, that the leave of absence paperwork was properly completed to cover my absence?" It was a gamble, but the knowledge that Sorensen had forged paperwork to cover her departure was the only card Tricia had to play at this point to cover her backside.

"It was," Clarissa agreed, taking a sip of her own tea. "Believe me, it is the only reason we are having this conversation instead of a much more difficult one." Tricia nodded.

"But know that I approved it because I trust you, Tricia," Clarissa continued. "I knew your reputation and how diligent you are in your duties here, enough to believe that if you needed to take a leave on such abrupt notice, it was truly very critical in some way. You aren't prone to flights of fancy, so I gave you the benefit of the doubt."

"I do appreciate that very much, Clarissa. Really, I do," Tricia replied gratefully.

"Of course, but I do want to emphasize again that the team was not set up for success while you were away," Clarissa said sternly. "You may have some damage control to do with them, to earn some of their trust back. Just be prepared for that. I also want to be very clear that if any other urgent issues arise in the future, we will have more advanced notice and preparation for extended time away. Can we agree on that as well?"

"Of course, Clarissa," Tricia said emphatically. "We definitely can. Should something like this come up in the future, I'll do my very best to handle it differently."

"Excellent," Clarissa said with a smile. "You know, Tricia, the silver lining of this is that it was a great learning and growth opportunity for the team. While it was somewhat chaotic at first, they stepped up while you were gone. In the end, all I really had to do was approve some things here and there that needed higher signing authority than the team had on their own. They ran things and have made excellent progress during your absence. They do you credit."

"Thank you, Clarissa," Tricia replied. "I can't say enough about how proud I am of them. Not just now but all the time. They are an amazing group."

"Indeed, they are," Clarissa agreed, "and a testimony to you as the lab director." She took another sip of her tea and shifted in her seat, crossing her legs. "Regarding your leave, is everything all right now? Have things resolved satisfactorily?"

Tricia nodded. "Yes. Everything is fine now. I'm quite ready for things to go back to normal again."

"Good, good," Clarissa replied, also nodding slowly. "Is there anything about it you'd like to talk about? I'm happy to listen if it will help with anything."

Tricia paused for a second, trying to read her, but it was impossible. "No, thank you, Clarissa. I'm ok. I just need to process a few things, but I'm fine. Really."

"I'm glad to hear that, Tricia," Clarissa said. She leaned back slightly and clasped her hands in her lap. "I know we still need to be acquainted more, Tricia, but I hope that someday we can build a relationship that goes beyond just Lab Chair and Lab Director. I think very highly of you, Tricia, and I think you have huge potential. Not just here but in the scientific community as a whole, and I'd like to do what I can to help you grow your career. I'm sure you have aspirations that extend beyond these laboratories, and I hope you can come to see me as someone who can help you achieve them."

Interesting choice of words, Tricia mused.

Clarissa then leaned forward slightly and rested her arm on the edge of the desk next to them. "And I am a very good listener as well. I do care, and I want you to know that if you ever need a sounding board or an ear to bend about anything, professional or personal, I'm here for you. My door is always open."

I didn't see this coming today, Tricia thought, smiling slightly. "Thank you, Clarissa. I think highly of you as well, and I deeply appreciate that offer. I will definitely keep it in mind."

"Please do," Clarissa said. She picked her teacup back up and sipped again. "Now, unfortunately, we have some other business to deal with as well. While you were away, Draconyx presented a proposal for investing in your lab. However, it seems that Director Sorensen had to take some sort of short-notice leave of absence—" Tricia raised an eyebrow and Clarissa nodded in acknowledgement "—so they withdrew. We are back to square one, and with the budget review cycles about to start, I want to make sure your lab is in a solid position."

Clarissa's face darkened. "It is serious, though, Tricia. We need to get sponsors and partners on board. If we don't, there will be cuts, and you'll have to make some tough decisions about your team. Am I clear?"

"Perfectly. I know that funding is an issue to take seriously, but in this case, Clarissa, I honestly think we might be better off without Draconyx," Tricia offered hesitantly. "I didn't get a good, um, vibe from Sorensen."

Clarissa nodded again, pursing her lips. "I definitely agree there was something off about him at the demo. I didn't get a good impression of him either."

"To say the least," Tricia added. "It makes me think, though, when we consider future candidates for a partnership, perhaps we can vet their interests a bit further...assure ourselves that their intentions are above board and that our work won't be, um, misused in some way."

"Given what we experienced, yes, I think that's a very fair suggestion," Clarissa said. She pushed her empty tea cup to the side, picked up her commpad, and lifted her glasses to the bridge of her nose. "Now, with the time we have left today, let's review the next steps for your team's programs and then discuss some of the potential partners I've been researching."

Monitors beeped softly next to the wall. Tricia sat on a small stool next to the bed. In front of her, Sofia lay motionless, her chest slowly rising and falling in cadence with the monitors. For the first time since Tricia had known her, Sofia finally looked genuinely at peace.

The attending physician, Doctor Schoenstein, stood beside Tricia. He looked down at her and nodded. *Are you ready?* his look asked her. Tricia sighed slightly and nodded back. Schoenstein inserted the tip of a syringe into the port on the IV running into Sofia's arm and injected a bluish solution. Tricia watched the solution traverse the tube and eventually flow into Sofia's outstretched arm.

District Attorney Harris was standing toward the back of the room, doing his best to look inconspicuous and blend into the background. He had traded in his signature tailored suit for a blazer, button-down shirt (which he wore open at the neck for a change), jeans, and a pair of boots. In the several days since the destruction of The Workshop, Harris had taken statements and asked questions of Tricia, Darci, and a few workers they had been able to track down who had evacuated The Workshop before it fell. The small number of people they'd been able to find so far had been relatively low-level technicians and, unfortunately were unable to give much in terms of the bigger picture of what Sorensen was doing, so when the decision was made to finally awaken Sofia, he insisted on being present to hear whatever she might say.

The monitors started to beep faster, and Sofia's breaths became deeper and more frequent. When they found her in the SUV she'd taken, she was comatose. They decided it was best to keep her that way as they removed the chip remnants and ran various tests to try to assess how much damage she might have sustained from the chip that had ruptured in her head. The medical team had finally exhausted their options and had decided they would not be able to assess her or treat her further until she was conscious and could respond – *if* she could respond.

Sofia's eyes fluttered and opened. She looked over at Tricia, her normally bright gray eyes looking a bit hazy and uncertain.

Tricia smiled at her. "Hi there. Glad you're back with us."

Sofia managed a small smile. "Hello," she said. She frowned a bit. "Do I know you? Are we friends?"

Tricia looked up at the doctor. He nodded to her to continue, so she looked back at Sofia and answered, "I'm Tricia. We, um, worked together for a little while, but, yes, I'd say we were—are—friends."

Sofia nodded slightly. Looking around, she finally asked, "Where am I? It looks like a hospital room?"

The doctor put a hand on Tricia's shoulder. He leaned down toward Sofia. "Can you tell us your name?" he prompted her.

Sofia thought for a second. "Sofia. Sofia Sorensen," she finally answered slowly and carefully.

Tricia breathed a sigh of relief as the doctor continued, "Good. Good. Can you tell us the last thing you remember, Sofia?"

Sofia scowled a bit again, clearly struggling to remember, to shake out the cobwebs and bring the world into focus. "I had just accepted a transfer from my old job and was getting ready to pack up my apartment," she offered. "My brother, Jonas, had convinced me to join a new project he'd been promoted to lead, so I was getting ready to relocate to their facility."

Sofia looked around again, more intently this time. She tried to sit up, but the doctor put a hand on her shoulder, urging her to lie back on the pillow. Settling back in, she looked at Tricia. "Do you know Jonas? Do you know where he is?" she asked urgently.

Tricia smiled weakly and put her hand on Sofia's hand. "I know your brother, but I'm sorry, I don't know where he is right now." It was the truth; no one, including Darci, knew where Sorensen was now, lost between the shadows. *Not likely anyone ever will know either.*

And I'd be a liar if I said I was the least bit sorry about it. Justice served.

"How did I get here? What happened?" Sofia pushed, now becoming much more alert and clearly much more concerned.

Doctor Schoenstein took over. "Shhh, just relax, Sofia. We will answer all your questions, but now that you're back with us, we need to have a closer look at you."

He turned to look at Tricia and Harris. "And we should avoid taxing you any further until we are sure you're up to it."

Harris took the hint. He uncrossed his arms and headed for the door. Tricia also took it. She stood up and once again patted Sofia's hand. "You're in good hands here, Sofia," she said softly. "The doctors will take great care of you, and when you're up for it, I'll come back and see you again, okay?"

Sofia nodded. "Yes, that would be nice. Thank you."

After the door closed behind them, and they were sure they were alone in the hall, Tricia asked, "You know, when you told me she was still alive, I was so thrilled and relieved to hear it that I never asked how she got here."

"She originally came in as a Jane Doe," Harris explained. "People had called in that a woman attempted suicide at a gas station several miles outside the city. When she was brought in, she was non-responsive, so no one knew who she was. Once you filled us in, we made the connection, and it became clear who she was. The doctors then did some more detailed imaging of her brain and found not only the remains of the chip you'd told us about but pieces of another device of some kind buried deeper in her head."

"Sorensen must have implanted a backup of some sort that she didn't know about. He was just the kind of person who would make sure he could kill his own sister if he needed to." Tricia shook her head in disgust and cursed under her breath

"Seems so. The doctors surmise that when she overpowered whatever the chip was doing, it overloaded, and she lapsed into a coma from the shock." Harris confirmed. "We are also guessing that when the chip overloaded, her hand jerked at the last instant. Judging from the bullet hole in the roof of the SUV she was driving, she was a fraction of an inch from not being with us at all."

"Well, I'm just glad she pulled through," Tricia said. "Without her, things would have gone very badly for all of us."

"Agreed."

"So, what happens with her now?"

"Once she's cleared by the medical staff, she's clear to go as far as I'm concerned," Harris replied. "I have no evidence at all related to her involvement beyond your and Darci's statements. We will want to question her, of course, but if her memory really is a wash, we probably won't get anything additional from her anyway. Besides, I think she's been through enough already."

"That's for sure," Tricia agreed. "No matter what cover story you come up with, suddenly being on her own, losing her brother, missing several months of her life...it's all going to be quite a shock for her."

"It will. So you know, we are already working on a cover for her. After all, as far as she knows, she could have been in a coma for several months instead of several days. We just need to get some pieces in place and finish the narrative. We'll likely break the news to her that she and her brother were in some kind of airplane accident. He was killed. She was injured, and we'll go from there."

Tricia nodded. "Ok, I can kind of take her under my wing, too. With a good cover, maybe she can go back to her life before her brother recruited her. If not, I can probably hook her up with something in one of the labs on campus and help her get back on her feet."

"Sounds good. We'll keep you in the loop on how the story plays out so you can help support the message," Harris said. "It goes without saying, though, if she shows any signs of remembering anything, we may have to revisit all of this."

"Agreed," Tricia consented, then furrowed her eyebrows thoughtfully. "Is Sofia in any danger?" she asked.

"Hard to be certain," Harris said solemnly. "It's clear whoever was behind that institute is quietly cleaning things up, so it depends on how much they believe she is something that needs to be cleaned up. On the one hand, she was in pretty deep, and somewhere in her head, there is a lot of damaging information. On the other hand, they know we'll be watching her closely, and not just Crystal Bay's finest either. All the three-letter federal agencies you'd expect to be interested in this are nosing around, and they'll be watching her, too."

"The feds?" Tricia asked hesitantly and sighed. "Do they know about me?"

"So far, no," Harris assured her. "The story we've crafted has you as a victim, and, of course, Beacon was undercover and got you and Darci Jackson out with an assist from Umbra. They're satisfied with that for now, so I'm very certain you and she are off their radar."

But it's only a matter of time, probably, Tricia resigned to herself.

"And, while we are on the subject of stories, I have to say that hearing Rene Thornton had come back from the grave was tough to swallow," Harris probed. "To think how deeply our services and systems have been compromised to make that happen is deeply disturbing."

"More for me than anyone," Tricia admitted. "Aside from all that, no matter what she'd done last year, we couldn't have stopped Sorensen without her. It was hard seeing her die a second time."

Harris nodded. "You might be happy to know, then, that I'm going to make sure her sealed file is updated with this information. No one will know right away, but someday all this will come out, and it's fitting that they know how she redeemed herself."

Tricia scowled. "For the record, I don't have much faith in your 'sealed files' these days, Harris," she retorted, pushing her pesky lock of hair back behind her ear.

"Yeah, I was waiting for that part to come up," Harris replied, obviously ashamed. "There are a lot of people who really lost their crap when they found out how much Sorensen and whoever he was working with had penetrated not only our files but secure files in a variety of systems.

"It wasn't just your files either," he went on. "They had put back doors in quite a few places. We are doing a full audit of our systems to clean them up and tighten the security protocols. Some heads have already rolled, and we are still looking into the records of a number of current and past employees to see whose financial situation might've drastically improved recently, too."

"Following the money," Tricia sneered.

"Absolutely. I'm confident we'll track down whoever did this—assuming they haven't been cleaned up already—and get it all straight again. I know it isn't anywhere near good enough, but I am sorry this happened."

Tricia sighed, "I know, and no, it isn't enough, but it will do for now."

"I'm going to be honest," Harris pressed on, "this has also made a lot of people nervous again about the potential of people like you."

Tricia snorted. "I think I've proven myself more than once, haven't I?"

"You have, but it's not just you anymore, is it?"

They both looked down the hall toward Darci. She was inspecting the contents of a vending machine by the small set of lounge chairs further down. She was wearing a plain T-shirt, jeans, and sneakers, a dramatic change from her typical black outfit. *She looks like any other ordinary college kid,*

Tricia thought. Darci turned and looked back at them, then sheepishly turned back to the machine; it must've been very obvious they were talking about her.

"No, it isn't," Tricia admitted. "However, I think she's learned a lot from all this, and I'm fairly sure with a little guidance and support, we don't have to worry about her."

Harris grunted.

"And, if one good thing came out of this," Tricia reflected, "it's that we now know more about these abilities and where they come from. That will help us keep the threat level down as well."

"Anything about that you care to share?" Harris asked with a coy smile.

Tricia didn't return the smile. "Not until you get your issues with your 'sealed records' taken care of."

"Not even off the record?"

"Is there such a thing?" Tricia challenged. Harris said nothing, but Tricia huffed a bit and pushed her fingers through her hair. "Look, Harris, it isn't you. You've been straight and honest with me from the start, but it's the system. The system is broken, and no matter how upright you are, a chain is only as strong as the weakest link."

Harris nodded. "I get it," he replied. After pondering for several seconds, he turned and looked her dead in the eye. "Tell me honestly, Tricia. Do these powers of yours and hers represent a threat?"

Tricia met his gaze. "In the wrong hands, of course, they do." She shrugged. "But then, what source of power doesn't? Money, politics, authority...they all can be, and have been, misused by people with bad intentions."

"What do we do to prevent that?"

Tricia paused a moment. "I think we keep doing what you and I have been doing, working together, cooperating, to bring about the best outcomes we can for everybody. If we let fear and paranoia, or worse, greed and exploitation, rule the day, well, we just saw proof that won't end well for anyone, will it?"

Harris shrugged a bit in agreement but said nothing.

Tricia looked back at Darci. She had made a selection from the machine and was now sitting in one of the chairs, snacking on something from a small bag. "What's going to happen with her?"

Harris looked in Darci's direction also. "Basically, we are in the same situation that we are with Sofia. I have nothing to charge her on right now."

"But she told you everything, didn't she?"

"She did, but a confession isn't evidence, and I did grant her a level of immunity for her cooperation. If you aren't going to press charges..."

"I'm not," Tricia emphasized, interrupting him.

"...then without any witnesses or evidence to back it up, nothing she or you said would hold up in court anyway. Furthermore, the facility is a total loss. There are a few odds and ends that somewhat corroborate your stories, but nothing solid to go on. It goes without saying, too, that the onsite systems were completely fried by the energy pulse, so there's nothing there either."

"How sure are you about your forensics team, Harris?" Tricia asked skeptically.

"In this case, very sure," he replied. Harris then frowned slightly and rubbed his chin. "The really strange and concerning part is that when we uncovered the network storage and penetrated the encryption, we found someone had beaten us to it and wiped it clean, so unless something turns up, she's free to go."

He then gestured casually in Darci's direction. "And, if she is going to get a fresh start, I don't think prison is where someone like her is going to find it."

Tricia grinned. "Why, Harris, it sounds like I'm starting to rub off on you."

"Maybe," he grinned back.

"Well, I'll see what I can do, too. I'm not sure who she has in the way of friends or family, but for me, having support was a huge part of getting me to where I am today, and as someone like her, maybe I can pay it forward and offer her a supportive relationship that others can't."

"Sounds like a plan," Harris agreed. "I'll also extend the same kind of cover to her that we give you and help keep her abilities off the radar."

"Thanks. I...we...appreciate it." Tricia extended her hand to Harris.

Harris shook it. "We'll keep you up to date on Sofia as well."

Tricia nodded and turned to walk down the corridor toward Darci.

As Tricia approached, Darci turned her head and looked up at her.

"Found something good, I see," Tricia said, smiling.

"Meh. It's ok," Darci said and offered the bag up to Tricia.

Tricia held up her palm and shook her head. "No, thanks. I appreciate the offer, but I've had my fill of chips recently."

Darci smirked and then stared down into the bag. "I saw you two talking. What's going to happen with me?"

Tricia sat down next to Darci. "Well, the DA isn't going to press any charges for starters."

Darci heaved a big sigh. "That's a relief."

"As for the rest, it's kind of up to you."

"What do you mean?"

Tricia turned slightly in her seat to look more directly in Darci's direction. "For starters, if you wanted to finish school, I could help with that. You've missed your finals at this point, but instead of failing you, I'm sure I could convince your professors and the dean to give you an incomplete. Some of them might let you make up some of the credit. Others, you'd probably have to repeat the classes, but you'd have the option."

Darci's face lit up. "Yeah, I'd really appreciate that."

"As for the internship, well, with your supervisor floating somewhere in limbo, I don't think he's going to sign off on the balance of your credits," Tricia continued, the corner of her mouth curled knowingly. "But, if your grades are good, I think I could arrange something in my lab to make up the difference."

Darci beamed and nodded enthusiastically.

"Lastly, I did some checking, and after the semester ended, the place you were staying figured you weren't coming back and put your things in storage at the university. Unfortunately, that isn't available any longer—they rented it out already to a summer student—but if you want any help with a place to stay or finding a place again, I'd be glad to do what I can there, too."

"I...I don't know what to say," Darci replied softly. "After everything that happened, after what I did, you're still willing to help me?"

Noticing that a few nurses and staff had started milling around the hallway, Tricia looked at Darci and nodded her head to the side. "Walk with me." They both stood up and followed the illuminated green arrows leading the way out of the hospital.

When they had cleared the hospital entrance, they found a deserted bench in the sun off to the side and again sat down.

Tricia put her hand on Darci's arm and lowered her voice. "It goes without saying, given how alike we are in, um, other ways, I'm more than glad to help out, work together, whatever, in that regard as well.

"I mean, I'm sure you have other friends and family too, but I know, at least for me, having another person like *us* would be really great. If you'd like that, of course."

Darci smiled and nodded.

"Have you explored any other aspects of your abilities?" Tricia asked softly.

"No, not really. Once I figured out the manipulation thing and the traveling, I pretty much stuck with that."

Tricia chuckled. "I have to admit that teleportation bit is pretty cool. It sure beats running across rooftops."

Darci laughed. "I suppose it is, but the way you fight is amazing. I really want to learn to do that."

"I'd be glad to show you what I can, but if you really want to learn, I'll introduce you to the guy who taught me. He believed in me and pushed me week after week. Pretty much everything I know, he taught me."

Darci smiled. "I'd like that."

"Super," Tricia said. "We can, you know, take it a step at a time, see how it goes. We'll get you set back up at school and take it from there. Don't forget, either, that Crystal Bay has a new superheroine, and Harris tells me they are getting calls day and night to learn more about Umbra."

Darci smiled and put her arm around Tricia's neck. She laid her head on Tricia's shoulder and gave her a small hug. Tricia squeezed her back.

"I think people like us will have to stick together," Darci said.

Tricia nodded in agreement.

Letting go, Darci sat back up and turned to face Tricia. Her face was more serious. "Do you think there are more people out there like us?"

Tricia turned to face her. "I honestly don't know, Darci. Sorensen implied that, while it was rare, there have likely been others like us. When it happened to me, I thought I was the only one. Now, there's you, too. In a population of billions, small probabilities imply a very real potential."

"Maybe then," Darci said tentatively, "the two of us can be the start of something bigger, then? Something done the right way."

Tricia smiled. "Two of us is already something bigger than just one of us, and even if it is just the two of us, then we'll have to make it the biggest something the two of us can make."

Darci took Tricia's hand and squeezed it firmly. Tricia smiled and squeezed back. *Definitely the start of something bigger...much bigger.*

The room was dark except for a single brilliant spotlight shining down from the ceiling at the center of the group. The members of the group sat at the fringe of the circle of light, just enough to be seen, but their faces and features were masked in shadow. A few of the seats were empty. Fewer still contained holograms dimly visible in the dark.

"Clearly, Sorensen ended up being a...disappointment," one voice said. "And the facility is a total loss."

"Worse," said another voice, "Sorensen's sister survived."

A tongue clucked from another member. "She's of no concern. Her memory of the project and participants is gone."

"And we do have the Emergents that were in stasis secure, do we not?" another voice inquired reassuringly.

The first voice responded, "We do, but Carling and Jackson, the assets known as Beacon and Umbra, have survived, and they have told the authorities everything about Sorensen's operation. Further, their continued presence constitutes a grave threat to our efforts."

"They must be neutralized," said a new voice.

"Neutralized?" exclaimed another voice, "But what of the Assurances in the *Arcana Elementalis*?"

"All in good time," the second voice said evenly, layering on a calming tone. "There is nothing for anyone to act upon, so the threat at this time is minimal."

"Correct," the first voice responded, "and our other facilities are still working on other options. Some are producing very promising results."

A raspy voice impatiently broke into the discussion, "We will focus our attention and resources there. Anything else that could compromise us has been contained, so for the time being, we are secure. Should Beacon or Umbra pose a more tangible threat in the future, we can deal with it then. Are we in agreement?"

"Agreed," all the voices said in unison.

"The Elementals shall be restored!" all the voices proclaimed together.

The holograms winked out, and the light went off.

After a couple of seconds, some dim bluish lights illuminated the walls at the edges of the room. Most of the people present took this cue to exit, all but two, a man and a woman. The man sat for a few seconds, clearly thinking about what had transpired. The woman sat watching him pensively and expectantly.

Finally, he sighed and stood. He was tall and well-built with wings of gray at his temples. The sheen of his expensive and well-tailored dark suit shimmered from the soft glow of the lighting. He buttoned the top button of his jacket and turned to leave when the woman called out, "Jeremy?"

Jeremy McKinley turned back to face her. "Yes, Clarissa?"

Rising to meet him, Clarissa Patel smoothed the skirt of her own exquisitely cut dark suit and tossed her long black hair back over her shoulders. "How do you feel about all this, Jeremy?" she asked, walking over to where he waited.

"About all of what, Clarissa?" he replied. "Do you mean about what we are doing, or how we are doing it?"

"Both."

Jeremy paused for a second and then answered her evenly, "Yes, I still firmly believe that restoring the Elementals will help recreate the balance between humanity and the planet that is essential for our survival and that it's critical we do everything in our power to realize the Assurances in the ancient texts. You know I've worked my entire career to help people live more harmoniously with nature, so yes, I'm still committed in spite of these recent setbacks.

"As for how we are doing it," he continued with a deep sigh. "I believe there are...opportunities to examine alternative approaches."

"I am still firmly committed as well, of course," Clarissa agreed. "I also believe when they are restored, we can learn much from them that can benefit humanity and society as a whole." She took another step toward him and lowered her voice. "However, I, too, cannot help but have serious reservations about how we are approaching our goals."

Jeremy looked down at her, pondered for a second, and then took a deep breath. "I can't argue that your concerns aren't valid. We have had two chances now to secure Beacon, and both times she, and now Umbra, have eluded us. Not to mention the manpower and money we've spent helping to conceal her identity, covering up her...lapses in discretion."

"Worse," Clarissa added, "with Sorensen going rogue and attempting to supplant our plan with his own agenda, our position has been seriously damaged, despite the assurances from our gravelly-voiced colleague."

McKinley nodded. "Yes. We can easily recover from losses of money and equipment, but now Beacon is alerted to something larger in play. She will be more aware and cautious going forward." He looked up at the ceiling for a moment, then looked back down at Patel. "Do you think she has any idea what she may be?"

Patel pursed her lips with a half-smile. "That she's potentially *elementalis bellatrix*, the incarnation of a prophecy from an arcane legend? The vanguard of an elite group of beings meant to dispel chaos and restore peace to our troubled world? No, definitely not, but she does have a strong sense of moral justice and a deep desire to use her abilities and leverage her image to make a difference to people. That can work in our favor."

"What are you suggesting?" he asked, narrowing his eyebrows.

Patel smiled and put a hand on his arm. "I'm suggesting that perhaps a change in strategy is in order. Instead of trying to "secure her" and treating her as an asset, we look for an opportunity to show her how her aspirations align with our goals."

"Yes, she would be a powerful ally," Jeremy agreed, "if we can do it. Needless to say, her trust level is very low, and she will be suspicious—if she'd consider it at all."

"True," Clarissa replied, smiling more, pressing her position, "but I am in a unique position to influence the situation. I have already taken steps to establish a positive rapport with Tricia Carling that eventually could help us lead her to see our position more clearly and more constructively."

Jeremy nodded in agreement. "It is definitely worth more thought." He glanced quickly at his watch. "I do need to meet Kym now, though. She was very disappointed to miss the Conclave today and is eager to hear how the conversation went. I'm sure she will be interested in this option as well."

"Excellent!" Patel responded, gesturing toward the exit. "Perhaps the three of us should meet soon," she said as they walked together, "I know a place that serves some lovely tea we can enjoy while we discuss how we can, um, coax the rest of the Circle toward this alternative."

Jeremy nodded. "Let's. The sooner Beacon joins us—and she *will* join us, one way or another—the closer we will be to achieving our objectives," he said as the door closed behind them, leaving the empty room in silence.

Epilogue

The spark flittered around the shimmering figure. The avatar was nascent, still newly formed. Through the shifting iridescent sections of its—her—body, the spark could see the faded outlines of the pinnacles and buttes in the shadowy, stony background.

Here in the realm of thought and spirit, the avatar bore the metaphors of her limitations in the substantive world. Her eyes were covered since she could not yet see the true nature of things or her place in them. Her mouth and wrists were bound, reflecting the fact that she could not yet access her power. Soon, though, she would Emerge, and her bindings would fade away.

Off to the side, several other figures stood. The spark did not understand them. They were different. Unnatural. They had started to Emerge, but, for some reason, stopped and now stood frozen, statuesque on the barren plain. The spark did not know if they would ever Emerge fully or even what they would become if they did.

They were a mystery, but this one, this one was true.

Thunder rolled across the landscape. On the horizon, the spark could see flashes of light and pulses of dark, casting sharp, deep shadows that shifted randomly on the ground and rocks behind. It was not a storm, however, at least not as humans think of them. It was from the Guardians and Champions that had already Emerged and were now channeling the elemental forces of the universe in the physical world.

The spark did not know why or even how mortals could be entrusted with such power, but it was how it had always been. Throughout time, they had risen and fallen, era after era, cycle upon cycle, and now it was time for them to rise once again.

The spark returned to the silent avatar standing next to it. This one, though, would soon Emerge. She would complete the Bonding, throw off her restraints, and join them.

Others would come, too.

And the Prophesies would be fulfilled once again.